COUNTING THE DAYS

After the fall of France, three young evacuees from the east end of Newcastle are sent to the safety of a country village. Billeted in a grand house with a spinster and her niece, Hazel, Irene and Carol's futures will be irrevocably changed by their new lives. When peace is declared, and Hazel and Irene return to their families they were forced to leave, they find Newcastle very different to the home they remembered. Mourning the people they love, they try to leave the past behind and start again. But it's never easy to forget...

3 8043 27007013 5

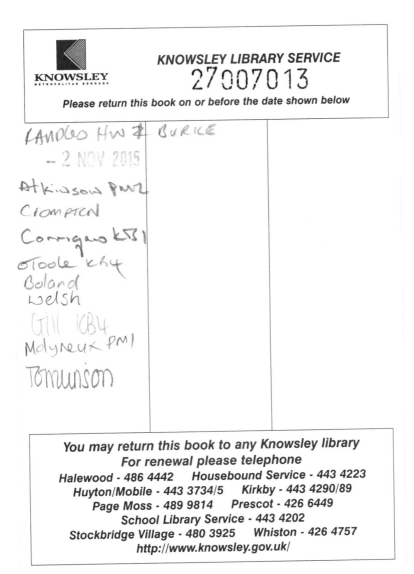

KNOWSLEY LIBRARY SERVICE

27007013

Please return this book on or before the date shown below

LANDEO HW # BURKE

– 2 NOV 2015

Atkinson PW2
Crompton
Corrigans KB1
OToole KH4
Boland
Welsh
Gill KB4
Molyneux PM1
Tomlinson

You may return this book to any Knowsley library
For renewal please telephone
Halewood - 486 4442   Housebound Service - 443 4223
Huyton/Mobile - 443 3734/5   Kirkby - 443 4290/89
Page Moss - 489 9814   Prescot - 426 6449
School Library Service - 443 4202
Stockbridge Village - 480 3925   Whiston - 426 4757
http://www.knowsley.gov.uk/

COUNTING THE DAYS

COUNTING THE DAYS

by

Benita Brown

Magna Large Print Books
Long Preston, North Yorkshire,
BD23 4ND, England.

British Library Cataloguing in Publication Data.

Brown, Benita
Counting the days.

A catalogue record of this book is
available from the British Library

ISBN 978-0-7505-4124-4

First published in Great Britain in 2014 by
Headline Publishing Group

Copyright © 2014 Benita Brown

Cover illustration © Gordon Crabb by arrangement with
Alison Eldred

The right of Benita Brown to be identified as the author of this work
has been asserted by her in accordance with the Copyright, Designs
and Patents Act, 1988

Published in Large Print 2015 by arrangement with
Headline Publishing Group Ltd.

Magna Large Print is an imprint of Library Magna Books Ltd.

Printed and bound in Great Britain by
T.J. (International) Ltd., Cornwall, PL28 8RW

To my darling husband,
with heartfelt thanks for his love and support.

Chapter One

Newcastle upon Tyne, December 1952

'Are you ready to order yet, madam?'

The waitress's thin smile veiled an air of impatience. Hazel was uncomfortably aware of the queue going all the way down the stairs. At lunchtime Pumphrey's coffee rooms above their shop in the Cloth Market were popular with people who wanted to have a light snack and savour some of the best coffee in town.

Hazel glanced at her watch, about to say that her friend wouldn't be much longer, but she changed her mind when she caught the waitress's irritated expression. She scanned the menu rapidly and then, giving the harassed woman an apologetic smile, asked for Welsh rarebit and a pot of coffee for one.

She looked out of the window. She had secured this seat because Kenneth, even though he was coming just across the road from his office, was often late, and while she waited she could entertain herself by looking out at the busy streets. Today lights were streaming from shop and office windows onto the rain-drenched pavements and everyone was hurrying along. The tops of large black umbrellas formed kaleidoscopic patterns with smaller coloured ones. People stopped, unfurled their umbrellas and shook them hastily

11

when they reached whichever door they had been hurrying towards.

It was past one o'clock and newspaper sellers with canvas sacks full of the early edition of the evening paper began to make their way from the nearby *Chronicle* office to their appointed pitches. Most were old men or young boys straight from school, but some were ex-servicemen whose previous jobs had gone to school leavers, and Hazel wondered if these men were at ease with the world they had fought to defend.

Kenneth had been lucky. Called up on his nineteenth birthday, he had fought steadfastly throughout the war and emerged unscathed at the age of twenty-three, with the rank of sergeant, then had walked back into his clerical job at the Town Hall. Now, seven years later, he was an important figure in the Housing Department.

Hazel's meal arrived and no sooner had the waitress left than a young woman wearing a damp raincoat approached her table. 'Look, you're on your own and this is a table for two – do you mind if I join you?'

'Oh, but ... I'm waiting for...' Hazel could see that the restless queue was now even longer, and she felt embarrassed.

'Well, you've been waiting a long time for your friend and I've got to get back to work.' She looked no more than sixteen but she was surprisingly self-assured. 'Are you sure you don't just want to keep this table to yourself?'

As the girl began to unbutton her coat before sitting down, Hazel was relieved to see Kenneth emerge from the stairway and weave his way through the tables to stand behind the persistent young woman.

To Hazel's surprise he said, 'Merle, what do you think you're doing?'

The girl turned to face him. Her bold air vanished. 'Mr Gregson!' She sounded shocked.

'Well?'

She recovered a little of her former confidence and said, 'I've been waiting for ages and this woman is taking up a whole table to herself.'

'And did this *lady* invite you to sit with her?'

Merle scowled.

'Did she?'

'No.'

'Then I suggest you get back in the queue.'

'But my lunch hour's nearly over!'

Kenneth's stern features relaxed a little. 'Then why don't you buy some sandwiches and take them back to the ladies' staffroom? You can make yourself a cup of tea. Tell Miss Thompson I said you could have an extra ten minutes.'

Merle grinned. 'Ta, Mr Gregson.' She turned to go.

'Merle.'

She looked round.

'Apologise to this lady for trying to barge in on her.'

'I wouldn't have done it if I'd known she was waiting for you.'

'You shouldn't have done it whatever the circumstances.'

She looked down at her feet sullenly.

'Take that look off your face and say sorry.'

Merle stared at Hazel. 'I'm sorry.'

13

'That's all right,' Hazel said. 'I realise you were pressed for time.'

'Good,' Kenneth said. 'Now, off you go, young lady.'

People on nearby tables who had been listening with amused curiosity turned back to their meals. Kenneth undid his overcoat and sat down. 'What is it?' he said when he saw her expression.

Hazel shook her head. 'Oh, nothing.'

'Was I too hard on her?'

'Not hard. It was just a little bit of a public dressing-down.'

'She's new. She's a clever girl but she's a bit rough around the edges for the Town Hall. She has to learn.'

'I suppose so. But you're not in the army now, Sergeant Gregson.'

'Now you've made me feel guilty. I've crushed the poor kid.'

Hazel smiled. 'No, you haven't. Not that one. She'll survive.'

Kenneth reached for the lunchtime menu. It never changed but he studied it as carefully as he always did, then looked up. 'I'm sorry I was late. The building regulations meeting went on and on and I couldn't get away.'

'No need to apologise.'

'I made it difficult for you.' Kenneth glanced at her plate. 'That must be cold by now.'

Hazel looked down at the spicy melted cheese. Wrinkles had formed across the top. 'I felt I had to order to keep the waitress happy.'

He frowned. 'You shouldn't have given in.'

'Given in?'

'I suspect she pressed you into ordering.'

'I didn't mind really. She has a hard enough job. I didn't want to make her life more difficult than it is.'

'Really, Hazel, it's her job to serve the customers, not to bully them.'

'She didn't bully me.' Hazel's heart sank. They were in danger of getting into one of their pointless tiffs, which usually arose when Kenneth thought he had the right to criticise her behaviour. Or 'put her straight about the ways of the world', as he would have phrased it. She had no wish to spoil both their lunch hours, so she picked up her knife and fork.

'Wait,' Kenneth said. His tone was conciliatory. 'Let's start again. I'll order you a fresh plate.'

'There's no need.'

'Yes, there is – to assuage my conscience. I'll have the same and we'll ask for a cake stand. You can take your pick.'

The waitress raised her eyebrows disapprovingly when Kenneth asked her to take Hazel's plate away, but she responded to what Hazel thought of as his 'masterful' tone and was actually smiling when she brought back their order with a steaming pot of coffee for two. They hardly talked while they ate beyond politely asking each other whether they were enjoying their meal.

Kenneth was probably thinking about the meeting that had taken up his entire morning and the report he would have to write; while Hazel grieved fleetingly about the shocking waste of food. She also felt a twinge of remorse over the fact that she had not told her mother that she was only working a half day today and could have gone straight home. She had decided to stay in town and do some Christmas shopping.

As she was signed up with a secretarial agency, she never had a consistent timetable. Hazel was an excellent secretary and had been offered a permanent job many times, but although some of the positions had been both enjoyable and interesting, there was something within her that prevented her from settling.

If I agree to stay, she often thought, *no matter how well paid and how good the prospects, I will be accepting that this is my life. This is how it's going to be, day in, day out, until I retire, and I can't accept that.*

Of course there was Kenneth. They might marry and have children. Pleasant though that might be, Kenneth was the type of man who would not want his wife to go out to work. He would be a generous husband who would expect her to devote herself to their home, just as his mother had always done. Hazel knew that she was not ready for that either.

They had met in a cinema queue. It was one of the rare times Hazel had gone to the pictures without her mother. Even though two of the stars were James Stewart and Farley Granger, Joan did not fancy seeing *Rope*, a film which had no light-hearted romance in it, nor what she considered to be an exciting story to tell.

'It's all about a dinner party,' she'd said when they'd seen the trailer the week before.

'There's a body in the trunk,' Hazel had replied.

'Yes, but as far as I can make out, nothing really happens. You go on your own, pet. I don't mind.'

16

Hazel knew that her mother had probably expected her to say no, it didn't matter, but she really wanted to see the latest Alfred Hitchcock film, so she took her at her word. Later that week, she went straight from work to the cinema and found herself in a queue that stretched right round the block.

Two girls in front of her had brought sandwiches with them and every now and then someone would peel off from the queue and come back with bundles of fish and chips for themselves and their companions. The smell was mouth-watering and Hazel wished she was not alone. If she left the queue to go to the fish and chip shop she would lose her place.

A young couple immediately behind her murmured something about going to see another film rather than wait any longer. When they left the queue Hazel was aware of someone moving up to fill the gap. She glanced round to see a tall man in a gabardine overcoat and a grey felt hat. He saw her glance and he tipped his brim politely.

The box office opened and, as the theatre filled, the queue began to move up slowly. Every now and then the uniformed commissionaire would walk along the line of hopefuls saying, 'Three together in the stalls.' Or 'single in the back circle.' There was always someone ahead of Hazel to take up the singles. Most people were in pairs. Then, with the foyer a few steps away, the commissionaire said, 'How about the front circle, ladies and gents?' The front circle was expensive but Hazel thought it worth it. She stepped forward but the commissionaire added, 'A few doubles going there.'

Before her disappointment registered she felt someone take her elbow and turned to see the tall gentleman smiling at her questioningly. *He's very good-looking*, she thought fleetingly, before nodding in agreement. And so, without even knowing each other's names, they found themselves sitting next to each other in the plush front row of the circle, just as the supporting film was about to begin.

Hazel felt vaguely embarrassed, but she still managed to enjoy the comedy about a panicking, scatter-brained hostess trying to arrange a society dinner party. When the film ended, her companion said perhaps they should introduce themselves, and after that they fell into an easy conversation. They chatted through the advertising films and exchanged views at the end of the newsreel. In the interval he insisted on buying them ice creams before the main feature began.

They both leaned forward and whispered, 'There he is!' when they spotted Alfred Hitchcock's trademark cameo appearance – in fact there were two in this film – and afterwards, following the crowd all the way out of the cinema, they discussed the film and how much they had enjoyed it.

'I think you could tell it started out as a stage play,' her new friend said. 'And did you know the inspiration for it was the Leopold and Loeb case?'

Hazel did know, but he seemed so keen to tell her that she didn't want to disappoint him. She raised her eyebrows slightly and said, 'Really?'

The cinema doors were closed behind them and the homeward crowd was dispersing rapidly.

Kenneth insisted on walking Hazel to her bus stop and then said hesitantly, 'It's been a pleasure to meet you. I wonder if we could see each other again sometime?'

As Hazel had no telephone at home they arranged to meet for lunch the next week in Mark Toney's on Grainger Street, and after that there had been films, concerts, the theatre and simple walks and picnics at the coast, where he lived. They sometimes went to the little café in Jesmond Dene. Kenneth loved to get dressed up and go to nice hotels, sometimes just for a meal and sometimes to a dinner dance. For such a big man he was a surprisingly good dancer. Hazel owed any dancing skills she had to practising to dance band music on the wireless with the other girls at Hillside House. Irene had been their tutor.

After about six months Kenneth took her home to meet his mother, yet now, nearly four years later, there had still been no talk of an engagement. Hazel knew that some girls would fret about this state of affairs but she was strangely untroubled.

I'm drifting, she worried sometimes. *I'm putting my life on hold, but I wish I knew what I'm waiting for.* And then she would remember what might have been.

'Penny for them?'

Hazel had been gazing out of the window. She turned to find Kenneth smiling at her.

'Oh, nothing interesting.'

'You looked so solemn. It's not more trouble at home, is it?'

Hazel hated the way he thought of her home

19

situation as troubled, but she knew he was trying to be kind. 'No, everything's fine. I think it's this gloomy weather. Cold, wet and miserable.'

'Well, it *is* December.'

'I know, but why can't we have crisp, bright days with a promise of snow now that it's nearly Christmas?'

'Snow turns to sooty sludge in the city.'

'Oh, Kenneth,' she gave an exasperated laugh. 'Can't you think of something to cheer me up?'

'How about the Christmas dinner and dance at the County? Me in my dinner suit and you in an evening dress and silver dancing slippers. And, of course, an intimate little table for two. Will that do?'

She smiled. 'Very nicely.'

'Good.' He looked at the flowered cake stand. 'And now, would you like that cream horn? I'll order a fresh pot of coffee.'

'I've already had a brandy snap.'

'Go on, be daring, my treat, and if you're worrying about your figure you've no need to. You're as slim as that top mannequin – what's her name? Barbara Goalen?'

'Thanks for the compliment but I really couldn't manage anything else. Why don't you have it?'

'I will.'

He grinned and took the cream horn and Hazel found her spirits lifting. Kenneth could be disarmingly nice and she sometimes wondered if the fault was in her that they seemed to be simply marking time. By the time the waitress arrived with their fresh pot of coffee Kenneth had already demolished the pastry, and he only took a quick sip from his cup before announcing that he had to go.

'Here again tomorrow?' he asked. 'Is that convenient?'

Hazel was working not too far away in a Norwegian shipping office. It wouldn't take her long to walk up the steep streets from the quayside. 'Yes, that's fine,' she said. 'But it'll be my turn to pay.'

'All right. Half day for you today, isn't it?'

'Mmm.'

'Then take your time over your coffee. There are plenty of free tables now.'

People were leaving to go back to work and the waitresses had begun to set up the tables for afternoon tea. A few women laden with shopping arrived and sat down wearily, but Hazel didn't think her waitress would mind if she stayed a little longer. Particularly as Kenneth had tipped so handsomely.

She filled up her cup and added a sugar cube. Then she reached into her shoulder bag for her notebook. Her Christmas list would not contain many names. Her mother, her father, Kenneth, Kenneth's mother, and the owner of the secretarial agency, Marion Grey.

Although Hazel and Miss Grey had never been truly close, they had fallen into an easy friendship over the years. Neither of them knew much about the other's personal life. They respected each other and they preferred it that way, though Hazel could not stop herself wondering sometimes about this husky-voiced, elegant businesswoman who wore no wedding or engagement rings, smoked incessantly and kept a bottle of scotch in her desk drawer.

Hazel took the cap off her fountain pen and concentrated on her list. A short while later she looked at it and sighed.

Miss Grey: Scarf clip – maybe cameo?
Kenneth: Leather gloves – silk lined?
Mrs Gregson: Box of embroidered Swiss handkerchiefs.
Father: Box of fifty Players and a scarf– Paisley or plain?
Mother: ? ? ?

What on earth could she get for her mother? Year after year, no matter what she bought, Joan would say, 'Hazel, pet, that's lovely, but you shouldn't have gone to so much trouble. A jar of nice bath salts would have done. Especially now that we have a proper bath.'

The landlord had recently converted the outhouses in the yard behind the scullery into a bathroom and indoor lavatory. Hazel and her mother considered it to be worth every penny of the extra rent.

In despair Hazel decided to get the bath salts her mother always insisted she wanted, but she would go to Fenwick's or Bainbridge's and find the most attractive jar they had. She'd seen some with different colour crystals swirled around in a pattern. She would also buy a large box of New Berry Fruits. Her mother loved them, and after all, Christmas should not be about the amount of money you spent, it should be about making people happy. She added the bath salts and the sweets to the list, then wrote *Christmas cards.* This reminded her of the hurried exchange they'd had that morning.

Her mother had come to the door with her, as she always did, and she was just about to give her a kiss goodbye when the postman had arrived with a handful of Christmas cards. Her mother took them, glanced through them and said, 'There's a couple here for you, pet.' She peered at them then held them out. 'Do you want to take them with you or wait to open them until you get home?'

Knowing very well that if she left them her mother would open them, Hazel pushed the cards into her bag. It didn't really matter who they were from; it was the principle of the thing. Much as she loved her mother, she resented being treated like a child. It seemed that Joan was forever trying to make up for the years she had missed when she had sent Hazel to safety in the country at the outbreak of war.

Hazel took the two envelopes from her bag and glanced at the postmarks. They had both been posted from the same place. The first one she opened had a picture of a steaming Christmas pudding topped by a sprig of bright holly. A brief handwritten message inside said: *Hope to see you soon, Love, Rita.*

Hazel frowned. Although she had exchanged Christmas cards and the occasional letter with Rita Bevan, she had not seen her for two or three years now. What could it mean?

The illustration on the next card showed the Holy Family with the shepherds and the wise men kneeling in the straw, a bright star shining in the sky above the stable. There was a letter inside. When she had read it, she understood Rita's message.

3rd December 1952

My dear Hazel,

I am pleased that we have managed to keep in touch over the years and I have enjoyed your interesting letters. The world is so different now, isn't it? I have often wished that you would come back for a visit but I fully understand how busy your life must be. However this time the invitation is a special one.

Withenmoor is to celebrate the coronation of our young queen next June, and many of us who were lucky enough to be host to children evacuated from the cities during the war have decided that it would be a marvellous idea to invite as many of you as possible to come and share the festivities.

Of course we realise that many, if not most of you, will choose to celebrate within your own community, but if there is the slightest chance of your deciding to come here, you will be very welcome. You could come just for Coronation Day, although you would have to set out very early, or better still, you could come for a whole week and spend some time at Hillside House. I'm hoping that this will be giving you plenty of time to arrange things with your employer.

In November we elected a Coronation Celebrations Committee. It is chaired by Mr Edwards. He is retired now, of course, but he is still active in village affairs. We have been collecting money by the usual means: bring and buy sales, jumble sales, cake stalls, and the schoolchildren have been making Christmas decorations to sell.

Please consider this very carefully, Hazel. I don't want to set the violins a-playing, but I am getting older and it would be wonderful for me to have you and Irene and Carol together again, even fleetingly, at Hillside House.

Yours sincerely,
Margaret Forsyth

Hazel folded the letter carefully and put it inside a zipped pocket in her bag. She had left Withenmoor when the war in Europe had ended in May 1945. She had not lingered as others had for the Victory celebrations. Her mother had wanted her to come home as soon as possible, and at the time she had been happy to leave. Could she face going back now? She wasn't sure. When she and thousands like her had left their homes all those years ago, the world had been a very different place.

Chapter Two

Sunday, 7th July 1940

Hazel pulled the blackout curtain aside and the morning sun streamed into the room, dazzling her. She fell back onto the bed and closed her eyes. She had not slept. The last week or two had been unusually hot, and anxiety about the coming journey and about her mother had kept her awake. Today she was going to be sent to the country and would not be coming home until the war ended.

Last night she had asked when that would be. Her mother had sighed and told her that no one knew the answer to that. Hazel had tried not to cry but a small sob had escaped her nonetheless.

Her father looked up from the racing results and snarled, 'For God's sake, stop that snivelling! You should think yourself lucky that you'll be out of reach of Hitler's bombs. To my mind you should have gone last September when the first lot were sent away. You got instructions from school but your mother ignored them. She obviously didn't care what happened to you.'

'That's not fair, Bill,' said Hazel's mother. 'There weren't any air raids then, and most of those bairns came home again before Christmas. So did the teachers.'

'And now that Hitler has the run of France, they've got to go back again. What sense is there in that? Go on, tell me!'

'Nobody thought that would happen so soon, and it was natural for folk to want their children at home with them.'

Joan Stafford did not usually challenge her husband's word, and Hazel held her breath. Her father pushed his chair back from the kitchen table and rose to his feet. Her mother remained silent, but it was already. too late. 'You want an argument, do you?' He took one step towards them, raising his hand and balling it into a fist, his shirt-sleeves rolled up to reveal his brawny arms. Hazel rushed forward and put herself between them.

'Don't hurt her!' she cried. 'It was my fault. I didn't want to go.'

His face purpled and her mother put her arms round Hazel protectively. 'Bill ... not in front of the bairn,' she pleaded.

Bill Stafford glared at his wife and daughter and they both flinched. But after an agonising silence he lowered his arm and laughed at them. 'What a pair. I can't be bothered with either of you. It's not worth wasting my breath.' He rolled down his sleeves, slotted his cufflinks in and reached for his jacket from the back of the chair. 'I'm off to the Hare and Hounds,' he said. 'Mebbees I'll get a bit of peace there.' He took his cap from the hook on the door and put it on before turning to face them. 'Don't bother to wait up for me.'

They remained silent until they heard the back door slam shut behind him and then her mother hugged her. 'Never mind, pet. You'll soon be off to the country. You'll like it there.'

'But what about you? Can't you come as well?

27

Some mothers do.'

'That's only if their children are babies or if they haven't started school. The younger bairns need their mothers to look after them. But you're a fine big girl of thirteen and you can manage without me.'

'I don't want to manage without you.'

'You'll have to, pet. There's nothing I can do about it.'

In her heart Hazel knew this was true but she went on regardless, 'I don't want to leave you alone with him. He's ... he's cruel.'

'Hazel! You mustn't talk like that about your father. He has his faults but he works hard and he brings home what he can. Times are hard. Often-times he has to walk miles to find a labouring job. It's no wonder he sometimes loses his temper.'

'But don't you see, if I'm going to be miles away, I'll worry about you?'

Her mother took hold of Hazel's shoulders. 'Look at me,' she said. 'You've no need to fret. He might raise his fist but it's only to threaten. The blow never lands.'

'But that's bullying!'

'Listen, pet, it won't be for long. They've started taking the older men – those in their thirties. Sooner or later your father will be getting his call-up papers.'

'What does that mean?'

'He'll be off to join the army.'

'Good!'

Her mother sighed. 'No, Hazel, it might make life easier for me, but it's not good. No matter what kind of man he is, we shouldn't be pleased

28

that he'll have to go and fight and maybe get killed.'

They looked at each other in perplexed silence and then her mother made an effort to smile. 'And just think,' she said, 'they're taking women on at the rope works.' Her smile widened. 'The money's good. Better than I get from my cleaning jobs. I'll be able to look after myself while your father's away and put a little bit by for after the war as well.'

So last night's conversation with her mother had ended where it had begun. It seemed to Hazel that everyone was talking about what it would be like when the war was over. But the trouble was no one knew exactly when that would be.

'Hazel! Time to get up!' Her mother's call interrupted her thoughts.

Her father was still in bed. He had a late lie-in on a Sunday, usually because his head was still groggy from the amount of beer he had drunk the night before. Standing at the scullery sink Hazel filled the bowl with cold water, took off her nightdress and used a clean facecloth to wash herself all over. The note from school had said the children should be clean. Her mother had been indignant. 'As if I've ever sent you out dirty!' she said. 'Although there are some who need telling, I suppose. Wouldn't know what to do with it if they were introduced to a bar of soap.'

Hazel had just finished wringing out the facecloth when her mother hurried into the scullery carrying a large towel. She was already dressed to go to work. On a Sunday morning she put in a couple of hours' cleaning in the Hare and

Hounds. She would joke to Hazel that she would be earning back some of the money Hazel's dad had spent there the night before. This morning her naturally wavy hair was drawn back from her face and rolled up neatly on the nape of her neck. In Joan's case this was as much for tidiness as for fashion. Her hair was the same chestnut brown as Hazel's but there were already premature streaks of grey.

She wrapped the towel round Hazel's shoulders and would have dried her and helped her to get dressed if Hazel had not objected. 'I'm not a baby,' she said.

'I know. It's just...' Her mother's voice trailed away. They looked at each other and smiled, but both were close to tears.

'Go on then,' her mother said. 'But mind you brush your hair.'

When Hazel returned to the kitchen, her clean clothes were in a neat pile on the armchair and the kettle was boiling on the range. Her mother made a pot of tea and sat down with Hazel. As they breakfasted on tea and bread and dripping, they tried to keep a conversation going, but her mother kept glancing at the clock on the mantelshelf.

'I suppose it's time for you to get along,' she said when they had finished. 'I'll just make sure I've packed everything you need.' She lifted a small suitcase from behind the armchair and put it on the table, then took a list from her apron pocket. 'Here, you read it out and I'll check that everything's there.'

When Joan was satisfied that all was present and correct, she went to the sideboard and took a small, pale blue folder from one of the drawers, then handed it to Hazel. On the front was a picture of a black Scottie dog with a tartan collar, standing on its hind legs as it tried to post a letter in a bright red post box.

'Go on, open it,' her mother said.

Inside the folder, a pad of writing paper was attached to one side and a pocket on the other side held a dozen envelopes.

'I've put a sheet of stamps in for letters home, but if you drop a line to Mavis, you'll have to ask at the post office how much it will cost to Canada. I'll send you more stamps when you need them. I hope you'll write to me every week and tell me how you're getting on.'

'I'll write to you every day!'

Her mother smiled. 'Once a week would be sufficient. And when you write you can tell me if everything is okay.'

'What do you mean?'

Her mother looked thoughtful.

'What is it?' Hazel asked.

'The people you'll be staying with – I've heard tales – they might read your letters before you post them. If they do, you might not be able to tell me the truth. So we'll have to have some secret way for you to let me know the state of things.'

'What can we do?'

'I've thought about it. When you sign your letter, if you're happy, put "Lots of love, Hazel". If there's a problem, just put "Love, Hazel".'

'Mam, you're brilliant! It will be like a secret code!'

'So don't forget.'

'I won't.'

'And now let's put it in the case along with your ration book and identity card. And would you believe it? As well as tying a label to the case I have to tie one on you just as if you were a parcel.' She looked perplexed for a moment then said, 'I know, I'll tie it through the top buttonhole of your coat.'

They laughed at that, although her mother's laughter sounded hollow. 'Do you want me to walk up to the corner with you?' she said.

Hazel looked up into her mother's kindly face and shook her head. She couldn't trust herself to speak.

'Off you go, then. Wait, don't forget your gas mask. There are some sandwiches in the string bag.'

'Should I say goodbye to Dad?' Hazel asked although she didn't really want to.

Her mother shook her head. 'He'd only complain if you woke him. It's best to let him sleep on when he's had a skinful.'

Her mother came to the door with her. They looked at each other uncertainly then Joan took her daughter in her arms. Hazel felt grief rising in her throat as if it would choke her. Her mother loosened her hold and stood back a little. She stroked a stray wisp of hair back from Hazel's brow.

'Remember, I'm only sending you away because I love you and I don't want any harm to come to you,' she said.

'I know, Mam, but I'll miss you.'

'And I'll miss you. I'll be counting the days until you come back to me.'

Hazel stepped out onto the pavement and the heat rose up to enfold her. The pavement was hot and dusty and tar was melting and forming little bubbles in the road. She blinked in the bright sunlight then set off for school.

Joan Stafford shielded her eyes with one work-worn hand while she watched her only child walk away. She had been wrong not to let her go last September. It had been pure selfishness. Some days it was only the love she had for Hazel that helped her endure the wasteland her marriage had become. But on a sunny afternoon last week, just a few streets away, all those people had been killed and injured during an air raid.

One detail in particular haunted Joan's dreams. The cries of a terrified baby had caused the neighbours to dig frantically at the rubble, but by the time they found the broken cradle the child was dead.

No matter how much it hurt her, she knew she had to send Hazel to a safer place.

'For heaven's sake, girl, shut that window!'

Irene looked round guiltily. Her mother was in the doorway holding a small suitcase. Edie Walker was still in her nightclothes. She wore a silky pale blue robe over matching pyjamas, and a pink and blue floral scarf was wrapped around her head like a turban to hide her curlers.

'But, Mam, I'm cooking in here,' Irene said.

'I can't help that. I'd rather put up with the heat than the smell from the glue factory. On a day like this, with not a breath of wind, let it into the house and you'll never get it out again.'

'I'm sorry.'

Her mother sighed and shook her head. 'And I'm sorry too. I shouldn't have yelled like that. It's just that I'm going to miss you.'

'And I'll miss you.'

'Never mind, just look on the bright side. No doubt the air will smell much sweeter in the country and no one will object to you opening a window. But we can't stand here blethering like this. Your case is packed and it's time to get ready and have your breakfast.'

Irene stood on tiptoe and pushed the top half of the window closed. 'Is Dad home yet?' she asked.

'He isn't.'

'Will he get back before I have to go?'

'I don't know. Night shifts, day shifts, they all seem to be running into one. He says the last few days and nights have been pandemonium. And it's not likely to get better until all the bairns are away, more than four thousand, he says, and maybe not even then.'

'Why not?'

'Because of all the men that have been called up for the forces. They're calling up the next lot now and they're shunting them to camps all over the place, poor beggars. Most of them end up miles away from their families.'

Irene's eyes widened. 'I never thought about that.'

'What do you mean?'

'Will Dad be called up?'

'There's no need to worry about that,' her mother said. She hugged her and Irene caught a waft of Californian Poppy, her mother's favourite perfume. 'They're not taking men who work on the railways. They're too important. Someone has to keep this country moving. So no, pet, your dad won't have to go.' Her smile faded.

Irene was puzzled. 'What's the matter?' she asked. 'Aren't you pleased about that?'

'I thank the Lord every day that he won't be taken from me.' Her mother pulled a silver lighter and a packet of her favourite cigarettes from her pocket. Irene thought the cigarettes must be posh: on the front of the packet a butler was pictured carrying the cigarettes on a silver tray. Her mother took her time lighting up, perhaps because her hands were shaking slightly. Her boldly attractive face was creased with worry.

'Mam, is something wrong?' Irene asked.

'It's Terry. He'll be nineteen soon, and if this blessed war isn't over by then, he'll be called up along with his pals, unless we can think of something to keep him at home.'

'What kind of thing?'

'I dunno. Some kind of important job that will mean he doesn't have to go away. Trouble is, since he left school he's never kept a job for more than a few weeks – and some a lot less than that. We might have trouble finding someone to take him on.' She sighed. 'We'll just have to hope your dad will be able to manage something. After all, he's got friends in the right places.'

Her mother took a long drag on her cigarette and then coughed slightly while she wafted the smoke away with one hand. She picked a flake of tobacco from the end of her tongue then smiled at Irene through the haze.

'Now you hurry up and get yourself washed,' she said. 'Get down to the scullery and back before Terry wants the sink. I'll put your clean clothes on your bed. And mind you comb your hair and put a ribbon in. Get a move on, or you'll miss the train and I'll have to put up with you for the rest of the war.'

Irene knew that her mother didn't really want to get rid of her. Neither did her dad, but he'd told her he knew things that other people didn't know, things that were happening right here in Newcastle, and he wanted her to be safely away. She had asked him what sort of things he meant and who had told him about them.

'Nobody told me. I use my own noddle. Working on the railways you find out about all sorts of things just by keeping your eyes and ears open. Things the enemy might be interested in. Places they might want to destroy. So just take my word for it, we wouldn't send you away if we didn't have to.'

By the time she had dressed and brushed her hair, her brother was sitting at the kitchen table waiting for his breakfast. He was in his shirt-sleeves, his hair smoothly Brylcreemed. Their mother, dressed now but still wearing the scarf around her head, was in the scullery frying bacon. The smell was tantalising.

Terry grinned up at her. 'Off on your hols, then? Some brats have all the luck.'

His slightly lopsided smile was infectious. The girls were charmed by it. But not Irene. Especially not this morning. She scowled. 'I'm not a brat, it's

36

not a holiday, and I don't think I'm lucky.'

Terry pretended to look thoughtful then he nodded. 'You're right. *I'm* the lucky one to be getting rid of you. Once you've gone there'll be no one here to pinch my fags.'

'Be quiet!' she hissed and nodded her head towards the open door that led into the scullery. She glowered at him and kept her voice low: 'I don't pinch your fags. Why would I when I don't even smoke? I'm not old enough.'

'Yeah? Well, that doesn't seem to stop you.'

Terry laughed but Irene's face flushed with fury. She clenched her fists and spat out, 'You're lying! I hate you!'

Their mother appeared holding two plates of bacon and eggs. She looked from one to the other. Terry was grinning; Irene was on the verge of tears. 'What have you said to upset her?'

Irene held her breath and stared at her brother intently. He met her gaze and then shrugged. 'Nothing much. You know how she flies off the handle if she thinks she's being got at.'

'So what did you say?'

He shrugged. 'I said I wouldn't miss her when she's gone but I was only teasing her. I'm sorry.'

'So you should be. Fancy tormenting her like that on her last day at home!'

Irene let her breath out slowly and relaxed. Her mother hadn't heard what the fuss was about and it looked as though she wasn't going to ask. She was used to the flare-ups between her two children and usually took Irene's side. Annoyingly Terry didn't seem to mind. It was all a joke to him. Like everything else. Even when he lost yet another job

37

he was always sure that something else would turn up. And now she supposed she ought to be grateful to him. He knew very well that she often took the opportunity to pinch one of his cigarettes, but he'd never told on her and it looked as though he wasn't going to give her away now.

Their mother put their plates on the table. 'Eat up,' she said. 'You'll not get breakfasts like that much longer. I paid a princely sum for the bacon that a certain grocer was keeping under the counter, and the eggs an' all. Shameful, isn't it?'

'What do you mean, Mam?' Terry asked. 'Do you mean the price of the bacon and eggs is shameful, or the fact that you were prepared to pay for them on the black market?' He grinned and, without waiting for an answer, reached for the HP sauce.

'Cheeky young devil!' Edie replied laughingly. 'If you say anything like that again I'll put you on basic rations. See how you like that!'

She made a pot of tea and joined them at the table.

'Aren't you going to have any breakfast?' Terry asked her.

'Not yet. I'll wait until your dad gets home. You know he doesn't like to eat alone. He likes me to join him and we can have a bit of a chat.'

She lit up another cigarette and turned away slightly so that she wasn't blowing smoke over the table. After a while she began to cough, and when the spasm ended she gulped down some tea. Even though she hadn't finished the cigarette, she stubbed it out in the ashtray they'd brought home from a holiday in Blackpool. Irene had always wondered how the picture of the tower had been put inside the glass.

Her mother shook her head. 'These damned ciggies. It says on the packet that they're good for your throat, but I'm beginning to have my doubts. Mind you never start smoking, Irene.'

'No, Mam, of course I won't.'

Terry almost choked on a mouthful of fried bread. Irene glared at him and breathed a sigh of relief at the sound of the back door opening. Their mother got up and when their father walked into the room she greeted him with a smile. Irene knew that women found her father handsome. Many had remarked how fine he looked in his porter's uniform of jacket, trousers, waistcoat and peaked cap. There were a couple of smart suits in the wardrobe along with her mother's fashionable dresses. When her parents were all dressed up to go out to the pictures or even to the pub, Irene thought they looked like film stars.

Leonard Walker had his canvas bait bag slung over his shoulder along with his gas mask. A rolled up newspaper was stuffed into a pocket and he was carrying a smart little suitcase that Irene had not seen before. 'Here you are,' he said, handing the case to his wife.

'What's this for?' she asked.

He put his newspaper on the table, and his bag, gas mask box and cap on a vacant chair, and turned to his wife. 'It's for Irene. We can't have her going away looking like a refugee with that battered old case of ours. I remember well what the last lot of bairns looked like. Elbows pushed out, buttons missing, and some didn't even have cases. They had all their clothes stuffed in shopping bags or pillowcases. God knows what the folks they're billeted with thought of them. If we want our Irene to be taken on by respectable people we'll have to make sure that she looks a cut above the other kids.'

Terry had taken the case from his mother and was examining it admiringly. 'Nice case, Dad. It looks like real leather.'

'That's because it *is* real leather.'

'Lost property, was it?'

'Been sitting there for months. No one's ever going to claim it. It would just be auctioned off.'

'What about the contents?'

'Women's stuff. Your mother can empty it, have a sort through.'

Terry had the case on his knee and he was just about to slide the catches along and open it when their mother took it from him quickly and said, 'Here, Terry, give it to me. I'll change cases and bring the new one back.'

'Can I help?' Irene asked. 'I'd like to see what's in there.'

Her mother was already halfway out of the door. 'No, pet, we haven't got time for all that. You stay here with your father.'

Terry picked up the newspaper and started to read it. Their father sat at the table and took something out of his pocket. He held his hand out towards Irene, palm up. There were three florins sitting there.

'Here pet, this is for you.'

Irene stared at the money. 'Six shillings!' she said. 'That's a fortune. What's it for?'

'Emergencies.'

'What sort of emergencies?'

'I dunno. You might want to buy a bar of chocolate or some toffees at the village shop.'

Irene frowned. 'I don't think that would be an emergency.'

'I was joking. Of course you can buy some sweeties but don't spend it all at once. The real reason is that I want you to have some money of your own so that you don't have to depend on whoever they put you with to give you pocket money.' He leaned towards her and took hold of her shoulders. 'And remember, if they don't treat you right you must write and tell us about it.'

Irene nodded solemnly. 'I will.'

Her father leaned back again and smiled. 'Right, where's your little Peggy purse?'

'It's with my watch in the drawer in the sideboard.'

'Well, go and get them both. That's right. Now, put your watch on and put the money in the purse.' Irene did so and her father put it over her head so that the strap was on her left shoulder. 'Keep it by you at all times. And don't ever leave your watch lying around. There are some dishonest scallywags about these days.'

Terry tried to smother a laugh. Irene turned to look at him. 'What's so funny?'

Her brother folded the newspaper and put it back on the table. 'Nothing much,' he said. 'Just the cartoon of Hitler and Mussolini in the paper.'

'Let me see it.'

'Nah, it's not for kids. You wouldn't understand it.'

Irene was about to protest but just then her mother came back into the room carrying the new case. 'I think that's everything,' she said. 'Now put your coat on.'

'Oh, Mam, it's too hot to wear a coat.'

'I know it is, but it's too big to go in the case and it would just be a nuisance to carry it. You might put it down somewhere and lose it.'

'I wouldn't lose it, I'm not that daft!'

'Irene, listen to your mother,' her father said. 'The train will be full and you've already got your case, your gas mask and your sandwiches to look after. There's no help for it, you'll just have to wear your coat.'

'Well, I'm not going to button it up!'

Her mother shook her head and smiled. 'That's all right, pet. As long as you let me tie your label on.'

A minute or so later Irene was ready to leave. Terry stood up and shrugged on his jacket. 'I'll walk to school with her, Mam. You have your breakfast with Dad.'

'Are you sure?' Her mother looked thoughtful and then smiled. 'I think that's best.' She turned to Irene. 'We'll say goodbye here, pet. You wouldn't want to see your mother crying in the street, would you?'

Irene gave both her parents a hug and then she and her brother set off together. It seemed strange to be going to school on a Sunday. Terry carried her case and joked that he was only looking after her like this to please their mam and dad. Irene knew better. Although she and her brother didn't always get on, it didn't mean that they didn't like each other. She knew that her parents spoiled her. The other girls at school often told her so. She thought maybe they were a little jealous. Terry wasn't jealous of her, and she thought that was because he was spoilt, too.

Mam and Dad didn't seem to mind that he never kept a job for very long. When he did work he handed most of his wages over to their mother. And yet he always seemed to have plenty of spare cash to buy his cigarettes and go to the pictures with his pals if the fancy took him. If he thought the picture was okay for kids to see he would take Irene along and they would have fish and chips with extra batter on the way home.

They had nearly reached school when Terry said, 'Hang on a minute.'

'What is it?'

'Wait and see.' He rested her case on a garden wall and slid the catches back, then, without lifting the lid, he kept the case steady with one hand and reached into his pocket with the other. 'These are for you.' He held up a packet of ten Woodbines, then slipped them into the case along with a book of matches.

'Thanks! What did you do that for?'

'For a treat and to stop you pinching fags from anyone else while you're away from home.' He closed the case and when he turned to look he found Irene was frowning. 'What's the matter, kid?'

Irene was troubled. 'Mam doesn't want me to smoke because she says it gives her a cough.'

'Nah, I've been smoking since I was your age, and they've never harmed me. Now don't smoke them all at once – and don't let the teacher catch you.' He grinned.

'I won't.'

'Good kid. I'll try and send you some more now and then, but you'll have to write home and tell us your address. And I've been thinking about that. Dad said to write home if things aren't right, but if that's the case, be careful. Don't let them see the letter, okay?'

'Yes. Okay.'

'Good kid. Now, I won't come any further with you or the other kids will think you're a softie. Here's your case. Off you go.'

Irene and Terry stared at each other for a moment and then she gave him a quick hug before turning and taking off without another word.

Terry lingered and watched her walk away. He almost called her back because there was something else he had intended to tell her. He had wanted to warn her to keep a hold of her temper. She lost it too easily – usually when she thought she was being criticised. He shrugged and decided that it was just as well he hadn't said anything. She would probably have flared up on the spot and then they might have parted bad friends.

Other kids appeared from doorways and began to walk in the same direction. As Irene mingled with the crowd he focused on the red ribbon tying up her curly blond hair. She was a good kid. He would miss her. He smiled and turned to walk home. He wanted to try to see what, apart from clothes, had been in the case that Dad had brought home from Lost Property.

The sunlight streamed through the cream-coloured net curtains onto the table. Carol Clark, dressed and ready to go, sat quietly waiting for her breakfast. She had offered to help but her mother wouldn't have it. 'Let me spoil you today,' Anne had said.

Across the table her father had lowered his newspaper and smiled at Carol over his reading glasses. He nodded as if to say *let her make a fuss of you, it will keep her happy.* Both Carol and her father knew that her mother was far from happy, and it wasn't just because Carol was being evacuated today. It was more complicated than that. Her father retreated behind the newspaper again. Carol stared at the headline: *2oz TEA RATION FROM TODAY.*

Further down the page there was a photograph of a smiling energetic-looking young woman in a pretty summer dress sitting on a garden bench with two dogs at her feet. They were looking up at their mistress adoringly. The caption above the photograph was: *Lone woman and her dogs capture German pilot.*

Carol couldn't read the rest of the story but she wondered why tea being rationed was more important than capturing an enemy pilot.

'Really, Brian, put the paper away! I should have thought you would want to talk to your daughter on her last day at home.'

Her mother had appeared with the tea trolley laden with a boiled egg each, toast and marmalade and a pot of tea. The blue and yellow glass beads on the crocheted milk jug cover sparkled as the sun caught them. Her father folded his newspaper and put it aside.

'I'm sorry, dear,' he said. 'I was just checking to see if there was any change of plan. The stationmaster phoned the Town Hall on Friday to inform us that no proper timetable had been sent along to the schools, and this meant they would all turn up together. It's going to be a proper muddle, what with soldiers and children all mixed up and not knowing which platform to go to.'

'That's dreadful. Poor children! They might have to wait for hours.'

'Exactly. That's why I thought it was worth checking the newspaper.'

Carol's mother started to put the food on the table. 'Well, is there?' she asked her husband.

'Is there what?'

She put on her fondly long-suffering look. 'Really, Brian! Is there any change of plan?'

'It doesn't seem so.'

Anne sighed deeply and began to pour the tea. Carol sliced the top off her boiled egg and cut a slice of toast into soldiers. They sat in silence for a while and she glanced at her parents, wondering whether the argument that had dominated their lives for several weeks would flare up again. Her father was concentrating on his toast and marmalade but her mother was only nibbling at her slice.

The home-made marmalade was good. Carol had watched her mother make it last year and now it looked as if the three jars remaining on the top shelf of the larder would have to last until the war ended. Whenever that would be.

'Have that last piece of toast, Carol,' her mother said. 'Goodness knows what time your next meal will be.'

Her father had just taken a sip of tea and he put his cup down and smiled enquiringly. 'You've made her some sandwiches, haven't you?'

'Of course I have.'

'Then there's no need to worry, is there? And I'm sure the children will be well fed when they reach their new homes. After all, the Government will be paying the families for taking them in – money for their board and lodging and some over to give them some pocket money.'

'Maybe so, but we have no idea what sort of home Carol will be going to. When some of the children came home in December there were some dreadful tales of dishonesty, neglect and downright cruelty. Children being used as unpaid servants and not allowed to sit with the family at mealtimes.'

They're going to start again, Carol thought. *Daddy will just tell her impatiently that she shouldn't listen to rumours spread by doom-mongers and Mummy will start crying.* She was wrong, at least wrong about her father. He kept his exasperation in check and reached across the table for his wife's hand. As Carol had predicted, her mother had started crying and she tried to snatch her hand away. He held onto it.

'Anne, don't get upset. You don't want to frighten Carol, do you?'

She sniffed. 'No. But–'

He shook his head. 'No "buts", please. We don't know whether any of those stories are true.'

47

'Then how can you let her go?'

'Let me finish. You know what a clever girl our daughter is?'

'Of course I do. I'll never know why she failed to get into the secondary school. I still think it's because of our address. We don't live in one of the better parts of town, do we?'

Carol saw her father close his eyes wearily. He had inadvertently started his wife off on another cause of marital conflict. Her mother hated living where they did, even though this was the house where she had been born. She thought she had gone up in the world when she married a man quite a bit older than herself – a man who had fought bravely in the last war and earned a battle-field commission. Her husband was not only college educated but had a respectable job at the Town Hall, where she had been working as a junior filing clerk.

When they married, Anne's widowed mother had been ill and had needed looking after. It had made sense to live with her and they had kept the tenancy when the old lady died. They had made it as comfortable as they could afford, and not a little stylish with luxuries like the fashionable chrome and glass tea trolley. Anne's favourite magazine was the *Lady's Companion* and she took the home and fashion features as gospel. That was where she had learned how to soak stark white net curtains in cold tea to give them a more sophisticated cream colour.

However, there was no bathroom. They kept a tin bath under the bench in the scullery and the lavatory was across the backyard. And depending which way the wind was blowing, you couldn't even hang the washing out because of the soot and the smell. That was bad enough, but once Carol had been born, her mother maintained that this part of town was no place to bring up their much-loved daughter.

When Carol started school she had begun to pick up the local accent. Horrified, her mother had sent her to Miss Donaldson, the same elocution teacher she had gone to herself. Emilia Donaldson was a retired classical actress who lived in Jesmond and who placed advertisements for her classes in the local paper. Anne had started going to Miss Donaldson not long after she had started work at the Town Hall and found herself mixing with girls from what she called the better parts of town.

Carol saw her father silently count to ten before he spoke. 'Anne, please stop this. You know very well we've nearly saved up enough to buy one of those houses you like at the coast. And before you say anything about schools, I think we could sort something out. After all, I'm due for promotion and there'll be no rent to pay.'

'Are you saying Carol could go to a private school?'

'Yes. We'll talk later. We're wasting precious time with our daughter.'

'I know we are, but surely you can understand why I'm so worried?'

'I do and I can assure you that she'll be all right. Carol is a sensible girl and I've told her that if she's worried about anything she must get in touch with us straight away. The people she's billeted with

49

wouldn't be allowed to stop her writing to us, and if there's a phone box in the village that's even better. I'm going to give her a purse full of pennies and my number at the Town Hall. Now, does that make you feel a little happier?'

Anne withdrew her hand from his and took a handkerchief from the pocket of her apron. 'Yes, it does,' she conceded, dabbing her eyes. 'But I still think we should have gone private. If you look in the papers there are lots of people who will take in children, and you can go to inspect the house before you agree to anything.'

'And you have to pay them.'

'Of course you do.'

Brian shook his head. 'Anne dear, I've already told you that no matter what the background of the family, not all the private placements have been happy. Wherever Carol goes we are going to have to trust the host family to look after her well and to be kind to her, although they will never love her as much as we do.'

Her mother stifled a sob.

'None of us know how long this war is going to last,' he said, 'but it won't be long now before we have a beautiful new home for her to return to.'

Carol had been silent throughout. No matter what her father said, she had agreed with her mother that they should have found her a good family, but her father, seemingly so easy-going, very rarely let her mother influence his decisions. *And I suppose he's right,* Carol thought. *He wouldn't make me stay if he thought I was being treated badly, and if I can just put up with things until the war is over, they will have moved away from*

50

here and I'll never have to go back to that horrible school where some of the children wear dirty, ragged clothes, and no socks, and shoes with holes in the soles. She had never told her father how she felt because he actually seemed to feel sorry for these people and she had been afraid that he would think less of her if she didn't feel the same way he did.

It was time to go. Carol was surprised but grateful that her mother wasn't going to walk to school with her. She guessed that her father had insisted that he should take her. At the door her mother hugged her. Carol hoped that none of the neighbours would come out of their houses and see the tearful scene. She knew that some people in the street thought that her mother gave herself airs, and they would find any occasion to criticise or laugh at her, or even mimic the way she talked. Carol, herself, had learned to keep quiet and keep out of the way.

Strangely, it seemed that these horrible people respected her father. They didn't mind that he spoke like someone on the wireless, and sometimes they would ask his advice about some problem or other. But now, thank the Lord, it seemed that they wouldn't have to put up with such common neighbours much longer.

'I won't come all the way to school with you,' her father said. 'If I did, your friends might tease you.'

Her father was right about the teasing but not about the friends. She didn't really have any friends. There was always someone to chat to during break, but none of the girls who were happy

51

enough to sit and gossip with her and even make up a party to go to the pictures on a Saturday morning, was what you would call a proper friend.

They stopped when the school was in sight. Brian was amused to see that the pupils were standing in regimented lines in the playground, as if they were about to go on parade. A queue of buses was lined up in the street, waiting to take the children to the station.

He smiled at Carol. 'There's no need for me to ask if you have everything. If you had left anything at home, your mother would have come running after us by now.' He paused and swallowed. 'You know we'll miss you, don't you?'

Carol nodded.

'We're only sending you away so that you'll be safe.'

'I know.'

He looked down at her composed little face, framed with perfectly cut, smooth black hair. Sometimes he had no idea what was going on behind those dark grey eyes. It was hot today, and even though she must be uncomfortable in her blue tweed coat with its velvet collar, she remained unruffled. Carol and her mother had the same refined beauty but they had entirely different temperaments. Anne was filled with nervous energy, whereas Carol was always calm and composed. They could not be more dissimilar, and yet he could not love either of them any more than he did.

Carol was looking up at him with a puzzled frown.

'What is it?' he asked.

'Why are we just standing here? They've started getting on the buses.'

'Of course. Sorry. Off you go.'

'Don't worry, Daddy,' she said. 'I'll be all right.'

Chapter Three

Miss Grace Norton put her suitcase down by her feet and surveyed the groups of children gathered around her fellow teachers in the station's lofty concourse. Some were chattering excitedly and others looked bewildered. Many of them, she imagined, did not really understand why they were being sent away. Grace quailed at the thought of the job ahead of her, but she accepted that it was her duty to do whatever she could to make it easier for these confused children.

Earlier, at school, her own group had boarded the last in the line of buses, so they were already on edge with having to wait for almost an hour in the unrelenting heat of the schoolyard. Even so, the journey had started cheerily enough, most of them enjoying the bus ride. Despite being asked to get on to the bus in an orderly manner, the boys, led by Billy Hobson and his gang, had shoved their way ahead and had commandeered all the seats on the top deck. When the journey began they gazed out of the windows and kept up a ceaseless flow of commentary as they drove past local landmarks.

But once the bus had pulled up inside the grand entrance portico of the Central Station, the noise from the upper deck died down and even the chattiest of the girls had fallen silent. No one actually said anything, but they suddenly seemed reluctant to go on with their journey. Grace's heart sank when she heard someone sobbing quietly and a little voice say, 'I want to go home.'

Grace got off first and, despite the unhappy memories this station evoked, she managed to smile as she turned round to face her charges. She called out encouragingly, 'Come along, boys and girls. We're off on holiday. We're going to the country. What fun it will be!' *Holiday? God forgive me for duping them like this*, she thought.

Her strategy might have worked if they had been able to head straight for whichever train awaited them. But the station was already swarming with men in uniform and with children from her own and other schools. Some mothers had turned up to say goodbye, although they had been advised not to. Many of them were crying and this had started their children off. Other children watched them, round-eyed and getting more miserable by the minute. Predictably, a growing number of children needed to go to the station toilets, and a small group of mothers had to be recruited to take them there.

As trains filled up and departed Grace glanced up at the station clock. Eleven o'clock. If they had to wait much longer she envisaged rebellion and the children demanding to be taken home. Some of them might actually make a break for it. That had happened when the first lot of children had been evacuated in September.

Suddenly the loudspeakers boomed into life and unintelligible instructions echoed above their heads. Grace could not understand a garbled word of it but someone must have done, because at last they began to move. A group of mothers with babies and children under school age were being led by an official-looking man in a bowler hat. They walked up the slope to the internal bridge that crossed over the main lines to the platform where their train was already building up steam. For most of the children the mood picked up again. Many of them stopped on the bridge to look down on the train. There were shrieks of delight and horror when a puff of steam engulfed them.

When it was Grace's turn to lead her group forward, one of the girls began to cry. Rita Bevan. *Oh no*, Grace thought. Once Rita turned on the waterworks it was hard to turn them off again. She was thirteen years old but she was a mousy little slip of a girl who looked at least two years younger. On most days she came to school unwashed and hungry, and Grace dreaded to speculate what the state of the clothes in her grubby pillowcase might be.

She had no idea what words of comfort might suffice to soothe the child, but just as she was about to go and deal with her, the girl standing in front of Rita turned round to face her. The girl smiled sympathetically and asked, 'Why are you crying?'

Grace recognised her and stopped to listen to their conversation.

'Because I'm afraid,' Rita said. 'Where are they taking us?'

'You heard Miss Norton. We're going to the countryside.'

'I don't like the countryside.'

'Have you ever been here?'

'No. That's why I'm afraid. What if it's horrible?'

'I'm sure it won't be.'

Rita sniffed and looked doubtful.

'Just think,' the other girl continued. 'There'll be flowers and trees and fields where we can play. We'll get fresh eggs and milk, won't you like that?'

Rita nodded. 'Mebbees I will. But that's not the only reason I'm afeared.' Rita's nose had begun to run and she paused to wipe her face with the back of her hand. A very dirty hand, Grace noticed.

'What else are you frightened of?' the girl asked.

'The train. I've never been on a train. Listen to all that hissing and look at the steam! It's like a dragon!'

Dragon? Not bad, Grace thought. *The poor little scrap has quite an imagination.*

The other children were becoming restless. Some of them were nudging each other and laughing, but the girl who was comforting Rita said, 'Oh, is that it? Well, don't worry, I've gone to the seaside on a train now and then, and there's nothing to be frightened of. In fact it was a lot of fun.'

'Really?' Rita looked unbelieving.

'Yes, it was.'

'Can I sit beside you?' Rita asked.

'Of course you can.'

The tears dried up and Rita smiled nervously. 'Right-oh, then,' she said.

Grace realised that the matter was settled. She went to the head of the line and told them in her no-nonsense teacher's voice to follow her, but before they set off she managed to catch Hazel Stafford's eye and nod and smile her thanks.

It was easy enough to get them on to the train but once they were in the narrow corridor of the carriage they began to push and shove and bang each other's knees with their bags and cases. By the time she had settled her brood into their compartments, Grace was exhausted. The journey itself shouldn't take too long, but nevertheless, it was going to be a long day ahead.

Hazel was aware that the other girls in her compartment were annoyed with her. All except Rita. As the train shuddered and gradually began to build up speed, Rita turned her head and stared out of the window. Soon they had left the station behind, and steep rows of soot-stained terrace houses and factories gradually gave way to stretches of fields, punctuated by pit villages, identified by the stark outlines of the pit head winding gear. And then there was only fresh green countryside. Rita seemed totally unaware of the disdainful looks being directed her way. Or perhaps she was so used to this kind of treatment that she had become hardened to it.

'Oh, what can that smell be?' someone said.

'Pooh, it's disgusting!' her neighbour chipped in.

Another girl said nothing, but she raised her chin and held her nose between thumb and forefinger.

Rita remained silent as she stared out of the window, entranced as Hazel herself was at the sight of sunlight dappling the river.

Hazel knew that it wouldn't help matters if she tried to stop them; it might only make things worse. So she kept quiet and eventually they got sick of taunting someone who ignored them so

58

completely and began to talk amongst themselves. Altogether there were eight girls in the compartment. Apart from Hazel, two of the others had not played any part in the cruel mockery.

Irene Walker, sitting opposite Rita, was scowling but Hazel wasn't sure where her anger was directed. Maybe she was cross with the others for behaving that way. Hazel hoped this was so, because she rather liked Irene. She could flare up sometimes but her anger never lasted very long. Carol Clark, sitting next to the door that opened onto the corridor, had not reacted at all. Her pretty face gave no hint of what she might be thinking. She wasn't exactly unpopular at school because she was never rude or actively unfriendly to anyone. She had a certain air of confidence which discouraged anyone who might wish to be unpleasant to her. None of the other girls ever asked her if she wanted to join in, but she seemed to be happy to keep herself to herself.

How much better this would be if Mavis could be here, Hazel thought. They had been friends since their first day at school, but last September Mavis had been sent to stay with her mother's sister in Canada. In her first letter to Hazel she had sounded very sorry for herself. The train journey to Liverpool had taken ages and the boat had been crowded and uncomfortable. However, once she had settled, she had soon cheered up and made friends with her cousins and at her school. Hazel looked forward to receiving her letters but neither of them knew when they would meet up again.

The sun was shining directly into their compartment and the heat was stifling. Irene opened the window but closed it quickly when they were all speckled with gritty soot. One by one the girls took their coats off and struggled to put them in the overhead racks. Rita turned her head to watch them but didn't attempt to remove her own coat. She must be boiling hot, Hazel thought, and she wondered if it was because everyone else was wearing newly washed dresses and Rita probably was not. No one felt like talking any more.

Hazel looked out of the window as the train slowed down to pass through a small station with tubs of bright flowers on the platforms. A woman in a flowered dress and a sunhat sat on a bench seat with her arm around a small boy who was clutching a teddy bear. There were suitcases on the ground at their feet. Hazel wondered if they were going to stay with family friends and thought how lucky the boy was to have his mother with him.

The train picked up speed again and the repetitive rhythm of the wheels on the tracks reminded Hazel of a poem they had learned at school. She began to recite it in her head:

Faster than fairies, faster than witches,
Bridges and houses, hedges and ditches;
And charging along like troops in a battle
All through the meadows the horses and cattle...

She leaned back and closed her eyes, trying to picture the images in the poem. The brambles, the daisies, the horse and cart, and the mill by the river. Soon she would be seeing these things in real life rather than just reading about them in a school book.

Grace, along with the other teachers, Moira, Jeanette and Peggy, spent most of the journey patrolling the long corridors and looking into the separate compartments to check on the children. Grace, at forty-nine, was much older than the other three women, who were still in their twenties. She was slimmer and her style of dressing was more reserved than that of the younger teachers who had taken up the more casual modern styles with enthusiasm. Even though she was told she looked young for her age she sometimes felt as though she had come from another age entirely.

She had been engaged to be married when the last war started, but after waving goodbye to her fiancé as he marched with his platoon into the station they had just left, she had never seen him again. Once in France, he had not lived long enough even to send a letter home to Grace or to his parents. Believing she could never love again, she had decided to train to be a teacher. She liked her job but she hoped the same fate of enforced spinsterhood was not awaiting any of the young women she was travelling with today.

As the train rattled along, Grace occasionally had to slide one of the doors open and deal with boisterous behaviour, but most of the children were too dozy with the heat to cause any trouble. Annoyingly, some of them had started to eat their sandwiches before the train had even left the station. The first group would be leaving the train in less than an hour; they had been told to keep their food until lunchtime as it might be a while before they were settled with their host families. Well, the little devils would just have to go hungry, Grace thought, and immediately felt guilty.

These children, bewildered by what was happening to the world they knew, had been torn away from their homes and families, most of them happy families as far as Grace could tell, for the duration of the war. Heaven knew what kind of homes they would find themselves in and how many of them would cry themselves to sleep in strange beds tonight.

The train steamed along, following the course of the river Tyne. Soon it was time for Peggy and her charges, the youngest children, to leave the train. This took much longer than it should have done because many of the children had shed their coats and some of them their shoes. There was a bad-tempered scramble to get ready. And then, just as the guard was about to raise his flag and blow his whistle, a minor panic arose because a few of them had left their gas masks on the train and had to go back for them.

Order was restored, but not for long. Some of the children gathered on the station platform realised that their older brothers and sisters were still on the train. Because of the hasty way this second evacuation had been arranged, no one had thought to make sure that siblings should be in the same group.

The little ones were weeping as the train pulled away from the platform, and their older brothers and sisters, seeing the forlorn group vanishing into the distance, began to cry too. All that Grace and the other teachers could do was assure them that they would sort things out as soon as possible and it wouldn't be too long before they would be reunited. Then they made sure that this wouldn't happen to the next group by frantically swapping children around until everyone was happy.

Even so, at the next two stations there was a fair amount of chaos, and the last group, Grace's own, did not arrive at Withenmoor until mid-afternoon, much later than they should have done. They were met at the station by a vaguely harassed-looking middle-aged woman, who nevertheless did her best to look welcoming. She approached Grace briskly.

'I'm Mrs Edwards, Dorothy Edwards,' she said. She offered a hand. 'And you are?'

'Grace Norton.'

They shook hands and Mrs Edwards shifted her gaze to the group of children who were looking up at her curiously.

She frowned. 'How many children are there?' she asked.

'Forty. Roughly half of them girls,' Grace replied.

'Oh dear.'

'Is there a problem?'

'Well...' Dorothy Edwards was hesitant. 'Not really. We weren't expecting quite so many, but I'm sure we'll manage.'

Grace's heart sank. She'd heard of the rumours circulating in school staffrooms about trailing round the streets with bands of bewildered and apprehensive children and knocking on strangers' doors and asking them if they would take a child in — maybe two. She hoped the stories were apocryphal but she didn't feel optimistic.

Mrs Edwards must have sensed her distress. 'Don't worry,' she said. 'We'll find decent homes for all of them. The local people are mostly kind and generous.' She turned to address the children. 'Now, girls and boys, if you follow me we'll go to the village hall. Two nice ladies have got sandwiches and milk waiting for you.' She paused and added smilingly, 'And home-made cakes.'

'How kind,' Grace said. She decided not to mention the packed lunches they had brought with them because, in any case, she suspected that most of them had probably been eaten by now.

The children had obviously appreciated the bit about home-made cakes because when Grace turned to look at them most of them had cheered up. Now was the time to rally the troops. 'Before we set off' she said, 'I want you to remember we are guests here in Withenmoor and guests must be polite. When we leave the station it will be the first time anyone here has seen you and I want you all to be a credit to your parents, to the school, and to me.'

They set off in their usual crocodile. They did not have far to go but by the time they reached the hall Grace had learned that Dorothy Edwards was the wife of the local head teacher and, as Grace would be taking up teaching duties in his school, she hoped Grace would agree to being billeted with them. And they would be glad to help in any way they could. Also that Grace must dispense

64

with formality and call her new hostess Dorothy.

Rita insisted on partnering Hazel. As Miss Norton's group trudged somewhat wearily through the pleasant, sun-filled streets Hazel watched her new friend gazing in wonder at the clean scrubbed doorsteps, the neat gardens full of unfamiliar flowers and the curtains twitching at windows as the small procession went by. She pulled at Hazel's sleeve.

'What is it?' Hazel asked.

'They're looking at us,' Rita whispered.

'That's all right.'

'I'm not so sure of that.'

'Why not?'

'If they don't like the look of us they might send us back and I've decided I don't want to go.'

'Don't worry. I don't think that will happen.'

'Are you sure?'

'As sure as I can be.'

Rita was silent for a while and then she said, 'They were daft, weren't they?'

'Who?'

'Them that was sent away before and ran home again. They didn't realise how lucky they were.'

'They were homesick,' Hazel said. 'They missed their families. That's natural, isn't it?'

Rita shook her head. 'Depends what sort of home they had. You know what I mean?'

Hazel didn't know what to say. After a pause she replied, 'I think I do.'

Rita was quiet after that. She seemed to withdraw into some troubled place inside her head. However, as soon as they entered the village hall

65

and saw two long trestle tables set up with plates of sandwiches and cakes she cheered up again.

Miss Norton told everyone to leave their coats and their belongings on the chairs set out along the walls then sent the boys to one table and the girls to the other. Nobody wanted to sit next to Rita. The girls made sure that she was at the end of the row. Hazel sat next to her.

The talk at the table was all about what sort of home they would be going to. Some of them had heard the stories about cruel people who had made the evacuees work and had not given them enough to eat. Really rough country folk, someone said, whose homes were no better than hovels. All the time they were talking they were attacking the plates of sandwiches greedily, as if they hadn't already eaten the sandwiches their mothers had given them.

Carol stared at the way some of her classmates were eating and made a moue of distaste. Very few of them had asked if they could go and wash their hands, as she had, and it seemed many of them had not been told that it was rude to speak with your mouth full. She realised that, momentarily, she had made no effort to hide her opinion of them and she darted a look across the table uneasily. She hoped no one had noticed her expression of disgust. She didn't want to antagonise anyone. Some of the girls in her class were quick to take offence, especially Irene Walker, and they wouldn't hesitate to deal roughly with anyone they thought was being snobbish.

A woman in a flowered wrap-around pinafore

came up behind her with a jug of milk. 'Would you like a fill-up, dear?' she asked. She spoke in what Carol's mother would call refined tones.

Carol turned her head. She saw a delicate china brooch – a posy of pink, white and blue flowers – pinned at the neck of her blouse. It was the kind of brooch her mother loved and Carol knew it must have been expensive. She smiled up into the woman's kindly face. 'Yes, please. That's very kind of you.'

The woman's answering smile showed her pleased surprise. 'Not at all, dear. We're all very glad to be doing something for you. It's our own chance to help the war effort.'

The jug was empty and she walked towards the door that led into the kitchen. Another of the helpers was just coming out with a plate piled high with currant buns. The two ladies smiled at each other and chatted briefly. Carol saw them glance her way and smile. They realise that I'm not like the rest of them, she thought. Hopefully they'll make sure that I go to a better sort of home. She returned to her sandwiches with a smile of satisfaction.

Irene had seen it all, starting with the sneering expression on Carol Clark's face when she'd looked at the other girls on her table. She had felt the heat spreading up from her neck to stain her cheeks with the tell-tale flush of anger and she lowered her head. She had almost shouted out: *What are you looking at, you stuck-up snob, and who do you think you are? Lady Muck?* But she had controlled herself. She didn't want to get into trouble on her first day away from home. Miss Norton had told them to remember they were guests here and that guests must be polite.

Irene liked Miss Norton, everybody did, even the roughest of the boys. She wasn't soft, she stood no nonsense, but she had a way with her that made everyone respect her and want to please her. It was rumoured that she had never actually used the cane that hung from a hook on the wall beside the blackboard. No one could remember a single occasion. Miss Norton wasn't young. She must be past forty, but she had a lovely complexion and shiny brown shoulder-length hair. Some of the girls had a bit of a pash on her and they loved to speculate on why such a nice-looking woman had never married. Their favourite explanation was that her sweetheart, a brave, handsome young soldier, had been killed in the last war and that Miss Norton, heart-broken, had vowed that she would never marry.

The exact details of the story often changed, depending on the latest romantic film they had seen at the pictures. Irene thought it was all a bit fanciful, but whatever the truth was, she knew that they were lucky to have Miss Norton here with them and she didn't want to do anything that would upset or annoy her.

So she held her peace but was sorely tested a moment or two later when she heard the way Carol smarmed up to the lady who came to pour her some more milk. *Yes, please. That's very kind of you*, she'd said in that ladylike little voice of hers. How she could put it on! Huh! Irene was pretty sure that Carol was trying her best to get chosen by one of the better-off folk; maybe by one of these woman who had been there to greet them and had been so nice even to poor, scruffy little Rita Bevan.

As soon as she had this thought, Irene felt uncomfortable. She could hardly blame Carol for wanting to go to a nice home when that was her own parents wanted for her – and, she had to admit, what she wanted for herself. But, unlike Carol, she hoped she would never look down on anyone who was not so lucky as she was. Kids like Rita Bevan. The thought of Rita made her feel even worse. When the other girls had been horrible to Rita on the train she had made no attempt to defend the poor kid. Not like Hazel Stafford. Hazel had sat beside Rita and treated her just like she would treat anyone else. *I did nothing to stick up for Rita,* Irene thought, *so in a way I was just as bad as the rest of them.*

Even before they had finished their sandwiches and cake, the hall started filling up with people who had agreed to take children into their homes. Grace was apprehensive. She had heard what had happened to some of the groups last September and she was determined that it wouldn't become a sort of beauty contest with the cleanest and nicest looking of the children being chosen first. However, it soon became obvious that Mrs Edwards had assumed that she was in charge of billeting, and all Grace could do was to unobtrusively gather together a small group of the better looking and brightest boys and girls and instruct them to help clear the tables, stack the chairs, and even to help with the washing-up in the kitchen.

The ploy worked better than she had hoped it would. Even the rough and ready Billy Hobson and his pals had found people willing to take them. Very soon Dorothy Edwards bustled up to her and told her that the only children left were the little work group and, 'One poor, benighted, runny-nosed little waif who might prove to be a problem.'

Grace sighed. 'Rita Bevan.'

'Yes, that's the name on her label.'

Poor little parcel, Grace thought.

Mrs Edwards was shaking her head. 'I reckon we've done well. I mean, not all the children were as clean as they should have been, even if they weren't as bad as Rita. I take it their parents were instructed to make sure they were clean and tidy?'

'Of course,' Grace answered tersely.

'Oh, my dear, I wasn't criticising you. Even here in Withenmoor we have some problem families. I can imagine only too well what you have to deal with in the poorest part of a big city. I hope I haven't offended you?'

Grace shook her head. 'You haven't,' she said but she couldn't help feeling slightly irritated by the woman's overbearing manner.

Dorothy sighed. 'Ah, well, if we can't find a home for Rita by the end of the day, I'll take her in myself, although Charles didn't think we should have any children at all. Having them in our house would mean that the poor little mites would have to be on their best behaviour at times. Also it wouldn't be fair on you. After school you need a break from duties.'

Grace's opinion of Mrs Edwards shifted a little.

I misjudged her, she thought. *I suppose I had decided she was a self-important do-gooder, but now I see that she is genuinely kind-hearted.*

'Now let me see who we've got left,' Dorothy said. 'As well as Rita we have three girls and a couple of boys.' She scrutinised them for a moment and then turned to smile at Grace. 'That was clever of you,' she said. 'Hiding the best looking until all the others had been claimed.'

The two local women who had been helping had already gone, each one taking a child with her. Grace was worried. 'Maybe not so clever,' she said.

'What do you mean?'

'It's been a good quarter of an hour since anyone else has come to take any of the children.'

Dorothy smiled. 'Don't worry,' she said. 'Some folk said they would be along later. Margaret Forsyth has a house big enough to take two or more and Jack Armstrong has a farm a little way out of town. I think he'll be very pleased to take both of the boys. Are they twins, by the way? They look so alike.'

'Joe and Jimmy Doyle. No, they're not twins. They're brothers with scarcely a year between them. Joe is in a class below but I arranged it so siblings could be together.'

She didn't admit that this plan had gone a little astray and had had to be sorted out when the journey was underway. She thought she might be haunted for life by the glimpse of those children weeping after the first drop-off.

'You're frowning,' Dorothy Edwards said. 'Why?'

71

'You say Mr Armstrong is a farmer. Will he expect the boys to work on the farm?'

'I expect he will. But I know what you're thinking and I can assure you it won't be a matter of slave labour. He's a good man, and his wife is a kind-hearted woman. They'll be well looked after.'

Grace became aware that the remaining children were laughing – and the spluttering noises they were making meant they were trying very hard not to. She looked across the hall to where they had been sorting out their bags and cases and putting on their coats as she had instructed them. They were staring in the direction of an odd-looking figure that had come in from the street and was walking towards them.

It took Grace a second or two to realise that, despite the masculine attire, what she was seeing was a comfortably rounded middle-aged woman. She was wearing corduroy slacks and an ancient tweed jacket with leather patches on the elbows. The jacket was open to reveal a checked shirt straining over an ample bosom. Her face was weather-beaten, and wisps of mousy hair escaped from under the brim of her felt hat. Heavy-duty boots completed the picture as she clumped across the polished linoleum-covered floor.

'It's Worzel Gummidge,' Joe, the younger of the Doyle brothers, said and he laughed openly.

Grace was mortified. It was very bad-mannered of the boy. She glanced at Dorothy. 'I'm sorry about that,' she said.

'Don't worry. Molly's used to that sort of re-action when people meet her for the first time. I think she enjoys being thought of as an eccentric.'

'You know her?'

'Everyone hereabouts knows Molly Watkins. She has a smallholding not far out of town and she makes a good living. I've often thought that she could go into Newcastle and get some really good clothes in Fenwick's French Salon if she wanted to. In fact I once asked her if she'd like to do that and I would go with her, but she told me that although she likes good clothes, she never goes anywhere where she would be able to wear them.'

'Were you expecting her?'

'No, not really. She values the peace and quiet of her little cottage.'

'But you think she's come to take one of the children?'

'She wouldn't waste her time otherwise.'

Grace leaned towards Dorothy and whispered, 'Look at the girls.'

Dorothy did so and laughed quietly. 'Two of them don't know what to make of her, one of them is horrified and little Rita is captivated. I think we've solved that problem.'

'Oh, but ... I mean...' Grace nerved herself to oppose Mrs Edwards. 'I couldn't let one of my children go with Miss Watkins.'

'Why not?'

'Well, I mean... I don't know how to put this, but Rita needs someone who will keep her clean and...'

'You don't think Molly will?'

Grace felt wretched. 'No, I don't suppose I do.'

'Look at Molly. Look at her properly. What do you see that you could object to?'

'Well ... she's, she's...'

73

'Dirty? Is that what you were going to say?'

Grace nodded unhappily.

Dorothy shook her head. 'Look again. She looks as though she buys her clothes from the rag and bone man, but if she does, everything has been washed and mended. Her unconventional clothes are as clean as Molly is herself. Look at her boots. Clean and polished. And her house – well, you would get a nice surprise there.'

'What do you mean?'

'I go up there now and then to buy vegetables or eggs, and I can assure you that I have no objection to sitting at her kitchen table and drinking tea with her. Everything is sparkling clean.' Dorothy smiled. 'Molly may not care too much about her own appearance, but her home is a different matter. All her furniture and furnishings are of the highest quality. You could even say tasteful. And she insists on having the best kitchen equipment that money can buy. Her cottage is a little palace. I doubt if Rita will ever have known such a clean and comfortable home.' She paused. 'Now why are you frowning?'

'If all that is true, why would Molly want to take Rita?'

'Because she has a soft heart. It's marvellous how stray cats and dogs find their way to her fireside. Look, I think she has already made her mind up.'

Grace looked and saw that Miss Watkins was helping Rita button up her coat. Rita's smile was radiant.

Dorothy turned to smile at Grace. 'Shall we make it official and let them go before Molly's hobnail boots do any more damage to this beautifully polished floor?'

Rita was ready to go. The two mismatched buttons on her coat were done up, her gas mask was over her shoulder and she was clutching the pillowcase that contained her clothes. Suddenly her smile vanished.

'What's the matter?' Miss Watkins asked her.

'Me friend – can me friend come too?' She pointed towards Hazel.

'I'm sorry, pet, but I haven't got room for anyone else.'

Rita looked as if she was going to cry. Her nose began to run.

'Listen,' Molly said. 'I haven't got a bed for her but you'll still be going to school together, and she's welcome to come and have tea with us whenever we can arrange it. How about that? Will that please you?'

Rita sniffed and nodded. She raised one hand and wiped her nose with her coat sleeve. Out of the corner of her eye Grace saw Dorothy shudder.

'Is it all right to go now?' Miss Watkins asked.

'Yes,' Grace and Dorothy said in unison.

'Has she got her ration book?'

'It's in with her clothes. I checked,' Grace told her.

'Then we'll be off.'

Molly took hold of Rita's hand. 'Say goodbye to your pals.'

Rita turned towards the others. 'Ta-ra,' she said waveringly.

Only Carol did not bother to reply.

Miss Watkins and Rita had only just left the hall

when two other people arrived in quick succession. Dorothy introduced them to Grace as Miss Margaret Forsyth and Mr Jack Armstrong. Jack Armstrong was a big, genial man and after the formalities the Doyle brothers went with him happily enough.

Miss Forsyth was well spoken and had the air of someone who was used to being deferred to. Nevertheless she gave every appearance of being genuinely delighted to help and, as Dorothy had predicted, had been quite happy to take all three remaining girls. Grace watched them leave the hall and wondered how they would adapt to their new life.

Hazel was thoughtful and intuitively intelligent, a thoroughly nice child. Irene was more mature than the other girls physically and good-natured at heart, but she needed to learn to control her quick temper. And Carol. Grace was perplexed. The girl was well-spoken and good-mannered, but she seemed to have erected some kind of barrier between herself and the world around her. These three girls, although they were not enemies, had never been close friends. And now they were going to have to live alongside each other, in a stranger's house, for the duration of the war.

Chapter Four

Letters home

Dear Mam,

We arrived safely in Withenmoor, and Irene Walker, Carol Clark and I have come to live with a lady called Miss Forsyth in Hillside House. She collected us from the village hall and we had a long walk past all the shops and houses and up a narrow country road to this house, which is perched on a hillside high up above the other houses. It's hard to guess how old Miss Forsyth is. She looks as though she could be the same age as our teacher, Miss Norton.

She is very fit. She strode ahead and expected us to keep up with her. 'Come along, girls. Don't dawdle!' she kept telling us. Have I made her sound fierce? Well, she isn't really. It's just her way. When we arrived at the house she told us that we were very welcome but that we must play fair and behave ourselves.

You would love this house. It's big and old looking, and has marvellous views over the countryside. Inside the house everything looks as though it's been there for ages. It's like one of those grand houses you see in the pictures. You can just imagine Margaret Lockwood coming down the oak staircase in a floaty evening gown and James Mason waiting in the hall to whisk her off to some grand ball.

We have a bedroom each! Even though the house is old, the rooms look very comfortable. Miss Forsyth warned us that even in the summer we might feel cold at night. The house, being up in the hills like this, gets chilly once the sun goes down. She said she was sorry she wouldn't be able to keep the fires in our bedrooms burning because she was saving the coal in case it was rationed.

After we had unpacked we had a meal in the dining room. Miss Forsyth called it 'dinner'. That's when we met Mrs Ellis who works here. She's round and plump just as you would expect a cook to be, but she didn't seem pleased to see us. We also met a girl called Bridget. Miss Forsyth told us that she was her niece from London who had arrived a few days ago and would be staying here along with us.

Bridget is slim just like her aunt and she has the same pale blond hair. There's a definite family resemblance. She was wearing a lovely pink woollen dress with a cream-coloured Peter Pan collar and long sleeves. I think she must be the same age as we are, but the dress made her look younger. She didn't say very much but then neither did we. I think Irene and Carol and I were all a bit overawed by where we found ourselves.

We had vegetable soup, home-made fishcakes with cabbage, and rice pudding. That doesn't sound very grand, does it? Miss Forsyth said it was because the rationing was beginning to bite. It was almost as if she was apologising to us as if we were proper guests and not just bothersome little vackies.

When Mrs Ellis came in to clear the table Irene and I got up to help her. Miss Forsyth looked puzzled for a moment and then she said, 'Oh, yes. Thank you, girls. That's quite right. Mrs Ellis has enough to do in this big house now that Pam and Maureen have gone to join the ATS. We must all do our share.' She didn't

78

explain, but Pam and Maureen must have been housemaids there.

Carol must not have heard her. She and Bridget were talking and they just sat there. Once in the kitchen Irene and I helped with the dishes. Mrs Ellis wasn't exactly friendly. She kept shaking her head and sighing. She told us that Miss Forsyth made her own bed and cleaned her own room now, although she had not been brought up to do housework. Mrs Ellis said that we should look after our own rooms and help in any other way we could.

Then Carol and Bridget came into the kitchen and said we had to come with them to the library. I didn't know what I was expecting. Maybe we were going to walk down into Withenmoor. You can imagine my surprise when we followed them across the entrance hall and into a large room with bookshelves all round the wall. I couldn't possibly count the number of books. Some of them looked very old.

Miss Forsyth was waiting for us at a table set into a large bay window. She told us that she thought we ought to write home and we were to help ourselves to the paper and envelopes she'd put there for us. It wasn't real notepaper. It looked like empty pages torn from old exercise books and there was plenty of it. There were some pens in a tray and pen wipers and blotting paper and bottles of ink. She said we must take a bottle of ink each because she didn't want any accidents caused by reaching over the table with dripping pens.

She told us she used to do her homework here when she was a child and so did her younger brother, Bridget's father. They had someone to teach them at home until they went off to boarding schools. The dictionary and the world atlas had been on the table ever since.

Miss Forsyth said we must tell our parents that if they wanted to come and visit us they would be welcome. Isn't that wonderful? Then she said if we put our letters in envelopes and sealed them she would stick on the stamps. She would do that for all of us once a week. Then she smiled and said that she wouldn't be censoring any of our letters. She meant she wouldn't read them. She said she thought that would be bad manners and in any case she didn't think any of us were enemy spies. We were quiet for a moment until we realised she'd made a joke, then we all laughed and she blushed and looked quite pleased.

I told Miss Forsyth I had my own notepaper and I would use that if I wrote to my friend Mavis. She smiled and said I could if I wanted to but I was welcome to use her paper when I ran out. She didn't say anything about buying my own stamps for any extra letters but I wouldn't dream of asking her.

I'm missing you already but you can see from this letter that I don't need our secret code.

Lots of love,
Hazel xxx

Irene stared across the table to where Hazel was scribbling away and wondered what on earth she had to say that took up so many sheets of paper. Of course Hazel was top of the class in English and Miss Norton often asked her to read her homework compositions out loud. Sometimes it was pretty ordinary stuff they had to write about, like 'A day at the Seaside'.

Irene had struggled with that one. She couldn't

remember ever going to the seaside with her mother, who had said that sitting on the beach and getting sand in your shoes and your hair was not her idea of a good day out. Terry had taken her to the coast once or twice but they had spent all their time and money in the amusement arcades on the promenade. Anything left over bought them a bag of winkles and a couple of pins.

Irene could still remember Hazel's composition about the seaside.

Hazel had started with her and her mam getting up early to make the sandwiches. Then the train ride from Newcastle to Cullercoats, finding a place big enough to spread their rug on the crowded beach. The small children building sandcastles and their dads wading into the sea with their trouser legs rolled up while their mams and their grandmas sat on deckchairs drinking tea from their Thermos flasks.

A dog had plunged into the sea after a ball then made everyone squeal when it came back and shook itself, sending out a curved spray of sparkling drops of salty water. That was how Hazel had described it. At the end of the day Hazel and her mam had stopped on the promenade to look down at the deserted bay. The tide was coming in and pushing the sandcastles over. It had been like a story and, listening to it, Irene had almost felt as if she was there.

Irene remembered that when Hazel had stopped reading and sat down again, Rita Bevan had started to cry. She was always doing that, you never knew what might set her off, and Miss Norton was always very patient with her. This time

81

Rita was blubbing because she had never been to the seaside and she didn't think she would ever have the chance.

Poor kid, Irene thought, and she wondered briefly how she was getting on with that funny-looking woman who looked as though she'd pinched her clothes from a scarecrow. All the same, she had a nice smile and was probably a decent sort. Irene wondered if the odd little woman was helping Rita to write a letter to send home and if Rita's mother would be interested enough to read it. She had a pretty good idea what went on in Rita's house. Everyone had.

But this wasn't getting the work done.

Irene looked down at the letter she had started writing and sighed.

Dear Mam and Dad and Terry,

I'm here in a place called Withenmoor. It was hot and stuffy in the train and some of the younger kids were crying, but apart from that the journey was okay. When we arrived we had to wait in the village hall until people came to take us away. Some ladies gave us sandwiches and cake.

Irene put her pen down on her sheet of blotting paper and sat there frowning. What should she say next? What would her family want to know? Then she remembered her father saying that he wanted her to look a cut above the other kids so that she would be taken in by respectable people. Well, she could set their minds at rest about that. She took up her pen, dipped it in her bottle of ink and began writing again.

The lady who came for me and two other girls, Hazel and Carol, is called Miss Forsyth. She speaks very posh and the woman who was in charge of boarding us out treated her as if she was an important person. Miss Forsyth is very slim and she looked very smart in a navy dress and jacket. You would have liked it, Mam, but her matching shoes were lace-ups with just a small heel. Which was just as well, because we had quite a long walk to her house and it was mostly uphill. Miss Forsyth's hair is a sort of faded blond and wisps of it kept escaping from her hair clips. She pushed it back from her face now and then but didn't seem bothered enough to fix it properly.

I think she must be in her forties but that didn't stop her from hurrying us along. We could see her house when we were about halfway there. Miss Forsyth turned to us and smiled and said, 'Not far now!' She pointed to a big posh house on the hillside. I couldn't believe it. It looked far too big for a single lady. I guessed she must be quite well off.

When we arrived I wasn't so sure. The house certainly looks grand from the outside but inside is a different matter. All the furniture is old-fashioned. She can't have bought anything new for years. I wondered if she had taken us in because she needs the money people get when they take vackies. But she has a woman working for her, Mrs Ellis. She's a cook and it seems there were a couple of maids who left to join up. I don't think Mrs Ellis likes us being here.

Miss Forsyth's niece is staying here, too. She didn't say much at first but then she began chatting to Carol Clark, who is a right little snob.

Irene paused and looked down at what she had written. She was quite pleased with herself. Miss Norton had often told her that she wasn't doing herself justice and that if she applied herself more she could be in the top set. She read her letter through and thought it would do. Then, remembering that Miss Forsyth had told them that their parents could pay a visit, she added that fact and then signed off with love and kisses.

Carol chose a pen from the tray and sat and thought for a while before she carefully opened her bottle of ink. She smiled because she knew that her parents, especially her mother, would be pleased with what she had to tell them.

'Dear Mummy and Daddy,' she wrote.

She paused and wondered where exactly she should begin. If she said that she had hated the crowded train journey and having to share a compartment with the smelly little Bevan girl, then having to wait for ages in the village hall with others nearly as bad, it would only start her mother wondering about such things as scabies and nits, and she might start nagging her father to bring her home and find a private place for her. Carol did not want to go home. She wanted to stay here at Hillside House. She knew her parents would want to know something about the journey, so she would just have to leave out the horrible bits. She began to write again.

The train journey wasn't bad. In fact once we left the town behind it was lovely travelling through the countryside.

Both her parents would like that. She remembered how much her father enjoyed taking her mother and herself on day trips and added:

Withenmoor is an interesting place. Too small to be a town but quite big for a village. I'm sure you would like to visit it on a day out.

Now in her stride, she began writing in earnest:

We were given sandwiches, cake and milk by some very nice ladies in the village hall and I think Miss Norton made sure that I didn't go to just any old family. I think she deliberately kept me until last with two other girls because she must have known somehow that Miss Forsyth was coming and Miss Forsyth would not have taken any but the most respectable girls. The other two are Hazel Stafford and Irene Walker.

Hazel's family are poor, her mother goes out charring, but Hazel is always clean and dressed nicely, and she is quite clever. Irene doesn't work hard at school and she can be a bit common at times, but she always has nice new clothes. She even has a wristwatch. I think her family must be quite well off. So you can see that you do not need to worry about the other girls I will be living with. I'm sure Miss Forsyth would not have taken just anybody, especially as she has her own niece, Bridget, staying with her. Miss Forsyth is a respectable lady and Hillside House is very grand. It is a good walk up the hill and well away from all the other houses. I think the Forsyth family must have lived here for many years, even a hundred or more, because some of the furniture looks like antiques. There are family portraits on the walls, real oil paintings. Bridget told me that the handsome man in naval uniform in one of the pictures is her father. She said that was his dress uniform. I didn't know what that means but I didn't like to ask.

Her father is Miss Forsyth's younger brother. She told me that her parents live in London. When her grandfather died he left the London house to Bridget's father and the house in Withenmoor to her Aunt Margaret, because he didn't think her aunt would ever get married and he wanted her to have a home. Bridget thinks that Hillside House must be left to her when her aunt dies.

I think Bridget was pleased to see me. She's hardly said a word to Hazel or Irene, but, after a while, she seemed to take to me. I think that is because I am the only one who speaks as nicely as she does. She told me that her father is in command of a destroyer and she and her mother are not allowed to know where in the world he might be. Bridget's mother is an admiral's daughter. She is an ambulance driver with the ARP in London. Bridget was sent here to stay with her aunt because they wanted her to be safe from the bombing.

Bridget didn't want to come. She said her whole school, a private girls' day school in London, is going to move to a castle in Wales and she wanted to go with them, but her parents were against the idea. Bridget said that being at the school in Wales would be like being at The School at the Turrets, which is one of her favourite books. I told her that you had given me The School on the Cliff for my birthday and that I loved boarding school stories. We discovered that we both like the Chalet School books.

While we write our letters we are sitting in the room

86

Miss Forsyth calls the library. I'm sure Daddy would like to see all the books. Bridget said she didn't think we would find anything that we would want to read there as Miss Forsyth had once told her that rather than reading schoolgirl stories she should be reading the classics. She means books by people like Charles Dickens and Sir Walter Scott. When Bridget told me that, she pulled such a face that I didn't tell her that Daddy had read Oliver Twist *to me and that I had really enjoyed it.*

If you are wondering why I am writing this on paper from an old exercise book it's because Miss Forsyth says it is part of the War Effort. We must not waste anything. Bridget said her aunt had been like that even before the war. She saves the wrapping paper from parcels and will spend ages untying knots rather than cut the string.

It seems that the servants have gone off to join up but there is a cook, Mrs Ellis, who is not very polite. Our dinner wasn't as grand as I expected but it was tasty, so I suppose that's why Miss Forsyth puts up with her.

Miss Forsyth says you are welcome to come and visit. I hope you do, because then you will see for yourselves that there is no reason to worry about me.

Love and kisses,
Carol

Carol blotted her letter, folded it and sealed it in the envelope. She looked up to see Bridget doing the same.

'Good, you're finished,' Bridget said. 'My aunt says we can all go up to the old nursery where there are some board games and books. What fun!

I'm sure Aunt Margaret thinks we're all children, when you and Hazel and Irene could probably leave school on your next birthday.'

'Oh, but I won't be leaving school,' Carol said, feeling flustered. 'My parents want me to go to a good secondary school and take the School Cert and then Highers. They have enough money to send me to a private school once the war is over. They don't need me to go and work for a living.'

'How nice for you,' Bridget said, 'but we don't talk about money, you know.'

Ignoring Carol's blush, Bridget led the way to the old nursery. On the way she revised her opinion of Carol slightly. At first she had been fooled by the way the girl spoke, but it was obvious now that her background might not be much better than those of the other two girls. Still, if she was going to have a friend here in the back of beyond, Carol might be the only girl her mother would approve of. Bridget thought back over the letter she had written:

Dearest Mummy,

Thank you for your very sweet letter but I am still trying to forgive you and Daddy for sending me here. You went to boarding school yourself, so you must know how much fun it would be if I could go with the school to the castle in Wales.

You didn't have to pretend that Aunt Margaret is lonely and asked for my company. She has made me very welcome but it's plain to see that she has no idea how to deal with a young person. Now she has four of us, because her evacuees arrived today. They are three girls about the same age as I am and they have come from Newcastle. Before you think how nice it will be for me to have company, I had better tell you something about them. They are called Hazel, Carol and Irene. I will try to describe them for you.

Irene is blonde and blue-eyed and pretty in a film actress sort of way. In other words, a trifle common looking. Her clothes all look new and expensive and she has a very nice wristwatch. That's a puzzle, because when she speaks she has a rough kind of accent. She looks older than her age. She's got curves, if you know what I mean (am I being vulgar?). I think she could even pass for sixteen if she put a bit of lipstick on and wore stockings instead of socks. I caught her scowling at me now and then as if she doesn't approve of me. But I don't care because I don't think that sort of girl could ever be my friend.

Hazel is quiet and has good manners. Her accent isn't as pronounced as Irene's but, although she is clean and tidy, her clothes are old and washed-out looking. She has wavy brown hair and unusual green eyes. I think when she is a little older she may be quite beautiful. She seems to be interested in this house and all that is in it, but she is not overawed. I think she's a confident sort of girl. The type that in a boarding school story would be described as a 'good sort'. I don't know if Hazel and I could be friends, our backgrounds are too different, but I think I might like getting to know her.

Carol and I got talking straight away. She is very attractive with smooth black hair cut stylishly, a pale complexion and grey eyes. She speaks very well and she likes to read the same kind of books that I do. She seems to hold herself a little apart from the other two and I suspect she thinks she is socially superior to them. She

89

certainly acts as if she is. I think it will be easier for me to be friends with her than either of the other two.

I don't know how Aunt Margaret is going to manage this house now that all the household staff have gone except for Mrs Ellis, the cook, and a woman who comes in twice a week to do the rough work. Ted, the gardener, is too old to be called up and he is turning most of the lovely lawns and flowerbeds into vegetable gardens. I heard Mrs Ellis telling Aunt Margaret that she ought to ask about getting some of the older boy evacuees along to help Ted, but Aunt Margaret said Ted would hate that. He guards his domain very fiercely.

I say my prayers every night and ask God to keep Daddy safe from the U-boats and to look after you when you're driving around London during the air raids. That's the real reason you sent me to Hillside House, isn't it? You want me to be with family if ever anything happens to you and Daddy. I couldn't bear it if I lost either of you. Darling Mummy, please, please, please take care.

Love,
Bridget

Margaret Forsyth sat at the table in the library and put stamps on the envelopes as she had promised. She would have liked to post them straight away, but she had no one she could ask to take them. Mrs Ellis had already gone home, and although home for her was a flat in the converted outbuildings across the stable yard, the poor woman worked hard enough and it would be quite wrong to ask her to walk down the hill to the nearest post box and back again. The letters would have to wait. She would sort something out tomorrow.

Although she would have liked a walk herself, she wasn't sure if it would be correct to leave the girls alone in the house. They were old enough to be left, she supposed, but three of the girls were strangers. Bridget would be all right, but she had only just met Hazel, Carol and Irene. Although first impressions had been good, she had no real idea of their characters or what trouble they might get into if left without supervision in a strange house. She sighed. Taking on these girls was quite a responsibility and she wanted to be worthy of their parents' trust. She had to accept that she could no longer order the days to suit herself. Her life would have to change.

But not as much, she realised, as the lives of the girls who would be here until the end of the war, plucked from the familiarity of loving homes and having to adjust to a different way of life, with no certainty that their homes would be waiting for them when the war was over. No matter how resilient the young could be, that would be a difficult path to follow. She must make it as easy for them as she could.

Chapter Five

December 1952

Standing behind the brightly lit wood and glass display counter, Irene glanced at her new wristwatch. Ten minutes to go and not a customer in sight. She began to tidy away and cover up the 'lipsticks, powder and paint' as Ray laughingly referred to the cosmetics she sold daily. There were some free samples with any Estée Lauder purchase: cute miniature lipsticks, rouges, eye shadows and face creams, and some leaflets from Revlon with a list of questions for customers to answer to make sure that the lipstick they chose would suit their personality as well as their face. Irene thought this a brilliant sales pitch and had even answered the questionnaire herself. The problem was that she no sooner got used to a particular colour than they brought out a whole new range.

She glanced at her watch again. Ray had given it to her in anticipation of Christmas. Its round face was framed with tiny diamonds and the bracelet was gold. 'It's time you had something more grown up,' Ray had said and, reluctantly, Irene had put aside the watch that her father had given her all those years ago. Len Walker had glanced at the new watch doubtingly and Irene could tell that he was wondering if the diamonds

92

were simply paste and the bracelet yellow metal instead of gold. But she also knew that he loved her far too much to spoil things for her, and his only comment had been, 'That lad must be really fond of you, our Irene.'

'And why not?' her mother had retorted. Edie Walker's eyes had widened when she saw the watch and there was no doubt expressed there. 'It's beautiful, pet. I really don't think you ought to wear it at work.'

Irene hadn't taken her advice. What was the use of having nice things if you just hid them away?

The minute the lights dimmed, signifying that the street doors were locked, Irene balanced the till and handed the money to the hovering supervisor, who was probably as keen to get away as she was.

'In a hurry, are you, Miss Walker?'

Her supervisor, Miss Barrett, was staring at her coldly. Tall, elegant and aloof, Dorothea Barrett had her black hair drawn back into a French pleat, and her face was skilfully made up. Privately, Irene thought she overdid the panstick foundation, but at her age – she must be well into her forties, maybe approaching fifty – she probably had the inevitable signs of ageing to conceal.

'No, Miss Barrett. Just checking if I had time to pop along and buy some shampoo.' Irene knew her answer was unsatisfactory and was relieved when Miss Barrett simply shook her head and sighed resignedly.

'Cut along then.'

'Thanks a ton!'

Irene took the few short steps to toiletries,

grabbed a few sachets of shampoo and a bottle of setting lotion, then thrust the money towards Sheila, who was in the process of cashing up.

'Irene!' she remonstrated.

'It's the right money. I don't need any change,' Irene said placatingly. 'Don't need a bag.'

She grinned and sped away.

The rain had turned into a fine drizzle and Irene didn't bother with her umbrella. The pavements were puddled, and before long her stockings were spotted with splashes of dirty rain. Damn. She wouldn't have time for a bath. She would just have to settle for an all-over wash with a hot soapy flannel at the bathroom sink. The important thing was to wash and set her hair. Thank goodness for her new hairdryer.

That was also a present from Ray. He had given it to her along with a really smart red leather vanity case. Ray had told her to fill the elasticated pockets inside with all her usual make-up and anything else she would need when she was travelling to engagements. She must always be prepared to make the best of herself quickly.

The bus was crowded. Irene managed to get a seat, but the man who was hanging onto the overhead rail just beside her was coughing and sneezing and probably spreading germs all over the place. She felt like telling him to use his handkerchief, but after a quick look at his miserable, angry face, she decided to keep quiet. She hoped to God that she wouldn't catch anything horrible. Not now, just when Ray was getting her bookings for the holiday season. Just when her

94

career as a singer might take off and she would never again have to stand behind the cosmetic counter at Brownlow's.

Not that she didn't enjoy her job. She loved knowing all about the new beauty products and experimenting with them. If she wanted to buy anything she had her staff discount, but even better, the reps were generous with their free samples and one chap in particular, a ringer for Stewart Granger, had shown a particular interest. Sheila from toiletries had warned her not to be taken in by him.

'He's probably got girlfriends all over the British Isles,' she'd said.

Her workmate need not have worried. After a couple of dinner dates Irene had decided that Jack Dawson was harmless. And dull. The next time he came into Brownlow's she had told him that she liked him very much but she didn't think they were right for each other. He hadn't pretended to be broken-hearted. And now, of course, there was Ray.

Her mother must have been looking out of the window for the moment Irene rounded the corner of the street. A sandwich cut into dainty triangles was waiting on the table.

'Oh, Mam,' Irene said as she got out of her wet coat.

'It's tinned salmon, your favourite. And look at you! Your face is damp and your hair's gone frizzy. You look as if you could do with a cup of hot tea.'

'I haven't time. I have to wash and set my hair.'

'What's the hurry? Surely you've got a couple

of hours yet?'

'I've got to get there before it opens to the public.'

'All right. Give me that coat. It needs hanging up to dry. Go and do what you have to do. As soon as you're ready I'll make the tea, and I'll dry your hair for you while you eat your sandwich.'

'I'm too nervous to eat. I might be sick.'

'You've just done a full day's work and you've got a long night ahead of you. If you don't eat now you might faint. Come on, Irene, when you're ready just nibble what you can.'

Irene filled the washbasin with warm water and picked up the bar of scented soap. Lux. She grinned. Doris Day said using it would make you just as lovely as a movie star. Well, tonight Irene was going to be just as lovely as Doris Day – or at least she was going to sing like her.

Shortly after, in fresh underwear, she tore the corner off a sachet of shampoo and leaned over the sink to wash her blond hair. After a couple of rinses, she towelled it roughly, smoothed in some setting lotion and then put pin curls in.

Sitting at the table in her robe, she picked the slices of cucumber out of her sandwiches and nibbled at them while her mother dried her hair as she had promised.

'What are you going to wear?' her mother asked.

'Ray wants me to look like the girl next door.'

Her mother laughed. 'He hasn't seen our neighbours.'

'You know what I mean! Fresh and wholesome and cute. Not too glamorous.'

'Pity. You can be a proper film star when you're

all dressed up.'

'Doris Day *is* a film star, and if I'm going to sing her songs, Ray wants me to dress in the same style.'

'You haven't got clothes like that.'

'Yes, I have. Just wait and see.' She stood up.

'Irene, finish your sandwich!'

'Haven't time. Back in a mo.'

Irene hurried to her bedroom, opened her wardrobe and took out a zipped bag. Ray had given it to her the night before and she had smuggled it into the house. She wanted to surprise her mother with her new appearance. She dressed carefully, applied her make-up, brushed out her hair and slipped her feet into her white peep-toe shoes.

She put her head around the kitchen door and said, 'Close your eyes.' She stepped inside, posed with one hand on her hip and the other behind her head and said, 'Okay, you can open them.'

Her mother opened her eyes, blinked and opened them wider still. She took in the short-sleeved, wide-skirted navy blue dress with tiny white polka dots, the broad white belt emphasising Irene's tiny waist, and the white bow at the collar. Her earrings were plain white clip-on discs.

'Well?' Irene said impatiently.

'You look just like her.'

'That's the idea. The question is, will I sound just like her?'

'You'll sound even better!'

'Wow! Is that my daughter or a real-life film star?'

The two women turned to see Irene's father standing in the doorway.

'Len, I'm so pleased you got back from work in time to see her,' Irene's mother said.

'What do you think, Dad?'

'I think you look a knockout.' He studied her for a moment and then asked, 'What coat are you going to wear?'

'My winter coat. What else?

'A star performer would wear something expensive. I think you should borrow your mother's fur coat. Don't you agree, Edie?'

'I do.'

Irene looked uncertain. 'Ray wants me to look like the girl next door. Would Doris Day have a fur coat?'

Her father smiled. 'More than one, I should say. That girl-next-door look is for the movies. When a star arrives at the dance hall or the theatre, she's got to look successful. I'm sure your Ray would agree with me.'

He did. When Ray arrived he smiled and said, 'That's my girl! You look a million dollars!'

'You don't look so bad, yourself, Ray,' Irene's mother said. 'New suit?'

Ray flexed his broad shoulders and fingered the wide lapels. 'Sharp, eh?'

'Very natty,' her father said and, fleetingly, Irene caught that look on his face again.

It was obvious that her mother adored Ray and loved to listen to the tales he could tell about the deals he had cut and the people he knew. But her father, while happy to have a laugh and a chat with him, seemed to be withholding judgement. Irene hoped that eventually the two men would grow closer. After all, they both loved her and she loved them.

Ray had carried his camel coat in with him and now he put it on. 'We'd better be off,' he said. 'We'll have to be there in time for Irene to have a quick rehearsal with the band.'

'The band!' Irene said. 'I still can't believe it.'

Until now she had been singing at working men's clubs and private functions. On these occasions Ray had arranged for her to be accompanied by a pianist, a double-bass player and a drummer. They were a world-weary group of middle-aged musicians in black shirts and white jackets who called themselves the Trio De Jazz. They never said much, even to each other, and as soon as they were paid at the end of the show, they would pack up and leave without further comment. Irene had no idea what they thought of her as a singer. Tonight she was going to sing with a proper dance band.

Ray went ahead to open the passenger door of the Buick and Irene hurried out, clutching her mother's fox fur coat to her body with one hand and carrying her vanity case with the other. She suspected that the rain glinting in the light from the street lamps might be turning to sleet. Once they were inside the car, Ray switched on the ignition, turned on the windscreen wipers and turned up the heater. The Buick was his latest acquisition, bought from an American airman, and it was the biggest car Irene had ever seen. Certainly nothing like it had ever driven down her street before. It was like the cars in American gangster movies.

Whenever Ray arrived a crowd of kids would gather to marvel at it, even on a night like this.

Irene's father had said something about it only doing twelve miles to the gallon, but that didn't bother Ray. He always seemed to have plenty of cash and sometimes Irene thought he liked people to know it. Tonight, before he pulled away, he wound down the window and beckoned one of the kids over. He dropped a handful of coins in the lad's palm.

'Go on, treat yourself,' he said.

'Thanks, mister.'

The small gang turned and raced as one to the brightly lit fish and chip shop on the corner.

Tonight they were travelling to the Roxy at Seaton, about ten miles away at the coast. There were three dance halls in the popular seaside resort, and in the summer months they were packed with summer visitors, but even in the winter you sometimes had to queue to get in. The Roxy was the smallest of the three but, as Ray said, you had to start somewhere.

Irene had been there a few times with Sheila from work, who was mad about dancing. They would travel on the train, hurry down to the dance hall and dance until their legs were aching. Then it would be a mad scramble to get back to the station in time for the last train home. They had never been short of partners, but they always headed for the cloakroom as the last waltz struck up in order to avoid any over-enthusiastic dance partner who would hold them too closely and might want to see them home.

Her visits to the Roxy meant that she was familiar with the dance band. She thought they were good and she admired their resident vocalist,

Peggy Carr, who was married to the bandleader, Melvin, known as Mel. But Peggy, apparently, had gone down with flu and Ray had moved quickly and arranged for Irene to stand in for her. Peggy's throaty-voiced seductive tone was completely different to Irene's. The regulars loved Peggy. Irene could only hope that Ray was right and that they would welcome a change.

The Roxy was on the promenade and when they got there it was raining hard. Ray parked right outside the main entrance and reached over to open the passenger door. 'We'll have to make a dash for it,' he told Irene.

However, the brass-buttoned commissionaire was already hurrying down the steps from the foyer carrying a large umbrella. As soon as Irene got out of the car she felt her breath snatched away by the wind, and she could hear the crash of the waves on the shore behind them. The marble steps were slippery with rainwater and halfway up she turned her ankle. She dropped her vanity case and yelped with pain.

Ray grasped her to stop her falling, but when she thanked him, she saw his expression of vexation. 'Stupid bitch,' he murmured impatiently.

The commissionaire did not hear him because he had stooped to retrieve her vanity case. When the man asked if she was all right Ray was all smiles. 'Miss Walker is fine. Be good enough to take us to her dressing room.'

'*Miss Carr's* dressing room,' the commissionaire replied, his tone implying that Irene was being granted a rare privilege.

Before he left them he asked again if Irene was

101

all right and Ray began to lose his patience. Nevertheless he tipped him generously.

'What does the stupid sod think he can do?' Ray fumed when the door closed. 'Strap you up in a bandage? That *would* look good, wouldn't it?'

'I'm sorry, Ray,' Irene found herself apologising, even though she was hurt by his lack of concern.

'You made a grand entrance there, didn't you? If you're going to wear heels as high as that you should learn to walk in them.'

Stung, Irene defended herself. 'They're no higher than the shoes I normally wear!'

'That's as maybe.' Ray was beginning to bluster. 'But they're not what I wanted you to wear, are they? I told you to get some of those new little flatties – ballerinas – perfect for dancing the modern way.'

Irene felt her eyes stinging. 'I haven't come here to dance, I've come here to sing, and right now I wish I hadn't!'

She saw the flash of alarm in Ray's eyes and his manner changed immediately. 'Baby, I'm sorry! I'm letting my nerves get the better of me. I'm so anxious that everything should go well for you tonight that I've scolded you when I should be comforting you. Will you forgive me?'

She looked up at him, wishing she could stay angry, but when he looked at her this way she melted. 'I suppose so,' she said.

'Let's get you out of that coat,' he said solicitously. 'Right, here's a hanger. Now, sit down at the dressing table and put your feet up on this other chair. Lift your ankles up – here's a cushion.

Which ankle was it?'

'The right one.'

'Poor baby, I should have taken better care of you.'

He ran gentle fingers over her ankle and Irene winced with pain.

'No bumps, no lumps,' Ray said. 'I don't think anything is broken. It will probably hurt for a day or two.'

Irene felt like asking him when he had become an expert on first aid, but he was being so sweet that she clenched her fists under the wide spread of her skirts and managed a smile. *A brave smile,* she thought to herself. *No matter what happens, the show must go on!*

'Feeling better?' Ray said.

'Yes,' she lied.

'That's my girl. Now, keep your feet up. I'll go and have a word with Mel and I'll come for you when the band's ready to have a quick run-through. And, remember, I've worked hard to get you this chance.'

Irene was left on her own. The tears she had been holding back spilled over, and to her horror when she glanced in the mirror she saw her mascara was running down her face like the tears of a clown. She rubbed her face and made it worse. There were now big black smudges under her eyes. She would have to start again. And she would have to be ready before Ray came back for her.

Panic made her tremble and she had to force herself to control her shaking hands, open her vanity case and take out everything she needed to make a proper job of cleaning her face and re-applying her make-up. Although no one could have foreseen what had happened, somehow Ray had made her feel as if she had let him down.

When it was time to meet the band, the pain in Irene's ankle was agonising, but she forced herself not to hobble. She remembered the story her mother had told her about Ginger Rogers dancing until her toes bled. *A real little trouper, that's me,* Irene told herself, and when the music started to play she threw herself into her performance, heart and soul.

The evening meal, an appetising Irish stew, had been keeping warm in the gas oven in the scullery, or the back kitchen as they called it. Len, not the sort of man who expected to be waited on, served up two plates and brought them through to the table.

'Sit down, Edie,' he said, and she decided to let him have his meal before telling him.

Later, when they were enjoying a ciggie and a glass of stout, Edie showed Len the Christmas cards.

'Both for Irene?' he asked.

'From Withenmoor. The usual.'

'Nice they should remember after all these years.'

'Yes, isn't it?' she said distractedly.

'Something wrong?'

Looking troubled, Edie turned back to the sideboard and took another card from one of the drawers. She sat down and slid it across the table as if she was afraid of it. Len picked it up. It was unopened.

'This came. I wanted you to enjoy your meal first.'

'No stamp? No postmark?' he asked, although that was obvious.

'Hand delivered,' Edie replied.

Len looked at the envelope. It simply bore their name in block capitals but he wasn't fooled. 'You haven't opened it.'

'I thought you should – once we were alone together. I don't want Irene to know anything. It's better that way.' Edie shook her head. 'Why couldn't he just come in the back door and have done with it?'

'They could still be watching out for him. Particularly at this time of the year. People get sentimental and go home for Christmas. He probably didn't bring it himself. He'll have got someone to deliver it for him.'

'But he must be here in Newcastle. Surely there's some way we could meet up with him!'

'No, there isn't, he's a wanted man. If they find him it will mean a long stretch in jail. In the first war he would have been shot.'

Edie winced.

'And in any case,' Len continued, 'he doesn't have to be here in Newcastle. He could be in London, Liverpool, or God knows where. As I said, there are folk who would help him out.'

'For a price.'

They looked at each other solemnly. 'Yes, for a price,' Len said.

For a moment neither of them spoke. They were remembering the day when the military police had come to the door. As Terry had approached

105

his nineteenth birthday Len had tried desperately to find him some sort of reserved occupation so that he wouldn't be conscripted. The trouble was, Terry had never been able to keep a job of any kind for long, and although most people liked him, no one would give him a reference – not even any of Len's influential friends.

Eventually the official-looking envelope they had been dreading dropped through the letter box: Terry's call-up papers and a travel warrant to an army reception camp. When the day came, Terry had set off cheerfully enough, promising his parents that he would write to let them know he had arrived safely. They never received a letter. Terry never arrived at the camp. He had gone AWOL. Absent without leave. He was a deserter. Officially. They had never seen him since and they had no idea how he was surviving, although judging by the money they received now and then, whatever he was doing, he wasn't short of a bob or two.

Len opened the envelope and took out a card with a picture of a stagecoach and a valiant team of horses puffing it through glitter-speckled snow on a starry night. Two pieces of folded white paper fell out. Five pound notes. The hand-printed message inside the card read: *HAVE A GOOD CHRISTMAS*.

No love, no kisses, nothing personal. Len had explained that if he had signed his cards someone might see them and discover their secret. Edie wept with despair. She couldn't imagine how they could ever see their son again.

Chapter Six

Rather than feeling cheered up by her Christmas shopping, Hazel was oddly dispirited. She had tried to respond cheerfully to the helpful shop assistants but came away thinking that she had behaved like the sort of hard-to-please customer who strained their goodwill and their training to the limit. She wished she could retrace her steps and make it up to them, but that was impossible. Life once lived had to be accepted. Nothing could be changed.

Once she got home she went straight to her room and put the parcels on top of her wardrobe. She would wrap them in Christmas paper another day. Her mother had the meal ready but was dithering about whether to sit down and eat with Hazel or wait until her husband came home.

'Liver and onions,' her mother said, 'and mashed potatoes – you like that.'

'What about you? Are you going to join me?'

Her mother hesitated and then said, 'I'll wait for your dad. You know he likes a bit of company at the table.'

Hazel tried to hide her exasperation. 'I wish you wouldn't wait. You know very well he'll just sit there and say nothing – not one word, not even thank you – and as soon as he's finished he'll go off to the Hare and Hounds.'

'He works hard, pet, no matter what the weather.

He never complains. He deserves a bit of consideration.'

'Oh, Mam, he never considers you.'

'He puts his pay packet on the table every week, doesn't he? And remember, he's not the same man that marched off to war.'

Hazel sat down. She conceded defeat and let her mother place a generous plateful of delicious-smelling liver and onions on the table in front of her. She accepted that her father was not the unyielding, short-tempered, sometimes violent man that he used to be before the war. He had been severely wounded and had come home with a metal plate replacing part of his skull. Thankfully, his hair had grown again to cover the scars. He never talked about it and, to his credit, he did not use his injuries as an excuse never to work again.

After he had been demobbed he had convalesced for almost a year. Then, after breakfast one day, he had put on his muffler and his cap and, without a word to his wife, he had gone out to seek employment. He had found labouring jobs with small builders and had hardly ever been out of work since. After all, there was plenty of rebuilding work to do.

However, his former unpredictable behaviour had been replaced by an impenetrable indifference. He did what he had to do and got through the days seemingly in no need of normal human interaction. Her mother often said that her life would be a misery if she didn't have Hazel to talk to. And that was the problem. She was living her life through her daughter, and Hazel found it suffocating.

'Who were your cards from?'

Hazel was surprised that she got as far as her rice pudding before she was questioned about the cards she had received that morning. She was pretty sure that her mother had glimpsed the identical postmarks, but she answered, 'The usual from Withenmoor. Miss Forsyth and Rita.'

'Miss Forsyth was fond of you, wasn't she?' Her mother said this grudgingly.

'She was very kind to us – all of us.'

'Well, having no children of her own...' Her mother let the sentence trail away then changed the subject abruptly. 'And fancy Rita Bevan never coming home again! Well, she did for a while, didn't she? And then she ran away.' She frowned.

They had had this conversation, or one like it, many times before, but it seemed her mother could not let go of a subject that obviously touched her deeply.

'She didn't run away, she just went back to Withenmoor, and surely you don't blame her?' Hazel said.

Joan shook her head. 'No, I don't. She was badly treated before she was evacuated and I've heard it was worse when she got back. Her mother never gave her any peace. She accused her of having airs and graces.'

'It was hardly airs and graces. Rita just didn't fit in any more. She'd become used to a clean house – and being fed properly. And not having the belt taken to her, even as a grown lass, for the slightest of reasons.'

'Poor bairn. There was no love in that house.'

109

'No matter what fuss her mother made at the time,' Hazel said, 'I suspect her parents were pleased to be rid of her. The only thing they regretted was not being able to send her out to work to bring more money in. That was the only reason they made her come home. Molly Watkins was overjoyed to take her back.'

'It's hard to believe, isn't it?' her mother said.

'What is?'

'That her mother let her go. I would have been heartbroken if you hadn't wanted to come home.'

Hazel had had enough of trawling through the past. 'I know, Mam. But I did. Now, why don't we have a cup of tea together? I'll put the kettle on.'

'No, you stay there, pet. I'll do it. You've been working all day.'

Hazel felt a twinge of guilt. She hadn't told her mother that she was working a half day, because if she had she would have been expected to come straight home. Or maybe her mother would have suggested meeting up in town to have lunch and then do some shopping together. Kenneth, in his usual kindly way, would have understood, although Hazel knew he was becoming increasingly impatient about her home situation. *I didn't want to tell her because I wanted to buy her Christmas present*, Hazel told herself, but she knew that wasn't strictly true.

She loved her mother, there was no question of that, and she admired the way she had worked and dealt steadfastly with hardship and a difficult marriage. But she seemed to have given up on any idea of having a life of her own. She was a slave to her husband's inconsiderate ways, and otherwise,

110

the sole purpose of her existence seemed to be mothering Hazel. And that was bad for all of them.

The matter of the Christmas cards had not yet been exhausted. As her mother sat down for her cup of tea, she continued, 'Strange that Carol never sends you a card, isn't it? I mean, Irene remembers you.'

Hazel smiled at the thought of Irene, who had certainly livened up the sober atmosphere of Hillside House, often infuriating Mrs Ellis, who thought that these girls from the lower orders should be kept in their proper place.

'Well, Irene and I have never really been out of touch,' Hazel said. 'If I need new make-up, I pop into Brownlow's and ask her advice. Sometimes we manage to have lunch together. Kenneth and I met her in the queue for the pictures once and we went in together.'

'Was she on her own?'

'She was that time.'

'Hasn't she got a boyfriend?'

'She's had a few. After all, she's very attractive.'

'And flighty.'

'She just hasn't found the right one yet.' Hazel frowned.

'What is it?'

Hazel shook her head.

'Go on. Something's bothering you.'

'Well, a month or two ago when Kenneth and I went to that dinner dance at the Grand in Tynemouth, Irene was there with a chap called Ray. He looked about ten years older than she is, his hair was slightly too long and he had gold cuff-

111

links and a flashy gold wristwatch. I think I even caught a flash of a gold tooth.'

'Never!'

'Kenneth thought he looked like a spiv or a minor gangster.'

'And is Irene keen on him?'

'It looked that way. But the greatest surprise was when this Ray went over in the interval and had a word with the leader of the band. We couldn't hear what he was saying but the man was shaking his head. Then Kenneth swears that he saw money change hands.'

'Go on!'

'The next thing was that Irene was on the little stage with the piano for accompaniment and she started to sing. One of your favourites, actually – "Too Marvellous For Words".'

'Was she dreadful?'

'No, she was really good. She got a nice round of applause. She came over to see us and Kenneth and I congratulated her. She looked really excited.'

'Well now, fancy that!'

Just then, Hazel's dad arrived home and she was saved from further questions. He looked weary, his spare features lined with brick dust. He stripped to his vest and had a quick wash in the scullery sink, then put on a clean shirt, rolled back his cuffs and sat down at the table. All without a word. Her mother served up two plates of liver and onions and then sat and picked at her own food while she kept up a constant flow of chatter about the weather, the news, neighbourhood gossip, and even what she had bought in the shops that day.

Bill remained expressionless throughout, barely grunting a reply if he was asked an outright question, and not offering any opinions of his own. He showed no sign that Joan's constant chatter was getting on his nerves. Hazel remembered the man he used to be when she was a child. In those days, if he lost patience with her mother, he would slam his fist down on the table and shout at her to stop blethering. There had been more than one occasion when he had picked up his plate and flung it in the direction of the hearth.

Tonight, he surprised them both. When his plate was almost empty he reached for a slice of bread, mopped up every last drop of gravy and said, 'That was good.'

Both Hazel and her mother stared at him expectantly but he didn't say any more. He got up, rolled down his sleeves and put his jacket and coat and cap on. He took a handful of coins from the Rington's jar on the mantelpiece and left the house.

Her mother sighed. 'He'll not be back until closing time,' she said resignedly.

Hazel had been flicking through the *Radio Times*. 'Good,' she said. 'We can listen to the wireless in peace and without a fug of tobacco smoke. Let me do the dishes while you look through this and choose whether you want to tune in to some nice dance music or a mystery play.'

Her mother chose the play and, like a child listening to a new story, was soon enthralled. Hazel liked radio drama but tonight she couldn't concentrate. She only hoped her mother wouldn't want to analyse it afterwards over their nightly cup of cocoa.

The play was set in an isolated inn on the moors, where a disparate group of people had gathered, with sound effects of howling wind and driving rain. Hazel started as the fire spluttered and spat, and looked into the burning coals, her eyes half closed. She remembered sitting by another fire in another room, with old but comfortable furniture, and listening to the wireless with Irene, Carol and Bridget.

At first Miss Forsyth had been sure they would want to listen to *Children's Hour* and had made sure that their afternoon tea of bread and butter (or butter mixed with margarine) was over in time for their five o'clock appointment with Uncle Mac. She did not approve of having the wireless switched on while they were at the table, although she relaxed this rule to accommodate the news programmes as the war progressed.

It was Bridget who had persuaded her aunt to allow them to listen to something more grown-up. After their evening meal, apart from classical concerts, the choice on the airwaves had been pretty much as it had been tonight. They danced to various dance bands and Irene, who seemed to be able to memorise the lyrics of a new song after hearing it once, would often sing along. After supervising a few of the dance sessions, Miss Forsyth left them to get on with it, but she always listened to the plays with them.

Initially Hazel thought that this was because there might be something unsuitable for their young ears, in which case she would switch the wireless off. But this never happened and it soon

114

became obvious that Miss Forsyth enjoyed the dramas as much as Hazel herself did.

Sometimes Carol and Bridget would get bored and they would retire to a corner of the room and gossip. Irene would shoot them furious looks if their voices rose and they would raise their eyebrows exaggeratedly but oblige by talking more quietly.

Carol...

It was true that she hadn't kept in touch. Hazel had not expected her to. Of all the evacuees, Carol's life had changed the most. Hazel wondered what it would be like to meet her again. And then she sighed, because it wasn't going to happen. No matter how much she would have liked to have accepted Miss Forsyth's invitation to go back to Withenmoor for the coronation celebrations, there was no way she could leave her mother to cope with her father's fluctuating moods by herself. Or so she told herself.

They were just about to leave when three young lads approached, smiling hopefully. Two of them pushed the other one forward and he asked Irene if she would dance the last waltz with him. Ray stepped in quickly.

'It's very kind of you to ask,' he said, 'but Miss Walker has to go home now. Her car is waiting.'

The youth looked embarrassed. 'Oh, of course,' he said and turned to go. Then he picked up a beer mat from a table under the balcony and said awkwardly, 'Would you sign this?'

My autograph, Irene thought. *Someone has asked for my autograph!*

Ray produced his fountain pen and Irene signed the beer mat.

The lad looked overjoyed. He shook it and blew on it to dry the ink, then put it in his breast pocket. He said, 'I think you're terrific!'

The other two had followed suit and thrust their beer mats towards her, but Ray took her arm and whisked her back to the dressing room. 'Can't get too friendly,' he explained. 'If you'd started that we'd have been here all night. Got to leave them wanting more.'

Irene's ankle was throbbing painfully so she was happy to take his advice. Ray helped her on with her coat and then surveyed it critically. 'Hopefully, we'll be able to get you something better than that before long. Something more up-to-date.'

Irene thought of how proud her mother was of that coat and how attractive she looked when she wore it, and she bit back an angry response. She was tired and her ankle was hurting and she didn't think she could stand a spat with Ray right now.

'Thank you for saving me,' she said instead.

'Saving you?'

'From that kid who wanted to dance with me. I don't think I could have gone round the floor once without tripping over.'

Ray frowned. 'What do you mean, tripping over? You're a good dancer.'

'Not when my ankle's twice the size it ought to be.'

'Oh, that. No, the reason I stepped in was because we can't have your fans getting too familiar.

You've got to keep a certain distance or you'll spoil the magic.'

'My fans?'

'Sure. That lad will be the first of many.'

'Do you really think so?'

'I was watching their faces while you sang. I could tell you were getting across to them, although I don't imagine Peggy Carr's dedicated followers will ever be won over.'

Irene wasn't quite sure what to make of this. Was Ray pleased with her or wasn't he? Looking at his thoughtful expression it was hard to tell. Suddenly she felt tearful. It had been a long day, her nerves had been wound up tight, and her right ankle was throbbing. She couldn't imagine how she was going to get through a full day's work tomorrow unless she kicked off her shoes the minute she was safely behind the counter.

Ray was still thinking about Peggy Carr. 'She has a proper fan club, you know, run by a couple of local girls. Signed photographs and all that jazz. Still, it will be pretty small potatoes compared with you when you take off.'

All that jazz – small potatoes – Irene looked away so he wouldn't see her smile. Sometimes Ray talked like a character in a second-rate movie. He didn't realise that people laughed at him for it, which embarrassed her, but it also made her feel protective of him. He had never said as much but she had guessed that he came from a poor background, and she respected him for wanting to make something of himself.

'Come on, baby, let's get to the car. We'll hang on until they start pouring down the steps. Then

117

I want them to see you driving away in style.'

When the crowd started to leave, Ray told her to wind down the window and give them a wave before they drove off. The rain had stopped but a mist had rolled in from the sea and followed them about halfway home. Ray tuned in to AFN on the car radio, and coincidentally, they were playing a selection of hits by Doris Day. Irene thought this was an omen. She settled back into the comfortable embrace of the leather upholstery and fell into a half-sleep.

'Wake up, baby, you're home.'

Irene opened her eyes and saw that the passage light was shining through the fanlight above the front door. They would have left the light on anyway, but Irene was pretty sure that her mother would be waiting up for her.

'We've got to get you a place of your own,' Ray said.

Irene knew what he meant but she didn't reply. She and Ray had indulged in passionate necking sessions – usually in the back of his car – but they hadn't gone any further, and she didn't want to. Not yet. He had promised to be careful but mistakes could happen. If she got pregnant that would put an end to her singing career and, although she tried to suppress the thought, she wasn't sure that he would do the right thing and marry her.

She waited for a moment to see if he was going to get out of the car and come round to help her out, but he leaned over her to open the passenger door and said, 'Off you go, sweetheart. Go and catch up on your beauty sleep.'

Irene was halfway out of the car when she remembered something and got back in again.

'What is it?' Ray asked.

'You haven't paid me.'

'Oh, didn't I tell you?'

'Tell me what?'

'We didn't get paid. I had to pay Mel, just like that time at the Grand.'

'No, you didn't tell me that.'

'Well, what did you expect? Mel was taking a chance. It took some persuasion.'

Irene was too tired to be angry. 'You mean you had to bribe him.'

'I wouldn't put it like that.'

'Well, I would.' She felt like crying. She didn't know how much she had been expecting, but she had never been good at putting something by every week and she had been counting on this payment to go towards her Christmas shopping.

'Look, you were great tonight. Word will get round. We'll soon be raking it in, I promise you.'

'Do you, Ray? Do you really promise me that?'

He lost patience with her. 'Pack it in, Irene. Instead of griping you should be grateful to me for working for you like this.'

She glanced at him and the interior light of the car lit up his scowl. She shuddered involuntarily. She had actually been frightened for a moment. Without another word she got out of the car and would have slammed the door behind her but Ray leaned across quickly and caught it.

'Good night, baby. You were swell,' he said, his tone appeasing, his anger apparently forgotten.

Irene was already at her front door, the key in

119

the lock. She opened it and went in without answering him.

'How did it go?'

Her mother was sitting by the fire but she looked around as soon as Irene walked in. Irene thought she looked tired; in fact she had probably been dozing. She was wearing her pretty silk robe and her hair was bound up in a chiffon scarf to keep her curlers in place.

'Okay. I think they liked me.' She decided not to tell her mother that she hadn't been paid and was grateful that her father had gone to bed, because he might have asked about it.

'Of course they liked you,' her mother said and then her tone changed abruptly. 'You're limping.'

'I went over on my ankle. I'm all right.'

'Take your stockings off, I'll strap it up.'

'Don't fuss, Mam.'

But Irene was grateful to do as she was told. They talked quietly because her father needed his sleep: he was on early shift for the next few days.

Her mother opened a tin of cream of chicken soup for her and buttered a couple of slices of bread. Irene found that she was hungry. A little later she tried to answer her mother's questions about how the night had gone, but she was concerned to see how tired Edie looked.

'Mam, go to bed,' she said. 'I'll wash up and see to the fire.'

'All right, pet.'

Irene was surprised that her mother raised no objections. She looked at her closely and realised that she looked strained. Perhaps it was what her mother referred to as 'the change' – or was there something else bothering her?

'Don't stay up too long, Irene. You must be exhausted.' Edie kissed her daughter's brow and went quietly to bed.

Irene was indeed exhausted but her emotions were in turmoil. She needed to wind down. She'd read articles in the *Picturegoer* about promising young stars whose careers had fizzled out because they hadn't been able to stand the pressure, and how they'd had to learn how to relax and even gone in for things like hypnotism and yoga. Others took to drink or drugs, although the film studios usually tried to cover that up.

Ray liked a drink. Irene was constantly amazed by the amount he could consume and yet stay steady on his feet. She'd never heard him slur his speech. The first time she'd met him had been at the Sunday night jazz club in an upstairs room at the Royal Hotel in Seaton. Sheila had persuaded her to go along out of curiosity. At the time, neither of them knew very much about jazz.

Irene liked to think that Ray had noticed her the moment she had walked into the room. He'd been surrounded by a lively crowd but he had kept glancing in her direction, and it hadn't been too long before he'd come over to their table and offered to buy them drinks. When it was time for them to leave to catch the train, Ray told them he was going to town himself and he would take them back in his car. It had been a different car then. Not quite so big, but certainly what Sheila had called 'flashy'.

They had told him they worked at Brownlow's but they hadn't been able to pin him down about exactly what he did. He said he was a businessman and that he 'promoted' things. And people. On the way home he turned on the car radio; Kay Starr was singing 'Nobody's Sweetheart'. Irene began to sing along and that was the start of it. Ray had told her that she had a terrific voice and ought to be singing for a living rather than working in a shop.

Irene had been flattered and had agreed to let him become her manager. They had to come up with some kind of act. Irene told Ray that she liked Kay Starr and her songs, but he'd said that with her natural blond hair she looked more like Doris Day and that she should model herself on her. That was how it had started.

While she was tidying up, Irene noticed the two envelopes on the sideboard. *Christmas cards*, she thought. They were addressed to her. Her mother must have been too tired to remember them. She looked at the handwriting and smiled as she opened the one she knew to be from Rita. She stared at the message written inside the cheery card.

Hope to see you soon.

She sat down again slowly. What could Rita mean? Were she and Miss Watkins going to make one of their rare visits to Newcastle? And if so, why didn't she give more details? Irene remembered the last time they had come to town. It must have been nearly two years ago.

They'd come to do some Christmas shopping and also to buy themselves some clothes, the sort of good quality stuff that would last for years. Neither of them worried about passing fashions, although Rita had long ago persuaded Molly to try and be a little less eccentric. They had even come into Brownlow's to treat themselves to some cold cream and face powder, and in Rita's case some foundation and a couple of lipsticks. They spent quite a lot of money, so Irene had had no compunction about filling up a bag of free samples.

Molly and Rita had been staying at the Station Hotel in old-fashioned grandeur and they'd invited Irene and Hazel along for dinner one evening and, on another day, lunch at the Tivoli in Fenwick's. Although they'd talked a lot about the old days and the people they had spent the wartime years with, Carol was never mentioned.

Two people who were mentioned were the Doyle brothers, who had been taken in by the farmer, Jack Armstrong, and his wife Ena. They had no children of their own and they doted on Joe and Jimmy. Nevertheless, Joe had hated life in the country and had gone home as soon as the war ended. Jimmy adapted to farm life as if he had been born to it, and he had stayed on. The Armstrongs regarded him as a son and went on doing so even when a miracle happened and they had a late baby of their own, a boy.

Irene had got the impression that Rita was sweet on Jimmy and he on her, but nothing seemed to have come of it. Or maybe it had by now. She suddenly realised how much she would like to catch up with her old friends at Withenmoor.

When she opened the second card and read the enclosed letter from Miss Forsyth, for a moment

123

she thought it might be possible to do just that. But the moment didn't last. A whole week away from home when Ray was already trying to get bookings for her to sing at coronation parties and dances would be very bad timing. It suddenly struck her that her career as a singer – the career she was so keen to pursue – would have to take first place in her life. She had been going along with Ray and his plans for her without really thinking about how her life might have to change.

A little later, in bed, she tried to hang onto the excitement and the glamour of the night. Singing with a proper dance band. Performing before an audience. Having fans asking for your autograph. That was what she wanted, wasn't it? Her purpose in life was to sing. She was as good as any of the modern-day recording stars, and she was much better looking than most of them. Ray had said so.

Then, as she was falling asleep, she remembered other voices, other tunes. Old tunes of haunting beauty ringing out clear on a frosty night under the stars. If she closed her eyes she could almost see the frozen breath of the children and hear their voices as they sang carols on that first Christmas away from home. Their first Christmas at Withenmoor.

Chapter Seven

December 1940

'You mean you're going to send them along to the woods on their own to get the holly?' Mrs Ellis stared at her employer doubtfully.

Margaret Forsyth tried to remember exactly when her cook had started questioning her decisions and why she thought she could. She decided it must be something to do with the war. Times had changed. Houses like this no longer had a full complement of servants. Now there was only Mrs Ellis to cook and housekeep and Hilda Barton who came twice a week, if she felt like it, to dust and polish, manhandle the vacuum cleaner, and get down on her creaky knees to scrub floors. The girls made their own beds and kept their rooms clean and tidy. Miss Forsyth would have been quite happy to do the same but Mrs Ellis wouldn't hear of it.

'Why shouldn't they go to the woods?' Miss Forsyth said. 'They're big girls and it isn't very far. When we were children my brother and I used to bring the holly home every year when we were much younger than they are.'

'I dare say you did, but you and the captain were brought up here in the country. These lasses have probably never seen a bunch of holly before.'

'Oh, I'm sure they have. They sell it in shops in

town, don't they? And besides, Bridget has spent Christmas here before. She can guide them.'

'That was a few years ago, and she went with her mother and father. She'll have forgotten all about it.'

'I don't think so. I'm sure she'll remember what fun it was. It was snowing and they brought the holly home on our old childhood sledge. Don't you remember?'

'I suppose I do.' Mrs Ellis paused and her disapproving expression softened a little. 'Very well, Miss Forsyth. I'll see to it they have a couple of trugs and a pair of secateurs from the garden shed, although I don't know what Ted's going to say.'

'I'm sure he won't mind.' It will save him the job, Miss Forsyth could have added. At his age he wouldn't relish the uphill tramp to the wood to find the wild holly.

A short while later the four girls set off with instructions to cut only the branches that were heavily berried – and to keep their gloves on. Bridget had been trusted with the secateurs and she and Carol were leading the way. Hazel and Irene followed, each carrying a trug.

Hazel noticed that Irene was frowning. 'What's the matter?'

'Why do we have to trudge around in the cold like this?' Then, loud enough for Bridget to hear: 'Why can't we just pop down to the shop in the village and buy some holly? Can't she afford it?'

Bridget turned and raised her eyebrows. '*Miss Forsyth*, not *she*, if you don't mind, and it's not a matter of affording it. You know it isn't. It's a fam-

126

ily tradition of ours to go and gather the holly. You should be pleased my aunt wants to include you.'

Irene thought about this. 'I suppose I am,' she said. But she couldn't help adding, 'So what do you do in London? Do you and your mam go and pinch it from the parks?'

Bridget looked at her for a second or two and then laughed. 'Shut up, Irene,' she said. 'You know very well we don't do that.'

She turned to walk on but Carol lingered a moment to look at Irene scornfully. 'Don't show your ignorance,' she said. 'It's embarrassing for all of us.'

'It was a joke!' Irene took a step towards Carol but Hazel put a restraining hand on her arm.

'Don't worry, I wouldn't have hit her,' Irene muttered.

Carol had already caught up with Bridget and they heard her ask, 'Where *do* you get your holly when you're in town? Do you get it sent up from the country?'

'Goodness, no. We buy it from Harrods along with anything else we need for Christmas.'

Carol didn't speak for a moment and then she said, 'Oh, of course. My parents get everything except the holly from Bainbridge's. That's a very good shop in Newcastle, you know.'

'Little fibber,' Irene muttered so that only Hazel could hear.

'Oh, I don't know,' Hazel replied. 'It could be true. Her mother probably does shop there. Our Carol is definitely a cut above the rest of us.'

They smiled at each other. *A cut above.* Between the two of them this was how they had started to refer to Carol, since it had become increasingly obvious that she was desperate to impress Bridget Forsyth and to be accepted as her equal.

'London must be splendid at Christmas,' they heard her say. 'I mean, the shop windows on Oxford Street. They've superb displays, don't they?'

Bridget was quiet for a moment. 'Not this year. The shops in the West End were bombed. Mother said when the ambulances arrived they saw some of the mannequins – the window dummies – lying amongst the rubble looking like real bodies. Now many of the windows are boarded or taped up.'

'Oh, how sad you must be.'

'Just listen to her,' Irene said. 'And where did *splendid* come from? Why can't she just say nice or lovely?'

'Hush,' Hazel said. 'Let her be. She hasn't done you any harm, has she?'

Irene scowled. 'She doesn't get at you, but she's always finding some way of putting me down. She tries to make out I'm common.'

'Well, you're not, and besides, do you care what she thinks?'

'No.'

'Well, then. Now be quiet and let's enjoy this holly hunt.'

Irene smiled. 'You're all right, Hazel. I think I would go potty here without you. Oh, drat it all!'

'What's the matter?'

'All this talk about holly and shop windows at Christmas, that's what the matter is.'

'What do you mean?'

'Mam and me usually get our holly from a stall in the Grainger market, and mistletoe, too.

There're rows and rows of plucked turkeys hanging up in the butchers' aisles and the whole place smells of Christmas trees and oranges. Then there's the windows at Woolworth's in Clayton Street. All that tinsel, the strings of lights, the Christmas crackers, the cotton wool snowmen with little strings to pull out the prizes they have inside them, and the boxes of shiny tree decorations. Just think what we're missing.'

'I'm afraid it won't be like that this year,' Hazel said. 'In her last letter my mother told me that there wasn't much in the shops and there was no chance of getting a chicken for Christmas Day because everybody is after them.'

'What's she going to do?'

'Sausages done in the oven with roast potatoes and sage and onion stuffing. And she saved up enough dried fruit to make a pudding. Dad's almost certain to be called up soon, and for his sake she wants to make Christmas as special as she can.'

Irene tried to imagine her mother managing like that and couldn't. Suddenly she knew with certainty that her dad would come up with something. Whatever happened, he would never let the family go without. How he would do it she didn't know, and she realised that it was better not to think about it.

Suddenly Irene felt forlorn. 'I wish I could be there in town, no matter what it's like. I've heard some of them are planning to sneak back home.'

'Me too, but Mam said I wasn't even to consider it,' Hazel told her. 'She said the worry would kill her if I were to put myself in harm's way.'

129

The four girls continued in silence for a while, the Segs on their shoes making metallic clicks on the frosty road. A cold wind came down from the hilltop to meet them. Irene turned her head and noticed that Hazel had gone all distant looking.

'What are you thinking about?' she asked.

'Oh, it doesn't matter.'

'It does. Tell me.'

'Well, don't laugh.'

'I promise not to.'

'I was thinking this is like a poem in a book I found in Miss Forsyth's library.'

'What's the poem about?'

'Walking up the hill like this in the winter.'

'Can you remember it?'

'I think so. Well, some of it.'

'Go on, then. Recite it.'

'All right. Just for you.'

The two girls fell back a little so that only Irene could hear. Hazel began:

'When winter woods are piercing chill,
And through the hawthorn blows the gale,
With solemn feet I tread the hill,
That overbrows the lonely vale.'

Hazel stopped when she realised that Bridget and Carol had stopped and were waiting for them to catch up.

'I liked that,' Irene said quietly. 'Maybe I should start reading poetry. I like the way it rhymes like songs.'

Bridget pointed to the entrance to a lane, little more than a cart track, with high hedges obscur-

130

ing the views of the land at each side. 'This is the way to the wood,' she said. 'It's not far now.'

'About time,' Irene muttered and hitched the trug she had been carrying further up her arm. Then she grinned. 'Well I never!'

'What is it?'

'Look who's coming down the lane towards us. It's Rita Bevan and she's got a wheelbarrow full of holly. 'Hi, Rita,' she called cheerfully. 'You look like Little Red Riding Hood.'

Rita came right up to them and stopped, lowering the handles of the wheelbarrow then straightening up. Her eyes were bright and her cheeks rosy. She was hardly recognisable as the skinny waif who had first come to Withenmoor.

She grinned. 'Like me red pixie hood, do you? I knit it meself. And these gloves to go with it.' She held her hands.

'You never did!' Irene was incredulous. 'All those fingers and thumbs!'

'Well, it took a bit of working out, but Aunty Molly said I'm a natural knitter!'

'Who's Aunty Molly?'

'Miss Watkins, of course. She said I was to call her that.'

'And that's a very nice coat,' Irene said. 'Is it new?'

'It came from the cupboard at school. Miss Norton sorted it out for me.'

'It's a Yankee coat, then?'

'Aye, it is. All the way from America in one of them clothes parcels.'

Carol had been hanging back looking bored, but now she suddenly stirred. 'Don't you mind wearing other people's cast-offs, then?'

Rita looked at her levelly and Irene was amazed at the change in her. Once Rita Bevan would have been reduced to nervous tears by Carol's superior attitude, but now she simply smiled and said, 'I'm used to wearing second-hand clothes, as you well know. It's nothing to be ashamed of.'

'No, of course it isn't,' Bridget assured her. 'It's a very nice coat. Passing on good clothes is a very sensible thing to do.'

Carol pursed her lips and looked acutely uncomfortable. Irene realised that Carol had been brought up to think that she was better than the other girls at school. Her parents considered themselves middle class, and yet she knew she was far below the Forsyth family in the social scale. And to her this kind of thing mattered. Carol wanted to be just like Bridget; she copied her manner of talking and copied her ways, but every now and then, like this matter of the coat, she got things wrong. Seeing how embarrassed she was, even though she understood why, Irene could only think it served her right.

She turned to Rita and asked, 'What do you need all that holly for?'

'Aunty Molly and me will make bunches tied up with red ribbon and mebbees a wreath or two and we'll sell them to her customers when they come for their eggs and their onions and their parsnips and sprouts and the like.'

'What fun,' Bridget said. 'And do you help Miss Watkins grow all that?'

'Aye, I do. Although at first I think I was not so much a help as a hindrance.'

Bridget smiled at her. 'I'm sure you learned quickly.'

Irene thought Bridget's tone of voice was a bit superior but she decided Miss Forsyth's niece was only trying to be kind. It was time to move on.

'Well, we can't stand here chatting like this,' she said. She stamped her feet in an effort to warm them. 'We'll all freeze to death.'

'Yes, we'd better go,' Bridget agreed.

As Rita picked up the handles of her wheel-barrow, Irene eyed its abundant load. 'I hope you've left some holly for us,' she said.

'Oh, aye. There's plenty. Though you might have to reach a bit higher than I did. You won't have any difficulty finding the good stuff. Aunty Molly said it's a long time since there have been so many berries and that means it could be a hard winter ahead of us.'

Irene laughed. 'You love all this, don't you?'

'All what?'

'Living in the country.'

'Aye, I do. It suits me fine.'

Irene grinned at her. 'Well, take care you don't turn into a country bumpkin.'

Rita's laugh was confident. 'Don't be cheeky. Well, I'll love you and leave you. I'm off for me dinner. Rabbit stew and steamed chocolate pudding. There might be a war on but Aunty Molly knows how to serve up good grub.'

They stood and watched as Rita guided her load over the frozen ruts and then they turned and headed up the lane.

That night, after their evening meal, they walked

down to the village hall to practise carol singing. The headmaster's wife, Mrs Edwards, and their own Miss Norton had got together a choir made up of local children and evacuees. The plan was to sing in the Market Square for an hour after school each day on the last week of term, and a collection would be taken to go towards helping refugee children. If the weather was bad they would retire to the village hall.

They were each handed a carol sheet as they arrived in case they didn't know the words. Hazel glanced at it quickly and said to Irene, 'They're just the same as we sing at school.'

'Maybe Mrs Edwards thought we were little heathens,' Irene replied.

'That's a funny thing to say.'

'I know, but they treat us as though we're different, don't they?'

'Well, we are, aren't we?' Hazel said.

'We're just as good as they are!'

'Of course we are, I didn't mean it like that. It's just that we've had a different sort of life in town, and we've had to get used to them just as they've had to get used to us.'

'Sometimes I think you're just too nice, Hazel. You never seem to get mad at anybody.'

'Oh, I do. It's just that I think there's no point in looking for trouble.'

'Like I do, you mean?'

Hazel sighed. 'Irene, stop this. You'll spoil it for everyone if you go on like that. We've come here to sing carols and I'm going to sing my heart out and then enjoy the cocoa and cakes they've made for us. Why don't you agree to do the same?'

She walked away to join some of the local girls she had made friends with at school, leaving Irene feeling upset with herself. She was forced to accept that Hazel had been right. She did look for trouble, not just here in Withenmoor but even when she had been a little girl at home. She remembered her brother saying that she flew off the handle when she thought she was being got at. He was right. In future she would have to try to be more like Hazel, who never seemed to get her feathers ruffled.

Although...

Hazel had just admitted that she sometimes got mad but didn't see any reason to go looking for trouble. Irene realised that sometimes it was hard to tell what Hazel was thinking. Maybe it was a matter of still waters running deep.

Miss Norton stood at one end of the hall and clapped her hands to draw their attention. Mrs Edwards was settling herself at the piano while a very good-looking older boy arranged her music for her. As the children fell silent Irene heard Mrs Edwards say, 'Thank you, Alan.'

'Who's that lad?' Irene asked the girl standing next to her.

'Alan Sinclair, the doctor's son. Lush, isn't he?'

'Why haven't I seen him around?'

'He goes to boarding school somewhere in Yorkshire. He's home for Christmas.'

The girl lost interest in talking to her and moved away. Irene realised she was surrounded by people she didn't really know. She felt too embarrassed to follow Hazel so she looked around for another friendly face and saw Bridget smiling at her. Irene

135

thought Bridget a bit toffee-nosed but was beginning to see that the girl couldn't help the way she had been brought up. Basically there wasn't much wrong with her, except that she didn't seem to be able to see through that little toady, Carol. Carol was with her now. Of course she was; she followed her like a shadow. And Carol had seen Bridget's friendly smile and was now scowling fiercely in Irene's direction.

Irene accepted that it was her own fault that Hazel was fed up with her and decided to stay where she was. Despite feeling sorry for herself, once she started singing the familiar carols she found herself enjoying the rehearsal. She liked singing and was very soon chosen to perform a solo part. Bridget congratulated her and Irene was pleased to see that annoyed Carol even more.

The cocoa made with condensed milk and the cakes were scrumptious. The four girls from Hillside House sat together at the trestle table, Bridget and Carol opposite Hazel and Irene. Hazel seemed to have forgotten their slight tiff but she didn't say very much to Irene; she was too busy talking to Alan Sinclair, who had brought his plate and his mug of cocoa and sat down next to her on her other side. They had only just met and Irene wondered how on earth they found so much to talk about.

Alan walked part of the way home with them and laughingly suggested that they should sing as they went along. So they sang the carols they had just been rehearsing, their young voices carrying across the lanes and the fields and echoing under the star-frosted dome of the winter sky.

Chapter Eight

December 1952

Hazel had just come home from work and she was sitting with her mother at the table while they waited for the evening meal, a lamb hotpot, to be ready.

'Why won't you come?' Hazel asked.

'It's very kind of Kenneth's mother to ask,' her mother replied, 'but I couldn't leave your father on his own.'

Hazel had been expecting this. 'Dad will be at the Hare and Hounds as he is most nights. He won't even notice that you're not here. And it's not as if you don't ever go out at night. What about when you and I go to the pictures?'

'We always get home before he does.'

'Not always.'

'That happens very rarely. It's only if there's a long queue at the bus stop and we have to wait.'

'But it does happen, and when we get back Dad is perfectly all right.'

'No, he isn't. He gets miserable.'

'What on earth makes you say that?'

'If he comes home and I'm not here he just sits and says nothing.'

Hazel felt like screaming. 'But he never does say anything, even when you are here!'

'I know, but it's different. I can tell.'

Hazel stared at her mother in despair. Mrs Gregson was having a small party and Kenneth had told Hazel how much his mother wanted to meet Hazel's parents. Kenneth had laughed and said that what his mother had actually said was that it was about time. Hazel got the impression it was going to be an inspection. That had filled her with unease but she had felt obliged to go along with it.

At least they had agreed that it would be a bad idea for Hazel's father to attend the party. Kenneth was quite happy to explain to his mother that Bill Stafford had been badly affected by his experience in the war and was reluctant to go anywhere unknown to him and mingle with people he didn't know.

His mother had accepted this. Kenneth's father had fought in the Great War and he had come home to his younger sweetheart with respiratory problems caused by poison gas and a bad case of shell shock. They had gone ahead with the wedding and had been happy enough for a few years, but she could never forget the robust, cheerful man who had marched off to war, a man who Kenneth would never know, because his father had succumbed to pneumonia and died before seeing his son take his first steps.

As he grew, Kenneth admired the way she had simply got on with life, surviving on a small pension and an inheritance from her parents. She made friends, she did voluntary work and she joined the local bridge club. Rather than clinging to her son as some bereaved women might have done, she wanted him to find a girl and have the married happiness that had been denied her. She wanted him to provide her with grandchildren while she was young enough to enjoy them. She couldn't understand why Kenneth and Hazel didn't just go ahead and make a match of it.

All this was on Hazel's mind while she was trying to persuade her mother to accept the invitation to Mrs Gregson's Christmas party.

'Mam, you like Kenneth, don't you?' she asked.

'Yes, pet, I do.'

'Then don't you want to see his home? Aren't you at all curious about his background?'

'You can tell he's a gentleman.'

'How?'

'He took all those exams at school, he's got a good job, he's got good manners and he speaks well and dresses smartly.'

'And that's enough for you?'

'I don't know what you mean.'

'Most of those things are true of John George Haigh, and yet he murdered six people – maybe nine.'

Her mother was shocked. 'Hazel, how could you? Comparing your young man to a murderer!'

Hazel made herself calm down. 'I'm sorry, that was silly of me, but I was only trying to tell you that, as my mother, you should be keen to know more about the man I'm going out with.'

'Well, that was still a wicked thing to say. Do you really think my judgement is so poor that I could be taken in by appearances?'

Hazel was overcome with remorse. 'Of course I don't, and I'm truly sorry. Put it down to the fact that Kenneth and I really want you to come to

139

the party, and it's just so frustrating to have you making all these excuses. They *are* just excuses, aren't they?'

Her mother looked down at the tablecloth.

'Aren't they?'

Joan sighed. 'Yes, pet, they are.'

'Why?'

'If you really want to know, it's because I don't want to let you down.'

'What on earth do you mean?'

'Well ... you know ... Mrs Gregson is quite posh, isn't she? I mean, she's bound to be. You said she never had to go out to work and they live in a nice little semi at Seaton. You've never said so but I bet she has a charwoman – or even a little maid-of-all-work.'

'She has someone who comes in twice a week to do the cleaning.'

'There, you see?'

'See what?'

'That's what I did from the moment I left school. Someone else's cleaning. Oh, I earned good money at the rope works during the war, but I don't suppose she would think much of that either, and when the men came back I had to leave and go back to cleaning. I mean, isn't she bothered about what her posh friends will think?'

'Obviously not. Mrs Gregson knows all about us. She wouldn't ask you to come to her party if she minded about that sort of thing. It's you that minds, isn't it? You've taken against her just because she's better off than we are. Don't you know that that's just another form of snobbery?'

Her mother shook her head. 'It's not that. I'm

140

sure she's a very nice woman. It's just … it's just that I don't want to let you down.'

'Whatever do you mean?'

'You're clever, you've made the best of yourself, you speak so nicely. Whereas I'm just ordinary. I left school when I was twelve, and as soon as I open my mouth you can tell where I come from. Nobody meeting us for the first time would think you were my daughter.'

'You're quite wrong! If I'm all the things you say I am, I owe it all to you.'

'No pet, not all of it. If you hadn't been evacuated during the war and learned to live a different sort of life, you wouldn't have grown up the way you have. Miss Forsyth had the making of you. Not me.'

Hazel felt like weeping. So many conversations with her mother came back to the years they had been parted. She knew she had lost the argument even before her mother surprised her by what she said next.

'So thank Mrs Gregson very nicely and say I'm not well or something.' She raised her hand as if to ward off Hazel's objections. 'And Hazel, pet, when the time comes, I'll make the effort and come to meet Kenneth's mother.'

'What do you mean, when the time comes?'

'When you get engaged. You've been going out for years now and there's no sign of a ring, is there? There was a time when I began to worry that he was stringing you along and that you might get your heart broken. But I know you well enough to see that you seem to be happy with the way things are. As I say, if I thought you'd set a

141

date, I would make every effort to be sociable with your future mother-in-law. That would be my duty and I wouldn't let you down. But as things stand, I don't see the point.'

Her mother got up and took the hotpot out of the oven. She filled Hazel's plate and set it before her, then said, 'I'll wait and have mine with your dad.'

Hazel was left with nothing to say. She had lost the battle and also any hope of changing her mother's mind. At least, not until there was a wedding on the horizon.

That night in bed Hazel worried over what she would say to Kenneth when they met for lunch the next day. She could hardly tell him that her mother thought it pointless to meet his mother until they became engaged.

Kenneth would almost certainly take it as some sort of hint, and that would be embarrassing. Worse still, if his mother had been putting pressure on him, he might actually propose, and that was the last thing she wanted. Until now she had been grateful that Kenneth seemed in no hurry to get married. In fact, when she thought about it she wondered if she could even call what they had a romance. They enjoyed each other's company and they got on well. It was convenient for both of them to have someone to go out with on social occasions. But were they really in love?

If they were, their love was not driven by passion. Every now and then, when his mother was at her bridge club, Kenneth would take her home and they would go to his room and make

142

love. He was a considerate and responsible lover, and there was never any danger of her becoming pregnant, but the experience always left her feeling empty somehow.

She had longed for someone to love and cherish her. For a while she had hoped she would find what she was looking for in Kenneth's arms. She knew that Kenneth did not deserve to be treated in this way. But was he just as guilty?

Her mother's words came back to her. Had he been stringing her along? Would they go on like this until one day he would meet someone younger and maybe more demanding, and then break it off with Hazel and get married, just as his mother wanted him to?

And if that happens would I be heartbroken?

Hazel asked herself the question, but she already knew the answer. Her heart had been broken once so badly that it had never mended. She knew she could never suffer the same soul-destroying grief again.

Meanwhile there was another Christmas to be endured. Sedate evening drinks with Marion Grey and her long-term employees at the agency; Mrs Gregson's celebrations with her friends and neighbours, and the Christmas dinner dance that Kenneth was so looking forward to.

And what of Christmas at home? Her mother would dress the tree with the same baubles they had had when Hazel was a child. Maybe she would buy a new packet of tinsel. She would have some coppers handy to give to any children who came carol singing, even though many of them didn't know more than a few lines and would ring the doorbell when they'd hardly sung one verse.

On Christmas Day they would open their presents while the house was filled with the smell of a roasting capon. There would be crackers and paper hats, sherry for Hazel and her mother, and a bottle of Newcastle Brown for her father.

After the meal Bill Stafford would sleep by the fire until opening time. Hazel and her mother would listen to the wireless, keeping it turned low until he had gone. Then what? A radio drama if they were lucky, maybe with a religious theme. And there would almost certainly be a live concert from Broadcasting House in London.

Joan would treat herself to another glass of sherry and then she would start talking about years gone by, especially the years before the war. Although she had heard the stories many times before, Hazel would listen and smile and try not to weep. She had her own Christmas memories but she could not share them with her mother – bittersweet memories of magical Christmases never to be experienced again.

Chapter Nine

December 1940

Grace Norton had been invited to call at Hillside House. Dorothy joked that it was a royal summons. After their high tea of scrambled powdered egg on toast, Grace offered to stay and help with the washing-up, but Dorothy insisted that she should get along as quickly as possible and find out the reason for the invitation. Dorothy's husband Charles, who was headmaster at the school where Grace was teaching, agreed. It might be something to do with the evacuees, he said, and he hoped there wasn't a problem of some kind.

'We were so pleased when Miss Forsyth agreed to take three girls,' Dorothy said. 'She also has her niece, and that's quite a handful for a spinster in her late forties who has never had very much to do with children.'

As opposed to this spinster of a similar age who deals with them every day, Grace thought, but she didn't say anything.

Dorothy looked thoughtful. 'Margaret Forsyth was engaged, you know. The usual story, I'm afraid. Her fiancé was killed in the last war. He was a politician, a Labour MP. They met when Miss Forsyth was involved in the Suffragist movement. It's said her family disapproved, but they were young and very much in love, and if he

145

had survived, I'm sure they would have married and had a houseful of children. It's very sad. So many women were left bereaved in that way. Oh!' She broke off, looking shocked. 'My dear – I'm so sorry! How could I have been so tactless? You were ... I mean, you told me about James...'

'Please don't say any more.'

Grace left the room abruptly and went into the cloakroom, a walk-in cupboard in the hall, to get her coat. She tied a warm headscarf under her chin and pulled on her gloves, then stood there for a moment amongst the coats and the shoes, the wellingtons and walking sticks, until she had her emotions in check.

I should be used to it by now, she thought. *The unintentionally thoughtless remarks of decent people who don't mean to hurt me. I shouldn't have reacted like that. Now Dorothy will feel wretched.*

Grace made herself go back to the kitchen. Dorothy was leaning over the sink. She turned to face her.

'It's all right,' Grace said. 'Really.'

The two women looked at each other.

Dorothy sighed. 'Okay. Take a torch, and if you have to use it remember to keep it pointed downwards,' she said.

'Of course. But do you really think there's any need for blackout here in the country?'

'It's regulations.'

They smiled tiredly at the words which had become all too familiar. Grace knew there was nothing more either of them could say about what had gone before.

She enjoyed the walk up the steep road that led

146

from the village, even though the wind tried to snatch her breath away and left her cheeks stinging. Once she left the comparative shelter of the houses and ventured onto the open road, she found herself leaning forward into the wind for fear of being blown over. She turned the collar of her coat up and pulled her headscarf forward so that in silhouette only the tip of her nose was showing. Glancing up towards the ruins of the ancient fort and settlement, tumbledown shapes on the crest of the hill, she wondered how the Roman soldiers and their families had managed to survive the northern winters.

Soon the house loomed ahead of her, a dark outline with no lights visible, but with smoke curling from one of the chimneys into the winter sky. Mrs Ellis, Miss Forsyth's housekeeper, opened the door and beckoned Grace to follow her. Grace thought she looked tired. 'Miss Forsyth is in the little morning room,' she said.

Grace untied her scarf and dropped it to her shoulders, then unbuttoned her coat. Mrs Ellis looked at her.

'I'd keep your coat on if I were you.'

In spite of the heavy curtains and the thick carpets, the room was chilly. Miss Forsyth was sitting in a wing chair by the hearth, where a small fire was losing the battle against the cold air. Miss Forsyth rose to greet her and indicated that she should sit in the chair at the other side of the hearth.

'I'll bring you a pot of tea,' Mrs Ellis said. 'That will warm you up, but don't stay in here too long, will you?'

Grace was surprised at the informal way the housekeeper spoke to her mistress, but when she saw the glance that passed between them she realised that they were more than employer and servant; they had become friends.

When Mrs Ellis came back with the tea and biscuits Miss Forsyth told her to go home as soon as she had given the girls their supper. 'They can do the washing-up,' she added, 'and don't worry about this tray. I'll see to it myself.'

For a moment it looked as though Mrs Ellis was going to object, but then she smiled and said, 'Very well, Miss Forsyth. I won't argue with you.'

After Mrs Ellis had left them, Miss Forsyth poured the tea.

'I don't want to keep you out late,' she said, 'so I'll tell you straight away. I'm going to have a party here on Boxing Day and I need your help.'

'A party for the children?'

'Of course. I've told Hazel, Irene and Carol that they may invite friends who came with them from Newcastle and I'm going to invite the children of local families. I want to make sure we have the right mixture.'

'You mean of the children who live here and the evacuees?'

'That's right. Much the best thing to do, don't you think?'

'Yes, I do. A few friendships have formed between the two groups but we ought to encourage more. This is very kind of you. What exactly do you want me to do?'

'I need you to come and help me organise the fun and games. My ideas are no doubt very old-fashioned. I mean, do they know how to play charades or blind man's buff?'

'I'm sure some of them do, and if they don't we can teach them.'

'You are much more in touch with today's youngsters than I am.'

Grace was silent. She stared down into her cup, thinking of the conversation she'd had with Dorothy.

The moment lengthened and Miss Forsyth stirred uneasily. 'Am I asking too much of you?'

Grace looked up. 'What do you mean?'

'Well, I'm sure you must have been looking forward to your Christmas break and here am I asking you to give up some of your precious time.'

'No, I'd like to help. I think it's a marvellous idea. But how are you going to feed them all?'

'Thank goodness bread isn't rationed. Mrs Ellis has promised to come up with all kinds of meatless sandwich fillings, and Molly Watkins has promised us some eggs for the cakes.'

'What about Bridget?'

'I beg your pardon?'

'You didn't mention your niece when you said that you'd told the girls they could invite friends from school. Is she going home for Christmas?'

'To London? No. That would be impossible. She will be staying here and she will be at the party, but she told me that she hadn't really made any friends at school, from either group, and there was no one she wanted to invite.' After a pause Miss Forsyth said, 'She hasn't really settled in, has she? I mean, how do you find her?'

Grace thought about it. 'She works hard, she's

149

always polite, and I think some of the girls are beginning to like her even though they find her very different from themselves.'

'She *is* different. This has been a great change for her. Her life in London was so unlike anything these girls have experienced.'

'You mean her private schooling?'

'That's part of it.'

'It's obvious that she sometimes feels out of place, but I don't think you have any need to worry about her. You must have seen for yourself that she gets on well with Hazel, and well enough with Irene, even though that young lady can be difficult at times. And of course there's always Carol. They seem to have formed a firm friendship.'

Miss Forsyth smiled. 'Ah, yes, Carol. She's very taken with Bridget, isn't she? I think there's a bit of hero-worship there, but my niece is too sensible to have her head turned.'

And maybe not aware of Carol's real motives, Grace thought. Of all her little band of evacuees Carol Clark was the odd one out, imbued with a sense of superiority. Grace could see only too clearly why Carol had attached herself to Bridget. Bridget Forsyth was everything Carol would like to be: well born, rich and privately educated. Once this war was over, she would return to a world that Carol could only dream of. For the moment Carol wanted Bridget all to herself and guarded her fiercely, and maybe that was one of the reasons that Bridget had not made any other close friendships.

After they had talked more generally about

what sort of entertainment they might devise for the party, the two women agreed to draw up some plans and then meet again to discuss them.

As Grace pulled on her headscarf, Miss Forsyth said, 'I think I'll go and have a bite of supper in the kitchen with the girls. So far we've managed to keep the fire in the old range going. Oh, I should have asked, would you like to join us?'

'No, thank you. Dorothy has already given me a high tea. She looks after me very well.'

'Yes, she's a very nice woman.' Margaret Forsyth smiled. 'I'll see you to the door.'

As they walked across the hall, a door opened somewhere in the house and there was a burst of dance music. Someone was singing along with the music. Grace listened. Whoever it was, was very good – probably Irene Walker.

Walking back down the hill to the village, Grace thought about the girls and how fortunate they had been when Margaret Forsyth had taken them to Hillside House. She wondered if they realised how much the course of their lives had changed, and would go on changing.

They were sitting round the fireplace in the old nursery. The coals burned brightly in the hearth, casting a rosy glow on their faces, and the black-out curtains had been drawn against the lowering evening sky. The weather forecast on the wireless had foretold snow. Hazel was perched on a well-stuffed leather pouffe, an old notebook resting on her knees. She was supposed to be making a list, but so far she hadn't written a word.

She looked at the other three girls. 'It's not just

up to me. Miss Forsyth said we should all choose who to invite to the party,' she said. 'So let me have some names.'

'I really don't want to invite anyone,' Carol told her.

'Why not?'

'I wouldn't know who to choose.'

'It should be easy enough. We can invite people we are friendly with in our own class for a start.'

'Well, there you are, then. You two can have my share of guests. I was never particularly friendly with anyone at school.'

'That's true,' said Irene.

She scowled at Carol. Hazel shot her a glance and interrupted before she could say anything more. 'If Carol doesn't want to invite anyone you can't force her to,' she said.

'She's just frightened that anyone she invited would turn her down.'

'Irene!' This time it was Bridget who spoke. 'Why do you always have to be so confrontational?'

Hazel saw the angry colour flood Irene's face. 'What does that mean?'

'It means argumentative,' Hazel told her. 'And Bridget is right. You're always ready to pick a quarrel.'

'And it's always with me!' Carol said, her voice sounding strained.

Hazel looked at her in surprise. Carol had lost her usual cool composure and seemed genuinely upset. Suddenly Hazel realised why. She was glad when Bridget took Carol's arm and said, 'Will you come up to the box room with me and help

152

me sort out the tree decorations? Aunt Margaret says it's my job to dress the tree and I'd like you to help me.'

Carol tore her angry gaze away from Irene and made an obvious effort to control herself. Then she smiled at Bridget. 'Of course I'll help you. It will be such fun!'

'Come along then, but we'd better go to our rooms and get some extra cardigans. It will be chilly up there.'

As soon as the door closed behind them Hazel said, 'You've got to leave Carol alone.'

'Why?'

'Because she can't help the way she is, and you can. I think you were probably right when you said that she was worried that no one would accept her invitation, but you didn't have to rub it in. She wouldn't want Bridget to know none of the others care much for her, would she?'

'But she asks for it, doesn't she?'

'Maybe she does, but we'll all have to learn to get on or we'll make each other miserable. Carol won't change, especially not if you bully her.'

'I don't bully her!'

'Sometimes the way you speak to her comes very near to bullying.'

Irene was shocked. 'I'm not a bully!'

'I know you're not. Not really. You just don't think before you speak. What harm does it do you that Carol wants to be friends with Bridget?'

Irene hesitated. 'None, I suppose.'

'I mean, you're not jealous, are you?'

'Of course not!'

'Then what's the point of trying to spoil things

153

for her?'

Irene was quiet for a moment and then she said, 'You're right, as usual. Should I say I'm sorry?'

Hazel had a vision of Irene apologising and choking on the words. She smiled. 'No, let it rest, but promise not to be so beastly in future.'

'I promise that I'll try.'

'I suppose that will have to do. Now why don't we get on with this list?'

'Okay.'

They had a good few names written down when Irene said, 'Let me see.'

Hazel handed over the notebook. Irene looked at the list and frowned.

'What's the matter?' asked Hazel.

Irene read out the names and said, 'They're all lasses, that's what's the matter. What about inviting some lads? I mean, what's the use of playing postman's knock or spin the bottle if everybody there is a girl?'

Hazel smiled. 'I'm not sure if we'll be playing those two games but you're right. Miss Forsyth did say to invite boys and girls that we know from home.'

'Right then.' Irene handed the notebook back to Hazel. 'Get writing.'

Hazel held the pencil poised. 'Who do you suggest?'

They thought hard and the moment lengthened. All that could be heard was the crackle of burning coals and the ticking of the old clock on the mantelshelf. Eventually they looked at each other and laughed.

'They're not a very promising lot, our lads, are

they?' Irene said.

'That's not fair. There's nothing much wrong with them.'

'Isn't there? What about Billy Hobson and his gang? Would you really want to invite them?'

'I don't think they would want to come. They'd find it cissy,' Hazel said.

'Who, then?'

'There's always Joe and Jimmy Doyle. They're okay.'

'I suppose so, and one or two of the lads they're pals with aren't bad. Hey! Why don't we invite some of the local lads?'

'We can't. Miss Forsyth wants to organise that herself.'

Irene sighed. 'Well, I just hope she puts that Alan Sinclair on her list. He's a bit of all right, isn't he?'

'What do you mean?'

'Come off it, Hazel. He's dishy and you know it. And furthermore, he seems quite taken with you. After that first rehearsal he made a beeline for you and made sure he sat next to you.'

'He was just being friendly. He said he was pleased to meet us.'

'Maybe he was, but it was only you he talked to. I didn't mind. May the best girl win. But Bridget couldn't take her eyes off him and Carol was getting really flustered.'

'Honestly, Irene! Now you're imagining things.'

'She was. I think she resented him for taking Bridget's attention away. Or mebbees she fancied him herself.'

'That's a load of nonsense!'

'Whatever you say. But you can't deny he always finds time to talk to you after choir practice, and you don't seem to object. And why are you blushing?' Irene grinned.

'I'm not!'

'Yes, you are. Your cheeks are all rosy.'

'That's because of the glow from the fire. Your cheeks look rosy, too.'

Hazel was saved from further discomfiture by Miss Forsyth coming to see how they were getting on. 'I think we're done,' she said and handed her the list.

Miss Forsyth glanced at it briefly. 'Good,' she said. 'We'll make the invitations ourselves using bits of old Christmas and birthday cards. I've kept so many over the years, we'll have more than enough. All we need is scissors and glue and lots of imagination.' She stood for a moment, gazing into the fire. Her enthusiastic smile died and she looked so thoughtful that Hazel began to think there might be a problem.

But then Miss Forsyth turned to look at them both and said, 'It's a long time since there's been a party here. When my brother and I were children we had birthday and Christmas parties every year. I have such happy memories. And now I have you girls to thank for bringing back some gaiety to this lonely old house. How lucky I am to have you here.'

After she had left them Irene said, 'Do you think she means that?'

'I'm sure she does.'

'Well, we're lucky too. Some of the others aren't in such friendly homes. But no matter how nice it is here, I still wish sometimes that I could go home. Don't you?'

Hazel nodded. She was at a loss for words. It would be disloyal to her mother, wouldn't it, to acknowledge that she was happy here even for a moment?

Irene looked thoughtful. 'Do you think we'll ever get used to it, being away from our families?'

'I think we'll have to.'

Irene looked glum for a moment and then she grinned again. 'Well, at least I'm going to make sure that I enjoy this party!'

Hazel couldn't sleep. She was tormented by guilt that she didn't feel as homesick as she thought she ought to be. She missed her mother and wished that there was some way they could be together, but she realised with dismay that sometimes whole days went by without her feeling as homesick as she had at first. She decided not to wait until they all sat down to write their weekly letters home but to write an extra letter now. Maybe that would make her feel better.

She sat up in bed, switched on the bedside lamp and reached for the writing paper that her mother had given her. She didn't own a fountain pen like Bridget did, so she would have to use a pencil for her letters. She could always address the envelopes in the morning. She plumped up her pillows and propped herself up against them, resting the note-pad on her drawn up knees. She shivered. The room was icy cold. She pushed the bedclothes aside, found a jumper and a cardigan, put them both on over her pyjamas and scrambled back into bed as quickly as she could. Her feet felt like lumps of ice and she moved them around in the bed until she found the hot water bottle to rest them on.

She glanced over at the hearth. Instead of glowing coals there was a vase holding an arrangement of dried flowers. The brass coal scuttle was empty; there was no need for the matching fire irons. Once a fire would have burned there night and day. A maidservant would have seen to it, often cleaning the grate and rekindling the coals in the early hours of the morning when whoever slept in this room was fast asleep. Hazel pushed the writing paper aside and hugged her knees while she imagined what it must have been like to live in a house like this in those days.

She let her imagination roam. She was Mary Lennox who had just come home from India to live in Misselthwaite Manor on the bleak Yorkshire moors. No, that wouldn't do; there were no locked rooms in Hillside House, and if there was a secret garden Ted was keeping it well and truly hidden. And as she remembered it, Mary had had a miserable time until she met Dickon.

As she reached for her writing paper a gust of wind rattled the window and she remembered a scene in a film she had seen with her mother not long before she came to Withenmoor. There was a scratching at the window which meant that someone was outside and trying to get in. It was a child who had lost her way on the wild moors. A ghost child called Cathy.

The windowpanes rattled more furiously and the curtains began to move. Hazel tensed, gripping the eiderdown with both hands, and watched them for a moment. Then she relaxed and laughed at herself. She would have to learn to control her flights of fancy when she was alone at night and everyone else was sleeping. After they had seen the film her mother had been worried that Hazel would have nightmares. She had felt guilty for taking her, but Laurence Olivier was the star and Joan was a big fan of his.

Hazel remembered they had bought chips and batter on the way home. The memory of the hot, salty chips and the crispy batter and the way they had eaten them straight from the newspaper brought tears to her eyes. No matter how happy she was here, she missed her mother. She began her letter.

Dear Mam,

We are almost ready for Christmas and I'm sure it's going to be lovely here. We are actually going to have a turkey. We're getting it from Mrs Ellis's brother, who is a farmer. But you know I'd rather be at home to eat sausages and stuffing with you!

On Boxing Day Miss Forsyth is going to have a party for us here in Hillside House. She says she wants the old place to look cheery, so as well as the holly there's going to be a Christmas tree and paper garlands. Bridget says that some of the glass tree baubles have been in the family for many years, since some time in the last century. They were made in Germany and Mrs Ellis thought we ought not to use them, but Miss Forsyth said that we hadn't been at war with Germany when her great-grandfather bought them, so she didn't think it would be

159

unpatriotic to hang them on the tree.

*I think I told you about us going out to get the holly.
Well, now we have branches arranged along the
downstairs mantelpieces together with pine cones.
Small twigs are balanced on the frames of some of the
pictures. Miss Forsyth has made a beautiful arrangement of holly and red satin ribbons in an old brass
vase. It's in the library at the moment but it's going to
be the centrepiece on the dining table on Christmas
Day. Mrs Ellis says if the weather gets any worse Miss
Forsyth should consider having Christmas dinner in
the kitchen, where it will be much warmer because of
the range, and the table is quite big enough.*

*Miss Forsyth couldn't decide who should put up the
paper garlands. She said Ted, that's the gardener, is
getting too old and stiff and she doesn't want him
climbing ladders. Mrs Ellis hasn't a head for heights
and the picture rails here are very high. Irene and I
both offered to do it but Miss Forsyth wouldn't hear of
it. So then she said she would put them up herself and
Mrs Ellis had a fit.*

*It looked as though we would have to forget the
garlands until Mrs Ellis had an idea. She suggested
that Miss Forsyth should ask the doctor's son to help
us. He's fifteen and tall for his age, and even though
he's almost grown up, he seems to want to be friends
with us. Miss Forsyth said that was a good idea and
that she would have a word with his father.*

*Our teacher, Miss Norton, is going to help at the
party. Miss Forsyth has asked her to organise the
games. There's a piano in the corner of the sitting
room which hasn't been used for years. Miss Forsyth
has had it tuned and Alan, that's the doctor's son, is
going to play the music for some of the games. That*

160

means he won't be able to join in but I don't suppose he will mind. After all, we must just seem like little kids to him.

I wish you would come and visit me. Miss Forsyth says all our parents are welcome. Carol's parents are going to come for a day and so are Irene's mother and her brother, Terry. Irene's father can't come because of his work on the railways. Keeping the trains going is very important. Irene says her mother told her that her father might as well be in the army the little she sees of him. Her brother Terry is coming because he wants to see Irene before he gets called up. Bridget has no idea where her father is and her mother, who is driving an ambulance in London, doesn't know when she might be able to get leave. She must be very brave.

Oh, Mam, please come and see me. You could leave early in the morning when Dad goes to work and get back just as he gets home. We would only have a few hours together, but that's better than nothing, isn't it? And if you don't come soon it might be months before it would be possible, because everyone here seems to think the weather is going to get worse and worse and we might be snowed in. Please come soon.

Tell Dad that I'm asking after him.

Lots of love,

Hazel xxx

Hazel gathered up the pages of notepaper she had filled and put them in an envelope. In spite of her woolly jumper she felt colder than ever, and she considered huddling down under the bedclothes and trying to sleep. She entertained that tempting thought for a moment then decided against it. She ought to write to Mavis.

At first Mavis's letters from Canada had been full of the wonderful things she was doing. Her aunt and uncle had a car and they would go for drives in the woods. In the summer they had rented a log cabin by a lake, which Mavis thought was like a cabin in a cowboy film. They had visited an Indian Reservation where she had seen wigwams and a totem pole. Apart from having to go to school, it was like being on an everlasting holiday.

But her letters were getting shorter and shorter. In the last one she mentioned a Christmas parade that was being planned to go through the middle of Montreal. She described the lovely warm clothes her aunt had bought her for the winter, and she said how pleased her teacher was with her progress in French. And that was all.

Mavis never commented on anything Hazel wrote in her long letters and she wondered if her old friend had found them boring. She decided to keep this one short. She wrote about going out for the holly, the Christmas decorations and the planned party. She would have liked to tell Mavis about her new friend, Alan, but found herself curiously embarrassed, so she just finished with: *Write soon. It's always good to hear from you. Love, Hazel.*

Hazel put both the letters on the bedside table. She took off her cardigan but decided to keep her jumper on. She lay down, pulling the bedclothes up around her shoulders and pushing the hot water bottle down with her feet. Luckily there was still some warmth in it.

While she had been writing she had forgotten all about the ghostly rattling of the window, but now,

162

as she closed her eyes and tried to sleep, she began to see scenes from the film. Young Cathy and Heathcliff riding across the moors on horseback, then, when they were grown up, Cathy, wearing a beautiful ball gown and sparkling jewels, telling Heathcliff that she never wanted to see him again. They were standing on a terrace and all the while in the background you could hear the wind wuthering across the moors.

Wuthering ... *Wuthering Heights,* the film was called. Her mother had told her it was a story from a book. Hazel decided she would like to read it, but not on a wild and windy night like this one.

The stories of Mary Lennox and of Cathy and Heathcliff both took place in Yorkshire, and, just like Alan's school, the old houses were out on the moors. Alan had told her that, although he liked being at home for the holidays, he was very happy to go back to school. He said he liked walking in the countryside in all seasons of the year. He always had a drawing pad in his haversack and he could spend hours sketching a simple scene. He said his friends called him 'the artist' and they teased him about it, but they were a good-natured lot. They got up to all sorts of high jinks, he said, and Hazel hadn't been quite sure what that meant.

She asked if they had midnight feasts like the girls in school stories, and he said that the little kids did things like that, but the only thing that kept him awake at night was reading by torch-light under the bedclothes. He told her that he always had a book on the go and that he'd love to have a look at the books in Miss Forsyth's library.

Hazel wondered whether he had read *The Secret Garden* or *Wuthering Heights*. If he had, she would love to talk to him about them.

Joan hurried home from work. The letter had arrived just as she was setting off for her first cleaning job. It had been in her pinafore pocket all day, but she had resisted opening it. She would get Bill's dinner on the go before she allowed herself the luxury of sitting down to read it.

Soon the vegetable broth was simmering nicely and there was a bread and butter pudding in the oven. Joan glanced at the clock on the mantelshelf, built up the fire and sank down into the comfortable chair which was reserved for Bill. As soon as he walked through the door whoever was sitting there would have to get up and give way to him.

First she stared at the envelope, putting off the pleasure for a moment longer. The coals glowed and the wind scattered sleet against the window. It was getting darker outside and she would need to switch on the light. That meant she would have to put the blackout board up and draw the curtains.

Back by the fire she opened the envelope carefully; with the help of a label it could be reused. She smiled with pleasure when she saw the number of pages and settled back in the chair to read them.

Hazel was very good at writing, and that didn't just mean the spelling and the grammar. Her descriptions of the people and places brought them alive. Joan felt as though she knew everyone Hazel wrote about and that she could have described Hillside House inside and out without ever setting foot in it. It was almost like reading a book, or rather a serial story in a magazine. Joan couldn't afford magazines herself, but her ladies would pass them on to her along with clothes that were out of fashion, although that might come to an end if the government decided to bring in clothing coupons.

Joan began to read and waited for the usual rush of happiness when she could feel close to her beloved daughter. But this time it didn't come. The letter was all about Christmas and parties and turkeys and all the wonderful things that Miss Forsyth was doing for the girls. She should have been pleased but Joan began to feel angry. She had never been able to arrange a party for Hazel, not even on her birthday. The best she could do was to invite Hazel's friend Mavis along for tea, although she always tried to have a cake with candles. The two girls' pleasure on these occasions was completely forgotten as her resentment of Miss Forsyth grew.

Childishly, she counted the number of times Miss Forsyth's name was mentioned in the letter and found it to be almost a dozen. Joan knew she ought to be grateful that Hazel was so happy but instead she was overcome with bitterness. She ignored the fact that Hazel had begged her to come for a visit – the girl ought to know by now that she couldn't leave Bill – and she stuffed the pages of the letter back into the envelope. It took all her self-control not to throw it in the fire.

Chapter Ten

December 1952

The party at Kenneth's house was not something Hazel was looking forward to. She was ashamed of herself for feeling that way about it and she had to accept that it was entirely her own fault. She had realised lately that she was suffering from some deep-seated sense of dissatisfaction with her life. However, she didn't want to let Kenneth down, so when the day came she was determined to make an effort and be sociable.

Mrs Gregson, almost as tall as her son and still attractive in a rather faded way, was a little formal, but she was friendly and welcoming. Her guests were decent people. There was a doctor, a retired schoolmaster, the owner of a menswear shop and the editor of the local newspaper. They all had their wives with them and Hazel learned without surprise that the doctor had married a nurse, the schoolmaster a teacher, the owner of the menswear shop the daughter of an old-established draper, and the editor of the newspaper, more adventurously, had married a former actress from the local repertory company. The latter wore green eye shadow, mascara, and red nail varnish. The only woman in the party to smoke, she carried a diamond-studded cigarette holder. On the face of it she was very different from the other wives, but she had made friends with them at the bridge club that Mrs Gregson attended.

There were also three neighbours: Effie and Cora, two elderly sisters from next door, and Arthur, unattached and silver-haired, who was renting a house across the road. His bearing was that of an old-fashioned British gentleman.

After the introductions were over Kenneth drew Hazel aside and told her that Effie and Cora devoted themselves to charitable causes and they were eccentric but delightful. He said that Arthur was a retired tea planter – or claimed to be. Hazel asked him what he meant, and Kenneth replied that Arthur's descriptions of life in Malaya, the bungalows in the hill stations, the mosquito nets, the ceiling fans, and the slightly racy lives of the planters and their wives, were all like something from the stories of Somerset Maugham.

'But that doesn't mean they're not true,' Hazel said.

'I suppose not,' Kenneth replied. 'And my mother certainly seems to believe every word. It's a good job old Arthur knows I'm keeping an eye on the situation.'

'What situation?'·

'It could be that for all his expensive clothes, his club tie and his gentlemanly bearing, he is in truth a penniless con man who sees my mother as an answer to his problems.'

'How cynical you are,' Hazel said.

'I'm just being realistic. After everything my mother has done for me, I owe it to her to look out for her as she approaches her dotage.'

Hazel smiled. 'She won't thank you for using

the word dotage but you're a good son,' she said, and she meant it.

However, she couldn't help feeling that instead of protecting his mother Kenneth might spoil things for her by putting a stop to a genuine romance – a late chance of happiness. And who was to say that Mrs Gregson wasn't intelligent enough to work things out for herself and maybe she had simply decided to enjoy Arthur's old-worldly attentions?

Kenneth was in charge of the radiogram and it was his duty to keep the background music playing. With his love of ballroom dancing, Hazel wasn't surprised to find a predominance of Joe Loss and Victor Silvester records, along with his mother's favourite Palm Court light classics. He kept the volume just right so that people could enjoy their conversations.

The buffet food was laid out in the dining room, and when they went through Hazel was surprised to find a smiling, bird-like woman in a neat waitress's uniform in charge of the table.

Kenneth saw Hazel's expression and leaned towards her to say quietly, 'That's Mrs Salkeld, my mother's domestic help. She loves coming along to do this sort of thing. She thinks it's very posh. If the phone rings on the days she's here to do the cleaning she makes a point of answering it and she says, "The Gregson residence". Once I asked her why she said that and she looked at me as if I were totally ignorant and said that she'd seen the household staff saying that in the pictures.'

Kenneth smiled in Mrs Salkeld's direction. It was obvious that he was fond of her, but Hazel

168

couldn't help thinking that his tone had been slightly patronising. She thought of her mother and how she'd probably been right not to accept the invitation. Joan might suffer from lack of confidence, but she was also an intelligent woman and she would have seen through such an attitude straight away.

Kenneth left her and went to change the record stack. With her plate in one hand, a glass of wine in the other and no convenient chair, she wandered through to the oak-panelled entrance hall and sat down on the stairs. She balanced her plate on her knee and took a sip of wine.

'What a good idea,' someone said and she looked up to find Tim Gilbert, the editor of the local paper, standing over her. He was also trying to manage a plate and a glass of wine. 'Go on, manoeuvre yourself up a couple of steps and I'll join you.'

Tim Gilbert was a nice-looking man in his fifties. Of medium height and perhaps a little overweight, he was the only man there who was wearing slacks and a sports jacket rather than a lounge suit. For a while they concentrated on their plates of party food while the conversation ebbed and flowed around them. The other guests were coming and going from room to room and at one point Kenneth passed by and gave her a wave.

Then, completely without warning, Tim said, 'Kenneth tells me you were evacuated during the war.'

Hazel looked at him in surprise. 'Why would he tell you that?'

Tim grinned. 'Well, actually, I asked him if you

had been.'

'Just now?'

'No, a week or two ago. It was obvious you would be about the right age and I was right. Kenneth said you spent the war years in Withenmoor.'

'Why does that interest you?'

'Well, actually...' his smile was hesitant, 'actually I'm writing a book.'

'About evacuees?'

'Yes. About children from Tyneside. Particularly those children who had never seen the countryside before. I put a piece in all the local papers for people to come forward with their memories, and I've already had some responses. Happy memories, sad memories and even tragic memories. We should tell these stories before people forget them.'

'Maybe some people don't want to remember,' said Hazel. 'They would like to put it all behind them. And not everyone wants to share their memories for fear of hurting other people.'

Tim frowned. 'I'm not sure if I understand you, but if you agreed to talk to me it would be in the most general way. You could set me off in the right direction. Practical things. You know: the journey, the billeting arrangements, gas masks, grub, did you get any pocket money?'

'Surely there are records.'

'There are. But wouldn't it be great to see it from the kids' point of view?'

'I'm not a kid any more.'

'I know.' He grinned. 'But you're still young enough for the memories to be bright and clear. Will you at least think about it?'

170

'Okay.'

'Let me go and fill up your glass.'

Leaving his plate on the stairs, he took Hazel's empty wine glass and his own and disappeared into the dining room. It seemed only a few seconds before he returned. 'Well?' he said.

She laughed. 'I need longer than that.'

'But you're beginning to come round to the idea, aren't you?'

'I wouldn't say that.'

'And you could help me in other ways. You could be my research assistant. Kenneth has told me how wonderfully organised you are.'

'I have to work for my living, you know. I don't have much spare time.'

'I would pay you a fee.'

She smiled at his enthusiasm. 'What exactly would I be doing?'

'Collating the material, finding good photographs to illustrate each story. With any luck some of the children will have kept some photographs. Have you?'

The question caught her by surprise and it took her a while to answer. 'I don't think so.'

He looked at her quizzically for a moment and then said, 'That's a shame. Let's hope the other kids have hung on to some.'

'What other kids? So far you've only had a handful of answers.'

'Yes, but I'll start by asking everyone I talk to if they've kept in touch with any of their fellow evacuees. For example, have you? Would you know where to contact them?'

Hazel stared down into her wine glass. 'Maybe.'

171

'You could talk about the old days. The new friends you made there. It might be fun.'

The old days ... Irene and Rita, she thought, and couldn't help smiling.

But what of Carol and Bridget? Her smile faded. The new friends we made there ... *Alan* ... ice crystals formed round her heart.

Tim broke the silence. 'Something tells me you've lost any enthusiasm you might have had for my project.'

'Look, Tim, I think your book is a wonderful idea,' she said, 'and I hope you find someone to help you, but I'm not ready to share my memories yet. I don't know if I ever will be.' She stood up and motioned for him to move out of the way. 'So I'm afraid I can't help you.'

Kenneth opened the passenger door and waited for her to get into the car. Once he was settled in the driver's seat he turned and smiled at her. 'This is better than the train and the bus on a cold night, isn't it?'

Until now, no matter where they had been, he had always insisted on seeing her home to her door and then facing the journey home alone, often on the last train from the Central Station.

'Much better.' She tried to match his enthusiasm. He had just bought his first car; a brand-new Morris Minor.

'Just in time for the dinner dance,' he said. 'I'll be able to pick you up and take you there and home again in style rather than relying on taxis that smell like ashtrays.'

Kenneth had given up smoking not long after

172

he had left the army and Hazel had never started. Their dislike of the habit was one thing they were in complete agreement over.

'It went okay, didn't it?' he said.

'What did?'

'My mother's party.'

'Mm.'

'I think you made a good impression on my mother's friends.'

'That's nice.'

'For goodness' sake, Hazel, what's the matter with you?'

'There's nothing the matter.'

'Then why are you sitting there like a zombie, totally uninterested in anything I'm saying to you?' Hazel turned, and in the light from the dashboard she saw that slight tic in his cheek that meant he was becoming exasperated with her. 'After the effort my mother put into it you could at least have the good manners to pretend to have enjoyed yourself My mother's friends were genuinely pleased to meet you and I'm sure they all made you welcome.'

Hazel felt a pang of remorse. They *had* made her welcome and she had warmed to them. She had fallen into her usual habit of conjuring up their life stories. She had noticed that Effie and Cora, although unmarried, both wore engagement rings. In her imagination the two sisters had been beautiful, lively young women who, like many of their generation, had lost their sweethearts in the First World War, the war that was supposedly going to end all wars. As for the doctor and his wife, they looked young enough to have served in the armed forces in the second war, and maybe they had met in some field hospital when they were saving lives under fire.

Arthur left no room for her imagination. He had invented his own colourful history and could himself have been a character in a story. What about Esther Gilbert? Perhaps, for the love of Tim, she had given up the chance of stardom on the West End stage to settle for life in the provinces? Esther was very 'actressy' and called everyone 'darling', but was she star material? Maybe she had been pleased to retire from the spotlight and live a life more ordinary. Although it would undoubtedly please her to be the wife of a newspaper editor who would be prominent in the community.

As for her husband, Tim Gilbert was a little like a newspaperman in a film, enthusiastic and dedicated to getting a good story. Hazel could imagine him shouting out with relish, 'Hold the front page!' She would have loved to have carried on talking to him if only he hadn't thoroughly unsettled her.

She sighed and said, 'Kenneth, I'm sorry, they did make me welcome and I really enjoyed myself, it's just that...'

'Oh, so you've decided to speak. About time.'

'Please don't let's quarrel.'

'Then tell me why you look so miserable.'

'I'm not miserable, really I'm not, it was just something Tim Gilbert asked me.'

'What was that?'

'He said you'd told him that I'd been evacuated.'

'I did. Where's the harm in that?'

174

'No harm, it's just that he asked me to help him with a book he's writing about evacuees.'

'And you don't want to?'

'No.'

There was a moment's silence and then Kenneth took one hand off the wheel and reached for hers. He squeezed it briefly. 'Then don't.'

'You wouldn't mind?'

'Of course not. I imagine you felt awkward being put on the spot like that?'

'I did.'

'Hazel, I'm sorry. This was my fault. I knew he was going to ask you to help him and I should have okayed it with you. I didn't think it would upset you. Will you forgive me?'

'Of course.'

Hazel sensed that Kenneth's anger had drained away as quickly as it had come. His brief spurt of annoyance had followed the usual pattern. He thought she had behaved badly and he hadn't been able to restrain himself from criticising her. Then, after a word of explanation, his mood had changed swiftly and he had become reasonable again. Now he was genuinely sorry and she knew that he would be totally supportive of her decision.

The atmosphere in the enclosed space of the car lightened. Kenneth laughed. 'But apart from that, did you enjoy the party?'

She was able to tell him truthfully that she had.

On Monday Hazel finished work early and she hurried along to Brownlow's. The shop was busy. Irene was at her place at the cosmetics counter, and she looked up and smiled.

'Hazel – what are you doing here?' she asked. 'Have you come to buy Christmas presents?'

'I need some new foundation cream. Something very discreet, which looks as though I'm not wearing make-up and yet hides all my blemishes.'

Irene smiled. 'You haven't got any blemishes, but I know what you mean. Let me look at you.' She studied Hazel's face for a moment and opened one of the drawers behind her. 'Try this. A sort of creamy ivory. It's Elizabeth Arden. What do you think?'

'I think you're a genius. I couldn't have chosen better myself.'

Irene laughed softly. 'Of course you could. You have very good taste. But I'm the expert.'

'I'll take it.'

When Hazel had paid for her purchase and put the package in her handbag, Irene said, 'But that wasn't the real reason you came, was it?'

'Well, I really did fancy a new foundation cream but also I wanted to talk to you.'

'About Miss Forsyth inviting us back for the coronation?'

'Yes. Are you going to go?'

'Are you?'

'I don't know. That's why I want to talk about it.'

'Good idea.'

A man wearing a good overcoat and a trilby hat approached the counter and coughed politely to attract Irene's attention.

'Do you mind waiting a mo?' she asked Hazel.

Hazel smiled. 'Of course not. You just carry on.'

Irene gave her full attention to her customer, who it seemed knew exactly what his wife would like but was shocked when he discovered how much she had been paying for her cosmetics.

'Perhaps I've made a mistake,' he said. 'But I'm sure this is the stuff my wife has on the dressing table.'

He was looking at an arrangement of panstick, powder, rouge, mascara and lipstick. The items were set out temptingly on the glass counter with a bold red and white patterned make-up bag propped up behind them. A card beside them advertised the collection as a gift pack.

'Your wife has good taste,' Irene said, nodding approvingly.

He frowned. 'Expensive tastes.'

'Not necessarily.' Irene adopted a more serious expression. 'Not if she buys her make-up here. She probably takes advantage of our regular special offers.'

'Special offers?'

'Oh, we do them all the time. Our regular customers look out for them. On one occasion the new lipstick was actually half price.'

He looked at the items on display then at the price card displayed beside them. 'I don't see anything about price reductions here.'

'The make-up bag is free.' She picked it up and held it out to him. 'It has a zip and is a hundred per cent cotton. Look inside. It's fully lined. That would make a lovely Christmas gift in itself and you're getting it absolutely free.' She paused while he examined it then added, 'I'm sure your wife will be delighted with it.'

Suddenly he shrugged his shoulders and grinned at her. 'Okay. You've talked me into it. After all, it's Christmas.'

Irene smiled at him admiringly. Her voice expressed approval. 'You've made the right decision, sir.' She turned and reached down to open a cupboard behind her. 'Here you are, all boxed up and ready,' she said as she placed the gift box on the counter. The box had a pattern of red and white stripes like the make-up bag, but with the addition of bows of red ribbon and sprigs of holly. 'Isn't that attractive?' she said. 'Something to keep and store your bits and bobs in.'

'Look, miss, you've persuaded me. Just wrap it up and I'll take it.' The customer was beginning to look weary.

Irene nodded and wasted no more time. She popped the box in one of Brownlow's printed carrier bags and took the money. 'Merry Christmas,' she said as the customer turned to go.

'Yes, you too.' He turned and hurried away.

Irene glanced at Hazel. 'Did I overdo things there? Sometimes I get carried away.'

'You made the sale.'

'But will he ever come back?'

'Maybe next Christmas. Or for her birthday.'

'And that's another thing.' Irene looked worried.

'What is?'

'Maybe the poor woman will be in deep trouble now that he knows how much she's been spending on herself.'

'That's not your fault. She shouldn't keep secrets from him. Husband and wives should be totally honest with each other.'

178

Irene gave Hazel what could be described as an old-fashioned look. She shook her head. 'Sometimes I think you live in a different world than the rest of us. Life isn't like that.'

'Miss. I've been waiting for ages. Are you going to serve me?'

A girl aged about fourteen stood by the counter. Her coat was clean but shabby; the top button was hanging by a thread. Her socks had concertinaed around her ankles. Her hair was dragged back and up into a ponytail and her sharp-featured little face was marred by a scowl.

Irene looked apologetic. 'Oh, I'm sorry. Really I am. I thought you were with someone.'

'Who?' The girl looked belligerent.

'I thought you were with one of those ladies looking at the perfumes. I didn't realise you were a customer.' She hurried on before the girl could say anything else, 'Are you looking for a present for someone? Your mother, your sister? Have you been saving up?'

The girl's scowl deepened. 'I'm not a kid. I can afford to buy what I want, you know.'

'I'm sure you can.'

'And it's not a present for anybody. I want a lipstick for meself.'

'For yourself?'

'That's what I said.'

'But aren't... I mean, aren't you a bit young for lipstick?'

The girl looked Irene straight in the eye. 'I'm sixteen.'

'Oh, well, in that case.' Irene raised her eyebrows and shot an amused glance at Hazel. She

179

turned her attention back to her young customer. 'Have you any particular lipstick in mind?'

'The new Cutex one.'

'Oh.'

'What's the matter? Haven't you got one?'

'Yes, we have, but it's a very bright red, isn't it?'

'So what?'

'Well, you're so young.'

'I telt yer, I'm sixteen.'

'Well, girls your age usually go for something a little more delicate. How about rose pink?'

The girl snorted in disgust.

'Pale colours can be very attractive.'

'Do you want me money or don't you?' The girl scowled and put the exact price down on the counter.

'Oh, very well.' Irene shrugged and gave in gracefully. She popped the lipstick in a bag, but before she handed it over she said, 'Do your parents know that you're buying this?'

'What do you think?'

'So what happens if they see you wearing it?'

'Me mam would hold me down and wipe it off with a wet flannel and me dad would probably take the belt to me. But divven't fret.' Her scowl vanished. She grinned and suddenly looked quite pretty. 'They'll never know. I'm not so daft as to let them catch me.'

The girl walked away and Irene said, 'Oh dear, maybe I should have talked her out of it.'

'Not a chance!'

'What do you suppose she's up to?'

'Nothing much. She's just experimenting.'

'I hope you're right.' She smiled and shrugged.

'So what are we going to do?'

'Why don't we discuss things over tea and toasted teacakes?'

Irene started to tidy the counter. 'Yeah, that would be nice.' She glanced at her watch. 'Only another ten minutes and we'll be closing. And talking about closing time, where shall we go?'

'The snack bar in the station. They don't close.'

Irene smiled. 'Of course. If you wait outside we can hop on a trolleybus. I'll be as quick as I can.'

The bus was crowded. There were no seats and they had to hang onto the overhead straps. Other passengers pushed past them at every stop, so they abandoned trying to talk to each other.

The snack bar in the station was busy as they had expected it would be, but most of the customers were waiting for their trains, so none of the tables was occupied for too long. Hazel and Irene queued at the counter for their pot of tea and toasted teacakes. The hot water urn steamed and hissed and the sound of many conversations echoed around under the high ceiling.

Carrying their trays, they looked around for a table. One table up against the wall had a lone woman sitting at it. They made their way towards it, but then they saw that the two unoccupied chairs were piled high with shopping bags. They stared at her speculatively. The collar of her camel coat was turned up and she was wearing a silk headscarf with red and gold patterns on a deep blue background. They couldn't see her face.

'That's a Hermès scarf,' Irene said. 'And that

coat must have cost a fortune.'

'Rich then?' Hazel said.

'Loaded, I would say.'

'Shall we ask her to move her shopping bags?'

'Nah.'

'I'm sure she wouldn't mind sharing the table with us.'

'Maybe *I* don't want to share a table with *her*.'

'Because?'

'I don't like snobs.'

Hazel was exasperated. 'Keep your voice down, she'll hear you.'

'So what?'

'Irene, you have no idea whether she's a snob or not.'

'Yes, I do. Women dressed like that come into Brownlow's and they treat the assistants like some lower form of life.'

'Not all of them, surely?'

Irene hesitated. 'No, but most of them do. And that one's the same sort, I can tell, otherwise she wouldn't take up the whole table the way she's doing at such a busy time.'

Hazel was spared from further argument when two middle-aged ladies vacated a table next to where they were standing. A tired waitress appeared immediately to clear the empty cups and plates away.

'Quick!' Irene said. Laughing, she plonked her tray down with a defiant, 'There we are!'

Forgetting all dignity, Hazel joined her swiftly, to the amusement of two schoolgirls who were occupying the other two seats. The girls were eating iced buns and they seemed to be helping each other with their homework. The exercise books were open on the table. It looked like algebra. A flake of icing fell on one of the books and the girl it belonged to blew it off gently.

Irene smiled at them. 'Are you supposed to do that?' she asked.

Both of them glanced up. 'Do what?' one of them asked. 'Eat currant buns?'

Irene laughed. 'Cheeky monkey. I meant, are you supposed to do your homework together?'

The other girl grinned. 'I don't see why we shouldn't help each other, do you?'

'That's not an answer, but I don't blame you,' Irene said. She picked up her knife and cut her teacake in half. 'As a matter of fact, my friend Hazel and I used to help each other too, didn't we?'

Hazel nodded and smiled as she poured the tea. Both girls looked at Irene and Hazel as if they were trying to imagine these two grown women as schoolgirls.

'That was a long time ago,' Hazel said.

'And to tell the truth,' Irene added, 'it was mostly Hazel who used to help me.'

One of the girls glanced up at the clock on the wall behind the counter, then nudged her friend, and they shoved their books into their satchels. 'We'll have to finish this on the train.' She glanced at Irene and Hazel. 'We've got to hand it in before the end of term.'

As soon as they left, one of the seats was taken by a young woman wearing businesslike spectacles. She poured her tea, stirred in a generous spoonful of sugar and then took a paperback book

183

out of her large shoulder bag. Hazel recognised the green and white cover of the Penguin mystery series and immediately imagined this sensible-looking woman, a secretary perhaps, being transported into a world of murder and mystery. She looked the type who would follow every clue and possibly solve the crime long before she got to the last page.

'Cute kids, weren't they?' Hazel said. 'How old do you think they were?'

'About fourteen.'

'So at least another year of school to go. Another two years if they're going to sit the School Cert.' She shook her head and smiled over her cup. 'Not like in our day. I had a job in the village shop when I was their age.'

'That was your own choice. You could have stayed on for another year or longer for the extra classes Miss Norton and Mrs Edwards arranged.'

'Shorthand? Typing? Bookkeeping? French, for goodness' sake! You know I couldn't have managed that.'

'I know no such thing. You never gave yourself a chance.'

'Are you scolding me?'

'No.' Hazel smiled at her affectionately. 'I would never do that. But I still think you should have stayed on with Carol and Bridget and me.'

Irene looked thoughtful. 'Yeah, that was a surprise.'

'What was?'

'Bridget learning about all that stuff. I mean, Bridget Forsyth was never going to work as a secretary, was she?'

'I think she quite enjoyed being with the rest of us.'

'The riff-raff.'

'Don't say that. Bridget was never a snob. She was just used to a different way of life. Before the war girls like Bridget would probably go to a finishing school in France or Switzerland and then just mark time until they got married.'

'That's still the same for some. What about the debutantes, you know, the girls who get their pictures in *Country Life* along with the chinless wonders they call debs' delights?' Irene looked thoughtful. 'Do you think Bridget would have been a debutante? Presented at court and all that, and then settled for some chap with a title, or a fortune, or both, rather than marry for love?'

The chatter and the clattering of plates and cups surrounding them seemed to fade away and they looked at each other solemnly.

'We'll never know, will we?' Hazel said.

'No, we won't. Thanks to Carol.'

'Don't,' Hazel said. 'We don't know the truth of what happened, so don't say any more.'

Both of them were silent. They drank their tea. Irene looked down at her plate. A fat currant had escaped from her teacake. She picked it up and put it into her mouth. After a moment she said, 'So are you going to go to Withenmoor?

'I don't know,' Hazel said. 'I'd like to because it would mean so much to Miss Forsyth. She was so good to us.'

'I know. Much better than *I* deserved. So what's stopping you?'

'My mother, Kenneth, life.'

Irene grinned. 'You can say that again. Life, I mean. My career is taking off. Ray would go spare if I suddenly took time out.'

'Couldn't you manage just a couple of days? I mean, you could probably sing at the party.'

'What party?'

'They're bound to have a party!'

'If I sang Ray would expect them to pay for the privilege.'

'Do you always have to do what Ray tells you?'

Irene's glance was sharp. 'What if I do? He's my manager. He only wants the best for me. I'm lucky to have someone who believes in me and is prepared to work hard to make me successful. To make me a star.' She paused and looked at Hazel challengingly. 'And anyway, I don't see you telling your Kenneth where to get off,' she said.

'Don't take offence, Irene. I don't want us to quarrel.'

Irene glared for a moment and then her features relaxed into a smile. 'I haven't changed much, have I? I still fly off the handle too easily.'

Hazel glanced up at the clock on the wall behind the counter. 'Ten to six. I'll have to go. My mother worries if I'm late home.'

'We'll have to let Miss Forsyth know soon.'

'I know.'

'Let's get Christmas and New Year over and then decide.'

'All right.'

'You could pop into Brownlow's at closing time some day and we'll do this again.'

'Good idea. I will. Are you coming for the bus?'

'No.' Irene glanced up at the clock. 'I think I'll

wait for my dad. He gets off at six. I'll go home with him.'

They walked out into the busy station concourse and paused to listen to a children's choir singing carols beside the giant Christmas tree. The tree had come all the way from Norway. Each year since the end of the war, the people of Newcastle had received a Christmas tree from the people of Bergen. Each year the tree was decorated with traditional Norwegian white lights, a symbol of peace and goodwill.

'The kids are good, aren't they?' Irene said. 'And don't you think the girls look sweet in their little pixie hoods and mitts?'

'Yes, I do.'

'Do you remember that night when we walked all the way home to Hillside House singing our little hearts out?'

'Mmm.'

'Oh, Hazel, I'm sorry. I forgot that was the night when you first met Alan.'

'It's all right. It was a long time ago and time heals all wounds, isn't that what they say?'

'They may say it but it isn't true, is it?'

'No.' Hazel shook her head. 'Maybe the pain lessens but the wounds remain.'

They looked at each other, smiled sadly and then, after a brief hug, they said goodbye.

The woman in the silk headscarf watched them hug then walk away in different directions. She had waited in the café until she thought they would be gone but, seeing them standing talking, she had melted back into the crowd. She had

187

recognised them as they queued up at the counter and she had immediately pulled her headscarf forward and placed her shopping bags and parcels on the two recently vacated chairs. It was only when she saw them approaching with their trays that she realised her subterfuge would not work. Irene or Hazel would simply ask her to remove her bags. She contemplated gathering all her parcels together and making an undignified run for it but it was already too late.

At the last minute she was saved by Irene's ill-nature. They hadn't changed. Neither of them. Irene was still unpleasantly combative and Hazel was still acting like Miss Goody Two-Shoes. She had heard what they had said when they were standing near her table, and once they found their own table she had strained to listen. She didn't like either of them. She never had, and couldn't bear to face them now and ruin a marvellously indulgent day of shopping at Newcastle's best stores, made even more enjoyable by lunch at the Tivoli.

While they had waited at the counter she'd watched them surreptitiously. She decided that Irene looked as common as ever. There was no denying that her clothes were fashionable, but they looked cheap, and her hair and make-up looked showy. She admitted grudgingly that Hazel looked stylish and even elegant, but then, Hazel had never looked or talked like a girl from one of the poorest streets in Newcastle.

And now Miss Forsyth had decided to invite them to join in the coronation celebrations at Withenmoor. If they accepted she would have to pretend to be pleased and be all sweetness and light. Miss Forsyth had told her she would be relying on her to help with the arrangements and she could hardly refuse.

Maybe they wouldn't accept. She had heard enough of their conversation to learn that they both had problems. Hazel had mentioned difficulties with her mother and a boyfriend. And it seemed Irene had some sort of singing career and a manager who sounded like a money-grubbing wide boy. She wasn't surprised; Irene had always been a show-off and now it seemed she had delusions of becoming a star.

Her parcels and bags were getting heavy and she was relieved when Hazel and Irene had finally gone their separate ways. She waited until there was no sight of them and made her way to her platform. The train was crowded but there were one or two seats left in the first-class carriage. These days Carol always travelled first class.

Chapter Eleven

December 1940, January 1941

On Christmas Day Mrs Ellis had worked wonders. No one looking at the festive spread on the table would have thought there was a war on. Miss Forsyth had found a prewar box of crackers containing silver charms, paper hats, and the usual riddles and jokes. The jokes were as feeble as cracker mottoes always were, but all the girls made the effort to laugh. They didn't want Miss Forsyth to guess how much they were missing their families on their first Christmas away from home.

The party on Boxing Day had been fun. Even Carol joined in when she saw how enthusiastic Bridget was. Village children and evacuees united in enjoying themselves. Miss Forsyth and Miss Norton organised games such as blind man's buff and pin the tail on the donkey, and those who'd never played it before soon got the hang of charades. Alan played the piano for musical chairs and for a final sing-song before the young guests went home clutching small bags of cinder toffee provided by Molly Watkins.

On the first Sunday of the new year, Carol's parents and Irene's mother and brother visited Hillside House. Joan Stafford, in spite of Hazel's pleading, did not come, and of course it was quite impossible for Bridget's parents.

Miss Forsyth and her housekeeper had had a querulous discussion about whether Twelfth Night was on the fifth or sixth of January. Mrs Ellis insisted that it was the fifth, the very day of the visit, and that the Christmas decorations should come down and the tree and all the greenery be put outside. Not to do so would be inviting disaster. Miss Forsyth said that these days people said it was on the sixth, but even if Mrs Ellis was correct, they should leave everything in place until their guests had gone home, and not to worry because Alan Sinclair had offered to come along and help. Everything would be in order before midnight. Disaster would be averted.

Instead of being pleased that Alan would come to help, Mrs Ellis had grumbled about another mouth to feed and that she didn't have a magic ration book. Then she had retired to the kitchen to do the best she could. Miss Forsyth said all the girls must clean and tidy and make the house look inviting. Ted had braved the icy roads from his cottage and he saw to it that the fires were kept going. Miss Forsyth wanted the old house to be warm and welcoming.

Straight after an early breakfast, Hazel had taken on the task of vacuuming the carpet in the library. She was surprised when Bridget sought her out. 'Hold on a moment,' the other girl said. 'I'll pick up those stray strands of tinsel. Most of them look good enough to save for another year.'

Hazel switched off the vacuum cleaner and sat down on one of the footstools. She welcomed the break.

'There,' Bridget said as she draped the salvaged strands over the branches of the tree. She turned to Hazel. 'Do you think we'll still be here to dress a tree next Christmas?'

The question took Hazel by surprise. 'I don't know.'

'This wretched war. There seems to be no end in sight. When I first came here I was counting the days until I could see my parents again, but now I don't know if I ever will.'

'You mustn't talk like that. Of course you will.'

'How can you say that?' Bridget asked angrily. 'Nobody knows what's going to happen. Oh, I know you think you're smarter than the rest of us, but even you can't see into the future.'

Hazel was shocked. 'Is that what you think of me? Are you saying that I'm conceited?'

Bridget regarded her for a moment and then sighed. 'No, you're not conceited. But the truth is you are smarter than the rest of us and sometimes you seem to, I don't know, hold yourself a little aloof.'

'I don't mean to.'

'I know, and I'm sorry.' Bridget walked over to the window and gazed out unseeingly. 'Seriously, Hazel, I know the dangers my parents face every day. My father could be lost at sea, his ship sunk by some ghastly U-boat, and my mother might not be able to dodge the bombs forever. She could be killed while she's saving other people's lives.'

Hazel looked at Bridget helplessly. There was nothing she could say.

'And what about you?' Bridget asked.

'What do you mean?'

'Your mother has to stay in town and work in spite of the air raids and your father's waiting to go into the army, isn't he? Don't you worry about them?'

Hazel remembered a conversation she'd had with her mother:

'Sooner or later your father will be getting his call-up papers.'

'What does that mean?'

'He'll be off to join the army.'

'Good!'

Her mother had sighed. 'No, pet, it's not good. No matter what kind of man he is, we shouldn't be pleased that he'll have to go and fight and maybe get killed.'

Now she felt ashamed that she had ever wished him ill. No matter that her parents' marriage was far from happy, her mother was right. He was surly and awkward and sometimes frightening, but he was not a wicked man and he did not deserve to die.

'Yes, I do worry about them,' she said. 'But I have to go on hoping that we'll all be together again one day.'

Bridget turned to face her. 'Look, forget what I said. The fact that the other two are having their families to visit set me off, but you're in the same boat as me, so why don't we stick together today?'

Hazel rose to her feet. 'Okay, and you can help me finish in here if you like.'

'What shall I do?'

'Move the chairs around while I vacuum the floor. If we work together we'll be finished in no time.'

'But then Mrs Ellis will find us something else to do!'

'Not if we don't report back straight away.'

Bridget laughed. 'That's more like it! Sometimes, Hazel, you're okay.'

Hazel wasn't too happy about the word 'sometimes' but it wasn't worth getting upset about. The two girls finished their task, stole ten minutes to sit by the fire and then reported back to Mrs Ellis.

Irene's mother and brother were the first to arrive. Carol was waiting in the morning room with Miss Forsyth, but Irene, hardly able to contain her excitement, had actually been sitting on the stairs waiting for the bell to ring. When it did she rushed across the hall to open the door. She flung herself into her mother's arms and breathed in the wonderfully familiar smell of Californian Poppy.

After a while Terry, who had been standing outside, stamping his feet to keep warm, said, 'I'm here too, you know. Are you going to let me in or shall I turn round and go back to the station?'

'That's right, our Irene, let's get in and shut the door before we let all the warmth out,' her mother said.

Irene stood back and her mother and brother entered the house accompanied by a gust of frosty air. Miss Forsyth emerged from the morning room to greet her guests and Irene stood back and watched the scene proudly. She thought her mother looked like a film star in her fur coat and her matching pillbox fur hat. Her shining blond hair was set in pageboy style, and as usual she was beautifully made up. When Irene finally noticed

Terry her eyes widened. He wore a belted raincoat that looked brand new and, of all things, a trilby hat. The hat was tilted to one side as if to echo his lopsided grin.

'What do you think?' he asked Irene.

'You look so grown up.'

'I *am* grown up. Any minute now I'll be off to fight for King and Country, so I've damn well got to be grown up.'

'Terry! Language!' his mother breathed, but if Miss Forsyth had heard it she pretended that she hadn't.

Miss Forsyth made them welcome and told them that Irene would show them where to put their coats and then, if they liked, she could show them round the house.

Her mother was carrying a shopping bag. She dipped a kid-gloved hand into it and brought out a box of chocolates. 'This is for you,' she said and handed it to Miss Forsyth.

Miss Forsyth looked down at it in surprise. '*Liqueur* chocolates! My dear Mrs Walker, that's very kind of you, but I can't accept it.'

'Why ever not?'

'Because it must have taken all your sweet coupons, and perhaps those of your family as well.'

'Oh, that. It didn't cost me any coupons at all. My husband won them in a Christmas raffle at his social club. The money collected was for the children's refugee camps. People donated whatever gifts they could.'

'How kind of them.'

'So I hope you'll accept them. You've been so kind to Irene.'

Miss Forsyth nodded and thanked her and then said, 'As soon as you've shed your coats and had a little tour of the house, Irene will bring you back to the morning room for a cup of tea and a chat. You must have so many questions to ask me.'

When they reached the cloakroom her mother took off her coat and hat and became engrossed in touching up her make-up. She stared into the mirror of her gold compact and dabbed at her nose with the powder puff.

'Did Dad really win the chocolates in a raffle?' Irene asked Terry quietly.

Her brother grinned and winked at her. 'What do you think?'

'Lost property?'

Terry laughed. 'You've got it in one.'

'What are you two on about?' Edie asked as she snapped her compact shut and slipped it back into her handbag.

'I'm just asking my little sister where I can go for a smoke.'

'Wherever that is I'll join you,' their mother said. 'I'm gasping for a ciggie.'

'You can't smoke here,' Irene told them. 'At least not in the house. Ted has to stand out in the stable yard.'

'Who's Ted?' Terry asked.

'The gardener, the odd job man, I think I told Mam in one of my letters.'

'He's not the groom, then?'

'What's a groom?'

'The man who looks after the horses.'

'There aren't any horses. Not now. Mrs Ellis told us that they were all taken away during the

196

Great War and they never came back.'

'Poor things. Perished in France, no doubt.'

'I suppose so.'

'Cheer up, kid, it was a long time ago. So what does Miss Forsyth keep in the stables now?'

'There are a couple of old cars but Miss Forsyth never learned to drive.'

Their mother was satisfied with her appearance. 'Let's go,' she said. 'Now show me the way to the kitchen.'

'You're not going out to have a ciggie, are you? You've only just arrived.'

'All right, I'll wait until later.' She picked up her shopping bag. 'I've got a little present for the cook.'

Mrs Ellis looked up in surprise. So did Bridget, Hazel and Alan Sinclair, who were sitting at the table with toast and mugs of hot Bovril.

'This is my mother,' Irene said nervously. 'And, er, my brother.'

'Pleased to meet you,' Mrs Ellis said but she didn't look that pleased.

'And I'm very pleased to meet you. Irene has told me what a grand job you're doing in these difficult times.'

'Really?' Mrs Ellis's eyebrows shot up.

To Irene's further discomfort she could sense her brother holding in his laughter. She didn't dare look at him. Her mother put the shopping bag on the table and took out the contents: a two-pound bag of sugar, two quarter-pound packets of Rington's tea and then, amazingly, wrapped in butcher's paper, a whole boiled ham.

'My way of saying thank you,' her mother said.

197

Mrs Ellis stared at the goods on the table. Irene was sure that she would ask her mother how she came by them and was dreading both her mother's answer and the cook's reaction. But to her surprise Mrs Ellis said nothing at all. She put the tea and the sugar in the pantry and the ham on the cold shelf in the larder then turned round and actually smiled.

'Very good of you,' she said. 'I suppose you'll be wanting a cup of tea? One of these lasses will bring a tray to the morning room.'

'That's so kind of you, but Irene is going to show us round first.'

'Righto. She can come and let me know when you're ready.'

They turned to go but Terry said, 'Look, I'll skip the tour. I think I'll pop outside for a smoke. Anyone want to join me?'

The group of young people shook their heads. 'Are you sure?' he asked, directing his question to Alan as he held up a pack of Players Navy Cut. 'My treat.'

Alan smiled and said, 'No thanks.'

Irene, deeply embarrassed, said, 'No one here smokes.'

'Really? No one at all?'

There was no mistaking the way he looked at her and she was dreading what he might say next, but he simply took a cigarette from the pack, put it in his mouth and reached for his lighter. Before he could light up, Mrs Ellis said, 'Outside if you don't mind, young man.'

'Of course.'

'Serve you right if you freeze out there,' Mrs

198

Ellis said.

'If I do you can make me a nice hot drink when I come back. I'll have whatever they're having.' He made for the back door, turned and said, 'See you later.'

Irene saw that Mrs Ellis was actually smiling broadly. It seemed that Terry could charm anyone.

Her mother was impressed with the house. She kept up a flow of questions as they went round.

'You fell on your feet when you came here, didn't you, pet?' she said.

'Yes, I was lucky.'

'And do you get on well with the other girls?'

'Yes.'

Irene bit her lip. That wasn't quite true. She liked Hazel a lot and she was lucky that Hazel seemed to like her, but there wasn't much love lost between her and Carol. And as for Bridget, she had never been quite sure what to make of her.

'Well, most of the time,' she added, wanting to be honest.

Her mother laughed. 'Four young lasses – there's bound to be a bit of bother now and then. But you never told me there was a lad here.'

'There isn't.'

'Well, who was that good-looking young man in the kitchen?'

'That's Alan, the doctor's son. He's just come to help around the house today.'

'Does he do that often?'

'He's been coming during the holidays but he'll be going back to boarding school soon.'

'Is he earning pocket money?'

'What do you mean?'

'Does Miss Forsyth pay him to help?'

'I don't think so. He just likes coming here.'

'Which one is it?'

'I don't know what you mean.'

'Oh, come on, our Irene. Four bonny young lasses in the house. Maybe he has his eye on one of you.'

'Mam, he's nearly sixteen. We're just kids compared to him.'

'Listen pet, I was exactly your age when your dad first came calling. He was a year older. We were childhood sweethearts, and what innocents we were. Nobody thought it would last. They were wrong. We got married as soon as I was sixteen. We grew up together and found we suited each other very well.' She paused. 'Is it Miss Forsyth's niece?'

'Bridget? Why do you think that?'

'Because she's posh like he is. Good family and all that. Well, what do you think?'

'No, I don't think he comes here to see Bridget. It's Hazel he likes to talk to. They get on very well together.'

'Then good luck to her.'

'Oh, Mam, you make it sound as if she's out to get him. Hazel isn't like that.'

'What is she like?'

'She's clever and kind and sensible and much nicer than the rest of us. If you're right and Alan Sinclair is sweet on her, and if she likes him, then he's the lucky one.'

While Miss Forsyth was talking to Irene's mother and brother in the morning room, Carol's parents arrived. When they took their coats off Carol was relieved to see that they both looked very smart. Her father was wearing his best navy blue pin-stripe suit and her mother wore a grey fitted jacket with a straight skirt. Her blouse was a soft pearly colour and she wore her cameo brooch with the pale blue background at her neck. Her black court shoes had a stylish Cuban heel and her dark hair was swept back into a neat chignon. Her make-up wasn't plastered on like that of Irene's mother.

Carol thought Mrs Walker looked a bit common with her tight-fitting emerald green dress and her peep-toe shoes. She wondered what Miss Forsyth and Bridget would make of her.

After the initial introduction Carol took her parents round the house. They admired the Christmas decorations. 'Very tasteful,' her mother said. 'Just right for this lovely old house.' She was impressed with the curtains and the carpets. 'Such good taste,' she said. 'You can tell the Forsyths are an old established family.'

Carol's father recognised some of the furniture as being genuine antiques but most of all he was interested in the paintings, just as Carol had thought he would be.

Their visit to the kitchen was brief because it was nearly time for lunch. Carol's father didn't say much. He just stood there and smiled, but her mother was really nice to Mrs Ellis. At least that's what Carol thought. She thanked the cook for coping so well with wartime conditions and said it was encouraging to find such loyal staff in these uncertain days. Staff you could rely on.

Carol was startled when her father coughed

loudly and said, 'I'd like to add my thanks, Mrs Ellis. We're grateful that Carol is being so well fed.'

Carol led the way back to the morning room and became aware that her parents had stopped in the middle of the hall. She turned and saw her father put his arm round her mother and draw her towards him. He spoke very quietly. 'Tone it down a bit, Anne.'

'What do you mean?'

'In the kitchen there. You were acting like the lady of the manor. Or at least trying to give the impression that we have a houseful of servants at home.' Her mother gave a half sob and pulled away but he held onto her. 'Don't be upset. I know you're trying to make a good impression for Carol's sake, but you don't have to pretend to be someone you're not. You're perfect as you are and I'm proud of you.' He pulled her close, kissed her forehead and then looked up and smiled towards the doorway. But Carol had already hurried into the morning room.

Miss Forsyth had decided that Hazel and Bridget and Alan could help Mrs Ellis by carrying the dishes to and fro and then have their own lunch in the kitchen. Bridget thought this was the right decision. 'We'll just feel out of place when they're playing happy families, won't we? she'd said and Hazel had agreed with her.

On her brief visits to the dining room Hazel noticed that the conversation was flowing easily. Miss Forsyth had the knack of putting everyone at their ease. She also noticed how different the two mothers were. Irene's mother was lively and completely at ease in a way her mother never could have been. Her own mother would have been overawed and uneasy and would probably have been too frightened to open her mouth because of the way she talked.

In fact, if such things were important, Hazel's mother spoke in a more acceptable manner than Irene's mother, whose accent was rather broad. But it had obviously never occurred to Mrs Walker that she should be judged a lesser person because of her accent. Carol's mother, on the other hand, spoke very carefully and precisely, her rather thin tone sounding as if it was straining to get out.

'That woman's had elocution lessons, just like her daughter,' Bridget said when they met up in the kitchen. 'I can tell.'

'There's nothing wrong with that,' Hazel replied.

'No, I don't suppose there is, but she's over-doing it a bit and it's irritating. Why can't people like that accept their place in life like you do?'

Hazel didn't know whether to laugh or cry. Should she be offended by Bridget's snobbish remark or just accept that Miss Forsyth's niece had no idea that what she had said was insulting? She felt like bobbing a curtsey and saying, 'Yes, miss, you're quite right, miss,' but she realised the gesture would be entirely wasted on Bridget, so she let it go. But she couldn't help wondering, if Bridget felt this way about Carol, why she had become so friendly with her.

As if Bridget had read her thoughts she said, 'I quite like the girl, you know. I mean, if she didn't have me she'd be utterly miserable. Irene is so beastly to her and you don't leap to her defence as often as you should.'

Hazel was thoroughly taken aback. In one stunned moment she realised that Bridget had told the truth. She resolved to try and be kinder to Carol, although she knew in her heart that she wouldn't appreciate any attempt she made to be more friendly.

After they had cleared the dining room table, Hazel, Bridget and Alan helped with the dishes and then sat down at the kitchen table with their own meal. When they'd finished Bridget declared herself exhausted, and she went to her room to curl up with a book until she was needed at teatime. Mrs Ellis went across to her own quarters to put her feet up for a while. Hazel and Alan were left to tidy the kitchen.

'What was all that about?' Alan asked once they were alone.

'All what?'

'I saw you having a pretty serious conversation with Bridget.'

'We were just talking about Irene and Carol's families.'

'And let me guess. Bridget doesn't approve of any of them.'

'Well...'

'It's all right. I know you're not the sort to criticise people, but I do find that girl a bit of a snob, don't you?'

'I thought so at first, but it's not that. It's just the way she's been brought up. Her life in London, the kind of school she goes to, the girls she mixes with.'

'You think she'll ever change?'

'I think that deep down she's all right and that we should give her a chance.'

'You're all right, aren't you, Hazel?'

She didn't know why but his smile disconcerted her. She felt flustered. 'What do you mean?'

'I mean I'm glad that I met you and I like you a lot. I hope we can be pals.' He paused. 'Can we?'

She smiled and nodded. Neither of them could think of anything else to say.

After lunch Miss Forsyth said she had some letters to write and she suggested that Irene and Carol find somewhere to have an hour or two with their parents privately. She asked them where they would like to go. Carol chose the library, where her father could look at some of the books, and Irene settled for the old nursery, which would be nice and cosy.

They hadn't been upstairs more than a couple of minutes when Irene's mother said she was absolutely gasping for a ciggie and she would find her own way back to the kitchen and go out to the stable yard.

'Mind you put your coat on,' Terry told her. 'It's really cold out there.'

'What about you?' Irene asked him when they were alone. 'Don't you want a smoke?'

'I do, but not as much as I want to talk to my kid sister. I mean, God knows when I'll see her again.'

There was something in his tone of voice that alarmed Irene and she looked at him for reassurance, but there was no trace of his usual cheery expression.

'Don't talk like that, Terry. You're scaring me,' she said.

Terry sighed. 'Sorry, I didn't mean to. It's just that I'll be off to the army soon and I have no idea when I'll get any leave.'

'But you'll come and see me when you do?'

'You bet.'

'And will you write to me?'

'I'm not much good at that sort of thing.'

'You're better at writing than I am!'

He grinned. 'Okay, you win. I'll drop you a line if and when I can. But now you've got some explaining to do.'

'Me? What do you mean?'

'Where do you go for a sneaky smoke?'

'Oh, that.' She laughed. 'I don't.'

'Go on!'

'Honestly. Somehow I've never even thought about it. I don't know why I started smoking in the first place – maybe because I thought it made me seem grown up and because I didn't have enough to do. But ever since I came here there's been so much going on and so much to think about, I just didn't need to.'

'Well I never. I'm really glad for you. I'm beginning to think that Mam's right when she calls it a filthy habit but I just can't give it up – and neither can she.' He thought for a moment and then said, 'So what did you do with the ciggies I gave you?'

'I gave them to Ted.'

Terry stared at her for a moment and then he guffawed. 'Ted? The gardener?'

Irene nodded.

'What did he say?'

'Oh, I didn't give them to him face to face; I left them in the shed where he keeps his tools. They're the same kind he smokes, so maybe he thought he'd just forgotten about them. Anyway, nothing has been said.'

Terry shook his head. 'You're a proper card, our Irene.'

He picked her up easily and twirled her round. He had just set her down and they were both laughing when their mother came back into the room. She smiled at them. 'What's the joke?' she asked.

'No joke,' Terry said. 'We're just happy that we've had the chance to see each other before…'

'Before what?' his mother asked.

'You know.' He grinned but Irene noticed that the smile didn't get as far as his eyes. 'Before I go off to be a hero.'

Suddenly the room seemed cold and her mother must have noticed it too, because she went over to the hearth and put some more coal on the fire. She turned and her smile was not as bright as before.

'Let's sit by the fire and have a good old gossip,' she said. 'Let's make the most of the time we have left together before it's time to go down for tea.'

Irene let her mother and brother have the two armchairs and sank down on the hearthrug at her mother's feet. She lifted one arm and rested it on her mother's knees. They were happy to talk about people they knew: neighbours, friends and relatives, although Irene had the feeling that some of the time her mother hesitated and changed her mind about what she had been going to say.

She doesn't want to upset me if the news is bad, Irene thought, and she was happy enough not to ask any questions. The little clock on the mantelshelf ticked the minutes away and Irene realised that as their visitors would have to leave straight after tea in order to catch the train back to Newcastle, she was not going to have any more time alone with her brother. And there were things she needed to ask him.

For as long as she could remember, she had accepted that the treats her father had brought home had come from the lost property department at the station. Her father had always said they were unclaimed items that had been there a long time. As a small child she had never questioned this, but as she grew up she had begun to wonder whether her father had the right to take these items. She had once seen him wink at her mother and smile when he handed something over. She hated to think that the father she loved so much would do something dishonest.

Since leaving home and coming here to Withenmoor she had been able to put it out of her mind, but today, her mother's gift to Miss Forsyth of expensive liqueur chocolates had made her feel uneasy. She thought back to her earlier exchange with Terry while their mother had been busy with the powder puff. Lost property – the usual story. Her brother had grinned and winked at her – when he smiled and winked like that he looked just like their father.

She'd known then that she had been right to be suspicious, and it was worse than that. She remembered the breakfast her mother had cooked on her last day at home. She'd put their plates of bacon, egg and fried bread on the table.

'*Eat up*,' she had said. '*You'll not get breakfasts like that much longer. I paid a princely sum for the bacon that a certain grocer was keeping under the counter, and the eggs an' all. Shameful, isn't it?*'

'*What do you mean, Mam?*' Terry had asked. '*Do you mean the price of the bacon and eggs is shameful, or the fact that you were prepared to pay for them on the black market?*'

At the time Irene hadn't really known what the black market was. Her mother often took her into town to shop at the Grainger market or the Bigg market. Once or twice she had gone with her mother to the fish market, but Irene hated seeing all those open mouths and those glassy eyes staring at up her from the marble slabs. She couldn't remember when she'd first heard anyone mention the black market but she'd had no idea what they were talking about until she'd come to Withenmoor.

Miss Forsyth allowed them to listen to the news on the wireless. She thought they were old enough to follow the reports of the progress of the war. She also allowed them to read her newspaper. Irene's attention had been caught by an article about people who were making money by selling stolen goods, mostly food. These goods had often been stolen by railway workers and then sold on. The newspaper called them nothing less than traitors to line their own pockets in such straitened times.

When Irene had finished reading that report

she had felt physically sick. Had her father, who she had come to believe had not been completely honest about the things he brought home from lost property, become an out and out thief?

And now her mother had brought chocolates, tea, sugar and a boiled ham. All these things were rationed. It was obvious that Miss Forsyth had been taken in by the story of the raffle, but it was equally obvious that Mrs Ellis had suspected they had not been come by honestly but was willing not to ask any questions.

Although she was almost certain that what her parents were doing was wrong, this didn't mean that she loved them less. All she could do was hope that her father would not get caught. They shot traitors, didn't they?

The clock ticked and the fire crackled. Outside the sky darkened and the room grew shadowy.

'Do you think we ought to draw the curtains?' her mother asked. 'I mean, are they fussy about the blackout here?'

'They are,' Irene replied. 'Even though we've never had an air raid.'

'Nor likely to. That's why I agreed to you coming here.' Irene got to her feet. 'I'll put the boards up and draw the curtains,' she said.

Terry surprised her by offering to help.

'I don't need...' she began but he was already halfway to the windows.

He put the boards up, one in each window, and said, 'What's the matter?'

Irene drew the curtains and shook her head. 'Nothing.'

'Don't fib.'

'Really, I'm okay,' she said.

'Good. Then will you just point me the way to the bathroom?'

'It's just along the corridor. You've already been there.'

'I know, but this is a big house. Do me a favour and remind me, will you?'

Something about the way he looked at her made her walk to the door. Once they had left the room, Terry said loudly, 'Now then, right or left?' Then he took a few steps in the right direction and beckoned her to follow him. They stopped outside the bathroom door and he said, 'Something's up. I can tell. Aren't they treating you right?'

'Of course. I'm very lucky to be here.'

'Then what is it?'

She glanced back towards the open door of the nursery and said quietly, 'It's Mam. The things she brought today.'

'What's wrong with them?'

She felt an unexpected rush of anger. 'You know what's wrong with them!'

He looked at her through narrowed eyes. 'Does it bother you?'

'Very much.'

'Why?'

'It's wrong. You know it's wrong, and I love Mam and Dad and I don't want them to go to prison. A man on the wireless said that they should serve five years at least!'

'Phew! Glad you've got that off your chest?'

'It's not a joke, Terry.'

He stared at her for a moment and then he

shrugged. 'Sometimes I forget you're just a kid, and a very nice kid at that. I hate to see you upset like this and I wish I could tell you what Dad does is all above board, but I can't. But I can tell you that what he does is pretty trivial compared to what the real villains get up to. He has enough sense not to get involved with the real gangsters. Does that help?'

Irene sighed. 'I suppose it will have to.'

'Then get along back to our mam. She'll be wondering what's keeping you. And Irene...'

'What?'

'Cheer up and let's have a smile. A smile to remember you by.'

'I wonder if all these books have been read or if they were bought simply to fill the shelves,' Carol's father said.

Her mother frowned. 'That's a funny thing to say. Why would anyone do that?'

He reached up and ran his hand over a row of dark red leather-bound books with gold lettering on the spines. 'The owners of grand houses, even a moderately grand house like this one, used to buy books by the yard just to fill the shelves and make the room look impressive.'

'Well I never!'

'That didn't happen here,' Carol said. 'I once asked Bridget whether she knew if anyone had ever read all these books and she said the Forsyth family had been real bookworms since time began and that her grandfather had actually written some himself.'

'Really?' her father asked. 'What kind of books?'

'Not story books. I think they were history books, about this part of the world in ancient times. Romans and all that. She says there are a lot of Latin words in them, names of people and places.'

'Has Bridget read any of her grandfather's books?'

'No, although she's promised her father that one day she will.'

'Doesn't she like reading?'

'She does. She's always got a book on the go, but she likes school stories and adventure stuff. She says she prefers fiction to dusty old history. I ... I think I do, too.'

Her father smiled at her. 'There's nothing wrong with that. Reading stories can sometimes teach you as much about life as a work of non-fiction could.'

'Brian!' Her mother sounded exasperated. 'I don't know what you're on about and you're wasting time. You know we have so much to tell Carol. Why don't you come and sit beside us and we can give her the good news?'

'I'm sorry, Anne, of course we must tell Carol. I'll leave it to you; I know you want to. I'll just have a potter around these bookshelves for a little while. I don't know when I'll get an opportunity like this again.'

'There are plenty of books to look at in the public library at home.'

'I know, dear, but these books have been collected over the years by the Forsyth family. There are probably some first editions here. It's fascinating.'

'Oh, very well.' Her mother sounded exasperated but she looked at him fondly. 'Come along, Carol. Let's sit together on this old sofa by the fire.'

Carol was intrigued. She wondered what the good news could be and why they had waited so long to tell her. Her mother answered that unspoken question straight away.

'I wanted to wait until we could be sure of being alone for a while before I told you our news.'

'Get on with it, woman,' her father said laughingly, then he turned back to browse the bookshelves.

Carol was mystified. Whatever the news was, it had obviously made her mother very happy. Her usual look of vague disappointment with life had given way to genuine excitement. She placed her handbag on her knee, opened it and took out an envelope of photographs. She handed the envelope to Carol.

'Go on, look inside,' she said and moved up to sit as close to Carol as she could so that she could look over her shoulder.

Carol knew that her father liked taking photographs. They had albums full of snaps taken on holidays or day trips, especially if the trip involved a visit to what was called a 'beauty spot'. He especially liked taking pictures of her mother and her together in these places and he would sometimes ask passers-by to take the snap for him so that they could all be together.

So she was perplexed when she discovered that all the photographs seemed to be of a boring little semi-detached house. She looked at the

214

glossy black-and-white pictures, one after the other. There were snaps of the front of the house taken from different angles. 'Look at the bow windows,' her mother said, 'and that one shows the glass panel at the top of the front door. You can't see it properly in this snap, but it has a stained glass picture of a little sailing boat with white sails on a blue sea and a bright yellow sun in the sky. Oh, Carol, it's so attractive!'

Carol moved on to shots of the front garden with a crazy paving path, boring shrubs and a sundial in the middle of a tiny lawn. Her mother pointed to something in one of the snaps and said, 'You would have thought they would have pruned the rose bushes before they left, wouldn't you?'

Carol had no idea what to say. She was beginning to see where this was leading and her heart sank.

'The next ones are of the back garden,' her mother said. 'It's mostly lawn and the borders are boring but – look – there's a sweet little birdbath in the middle, and there's a shed by the back fence for your father to keep his garden tools in.'

'His garden tools?' In spite of the glowing fire, a cold dread was taking hold of Carol.

Her mother laughed. 'Oh, I know, he hasn't got many because we haven't got a garden, only a few pots in the backyard, but we'll be able to buy what we need once we move in. Isn't it exciting? We're going to leave the town and live by the sea!'

'You've bought this house?'

'Isn't it wonderful?'

Carol stared at her mother speechlessly.

215

'You're overcome, aren't you, pet?'

Carol nodded. That was true, she thought, but not in the way her mother wanted her to be.

'Go on, look at the other snaps taken inside.'

At last Carol found something to say. 'But the rooms are all empty.'

'I know. You'll have to use your imagination.' She reached over and picked up three of the photographs and handed them back to Carol one by one. 'These are the bedrooms,' she said. 'There are three bedrooms and yours will be at the back of the house overlooking the garden.' She took some more of the photographs. 'There's the bathroom – it's got cream and blue tiles. And now we go downstairs. There's a kitchen, a little scullery, a dining room with French windows opening onto the garden and a lounge looking out onto the front street. Look at the modern fireplace in the lounge.'

Her mother was getting more and more excited with every picture she showed her and Carol was getting more and more dismayed. Her mother didn't seem to notice her mood. 'Just think, Carol, once the war is over you'll have this lovely little house to come home to!'

'Have you told her?' At that moment her father came to sit beside them.'

'I have.'

'And are you pleased, Carol?'

'Yes.'

'You don't look pleased,' her mother said.

'I think Carol is a little overwhelmed with the news,' her father said. 'After all, it will be such a big change. She'll have to have time to digest it.'

Carol was grateful that her father wanted to

216

change the conversation and ask her all about her life in Withenmoor. They talked until Hazel came in to tell them that tea was ready. Later, when it was time for her parents to leave, her mother said, 'Don't look so downcast, Carol. Just count the days until you can leave here and come home to our nice little house by the sea.'

As soon as they had gone, Carol hurried upstairs to her room and flung herself down on her bed. How could anyone want to live in a poky little house like that after living here at Hillside House? She hoped the war would never end.

Chapter Twelve

At the end of February the snowstorms began. They seemed unending. To make things worse, gale force winds piled the snow up in drifts against the bare-branched hedges and the ancient drystone walls. The road down to Withenmoor was blocked and the girls were not able to go to school. By some miracle the telephone lines had not been brought down, and when Miss Forsyth contacted Grace Norton at the Edwards' house she learned that the classrooms were more than half empty.

'I wonder how long this is going to last,' Grace said.

'Who knows? All we can do is listen to the weather forecasts on the wireless.'

'It's too bad. The children have already had their education interrupted by the war and now this. Poor things.'

Miss Forsyth was amused. 'Really, Grace, I don't suppose any of them will mind very much, and the children from the town who are not used to such severe conditions will no doubt regard this as an adventure.'

'Maybe so, if it doesn't last too long. But eventually they will get bored.'

'You're right and that's one of the reasons I wanted to speak to you. I'm quite happy to give my girls some sort of lessons here in Hillside

House if you would trust me to do it and tell me what to cover.'

'That's good of you. I could bring some work up.'

Miss Forsyth chuckled. 'The roads are impassable. That's why we're having this conversation, remember?'

'Oh dear, I think my brain has gone into a deep freeze.'

'I have no idea when we'll see the postman or the milkman again.'

'It must be dreadful for you to be so completely cut off from the world.'

'It's not good to feel so isolated, but living here I'm used to it. It's happened before.'

'Have you plenty of supplies in?'

'Don't worry. Mrs Ellis is well stocked up. She's quite enjoying the situation. Now she's got the weather as well as Hitler to battle with and she's determined to win both wars. But what about these lessons?'

'I'll phone you in about an hour's time. Have a notebook ready.'

Miss Forsyth put the phone down and smiled. Not only did she like Grace Norton and enjoy talking to her, but now she could do something to help the girls. Her girls. She blessed the day they had come into her life.

They had their midday meal in the kitchen, all of them: Miss Forsyth, Hazel, Irene, Carol, Bridget and Mrs Ellis. The marrow bone broth had been simmering on the stove all morning and the smell was comforting. They had homemade bread with the broth and afterwards they had stewed apple rings and custard.

So far that morning it hadn't snowed, but the snow from the previous day had settled in the corners of the windowpanes, blocking out much of the light. It was only midday but the room was dark. The electric lights had been flickering uncertainly so Mrs Ellis switched them off and set an oil lamp in the middle of the table. It sent out a warm glow, but the corners of the room remained shadowy.

Carol looked around her. She was reminded of an oil painting she had seen on one of the occasions her father had taken her to the art gallery. The painting had shown a family in old-fashioned clothes sitting round a table just like this, but with candles on the table rather than an oil lamp. Her father had told her that the artist was known for the way he portrayed light. Her mother had given it a few moments' attention and then moved on restlessly.

Carol's mother never really enjoyed those outings. She liked to get dressed up in her best coat and hat and put her spectacles on to read the programme, but Carol thought she was pretending to be cleverer than she was. After a while she would abandon Carol and her father to go and look at the pretty things in the souvenir shop, then wait for them in the tea room.

Sometimes Carol wondered how her parents had got together. Her father was so clever – much cleverer than her mother, with his love of books and paintings and history and things like that. But she had to admit that her mother always

tried to do the best for her, to do things she believed would improve her way of life, even if it
sometimes meant quarrelling with her father.

And then, inevitably, the thoughts that she had
tried to keep at bay flooded in. She remembered
that her mother couldn't wait for the day when
the war would be over and she would have to
leave here – leave Hillside House, where she felt
so at home. Sometimes she felt that she had been
born to live in a house like this, but once the war
was over, she would have to leave here and go to
live in that horrid little house in a commonplace
little street by the sea.

Before her parents had left that day, her mother
had given her the photographs so that she could
look at them now and then to remind herself of
what she had to look forward to. Carol had left
them on the table in the library, saying that she
would take them to her room later. They were still
there the next morning. Waiting until she had a
moment alone in the room, she had thrown them
onto the fire, picked up the poker and pushed
them into the heart of the flames. Ever since then
she had tried to put the whole sorry business out
of her mind.

When any of the others wondered out loud
when they would see their families again, Carol
closed her mind and her ears. She supposed she
must love her parents. You had to love your
mother and father, didn't you? But she didn't
want them to come here again, not if it meant
that her mother would go on and on about that
house and all the things she planned to do to
make it nice for Carol's homecoming. She'd had

two letters from her mother since the visit. They were full of it. Carol had dealt with them the same way she had dealt with the photographs.

When the meal was over, Mrs Ellis opened the back door and looked up at the heavy clouds. She tut-tutted and told everyone to get their coats and wellies on and go out and get the washing in before it started snowing again. She didn't ask them; she told them. Carol glanced at Miss Forsyth, who was on her way out of the room, but she simply turned and nodded. Hazel and Irene were already on their feet and Bridget was getting up a little reluctantly. She looked resigned to it.

Carol leaned towards her. 'Mrs Ellis shouldn't tell you what to do like that,' she whispered.

'Why not?'

'She's only a servant and you ... well, you are one of the family.'

'Oh, that.' Bridget shrugged. 'Things have changed, haven't they? In the London house my mother's servants have deserted her. They've all gone to join up, even the chauffeur, who's almost forty but thinks he is fit enough to be a soldier. My mother is left with one girl to clean and cook, but although she's willing enough, the girl is a little slow-witted and she can't cook, so Mother has to do that herself – for both of them. I guess we're all in this together. My aunt expects me to be treated the same way you are.'

Carol drew back. That stung. All this time she had believed that Bridget had regarded her as a better class of person than Hazel and Irene, but it seemed she was wrong. Worse still, she was sure Bridget had not intended her remark as an insult.

It was just the way she had been brought up. Nevertheless, she hid her dismay and, once they had their coats and boots on, she suggested that she and Bridget should share one of the laundry baskets.

Hazel and Irene had gone out ahead of them, each footstep sinking into the snow so deeply that some snow tipped over into their wellingtons, making them squeal. Carol didn't think this at all funny and Bridget looked pained, but Hazel and Irene were laughing about it. They laughed even more when they found the clothes were frozen as stiff as boards on the washing line. As the various garments swung to and fro they bumped into each other and made crackling noises. Irene could hardly contain herself, especially when she found icicles hanging down from the cuff of a long-sleeved blouse.

'They look like fingers!' she exclaimed and her breath misted in the dense, frosty air. 'Jack Frost's fingers!'

To Carol's annoyance, Bridget smiled. 'Look, this one's the same,' she said. She unpegged the garment and waved the sleeve in Irene's direction. 'Shake hands and say how do you do!'

'Never mind how do you do, hurry up and get the clothes in before Jack Frost runs off with the lot of you!' Mrs Ellis snapped at them from the kitchen doorway. She was pretending to be cross but she was smiling.

They piled the unyielding clothes in the laundry baskets, and when they got back inside they found that Mrs Ellis had lowered the overhead clothes airer.

'There's still too much water in them,' she grumbled as she began folding each garment over the wooden struts. 'They're going to drip all over the floor. A couple of you girls, get that old tin bath out from under the bench, will you? I'll set it underneath.'

Hazel and Irene obliged. They would, Carol thought. When they had taken off their coats and their boots, they were all treated to mugs of hot Bovril. Hazel and Irene were still laughing about the frozen clothes and Bridget joined in their conversation. Carol had nothing to say. She had not found it at all funny and she thought they were being childish. She couldn't understand why Bridget could be bothered with the other two, but she sipped her Bovril and was careful not to show her displeasure. Bridget's friendship was important to her. She believed that socially she was much closer to Miss Forsyth's niece than she was to Hazel and Irene, and that one day everyone, even Bridget, would recognise that.

Every morning the fire was lit in the library. It was kept going with a plentiful supply of logs from the woodshed. They did their lessons at the table where Miss Forsyth and her brother had done their lessons as children all those years ago. After lunch they would go back to the library to do some homework and when they had finished, the fire was allowed to go out. After tea they spent the rest of the day in the old nursery, which was easier to keep warm. Miss Forsyth would join them there. Some days, if Mrs Ellis wanted to get away early, she would bring up sandwiches and mugs of cocoa

224

before she went back to her own cosy quarters at the other side of the stable yard.

It was Mrs Ellis's job to see to the fires. Ted had not been to the house since the worst of the blizzards and Miss Forsyth had assumed the road leading to his cottage, little more than a farm track, would be impassable. Miss Forsyth could see that her old friend was growing more and more weary. She wondered if she could remember enough about firelighting from her Girl Guide days and also, if she offered to take over, what Mrs Ellis's reaction would be. Thankfully the problem was solved before it came to that.

Early one morning, before her housekeeper had trudged across the snow-filled yard, Miss Forsyth went into the library, determined to at least try to get the fires going, and she found Hazel and Irene kneeling in front of the fireplace. The grate had been swept clean and both girls were rolling sheets of newspaper into long, tight twists and then folding them in two. A small pile of sticks waited on the tiled hearth and the old basket was full of logs.

'Of course,' Miss Forsyth said. 'I remember now.'

The girls looked up and smiled. 'We can do this,' Irene said. 'Or at least Hazel can. I've never had to light a fire in my life. My mother said there was time enough for me to learn. Terry said she was spoiling me. Mind you, she spoiled him, too.'

'Your brother. He's waiting for his call-up papers, isn't he?'

Irene nodded. 'He could be in the army by now.' She frowned. 'Mam hasn't mentioned him in her

225

letters since they came to visit, I don't know why.'

'Perhaps she doesn't want to worry you.'

'Well, she should realise that it's worse not knowing.'

Miss Forsyth looked at Irene sympathetically. 'You're quite right. All I know about my brother is that he's somewhere on the high seas. If he were engaged in some kind of battle we won't know until it's over.'

While they had been talking Hazel had been getting on with laying the fire. First the twists of paper, then the kindling, then finally one or two logs. A gust of wind blew down the chimney and sent a drift of smoke across the room. They turned to see the first, hesitant flicker of flames.

'Oh, well done, Hazel!' Miss Forsyth exclaimed.

Hazel half turned, looked up and pushed a stray lock of hair back from her forehead with the back of her wrist. She smiled. 'I used to help my mother with the fires at home. I don't mind taking over here.'

'That's very good of you. But I think you should teach the other girls to do it and they should take their turns, don't you?'

'All of them?' Irene asked.

'Of course. Why not?'

'Even Bridget?'

Miss Forsyth chuckled. 'You might find that my niece already knows how to light a fire, at least a camp fire. She's in her school's Girl Guide pack, after all. So, Hazel, what do you say?'

'I'm willing to show them.'

'And I'm willing to learn,' Irene said.

'There, you see?' Miss Forsyth said. Then she

glanced at Hazel. 'You look doubtful. Tell me why.'

Before she could reply Irene grinned and said, 'I think she's worried that Carol might not be so keen to dirty her hands, but I don't think there'll be a problem. If Bridget can stoop to such a lowly task, Carol will suddenly find that lighting fires is *soooper* fun!'

Miss Forsyth flinched at the hint of animosity in Irene's tone. She would have been foolish to imagine that there would not be occasional quarrels amongst a group of adolescent girls penned up together in this old house. She had been relieved that most of the time there had been no serious problems. But as the months went by she had realised that Irene, a lively, head-strong creature who sometimes spoke out without pausing to weigh up her words, had taken against Carol. As far as Miss Forsyth was concerned, Carol was trying her best to adjust to her new surroundings, but she had probably antagonised Irene by seeking Bridget's friendship, so there was a bit of inverted snobbery there.

Bridget, her beloved younger brother's only child, was very dear to her. She wasn't surprised that Carol had been attracted to her and wanted to be just like her. Irene, on the other hand, could be scornful of any behaviour that was outside her field of experience. Miss Forsyth sighed and looked down at the two girls who were now sweeping and tidying the hearth, Irene willingly following Hazel's directions.

Hazel was undoubtedly the most intelligent of the four girls, Miss Forsyth acknowledged, but she was also the most tolerant and had the kindest heart. Luckily Irene seemed to respect her and was prepared to listen to her and be guided by her. Thank goodness for Hazel!

'Well, look at that!' Mrs Ellis spoke from the doorway. They turned to see one of her rare smiles. 'You've got the blessed fire going.'

'It's thanks to Hazel,' Miss Forsyth said. 'And in future the girls – all of them – will see to the fires.'

Mrs Ellis raised her eyebrows, probably taken aback by the words, 'all of them', but then, if possible, her smile grew wider. 'Right then, extra porridge for the workers this morning, and black treacle all round.'

That afternoon Miss Forsyth took several books from the shelves in the library and placed them on the table. Bridget reached for one of the books and pulled it towards her.

'Poetry,' she said. 'We're going to have a poetry lesson.'

Hazel felt like laughing at Bridget's expression of dismay.

Her aunt smiled. 'Don't you like poetry, Bridget?'

'Not much, Aunt Margaret. At least, not the poems I've had to learn at school.'

'Well, today you're going to choose the poems yourself. I want you to look through these books until each one of you finds a poem that you like. Then copy it out and we'll discuss it.'

'Any old poem?' Irene asked. 'There are an awful lot of poems in these books.'

'No, not any old poem, Irene. I want you to

find seasonal poems. Poems about snow, about frost, about winter. Poems about this time of the year. Don't you think that's a good idea?'

'If you say so, Miss Forsyth.'

Miss Forsyth left them to get on with their task. Irene didn't sound convinced but she looked quite interested. Hazel remembered the day when they had gone to bring the holly home and Irene had said that she liked the way poetry rhymed the same way that songs do. Hazel was surprised to see that Carol looked quite keen. She had been expecting her to be as bored, or at least pretend to be as bored, as Bridget.

The only sound for a while was the shuffling of books and the turning of pages. Hazel's eye was caught by a slim, leather-bound book with gold lettering on the cover: *Classic Poems of the Seasons*. She had hardly turned more than a few pages when she discovered, to her delight, the poem she would choose. It was by Shakespeare and it was the very poem that Alan had quoted in his letter, which had arrived just before the roads became impassable.

She reached for her exercise book and her pen and began to write.

When icicles hang by the wall,
And Dick the shepherd, blows his nail,
And Tom bears logs into the hall,
And milk comes frozen home in pail...

Hazel continued until she had copied out the whole poem, blotted it carefully and looked around at the others. Irene was frowning as she regarded two books that she had obviously rejected. Hazel pushed the book she had been using towards her and flicked over a few pages. 'What do you think about this one?' she said quietly. She pointed to the open page. 'It's about a thrush bursting into song on a dreary winter's day.'

Irene glanced at the poem, then looked up and grinned. 'Thanks, you're a pal.' She began to write.

Carol and Bridget seemed to be working together. Or rather Carol, who had moved her chair so that she was right next to Bridget, was searching through the books while Bridget unashamedly sat back and read *The Mystery At The Moss-Covered Mansion*, one of the books her mother had sent her for Christmas

Irene saw the direction of Hazel's glance. Tearing a scrap of paper from the back of her rough notes book, she scribbled a message and passed it to her. *Little toady*, the note said. *Doing her work for her!*

Hazel shook her head and added the words: *What does it matter?*

Once Irene had turned her attention back to her work, Hazel reached down to pick up her schoolbag. She opened it and sorted through the bundle of letters she kept there: from her mother, from Mavis in Canada, and the letter from Alan. This was the one she took out to read, although she probably knew it by heart.

She had been surprised to receive it. They had become friendly over the Christmas holidays but they had made no promise to write to each other. The day it had arrived Mrs Ellis had placed the morning's mail on the hall table as usual. It was a school day and they had picked them up just before going in for breakfast.

Irene, who had got to the table first, called out, 'Two for you, Hazel.' But instead of just handing them over, she scrutinised the postmark on each envelope. 'Newcastle,' she said. 'That'll be your mam. But what's this? Castle Dale? Never heard of it.'

Alan had told Hazel that Castle Dale was the village nearest to his school in Yorkshire. There wasn't much there except for a railway station, a handful of shops, a small café and a post office. At the weekends the older boys were allowed to walk or cycle to the village to post their letters or maybe visit the Willow Café. When parents came to visit they often preferred to take their sons to the café rather than stay in the draughty old school, which never seemed to warm up, even on the most glorious of summer's days. It was the wind, Alan told her. Always wuthering about just like in the book.

Irene was still puzzling over the envelope. 'It's a nice fat one. Who do you think it's from?' she asked.

'I won't know until I open it, will I?' Hazel said. She held out her hand.

Irene passed the letters across but at the last minute she snatched them back. 'You're fibbing!' she said.

'Don't be silly.'

'It's from Alan Sinclair, isn't it? That's why you're blushing.'

'Pack it in, Irene. You're being a real pain.'

231

Hazel didn't want to give Irene the satisfaction of seeing that she was flustered, so, instead of trying to snatch the letters, she just held her hand out and waited patiently.

Eventually Irene, looking a little shamefaced, handed them over. 'Okay, here you are,' she said. And then she grinned. 'But don't go all secretive on me, will you?'

Hazel didn't deign to reply.

Irene picked up another letter. 'Just one for me,' she said, 'from Mam.' She looked really disappointed.

'What's the matter?' Hazel asked.

'Terry promised to write to me and I haven't had a word from him.'

'It isn't that long since he was here. Give him time.'

Irene sighed. 'Yeah, I'll just have to ask Mam if he's okay.'

While they were talking, Bridget arrived and picked up two of the three envelopes that remained. She glanced at them and said, 'The usual from Mummy and one from my father this time, although goodness knows when and where he posted it. They're not allowed to say. This letter could be weeks old. You never know what could have happened since then.'

Hazel knew what Bridget was thinking and she wished she could think of something to say, but she remembered the last time she had tried to comfort Bridget and how angry Bridget had been. She remained silent.

Then Bridget picked up the last remaining envelope. 'It's for Carol,' she said. 'I wonder why she hasn't bothered to come and see for herself. I suppose I'd better take it to her.'

Hazel had saved her letters until morning school was over. The pupils who lived nearby went home for their midday meal; others brought sandwiches or went to the community restaurant that had been set up in the village hall. For ninepence a day you could get a dinner and a pudding. Miss Forsyth insisted that her girls, as she called them, should have a nice hot meal rather than sandwiches and was happy to pay for them.

That day they'd had corned beef hash followed by jam roly-poly and custard. Feeling comfortably full and a little sleepy, Hazel dodged Irene and walked the short distance back to school by herself. She felt a little guilty about setting off alone, but Irene was talking to Rita Bevan, and from the laughter and the smiles it looked as if they were having a good old gossip.

The classroom was empty and Hazel settled down at her desk and took the two letters from her bag. She looked at the envelopes and hesitated, then decided to open her mother's letter first. She took out the sheets of lined notepaper and marvelled, as always, at how neat her mother's writing was. Much neater than her own. That was because she wrote too fast, trying to keep up with her thoughts, especially when she was writing a story. Miss Norton often told her to slow down and take more care, but Hazel was never able to explain how difficult that would be. She began to read:

Dear Hazel,

Your Christmas at Hillside House sounds lovely. You've described it so beautifully in your letter, I have to admit I cried a little when I read it. I don't think I'll ever get used to us being apart like this. But like I said I would, I made the best of things for your dad. I think he enjoyed himself although, as usual, he didn't say much. After Christmas dinner he went to the Hare and Hounds like I expected him to, but to my surprise, he came back well before closing time. He was a little unsteady on his feet but he mustn't have drunk enough to bring one of his rages on.

I was listening to a lovely carol service on the wireless and I got up to turn it off but your dad said, 'No, that's all right, Joan, you listen to it if you like. I'll read the football paper.' When it was time to go to bed he said, 'You go on up. I'll just sit here for a while and finish this. Don't worry, I'll see to the fire.'

Over an hour later he still hadn't come up. I was worried, so I went downstairs and found he had fallen asleep. I was afraid to wake him in case he lost his temper after all, but I felt I couldn't just leave him there. He grunted a bit but he didn't complain. His breath smelt of spirits. I helped him up to bed but all I could do was sit him down, take his boots off and push him over so that he was lying next to the wall and wouldn't fall off onto the floor. Then I went down to see to the fire. His football paper was lying on the hearthrug and so was my bible. It was open at the twenty-third psalm.

Hazel, pet, can't you just imagine what your dad and so many other men, knowing what they have to face, must be going through right now?

Hazel lowered the letter. For the moment she

couldn't bear to go on reading. She could imagine only too well the dread in her father's heart and she could also understand why her mother was so loyal to a man who treated her with so little consideration. She felt like weeping with frustration. It had taken the outbreak of war to make him talk to her mother in anything like a considerate way. She wondered whether his new mood would last or whether those few kind words would be all her mother had to remember him by.

She began to read what remained.

One of my ladies, Mrs Patterson, asked me if I would consider taking on another cleaning job. Her neighbour has lost her charwoman, who went off to work at the rope works where she'll be paid much more money. I had to tell her that I was planning to do the same, and that I had intended to give her notice once my husband was called up. She told me I would ruin my hands working there. I felt like asking her what did she think scrubbing and polishing for a living had done to my hands all these years, but I didn't want to be rude.

Then, can you believe it, when I finished work that day, she paid me and told me not to bother to come back. She said she would have to find another cleaner who wouldn't let her down and that she would prefer to do it right away. I've worked for that woman ever since the twins were toddlers. All those years, and that was that. But don't worry. I've a little bit put by, enough to see me through until I start my new job, and soon there'll only be myself to feed.

Well, that's all for the moment, Hazel, pet. I hope you and your friends are okay and please give my

235

respectful regards to Miss Forsyth.
  Lots of Love,
  Mam xxx

Hazel folded the pages and put them back in the envelope. The school bell rang and she could hear footsteps and voices in the corridors. A moment later the classroom door opened and her classmates began to stream in. Irene and Rita were still gossiping. Hazel put her letters away quickly. She didn't want to give Irene the opportunity to mention the letter from Alan again. She didn't have a chance to read it until she was alone in her room that night.

Dear Hazel,
  Well, here I am back at school and as usual the first few days are unsettling. This time it was worse because some of the boys in the upper sixth were missing. The headmaster told us that our head boy, two house captains and a prefect have all joined the air force. All four were in the school's cadet force and very keen, although I'm pretty sure they believed they would be going up to university later this year rather than going to war.
  After this dramatic announcement it took a while for everyone to settle down. Lots of boys said they would have done the same if they'd been old enough. After the initial excitement faded we talked about what kind of Christmas we'd had and I told my pals what fun it had been spending time with all of you at Hillside House.
  My parents are first rate but they married late and are a lot older than the parents of most of my friends.

They seem a little perplexed with what to do with a growing boy in the twentieth century. You see, life was very different in my father's day. That's why they sent me away to school. It's not because they're wealthy, they're not, it's because my father and grandfather both came here to Cragg Hall and it's the thing to do. A family tradition.

Life here isn't too bad. Cragg Hall isn't at all like Dotheboys Hall. That's the school in Nicholas Nickleby by Charles Dickens. Have you read it? It's a bit complicated and very melodramatic but it's a jolly good read.

Hazel, I do admire the way you put up with Carol and Irene. I mean, Carol is an utter little snob and Irene, although she's basically a good sort and can be a lot of fun, spends most of the time being indignant about Carol's airs and graces. I've seen the way you keep the peace. As for Bridget, she should feel the most at home – after all, Miss Forsyth is her aunt – but sometimes she looks very sad, doesn't she? It's like she can't let herself believe the world will ever be right again.

It must be strange for all of you being away from home and having to get on with other girls who you might not have anything in common with. It's a bit like me at boarding school, isn't it? I've been lucky; I've made some good friends while I've been here and I've never felt really homesick before. But now I can't wait until the Easter hols when I can see you all again.

Hope you like my drawings to go with Shakespeare's poem about winter.

Do write soon.
Yours sincerely,
Alan Sinclair

Separate from the letter was a folded sheet of drawing paper. Hazel opened it and looked at it wonderingly. There was a poem written out in beautiful lettering, and all around the poem were sketches. Going by the way the people in the drawings were dressed, they were obviously from a few hundred years ago.

There was a milkmaid wrapped up in a cloak carrying a wooden pail on her head, and a shepherd holding a crook in his hand and carrying a lamb under his other arm. He was trudging along a snowy track, followed by his dog. A stout woman stirred a steaming pot with a large wooden spoon. Icicles hung from the low eaves of a thatched roof, three tiny birds huddled together on a bare branch, and an owl flew across in front of a full moon. Here and there, were small sprigs of holly.

Hazel read the poem and stared at the drawings and was amazed at how talented Alan was. After a while she returned to the letter and read it again – and again. She wondered why her feelings were so mixed. She was happy to have received the letter, of course she was, but at the same time she was a little disappointed.

Alan had said that he had enjoyed visiting Hillside House, but she wished he'd said that he had enjoyed being with her rather than just being with everybody. And then he'd said that he couldn't wait to see everybody again. It would have been so much nicer if he had been more personal and said something like, 'I can't wait to see you again, Hazel.' At the end of the letter he had written 'Yours sincerely' rather than sending his love. And, of course, there had been no kisses.

Even though she was alone in her room Hazel felt embarrassed. Had she really expected love and kisses? Had she expected some kind of love letter? She was too young for that kind of thing, wasn't she?

Admittedly she had just turned fourteen and was old enough to leave school and work for her living, but that didn't mean she was grown up. Alan would soon be sixteen and she knew that boys of his age often had girlfriends. Did he think of her as a girlfriend or just a friend?

She had read his letter yet again and decided it was the latter. But that was all right, wasn't it? She wasn't ready for love letters. She just thought it amazing and totally wonderful that a boy as terrific as Alan Sinclair was looking forward to coming here again. And, even better, that he had asked her to write to him.

The shuffling of papers and the closing of books aroused Hazel from her reverie. Alerted to the fact that the others had finished copying out their poems, she returned her precious letter to her school bag, placing it in between all her other letters and the copy of *Nicholas Nickleby* she had borrowed from the crowded bookshelves.

'All ready, girls?' Miss Forsyth asked as she entered the room.

'Yes, miss,' they said in unison, just as if they were in the classroom at school.

Miss Forsyth took her place at the head of the table and smiled at each in turn. 'Good, let's start the lesson.'

Chapter Thirteen

December 1952

The passengers on the bus were a mixture of people going home from work and housewives who had been into town to do some late Christmas shopping. Some carried briefcases, some bulging shopping bags. One woman actually had a small Christmas tree, and wherever she tried to put it down it either blocked the aisle or was in danger of poking someone in the eye. Every time someone brushed past her there was a scattering of pine needles. Hazel couldn't find a seat but she managed to keep well clear, although she relished the evocative, dark green smell of the tree which, for a short while, overcame the fusty smell of damp overcoats and the ever-present stale cigarette smoke.

There were queues at every stop along the way and people squeezed and shuffled their way out before others crowded in. Hazel reckoned the journey was taking almost twice as long as it should, and steeled herself to face her mother's reproachful expression when she got home.

She thought back to her chat with Irene at the station café. It had got them no further forward in making a decision about whether to accept Miss Forsyth's invitation to return to Withenmoor for the coronation celebrations. She hadn't

240

responded to Irene's retort about Kenneth, but the truth of the matter was that she didn't want to discuss her relationship with Kenneth. She knew that he wouldn't like her to go away for a week, and if she asked him to come with her and stay in one of Withenmoor's comfortable guest houses, he would refuse to leave his mother alone for the celebrations. And Hazel could not have argued with that.

Kenneth had been talking about buying a television set so that they could watch the ceremony being broadcast from Westminster Abbey. They would invite one or two of the neighbours to join them, and his mother would provide tea and sandwiches and a bottle or two of her favourite cream sherry.

Just thinking about it made her feel guilty, for she knew that if she truly loved Kenneth she wouldn't even consider being parted from him on such an historic occasion.

The real problem would be her mother's reaction. Joan would object very strongly to her accepting the invitation. She had never got over the years that they had been parted from each other, and from early on had come to resent the influence that Margaret Forsyth had had on Hazel's life.

The two cheerful schoolgirls she and Irene had met in the station café suddenly came to mind. They must have been very small children, hardly more than babies, when the war started. They would probably have been evacuated, but, if they were lucky, their mothers would have gone with them. She wondered how much of the experience they remembered and if it had changed their lives as much as it had changed hers.

She found herself smiling as she remembered them helping each other with their homework. Algebra. They must be bright. Would they stay on at school until they were eighteen? Train to be nurses? Or maybe go to University? She hadn't had those options. If it hadn't been for the war, she would have left elementary school at the age of fourteen to find employment. If she was lucky it would have been a job with some kind of training, such as at the shirt factory. If she had wanted more from life there were always evening classes.

But Miss Forsyth had made a different sort of life possible for her. She had got together with Miss Norton and Mrs Edwards, the headmaster's wife, and they had roped in local people who could teach them office skills and even French. Miss Forsyth's girls had not been the only girls to stay on, and there had also been two boys, Gavin Pritchard and Paul Barton. They were teased by the other lads, who called them softies, but Paul had joked that the only reason they were there was to be near all the gorgeous girls.

Irene had hated the very idea of staying on at school and had found a job in a shop in Withenmoor that sold everything from pots and pans to ribbons and knicker elastic. It was a miniature department store, a little Aladdin's cave. Irene loved working there, despite the fact that she came home smelling of paraffin and mothballs. She was quick to learn and always helpful. She became popular with the customers.

Most of the girls who left school when they were

fourteen tried to find jobs in shops, at the woollen mill, or as maids-of-all-work in the larger houses. Some went home to Newcastle. Rita Bevan decided not to. Her parents could have insisted, but Rita told Hazel that Molly Watkins had written to them to say that Rita was working on the land, and that was valuable war work. They had no right to take her away. If they did they would get into trouble. Whether it was true or not, they had believed her. There were many new rules and regulations and it was best not to question them and draw attention to yourself. Especially as Rita's father had avoided joining up by breaking his ankle with a hammer and appearing at the medical on crutches.

So Rita had stayed to help Molly work her smallholding. After a year or two, you would have thought Rita to be a country girl born and bred. As well as working on the land, Molly taught her many of the old country crafts. She wanted to adopt Rita, but Rita's parents objected out of pure spite. When the war ended they insisted that she should return; as she was under twenty-one, they had the right to. But Rita had become both confident and courageous. She defied them and returned to Withenmoor.

Most of the boys found work on the farms. Joe and Jimmy Doyle stayed on with the Armstrongs but Joe never got used to life in the country. He would have gone home to be apprenticed in the shipyards or even joined the Merchant Service as a cabin boy, like the class bad lad Billy Hobson. Joe's parents convinced him that it was his duty to stay with his younger brother, and reluctantly he agreed. Perhaps it was just as well. Billy had only been at sea for three months when his ship was bombed by enemy planes and all hands were lost. Hazel believed Billy Hobson must have been one of the youngest to die serving his country.

Younger even than Alan, who had opened her eyes and her heart to a wonderful world beyond her imaginings, and then left her to face it alone.

Irene's father always took the local electric train home, although it meant a good walk from the station at Heaton. He had his pass and, in any case, he thought it better than the crowded buses and trams. As soon as she had said goodbye to Hazel, Irene bought her ticket and waited for him at the gate that led to the platforms for the local electric train service.

It had been good seeing Hazel and having a bit of a gossip, even though they hadn't resolved anything. Irene always came away from meetings with Hazel wishing they could see each other more often. Hazel would sometimes pop into Brownlow's and buy some make-up and suggest they have lunch together, but this didn't happen very often. Irene reflected that no matter how much they liked each other, they were not exactly bosom pals. Their lives were too different.

Hazel had soaked up all those extra lessons that were arranged for them, and when the war dragged on past her sixteenth birthday, she had got a job in the local solicitor's office. She had continued to study at the evening classes that the headmaster's wife had started up for anyone who was interested. Even then, it had been obvious how much Hazel had changed from the girl who had left the modest home in Newcastle's East End. She spoke well, she had good manners and she managed to look stylish, even in the second-hand clothes that the Yanks were sending over by the parcel load. And there was no denying that Hazel was beautiful, although in a quiet sort of way. No wonder Alan Sinclair had fallen for her. What a heartbreak that had been.

And now Hazel was signed up with Grey's, a top Secretarial Agency, and earning good money doing all sorts of clever jobs. She had a good-looking boyfriend who was a big noise at the Town Hall, and she would probably end up married to him and living in one of those white, modern-looking, flat-roofed houses along by the lighthouse at Seaton.

And as for me, Irene thought, *what path have I taken?* 'Do you really want to be a shop girl?' Carol had asked and Irene had felt like clocking her. In fact she would have done if Hazel hadn't taken hold of her arm and led her away.

'Oh, but it might be fun,' Bridget had said. 'Just think, you'll get all the village gossip!'

And that had been true. Many of the customers would stop and talk to each other, at first completely ignoring Irene. Then, so gradually that she didn't know quite how it had happened, they started including her in their conversations and sometimes even confiding in her.

'You have a way with the customers,' the shop's owner Jed Dixon had told her. 'And you're a good saleswoman. If you want to stay on after the war is over you've got a job for life.' He stopped and smiled broadly. 'Or at least until some likely lad puts a ring on your finger. That's bound to happen to a bonny lass like you.'

Irene had become part of village life much more than the other girls had been, apart from Rita Bevan, of course. Even so, she had often thought about going home as soon as she was old enough. She loved her parents and she missed them keenly. She could have found a job in a factory – they were even taking girls and women on in the shipyards – but her parents begged her to stay in Withenmoor.

I miss you more than I can say, her mother had written in one of her letters. *But I've got to know that at least one of my bairns is safe.*

So Irene had stayed and come safely home, although her brother hadn't. Carol would still call her a shop girl, but the cosmetic counter at Brownlow's was a world away from the village store.

Once back in Newcastle, her experience and a first-class reference from Mr Dixon secured her a job in a large department store. Parrishes on Shields Road was just a short walk away from home, but she didn't stay there long. It wasn't because she missed the gossip and cheerful friendliness of the shop in Withenmoor. She accepted that working in a shop on a busy street in town would be completely different, but she was an avid follower of fashion and devoured the articles in women's magazines, and she soon decided that Parrishes, old-fashioned as it was, was the kind of store you went to with your granny to buy your winter woollies or your Easter bonnet. She set out to find a job in one of the leading stores in the city centre.

She was taken on almost immediately by Brownlow's, on haberdashery at first, but her looks and style very soon got her moved to the cosmetics counter. She had been there ever since. Almost unknowingly, she had begun to adapt the way she spoke, taking the older, more experienced assistants as examples. But now, though many young women would envy her a job they believed to be sophisticated and glamorous, Irene had other ambitions. She wanted to sing. And not just in the local hotels and dance halls. She wanted to go to London and be a star of stage, screen, and radio! She wondered what Bridget would have made of that.

Irene had never quite made up her mind about Miss Forsyth's niece. At first, she'd been offended by the words she used and the posh way she spoke. She had thought her the most dreadful snob. Hazel had often had to persuade her that Bridget wasn't 'putting it on'; it was simply the way she had been brought up. Irene had eventually decided that it was Carol who was the real snob, pretending to be something she wasn't and attaching herself like a limpet to Bridget. Sometimes even doing her homework for her.

Irene had never understood why Miss Forsyth, who was so wise, had been taken in by Carol. But then, Miss Forsyth was far too nice a person to be suspicious about what had happened that dreadful day. Hazel had told Irene that no one would ever know the truth of it and that she shouldn't jump to conclusions. Irene supposed Hazel was right, but it annoyed her that she would never even talk about it. Irene had never been convinced that it was best to let sleeping dogs lie.

'Well, hello there! Could you be going my way?'

Irene's musings were interrupted. She looked up to see an impudent young fellow who, despite his lanky height, looked to be no more than fifteen, sixteen at most. Perhaps it was the pimples that gave him away. He was reasonably well dressed: his belted raincoat was cheap but decent enough, and at the neck there was a glimpse of a shirt and tie. Office boy or junior clerk, Irene thought. His smile broadened and he winked at her.

'Get lost,' she said.

'Aw, come on, you've been standing there for ages. He's not going to turn up, is he?'

'I don't know what you're talking about.'

'Your bloke. Your date for tonight. He's not going to show. Although he must need his head examining to let down a real looker like you.'

Irene couldn't help smiling at his sheer audaciousness. 'What makes you think I'm going out on a date?'

'Well, look at you. The way you're dressed – your hair – your make-up.' He gave a wolf whistle.

She laughed. 'For your information I'm no different than I am any other day of the week. I'm not going out on a date. I'm on my way home from work and, before you say anything else, the bloke I'm waiting for is my father. Now push off and don't bother me again.'

She thought she had dealt with the matter, but to her surprise the young pup didn't run off with his tail between his legs. He backed off a little

248

and stared at her, frowning. 'Haven't we met before?' he asked.

'For goodness' sake,' Irene said. 'What's your next line? "Do you come here often?"'

He looked hurt. 'I wasn't going to say that. I meant what I said. I'm sure I know you.'

'You don't give up, do you? No, we certainly haven't met before. If we had I'm sure I would have remembered you.'

'Would you?' His expression brightened.

'For all the wrong reasons.'

'Oh.' His smile faded.

'Now please, I'm asking you nicely, leave me alone.'

He sighed and turned to go and then he turned back to face her, looking as if a light bulb had been turned on inside his head. 'You're Irene Walker!'

Now it was Irene's turn to frown. Did she know this young rapscallion after all? She studied him closely. No, she didn't think so. 'What if I am?' she asked hesitantly.

'Irene Walker. The singer. It *is* you, isn't it? I heard you at the Roxy. I think you're terrific!'

'Don't shout!' Irene said. 'People are looking at us.'

'I'm so sorry, Miss Walker.' His whole demeanour changed. 'You're travelling incognito, aren't you? And I've given you away. I'm really sorry.'

'Look, that's all right. But please go away. You're embarrassing me.'

He nodded sagely. 'You'll have to get used to that. People noticing you, I mean. You're obviously going to go right to the top of the Hit Parade.'

'Please...'

He held his hand up, palm towards her. 'It's all right, I'll go.' He thrust a hand into an inside pocket and brought out a pocket diary. 'But first, can I have your autograph? I was going to ask you that night at the Roxy but I was too late. I saw you signing something for one lucky lad and I hurried over, but the old bloke you were with whisked you away.'

'My manager,' Irene said.

'I beg your pardon?'

'The old bloke was my manager.' She tried unsuccessfully to suppress a giggle.

'What is it?

'I'm trying to imagine what he'd say if he heard you calling him an old bloke. But okay, I'll give you my autograph.'

'That's great. I'll disappear as soon as you've signed it, I promise you.' He opened the diary at a blank page and suddenly a ballpoint pen appeared. 'Put "To Kevin". That's my name. Maybe you could add "With Love"? No? Oh, well, "Best Wishes" will do.'

Irene took the diary and signed it as quickly as she could. Kevin thanked her and then, true to his word, he left her and walked through the gate onto the platform.

As Kevin disappeared into the crowd, Irene turned to look across the main concourse, searching for any sight of her father. She glanced at her wristwatch. It was half past six. Surely he should have finished work by now – unless he had changed shifts or been asked to work extra hours. If that happened he would always telephone the shop at the top of their street and ask them to send the delivery boy down with a message so that her mother wouldn't worry, then her mother would give the lad sixpence for his trouble.

Irene had just decided that that was what must have happened when she caught sight of her father standing to the side of the Christmas tree. He was facing in Irene's direction but he hadn't spotted her, probably because he was concentrating on his conversation with a man who had his back to Irene. The man was not quite as tall as her father and he was wearing a dark overcoat with the collar turned up and a trilby hat. Irene could see nothing of his features or of his hair.

Something about the way they were standing made her uneasy. Her father's handsome features were drawn with worry and every now and then he would glance to either side. Her heart sank. She now knew for sure that even before the war her father had been engaged in activities that were not quite honest, and that when the war started and rationing was introduced, like so many other people, he had been involved in the black market.

She remembered how Terry had confirmed her fears when he'd come to Withenmoor with their mother, but he'd told her that what their father did was pretty trivial compared to what the real villains got up to and that he had enough sense not to get involved with gangsters. She had accepted his reassurance – she didn't think Terry would lie to her – and she'd convinced herself that what he was doing wasn't so bad after all. You couldn't blame folk for wanting to feed their families a little better. Even Mrs Ellis, Miss

Forsyth's own cook, hadn't blinked an eye when her mother had handed over all the goodies she had stashed in her bag.

When Irene started work in the village store she learned that the country folk were as deeply involved in the black market as people in the towns and that certain farmers were quite happy to sell their produce 'privately' at a good price rather than hand it over to the government. But none of this had made her any happier. Bridget and Hazel's fathers were fighting for their country. Carol's father had fought in the last war. Her own father might be doing an important job by helping to keep the railways going, but he was also taking advantage of the opportunities his job provided to help himself.

When the war ended, Irene had believed that her father had changed his ways. She learned from local gossip that while she'd been away, one of his friends from the social club had been fined the huge sum of five hundred pounds and been sent to prison for two years. She'd hoped this had shocked her father enough to make him stop what he was doing – but there was still the matter of the things he brought home now and then from lost property.

Irene had made it her business to find out what happened to the unclaimed goods. She had decided that rather than stealing them outright, as she had feared, her father was simply waiting until the holding time was up and then helping himself before they were auctioned. She had told herself that she would just have to live with it, even though he probably would not be paying for the things he took.

But even this had dropped off lately. Her father was well paid and every now and then he seemed to get a bonus, she wasn't sure why. Her parents wanted for very little and there was no need for him to pilfer from the lost property office.

She stared at her father, still engaged in conversation with the man in the dark coat, and her feeling of unease grew. She realised suddenly that it wasn't worry that had drained all the life from her father's face; it was shock. Had Terry been mistaken, or had he lied about her father not being involved with gangsters? Had someone from the past caught up with him?

And then, as she watched them, the two men shook hands. Now, rather than looking shocked, her father seemed resigned. Irene had no idea what had been going on, but something told her that her father would not have wanted her to see what had happened. She turned her back on the scene and pretended to be studying a wall where posters of seaside resorts were displayed.

It was summer in every boldly coloured picture. In Saltburn, Scarborough, Morecambe and Broadstairs, happy, brightly dressed families were walking along the promenade eating ice creams, or building sandcastles on the beaches, or paddling in the sea. A jolly fisherman was skipping along the shore at Skegness. All these people looked so happy and carefree. Irene couldn't decide whether looking at the posters was cheering her up or simply making her more acutely aware of her anxieties.

'Well, well, what are you doing here?'

Irene heard her father's voice and turned to see him smiling at her. He no longer looked shocked or worried.

'I had a cup of tea and a gossip with Hazel in the station snack bar. I thought I'd catch the train home and I wondered if I'd catch up with you, but I was beginning to think I'd missed you.'

'No, the London train was late setting off. I had to deal with some angry passengers.'

Irene knew this was a lie – she had heard all the announcements of arrivals and departures on the loudspeaker while she had been waiting – but she didn't challenge him. Nor did she tell him what she'd observed. If he had wanted her to know about it he wouldn't have made that excuse about the London train.

'Well, we'd better get home,' her father said. 'Your mother will have something good on the table.'

'Oh, no!'

'What is it?'

'I won't have time to eat. I've just remembered, I'm going out tonight. Ray's picking me up at eight o'clock.'

'Won't he wait for you?'

'It's not that. I've got a singing date at a club in town. I'll have to get all dolled up like Doris Day.'

Irene was grateful that her father didn't comment. He just took her arm and they walked through to the platform together where, luckily, a train was waiting. Once on the train Irene fretted over how on earth something so important could have slipped her mind. She hadn't exactly forgotten about the engagement, it was just that she

254

hadn't taken enough notice of the passing of time. If she wasn't ready Ray would be furious with her. He kept telling her that if she was going to succeed she would have to be more professional.

The train was packed but her father managed to find her a seat. Perhaps his being in his railway uniform helped. As they rattled over the rails, she considered what songs she might sing that night. She wondered if she could persuade Ray to let her sing something other than a song recorded by Doris Day. Maybe 'The Wheel of Fortune', made popular by Kay Starr. This was an ongoing tussle. Ray wanted her to take advantage of her resemblance to the popular blonde film star, but although Irene liked most of the songs they'd agreed on and thought Doris Day was fantastic, she didn't want to base her whole career on copying someone else. She had realised that she was in danger of becoming another singer's look-alike and sing-alike, a sort of novelty act. Irene wanted to develop her own style.

Her encounter with young Kevin just now had given her a glimpse of what it could be like. He thought she could go right to the top. She would always be grateful to Ray, who told people that he'd 'discovered' her and had worked hard to get her started, but she was beginning to realise that he wanted total control of her, and she didn't like that idea at all.

There was something else. She wasn't sure if he was always entirely honest about how much money she was making. A couple of times he'd told her that rather than being paid anything, he'd had to pay the bandleader to persuade him to give her a chance. He had started calling himself her agent, and Irene knew enough about show business to know that agents didn't work for nothing. They expected a percentage, which was fair enough. After all, they took charge of all the business side of things. But Ray had never told her exactly what his cut was going to be, or drawn up any kind of contract. You had to have a proper contract, didn't you?

Irene had read articles in the *Picturegoer* and *Melody Maker* about film stars and singers who had been swindled by their agents. Just when they thought they had everything that their hard-earned money could buy, they found their bank accounts empty and couldn't afford the long legal battle to get their money back. She felt guilty about the way her thoughts were taking her. She ought to trust Ray, but she had to admit that she knew very little about him. He never spoke about his parents or the existence of any brothers and sisters, and the fake American twang he adopted disguised any regional accent he might have. Irene didn't even know how old he was.

She had guessed he was old enough to have served in the war and once, when she had asked him whether he had been in the army, he had said, 'Don't worry, kid. Ray Regan did his bit for his king and country, you gotta believe it.'

In her heart Irene wanted to believe that he was telling the truth, and the fact that he would never talk about it wasn't that unusual. A lot of men were like that. Sheila, Irene's friend from work, had a brother who had fought his way across Europe and had been decorated for his bravery, but he refused outright to tell anyone anything about it, even his own family.

When they reached their station Irene pushed all these treacherous thoughts aside. As they walked home, she began rehearsing in her mind the songs she would sing at the club. The club, the Cask, was in an ancient wine cellar in an old cobbled street not far from the cathedral. Most of the members were wealthy, but some of them were not entirely respectable. When Irene had mentioned the club's reputation, Ray had told her not to worry, he would look after her, and that it might be an advantage to be taken up by these influential people.

'Influential? Don't you mean criminal?' Irene had blurted out, and Ray had laughed at her.

'Don't let that worry you,' he'd said. 'I could tell you of more than one Hollywood star – and British ones, too – who've had to quiet their consciences and mix with people like this.'

'I refuse to mix with them!' Irene had flared up in her characteristic way.

Ray had raised his eyebrows, no doubt surprised by her rebellion. 'Okay, kid,' he'd said. 'You sing your songs then I whisk you away. That's a promise.'

Irene was left wondering why Ray had given in so easily and it began to occur to her that he might need her more than she needed him. But she would have to bide her time and get as much experience as she could before even thinking of parting company with him.

Do you always have to do what Ray tells you? Hazel's words came back to her and Irene smiled when she remembered her outburst in response.

257

It was a good job Hazel knew her of old or they might have quarrelled, and that would have been a cause for regret.

Once they left Shields Road with its brilliantly lit shop windows, the street lamps were fewer and further between. Irene linked arms with her father so that she wouldn't trip on the old, uneven paving stones. In some backyard a dog was barking relentlessly, and as they walked past one house with thin, cheap curtains, a man and a woman could be heard screaming angrily at each other. *When I'm rich and famous*, Irene thought, *I'm going to buy Mam and Dad a nice little bungalow far away from here and the smell of the glue factory. Perhaps somewhere by the sea. And I'll buy Dad a car, and maybe I'll take driving lessons myself.*

By the time they reached home, she was full of hope and enthusiasm for the night ahead of her. She was so taken up with her own thoughts that it never occurred to her until much later that all the way home, her father had never said a word.

Hazel could see how much it cost her mother not to ask why she was late home. She decided to put her mind at rest by telling her a half truth.

'Sorry I'm late. I popped in to Brownlow's after work to buy some new make-up, and Irene and I decided to have a cup of tea and a chat.'

'Where did you go?' her mother asked querulously.

'To the café in the station.'

'The Central Station?'

'Yes.'

'During rush hour?' Joan raised her eyebrows.

Hazel held onto her patience. 'It wasn't so bad, and the carol singers by the Christmas tree were lovely.'

Her mother was quiet for a moment. She looked down and Hazel had the uncharitable thought that she was searching for something else to question or complain about. She was relieved to find that she was wrong when her mother smiled and said, 'So, did you have a nice chat?'

'Yes.'

'Put the world to rights?'

'We did.' Hazel realised that her mother was trying to make amends for her fractious welcome. Instinctively she stepped forward and hugged her. 'But I'm really glad to be home.'

'Right then, how about setting the table for me? Your dad will be home any minute now and he'll want his dinner.'

Hazel obliged, and when her father came home he went to the bathroom, took off his work clothes and washed himself thoroughly. Hazel remembered when they'd had to use the sink in the scullery. His clean clothes were waiting for him and when he emerged his meal was on the table.

Later, when he had gone to the pub, Hazel and her mother sat by the fire. Her mother listened to a light music programme on the wireless while she skimmed through a magazine, and Hazel began to read a murder mystery she had borrowed from the library. Set in an English village with a typical cast of disparate characters, an old manor house and a snowstorm, it should have been the perfect book for escaping from everyday matters for an hour or two.

Normally she loved books like this and enjoyed the challenge of picking up on the clues and solving the mystery before the detective revealed all. The stories were not to be taken seriously. The villages, the characters, the old houses, were never meant to be realistic. Certainly she had never been disturbed by them before, and this book had promised to be as entertaining as all the others of its kind, until she turned the page and came across a frozen lake.

She closed the book and told her mother that she was tired.

'Go on up to bed, pet,' her mother said. 'I think I'll wait up for your dad.'

Hazel felt like asking her why. He wouldn't appreciate it, might not even speak to her. But she knew nothing she said would change her mother's mind, so she kept quiet. Lying awake in bed, she fretted over Miss Forsyth's invitation to return to Withenmoor and the fact that she had not made a decision.

She loved and respected Miss Forsyth and would be eternally grateful for the opportunities she had provided and the way she had changed her life. She also knew that Miss Forsyth had grown to love her wartime charges and it seemed mean not to grant her the pleasure of seeing them again.

Hazel began to examine the reasons why she could not go. She knew how much it would upset her mother. She thought of Kenneth's plan to buy a television set and have a few people in. She had told him that she ought to spend the day with her mother and he had said that was no problem, her mother was invited too.

'But my mother won't leave my father,' she had told him, and Kenneth had lost patience with her.

'Well, bring him along as well, but really, Hazel, when are you going to cut the apron strings?'

As usual, he had calmed down quickly. Trying hard to be reasonable, he had told her they would work something out. She hadn't told him that she didn't have much hope of finding a solution.

I can't please everybody, she thought. *My mother, Kenneth, Miss Forsyth. But what about me? What do I want to do?*

Suddenly the sound of the children singing carols near the Christmas tree echoed in her mind. Irene had asked her if she remembered the night they had walked home to Hillside House singing carols as they went, then she had apologised for mentioning it. But there had been no need to apologise.

If she couldn't have memories of Alan it would be as if he had never existed. All that talent and lively intelligence would have been meaningless. All that love and hope shot down in flames. His parents were dead. There was no one else to remember him. No matter what pain it caused her, somehow she must keep him alive in her heart.

Chapter Fourteen

April 1942

Hazel, Alan and Rita were sitting at the table in Molly Watkins' kitchen. The comforting aroma of something cooking in the oven enfolded them, and a wire tray of scones was cooling on the bench. Molly's latest feline guest, a skinny tabby, was curled up with her kittens in an old basket near the range. A very old dog twitched in his dreams in a blanket-covered armchair.

The previous months had been bitterly cold, with snow as late as the beginning of March. It had been another severe winter. The sheep farmers had been hard hit again with thousands of sheep and new-born lambs found dead in the snow. There were still drifts piled up against the old stone walls but the skies were beginning to clear and a thaw had set in, turning the steep country roads into mountain streams.

Today the sun was shining brightly. Molly was hoping that the better weather would last for the next few days. Folk needed cheering up and she would do what she could. She had planned an Easter Sunday treat for the younger bairns in the village and, only two days ago, she had told Rita of her plan and asked her who she thought would be the best ones to help her.

'Hazel Stafford and Alan Sinclair,' Rita had

said without hesitation.

'Why those two?' Molly had asked.

'Hazel, because I like her,' Rita replied.

'That's a good enough reason. And the lad?'

'He's very artistic.'

'Just the fellow we need, then,' Molly said. 'So off you go to Hillside House to ask Hazel, and you know the way to Dr Sinclair's, don't you?'

Rita nodded her reply.

'Now wrap up warm. Just because the sun is shining it doesn't mean that winter is over.'

Rita put on her winter coat, wrapped one of Molly's long woollen scarves several times around her neck, then pulled on the latest hat and glove set that she had knitted for herself. This time she had attempted a Fair Isle pattern which was just complicated enough to cover up the few mistakes she had made.

'Better put your wellington boots on,' Molly said, 'and a thick pair of socks.'

'When do you want Hazel and Alan to come here?'

'It will have to be tomorrow, won't it? I mean, the day after that is Good Friday.'

Rita nodded. 'Yes, of course.'

'Here,' Molly said, 'you can take Mrs Ellis some Brussels sprouts. Tell her it's the last of them and I don't want paying.'

Rita put several stalks of sprouts in a wicker trug and set off on her errand glowing with happiness. She loved it when Molly asked for advice or for her opinion. No one had ever cared enough to bother before.

She was fairly sure that she would not have to go to the doctor's house. Alan Sinclair, who was home from his boarding school for the Easter holidays, seemed to spend all his time at Hillside House. Apparently he made himself useful while he was there, chopping logs on the days when old Ted's rheumatics got the better of him, and climbing ladders to change light bulbs and to check that the blackout curtains were fitted properly. Sometimes, along with Hazel, he even peeled potatoes for the midday meal. Hazel had told Rita that Miss Forsyth was very grateful for his help and that Mrs Ellis no longer begrudged having an extra mouth to feed.

Rita had learned these things on her visits to Hillside House with fresh produce from Molly's smallholding. Mrs Ellis was one of their best customers. Rita had also observed the growing friendship between Hazel and Alan and it hadn't been hard to work out that the doctor's son was really keen on Hazel – and she on him.

She was right about not having to go to the doctor's house. Alan had gone out walking with the girls and would be coming back with them for tea. Mrs Ellis had wanted them out from under her feet for a while.

'A bit of peace and quiet,' she told Rita. 'A rest from their eternal chattering. I told Alan to show them the tarn.'

'I've never been up to the tarn.'

'You should take a look sometime. The views are famous. They sell picture postcards of them in the shops in Newcastle.'

Rita gave Mrs Ellis the sprouts and then asked

if she could wait because she wanted to see Hazel and Alan.

'What do you want them for?' Mrs Ellis asked.

When Rita explained Molly's plan Mrs Ellis was incredulous. 'What? Doesn't she know there's a war on?'

'Of course she does.'

'This isn't an April fool's trick, is it?' She glanced at the mantel clock. 'If it is, you're too late; it's after twelve noon.'

'No, it's not a trick. Molly is serious about it.'

'After your own rations she's supposed to hand over all surplus eggs to the Ministry. How come she's got enough eggs for this hare-brained scheme?'

'I don't think it's hare-brained,' Rita said loyally, 'and anyway, I haven't heard you complaining when you buy eggs from us. Eggs that haven't been handed over!'

Mrs Ellis made no reply. She frowned as if she were trying to come up with a clever retort, but after a while she shook her head and smiled at Rita. 'So it's "us" now, is it? Molly's little business partner, are you?'

Rita looked uncomfortable. 'Molly says I'm a real help to her.'

'Of course you are. I was just teasing. I'm sure she's very pleased you came to live with her. It was a lonely life for her before – except for all the stray animals she takes in! Now then, if you're going to wait for them how about a cup of Bovril and a slice of bread and dripping?'

'Yes, please,' Rita said. 'I could do with warming up. It's proper parky out there.'

'You'd better take your coat off, then, or you won't feel the benefit when you go out again.'

Mrs Ellis filled the kettle and placed it on the hob, and a short while later Rita was dipping a knife into the bowl of soft pork fat and spreading it on a thick slice of bread.

'Go on, don't be shy,' Mrs Ellis said. 'Take some of the jelly from the bottom of the bowl. It will do you good. You're such a skinny little thing.'

Rita frowned. 'It's not for want of feeding,' she said.

'Don't take offence, lass. I know you've found a good billet with Molly Watkins. Some folk are just naturally thin, like Miss Forsyth and her niece, Bridget. And nobody can say they go without as long as I'm in charge of the kitchen.'

Rita finished spreading the dripping and then she sprinkled it with salt and pepper. Mrs Ellis joined her at the table.

'So Molly really intends to make paste eggs?' she said.

Rita nodded, her mouth full.

'How many?'

'She plans on three dozen.'

Mrs Ellis's eyes widened. 'And who's she going to give them to?'

Rita finished her mouthful and said, 'The nursery class at school and the younger children at the Sunday school. She's hoping the weather holds so that we can have egg rolling on the green.'

'And she wants Hazel and Alan to help her decorate the eggs?'

'Mmm.'

'Well, I don't suppose Miss Forsyth will object.

She'll think of it as a good cause. And to tell the truth, she doesn't know the ins and outs of this rationing business. I keep the ration books and she leaves it all to me.'

Just then the back door opened and there was an icy blast as Bridget led the walking party into the kitchen.

'For the Lord's sake shut that door!' Mrs Ellis said.

'Right-oh,' Bridget said cheerily.

They removed their outdoor clothes and took them through to the cloakroom. When they came back into the kitchen Bridget blew on her hands and gave an exaggerated shiver. 'Mrs Ellis,' she said, 'I don't suppose we can bother you for a hot drink? It's jolly cold out there.'

'Bloomin' perishing,' Irene added. 'I got chilled to the bone while Alan messed about sketching things. He's always doing that sort of thing even when there's a howling gale.'

'But it was beautiful,' Hazel said. 'And the water was frozen over. It must be fun to go skating there.'

'My father and my aunt used to skate there when they were children,' Bridget said. 'I wonder if their skates are still in the house somewhere.'

'Even if they are I would forget about it. The ice isn't firm enough. The thaw's setting in,' Alan said.

'Oh well, never mind. One day we'll do it. And if we do, who will come with me?'

'Oh, I will,' Carol said. 'I've been skating at the rink but never out of doors.'

'That's a date, then.'

Bridget seemed to notice suddenly that they

had a guest. 'Ooh, what's Rita been eating?' she said. 'Bread and dripping, is it?'

Rita nodded.

'Just the job!'

Rita was amused to see a look of distaste pass over Carol's face. *She can't understand why someone posh like Bridget Forsyth would like bread and dripping,* Rita thought. *I'm sure she never had it before she came to live here. Her mother would think that only common people like me would eat such a thing.*

'Hello, Rita,' Hazel said. She glanced at the wicker basket on the bench near the sink. 'I see you've brought us some lovely Brussels sprouts.'

Irene pulled a face and Alan said, 'Ugh!'

'Sprouts are good for you,' Rita said. 'Molly says so.'

'It must be true then,' Carol said sarcastically.

'Oh, I'm sure it is,' Bridget said. 'Molly Watkins is quite a wise old bird, isn't she?'

'She's not that old,' Rita said loyally.

Bridget smiled at her. 'It's just a saying. I didn't mean it as an insult.'

Behind her back, Carol scowled.

'I didn't come just to bring the sprouts,' Rita said. 'I want to ask Hazel and Alan a favour.'

'What's that?' Hazel asked.

'Molly wants you two to help her with something. She needs you to come to the cottage tomorrow morning.'

Then Rita explained her mission all over again. Hazel and Alan needed no persuading.

Bridget said, 'Oh, what fun you'll have!'

And Irene and even Carol had looked as though they would have liked to have been invited, but any more helpers would have been too many for Molly's small kitchen.

So now, Hazel, Alan and Rita were gathered round the table watching as Molly filled several pans with water and set them on the stove.

Hazel was pleased that she had been asked to help, though she wasn't sure why. She had enjoyed art lessons at school, but she had never had one of her paintings pinned up on the wall. And Rita, despite the bright primary colours of the poster paints, had usually managed to produce drab pictures in shades of watery brown and grey. If these eggs were going to be a success it would be up to Alan to inspire them.

'Have any of you done this before?' Molly asked.

Rita was sitting across the table from Hazel and Alan. She shook her head and sighed. 'My mam could never be bothered with something like that.'

Alan looked at her kindly. 'Neither could mine. According to her, it was all nonsense and nothing to do with Christianity at all. She said it was an old pagan custom and that decorated peacocks' eggs had been found in the graves of people who had been buried more than five thousand years ago.'

Rita looked shocked. 'Do you think that's true?'

'My mother studied ancient history at university so she's probably right, but I certainly don't think it was wrong of the early Christians to adopt the custom and make it part of their beliefs.'

'What about you, Hazel?' Molly asked.

'My mother used to make paste eggs. Usually about half a dozen, more if she could afford it.

269

One of them was for me and one for my friend Mavis.'

'And the others?'

'She would take them to work and give them to the children in the houses of people she cleaned for. I remember there were some twin girls at one house. My mother used to talk about their funny little ways. I never told her, but I felt a little jealous of them.'

'And you helped her?'

'Well, I peeled the onions, but then my mother took over. All I was allowed to do was fill the pan with water.'

Suddenly Hazel remembered how much her mother had enjoyed decorating the paste eggs. She had been like an excited child. And then, one night, when the coloured eggs had been left nestling in a paper doily in a nice little basket on the sideboard, Hazel's father had come home from the pub and eaten every one of them. The next morning Hazel and her mother had found the basket full of broken eggshells. Her mother had not remonstrated with him. She had disposed of the shells, bought Hazel and Mavis a chocolate egg each at Woolworth's, and never bothered with paste eggs again.

The warmth and chatter in Molly's kitchen faded as Hazel was overwhelmed by this dismal memory. She thought of her mother at home alone in Newcastle while she was here with her friends and felt dangerously near to tears. She clenched both hands under the cover of the table but Alan must have sensed her distress, because he put a hand on her shoulder and said, 'Think of the happy times.'

She turned to look at him and saw that he understood why she was upset. She ignored the ache in her throat and smiled at him. 'I will,' she said.

If Molly had noticed Hazel's momentary distress she didn't remark on it. 'Right, now, let's get started,' she said.

They watched as Molly placed onions, carrots, parsley, apples, a jar of pickled beetroot, a small bottle of cochineal and a larger bottle of coffee essence on the table. She stood back and looked at them.

'Can you think of anything else?' she said.

Hazel was as puzzled as Rita looked, but Alan said, 'Have you got any red cabbage?'

'Aye, I've got some stored in the shed.'

'It's worth a try, don't you think? Although I'm not sure what colour it will result in.'

By now Hazel had worked out that rather than just using onion skins which dyed the eggs a sort of mottled orange colour, they were going to try to dye the eggs other colours by using the things Molly had put on the table. That was why they needed more than one pan.

'We'll start with the onion skins,' Molly said. 'And it's better if you soak them first.'

'We'll need some rubber bands or some wool,' Hazel said. 'My mother used to tie the skins around the eggs before boiling them.'

'Go and get the eggs from the pantry, Rita,' Molly said.

Rita stood up and smiled broadly. 'Right then, let's get cracking!'

Hazel and Alan burst out laughing and Rita stared at them in bewilderment. 'What's so funny?'

'It's what you said, pet,' Molly told her.

Rita frowned then a moment later she grinned. 'I get it. Cracking. Let's get started, then.'

Their cheerful mood lasted while they boiled the eggs and experimented with all the things Molly had put on the table. The outcome was a variety of different coloured eggs. They were surprised and pleased with the results. As well as the marbled orange produced by the onion skins, they had yellow from the carrot tops, green from the parsley and the apple skins, brown from the coffee essence, pink from the beetroot juice, and deep red from the cochineal. A surprising result was the beautiful deep blue colour produced by the red cabbage leaves.

While the eggs were boiling they kept looking in the pans, and as soon as Alan was satisfied with the colour of the eggshells they lifted them out carefully and placed them in a row of old cast-iron egg holders, then left them there to cool. Then they cleared everything from the table and wiped it clean. Rita brought out the cutlery box while Molly served them heaped plates of rabbit stew.

When they'd finished their meal, Rita told Molly to sit with her cup of tea while she and Hazel cleared up and washed the pots. They didn't ask him, but Alan insisted on helping.

Molly lifted the egg holders onto the table and said, 'What do you think?'

'The marbled ones are okay,' Alan said, 'but if you'll trust me, I can do something with the plain

272

ones. Especially the deep pinks and the blues.'

Molly gave him the go-ahead and they all watched as Alan took a penknife from his pocket, took one of the deep blue eggs and began very carefully to scrape away the colour with the point of the smallest blade. No one spoke and when he held up the egg to show them the result they were amazed. He had created an intricate design with the original white of the shell showing through the colour.

'That's beautiful, lad,' Molly said. 'It reminds me of them posh jewelled eggs you can buy in the fancy goods shops. But I have to say, the bairns won't appreciate it. They'll just roll it and crack and eat it like all the others.'

Alan wasn't a bit offended. 'You're right. I'll do some more simple designs. Stripes and dots and zigzags. And how about baby bunnies and ducklings?'

'That'll do nicely,' Molly said.

While Alan worked, Molly, Rita and Hazel sat at the other end of the table and talked quietly.

'You're wise to stay on at school,' Molly told Hazel. 'It will get you a better job when this dratted war is over.'

'Whenever that will be,' Hazel said.

'The last one went on for four years.'

They looked at each other and for the moment no one felt like talking. Then Molly went back to the subject of schooling. 'I told Rita she could stay on for those extra classes if she wanted to, or mebbees go after a well-paid job in the woollen mill.'

Rita looked scornful. 'Shorthand? Typing?

273

Bookkeeping? That's not for me, and no matter how good the pay, I don't want to go deaf working in the mill. I'm perfectly happy working here with you, the two of us digging for victory!'

Hazel saw how they smiled at each other and reflected, not for the first time, that the war had changed Rita's life for the better. And there would be other children whose lives had improved, just as there were those whose lives had become a misery. For herself, she did miss her mother, but she had much to be thankful for. As soon as she thought this the guilt kicked in again. When the war was over, she wanted to do the best she could to make things better for her mother.

'I didn't have much choice, you know,' Molly said. 'I left school when I was twelve, and as I had no brothers or sisters, I had to help my mam and dad with the smallholding. They were quite old when they had me, so their pins were getting a bit creaky and they were short of breath.'

'Did you mind having to help them?' Hazel asked.

'I loved it. This bit of land has been in my family for generations. I knew it was mine to treasure. My young man was a younger son with no prospects, so when we got married he was going to come here and work with me.'

'I never knew you had a sweetheart,' Rita said.

'John Jopson. We started walking out when I was fifteen, the same age as you two lasses. My mam and dad took to him straight away. It wasn't long before I started a bottom drawer. A couple of bonny tablecloths, some bed sheets, a fine quilt. They're all there to this day. Kept sweet-smelling with lavender.'

Molly shook her head and smiled sadly.

'What happened?' Hazel asked.

'Before we had saved enough to get wed, John went off to war. He died in the trenches.'

Neither Hazel nor Rita knew what to say. Hazel saw Alan glance up from his work and look at Molly sympathetically.

'So when my parents passed away I was left here on my own.' Molly paused and looked at Rita. 'Until you came along.'

Molly got up and filled a plate with the scones she had baked that morning. She put them on the table along with the butter dish and a jar of plum jam. By the time Alan had decorated his last egg, she had made a pot of tea.

It seemed that no one wanted to bring such a happy day to an end and it was dark by the time Hazel and Alan were ready to leave the cottage.

'Mind you see Hazel all the way home,' Molly told Alan.

'Happy to oblige, ma'am,' Alan said, and he gave a slight bow just like an actor in a film about days gone by.

Molly thanked them for their help and told them that she would like them to come to the egg rolling on the green on Sunday. 'I'll probably need some help with the bairns. You know, making sure that they all start off properly and that they don't cheat and bash each other's eggs when no one's looking.'

'As if they would,' Alan said, and they all laughed.

'Do you think the other three lasses would like

to come?' Molly directed her question at Hazel.

'I'm sure Irene would, and I think Bridget would think it would be good fun.'

'What about Carol?' Rita asked. She looked doubtful.

'If Bridget approves, so will Carol,' Hazel said.

'Pals, are they?' Molly asked.

Hazel hesitated for a moment then said, 'Yes, they are.'

'You'd best be off, but don't be strangers. You're welcome to come and visit Rita any time you feel like it. It's good for her to have company her own age. I worry that she spends too much time with an old crock like me.' She smiled at them. 'Now have you got a torch?'

'Yes,' Alan said.

'Well, if you have to use it remember to keep it pointing down at the ground.'

In fact they didn't need a torch. The skies were clear and the moon was bright. It had been like that for almost a week.

'It's a bomber's moon,' Alan said, looking up at the sky. 'The Luftwaffe will be able to zero in on their targets.'

'Don't,' Hazel said.

'I'm sorry. You must be worried sick about your mother on nights like this.'

'There's an air-raid shelter in the back lane behind our house. My mother wrote and told me that on nights like this all her neighbours hurry to the shelter even before the sirens go off. She always phones the morning after a bad raid, to let me know she's all right.'

Alan reached for her hand. 'Sometimes I forget

how lucky I am that my father is too old for the forces and that we live so far away from the air raids.'

'We'd better go,' Hazel said. 'I didn't think we'd be as long as this. It's nearly time for supper.'

'I thought Mrs Ellis left something out for you before she went back to her own rooms across the yard?'

'Sometimes she does, but sometimes she stays and talks to us for a while. You know, I actually think she likes us being here. Or at least she's got used to us.'

'Have you enjoyed yourself today?' Alan asked.

'I have.'

'So did Miss Watkins, didn't she? If her sweetheart had survived the Great War I'm sure they would have had a houseful of happy children instead of all those stray cats and dogs.'

'But now she's got Rita,' Hazel said. She looked up at Alan's face, his intelligent and kind-hearted expression so clear in the moonlight, and they smiled at each other.

'I suppose we'd better get back to Hillside House,' he said.

'You sound reluctant.'

'I am. It's good to have you to myself for a while.' He paused. 'Please say you feel the same way.' He looked at her anxiously.

Hazel sensed that her answer was important to him. 'I do.'

He smiled with relief. 'I'm glad that's settled. Still, it would have been nice to go up to the tarn, wouldn't it, to see it in the moonlight?'

They looked at each other ruefully and then set

off along the rough track. Somehow it seemed the most natural thing in the world for Alan to keep hold of Hazel's hand.

The lane joined the road that led to Hillside House. Just before they reached the junction a large black car drove past.

'I wonder who that can be?' Alan said.

Hazel suddenly felt anxious. 'Or where they're going?'

'There are a couple of farms over the brow of the hill. Otherwise...'

They began to walk more quickly, still holding each other's hands. A minute or two later they could see Hillside House and the car parked at the door.

'Is it your father?' Hazel asked. 'Has he come for you because you've been out too long?'

'No, that's not my father's car, and in any case, Dad wouldn't do that. He needs his petrol ration for when he does his rounds. He wouldn't waste them on an errant son. No, if he thought I'd overstayed my welcome, he would simply phone Miss Forsyth and tell her to chuck me out.'

Hazel glanced at him and saw that he was grinning. 'But who can it be?'

Alan peered ahead and then he stopped so suddenly that Hazel bumped into him. 'I recognise the shape. It's a police car.'

Hazel felt a lump of ice forming inside her. 'Are you sure?'

'I'm sure.'

'That can only mean bad news.'

Alan put his arm around her and pulled her

278

close. 'Not necessarily.'

Anger flared. 'What else could it possibly be? It's something about one of our parents, it must be.'

He must have sensed her panic and perhaps he was anxious too, but he spoke calmly: 'Then we'd better go and find out.'

The house was a large black shape merging with the darker shape of the hills behind it. Not even the tiniest chink of light escaped from around the edges of the blackout curtains. Never before had Hazel thought of Hillside House as forbidding.

When they reached the car Hazel and Alan walked all round it and, sure enough, a metal plate bearing the word POLICE was attached to the radiator. They approached the old stone entrance steps and stopped. They looked at each other and some instinct made them go round to the stable yard. When they reached the back door Hazel pulled back.

'For someone here everything has changed,' she said. 'Their life will never be the same again.'

Alan rested his hands on her shoulders and looked at her solemnly. 'You don't know that,' he said.

'I can't think of another reason why the police would come here at this time of night, can you?'

He shook his head.

'Bridget's father is at sea; her mother drives ambulances in London; Irene's parents, just like my mother, have to face the air raids. My father is fighting in North Africa and Irene's brother hasn't written home since the day he left to join the army.'

'And Carol?'

'Her parents have moved to a house by the coast. There's nothing worth bombing there.'

Alan took hold of her hand again. 'We'd better go in.'

The kitchen was warm and smelled of freshly ironed clothes. The people sitting round the table looked up as Hazel and Alan entered. Nobody was talking. Hazel looked at their solemn faces: Mrs Ellis, Irene, Bridget and Carol.

'The police are here,' Hazel said.

Irene nodded. 'We were all in here about to have our supper.' She gestured towards the plate of uneaten sandwiches. 'Miss Forsyth had joined us. When the doorbell rang I went through to answer it, and I got the shock of my life. There was this policeman standing there. I just stared at him. I thought ... I thought...'

Hazel saw the remembered fear in Irene's eyes and knew what her friend had been thinking.

'I put him in the morning room,' Irene continued. 'The fire was nearly out and it was cold in there but I couldn't think of anything else to do with him. I came back here and told Miss Forsyth.'

Irene faltered and looked down at the table. She had both hands cupped round her mug. Hazel could see the skin stretched tight across her knuckles.

'My aunt went to the morning room to deal with him,' Bridget took up the tale, 'and we all sat here fearing the worst. He hasn't been here very long but it seems like ages.'

As if to emphasise the point, Hazel suddenly

280

became aware of the ticking of the clock.

'Sit down, you two,' Mrs Ellis said. 'Standing over us like that makes me nervous.'

Hazel and Alan did as they were told. Nobody spoke. Hazel realised that they were all watching the door that led into the hallway. The clock ticked on until, suddenly, the door opened and Miss Forsyth came into the kitchen. She looked drawn and anxious. Hazel felt her breath catch in her throat. So much depended on what happened next.

'Carol, dear,' Miss Forsyth said. 'I need to talk to you.'

Chapter Fifteen

Margaret Forsyth wondered if the poor child had understood a word she had said. Carol was sitting straight as a poker in the wing chair staring into the dying fire. She had not wept and there was no sign of any sort of emotion on her young face.

'My dear...' Miss Forsyth began tentatively.

Carol made no response.

Sergeant Jameson, standing awkwardly a little distance away, said quietly, 'The lass is in shock.'

A shiver ran through Carol's body from head to toe.

'She needs to be kept warm,' he said.

'Of course, I should have thought.'

Miss Forsyth started towards the log basket at the side of the hearth but the policeman got there before her.

'I'll see to the fire,' Sergeant Jameson said. 'You go and make her a hot drink. A nice cup of tea, perhaps, with plenty of sugar in it.'

'Of course.' Miss Forsyth picked up a little tartan rug from an armchair and draped it round Carol's shoulders. 'I won't be long.'

Carol remained speechless and motionless.

When Miss Forsyth entered the kitchen everyone looked at her. For a moment she did not know what to say. The news the police sergeant had brought had shaken her to the core.

'Miss Forsyth?' Mrs Ellis said enquiringly.

'I need to make a cup of tea.'

'Just one?' Mrs Ellis asked.

'For Carol.'

'You look as though you could do with one yourself.' The cook rose and lifted the kettle onto the hob. 'Sit down and give yourself a moment or two to collect yourself. When the tea's ready I'll come in with you and bring a tray. I suppose the policeman ought to have one as well.'

'Oh, of course. I should have asked him. My manners seem to have deserted me.'

Mrs Ellis spooned tea into the pot and began to set up a tray. 'It's bad news then?'

'I'm afraid so. The worst.'

'Carol's dad?' Mrs Ellis asked. 'He works in Newcastle, doesn't he? There was a bad raid there a few days ago. The news on the wireless said some of the fires are still burning.'

Miss Forsyth sighed. 'I suppose you will all have to know. It's not just Carol's father. It's her mother as well.'

'Dear God,' Mrs Ellis said. Hazel, Irene, Bridget and Alan stared at her in horror.

'And it wasn't in Newcastle. They were at home in their house in Seaton. Apparently three whole streets were hit. There were ... there were many deaths.'

No one seemed to know what to say. Eventually, Mrs Ellis asked, 'Why would anyone want to bomb Seaton? There's nothing important there. It's just a little seaside resort.'

'Apparently it happens now and then,' Miss Forsyth said. 'Sergeant Jameson told me that sometimes, when the German bombers are returning from their raids on the shipyards or the factories, they jettison their remaining bombs anywhere they can before flying post haste across the sea.'

Mrs Ellis was pouring boiling water into the teapot. Her hand shook and water splashed onto the table. 'Wicked,' she said. 'May they rot in hell.'

Miss Forsyth noticed the expressions on the faces of the youngsters seated at the table. It occurred to her that all the girls must have wondered if the bad news was for them, and now their faces showed a mixture of shock and relief. That was quite normal. She hoped that when they admitted to themselves how relieved they were, it would not make them feel guilty.

'I'm sure I don't have to ask all of you to be kind to Carol?' she said.

'Of course not,' Bridget replied.

'She's very attached to you, Bridget,' her aunt said. 'At the moment she seems to be in a state of shock but you may be able to get through to her better than I can.'

'I'll do anything I can.'

Her aunt looked at her wonderingly. 'You're just a child yourself.'

'I'm fifteen years old. Don't worry.'

'The tray's ready,' Mrs Ellis said.

Miss Forsyth stood up, put her hands on the table and leaned forward for a moment before standing up and straightening her shoulders. 'Very well, let's go.'

Sergeant Jameson had performed a small miracle with the fire but his worried expression told her

284

that there had been no change in Carol's condition. Mrs Ellis gave her a cup of tea without the saucer and hovered over her while she sipped it.

She turned to look at Miss Forsyth. 'I think I ought to fill a couple of hot water bottles and settle the lass in bed.'

'Would you like that, Carol?' Miss Forsyth asked.

Carol closed her eyes as if she were thinking, sighed deeply, and then said, 'Can Bridget come and keep me company?'

'Of course, my dear. I know, why doesn't Mrs Ellis bring the two of you a plate of sandwiches and perhaps some cocoa?'

'I can manage that,' Mrs Ellis said.

Carol gave her cup to Mrs Ellis, then, without another word, she left the room. The three adults looked at each other thoughtfully.

'She hasn't cried,' Miss Forsyth said.

'Shock takes people different ways,' Sergeant Jameson told her. 'I should know. I've had to deliver a lot of bad news since the war started. Some people scream, some suffer in silence, and some simply refuse to believe you. "Are you sure?" they ask me. "Are you *absolutely sure?*" It's heartbreaking.'

'I'll go and make the cocoa, and do you want me to ask Bridget to go up to her?' Mrs Ellis said.

Miss Forsyth nodded.

'And what about your own supper?'

'I beg your pardon?'

'We hadn't started eating when the sergeant arrived, remember?'

'I'd forgotten.'

'Are you coming to the kitchen to join us?'

'There are still a few things I must discuss with Sergeant Jameson.'

'Right, I'll save you some sandwiches, but mind you come and eat them.' Mrs Ellis hurried out of the room.

Margaret Forsyth sank wearily into the chair that Carol had just vacated. She gestured for the sergeant to take the chair at the other side of the hearth. 'I don't know what I'd do without Mrs Ellis,' she said. 'Sometimes I think she's the one in charge of this household rather than me.'

Sergeant Jameson sat down and placed his cap on the floor underneath his chair. 'She must be a big help with your evacuees.'

'She is. She's quite taken to them, although at first she was very suspicious about what kind of homes they came from.'

'In my opinion she had every right to be. Some of these kids come from the worst kind of homes you can imagine. It's not their fault, poor bairns, but many of them have never been taught table manners or even how to keep themselves clean. Respectable ladies like you have had to deal with things like impetigo and ringworm. Not to mention head lice.'

'If I'd been sent children like that I'm sure we would still have welcomed them. As you say, it's not their fault.'

'You have a decent bunch, then?'

'I think I've been lucky. And I've become very fond of them. This big old house needed the sound of young people's laughter. And now...' She sighed. 'I'll do anything I can to help Carol.

286

So you must tell me everything I need to know.'

'Very well.' The sergeant took a notebook from one of his pockets and flipped it open. During the ensuing conversation he was to refer to it every now and then. 'When the police in Seaton phoned us,' he began, 'they said the house wasn't too badly bit but unfortunately half of the top floor was demolished. Mr and Mrs Clark were in bed. For some reason there was no air-raid warning. That happens sometimes. Tragic.' He paused and shook his head, then seemed to pull himself together. 'I suppose you know that there are folk who steal from bombed houses?'

'I know. My sister-in-law drives an ambulance in London. She's seen it happening.'

'Some of them are just kids, although I'm sure they've been put up to it. They'll take anything they can find. Coins from the gas meters, clothes, jewellery, some of it from the dead bodies.'

Miss Forsyth looked horrified. 'Are you trying to tell me that Carol's parents were robbed this way?'

'No, no, forgive me, I've made a mess of things. I was going to assure you that, in this case, nothing like happened. The Home Guard was sent round to rope off the area and to prevent looting. They looked for anything that could help identify the victims or their relatives. It seems Mr Clark was a very well-organised sort of chap. They found neatly filed letters in a bureau in the sitting room. There was also a photograph album.

'More importantly, there was a tin box containing all his important papers such as his bank book, his will, birth and marriage certificates, and papers to do with the purchase of the house. The little lass should have no trouble getting a grant to help with the repairs. Shall I tell them to send everything here to you?'

'Please do.'

Sergeant Jameson put his notebook away, retrieved and replaced his cap, then stood up. 'I'll go now, Miss Forsyth, but if there's anything we can help you with, just phone the local station.'

'I will, thank you. I'll see you out.'

They got as far as the front door when the sergeant stopped. 'There's something I need to know.'

'What is it?'

'The funeral. Who will...'

'Presumably the name of Mr Clark's solicitor will be in his address book and on his will?'

'I believe so.'

'Then, unless a relative comes forward, I'll ask him to arrange the funeral. I'll also write to inform everyone in the address book.'

A wind had sprung up and it snatched the sergeant's cap from his head as soon as he stepped outside. He grabbed at it and hung onto it while he walked to his car. He waved to Miss Forsyth and she inclined her head, then shut the door. As she turned, she saw Bridget coming down the stairs carrying a tray.

'How is Carol?' Miss Forsyth asked.

'I'm pleased to say she managed to eat all her sandwiches and drink up her cocoa. However, she's hardly spoken a word. I'm not sure why she wanted me there.'

'She probably just didn't want to be alone.'

'Well, I offered to stay as long as she liked,

perhaps read to her from the latest book Mummy sent me, but she thanked me in such a polite little voice, and said she just wanted to go to bed.'

'Poor child. I'd better look in on her.'

'No, Aunt Margaret, I don't think you should. At least, not immediately.'

'Why not?'

'She hasn't shed a single tear. I think she feels that she's got to be brave. All this chin up and stiff upper lip nonsense, you know. I believe the poor girl thinks it's simply not done to show your emotions. If this had happened to me I'd be howling with pain and I wouldn't care who heard me. I think we should leave her alone for a while so that she can cry her heart out all by herself.'

'You're a wise child, Bridget.'

'I'm a Forsyth, aren't I?'

They went to the kitchen together. The others were still sitting round the table. No one felt like talking, and when Alan took his leave, Bridget, Hazel and Irene went quietly to bed.

The windowpanes began to rattle. Carol burrowed down into her pillows and pulled the bedclothes up over her ears to shut out the unnerving, high-pitched howling of the wind. She didn't hear the bedroom door open but when she heard Miss Forsyth say, 'Carol, dear?' she lay quite still and pretended to be asleep. She held her breath and strained to listen to the departing footsteps and then the door closing.

They expected her to cry, but she couldn't. She had loved her parents, especially her father, but they had become like strangers to her. She never

289

felt that she missed them and wanted to see them like the other girls did. She felt more at home here in Hillside House than she ever had in Newcastle. And she hated the idea of that commonplace little house in Seaton. She hoped she wouldn't have to go there now. They couldn't expect her to, not when her parents had died there. She was sure Miss Forsyth would let her stay here for as long as the war lasted. But when it ended, where would she go then?

One month later

Miss Forsyth settled herself in the morning room, and after Mrs Ellis had brought her a cup of coffee, or rather whatever masqueraded as coffee these days, she sat at her small writing desk to reread the letter that had arrived the day before. The lined paper was cheap and flimsy and the writing ill-formed.

She put it down on the desk's tooled leather writing surface while she drank her coffee and allowed herself to look out of the rain-speckled window at the welcome sunshine. *Sunshine and rain*, she thought. *Maybe there's a rainbow out there.* She resisted the temptation to go to the window to look into the sky. She mustn't procrastinate any longer. She had a decision to make, and before she could do so, she needed to read the letter again.

Dear Miss Forsyth,
Thank you for writing to tell me of the death of my dear cousin Anne Clark and her husband Brian. We

were very shocked. We read about the raid on Seaton in the newspaper but we had no idea that they had moved there. Perhaps they just had not got around to telling us.

My husband and myself and our daughter Janet went to the funeral. I thought you might attend yourself and bring Carol. We were surprised not to see her there at her own parents' funeral, but I suppose she must be too upset. All the same, it was a pity, because our Janet is the same age as Carol and I think it might have been nice for her to meet her cousin.

Be that as it may, I'd like to assure you that the funeral parlour arranged things very well, including the reception at the Royal Hotel after the service. It's just a pity that so few mourners turned up, but then Carol's father's only living relative is a brother, and I understand he lives in Australia. The only person there to grieve for Brian Clark was a man who said he was his solicitor, Mr Robert Golightly. I told him that I would do anything I could to help Carol. It was my duty. I had a good chat with him. As I am a first cousin of her late mother I am Carol's nearest relative. I asked him to be sure to keep in touch with me.

A few more distant family connections of Anne's turned up. They all told me that they were surprised you had found them in the address book, because once she got married to Brian Clark she gradually cut herself off from her family. There are those who thought she'd had her head turned. I suppose she could never have imagined something like this would happen, which is a pity, because Carol now finds herself alone in the world.

Of course Carol is lucky to have you. It is very good of you to help her continue her schooling when most girls of her age would be working in proper jobs. My

291

Janet is just a little slip of a lass, but she's doing her duty helping to win the war, like you're supposed to, by working at Vickers Armstrong making shells.

You must be wondering what do with Carol when the war is over. Well, there's no need to worry. No doubt she will want to go to the house in Seaton. I understand she has inherited it. If she does go there to live, I can assure you that I will keep an eye on her. She will need someone to see to her affairs until she is twenty-one, won't she? Janet and I will visit her regularly, or we could even move in with her to keep her company if that is what she would like.

As far as arrangements for the repairs and rebuilding are concerned, my husband, Cyril, who was not fit enough for the army and can only do light work, would be perfectly happy to keep an eye on the house while it is being repaired. He could look after it like a caretaker until Carol wants to move in. He would want no more than his expenses. I mean train fares and the like.

But as for the present, I'm sure you will agree that I should come along and meet Carol as soon as possible. There's no point in delaying things. If you would make it a Sunday then Janet could come as well. She is as impatient as I am to meet her.

To conclude, please give Carol my love and tell her that her Aunty Ada is looking forward to meeting her as soon as possible.

Yours truly,
Ada Wilson

Miss Forsyth folded the flimsy pages and put them back in the envelope. What was she to do? Ada Wilson was the only relative of Carol's who had replied to the letters she had sent to everybody in the address book. On the face of it, it seemed perfectly in order that she had offered to help Carol, but the tone of the letter was deeply unsettling.

Maybe I'm getting cynical as I grow older, Miss Forsyth thought, *but my instinct tells me that this woman is out to see what she can get for herself. She hasn't even met Carol and she's suggesting that she should move into the house in Seaton, lock, stock and barrel.*

She was tempted to throw the envelope on the fire or at least stuff it at the back of a cubbyhole and conveniently forget about it. She sighed. In all conscience she could not do that. Carol had a right to know that a relative of her mother's wanted to meet her. She would have to tell Carol about this and then invite the woman and her daughter to come to Hillside House. It was only right that she give Carol a chance to get to know them. She would try to stay out of their way for an hour or two, and then she would leave it to Carol to decide whether she wanted to keep in contact with them.

But then, would Carol have any choice? Miss Forsyth gripped the envelope, wrestling with the many worries that sprang to mind. In her letter Mrs Wilson had brought up the fact that Carol was a minor and could not be in charge of her own affairs. Was she hinting that she should be her guardian – it certainly looked that way – and if so, would she have any legal claim to the position? Miss Forsyth was convinced that that would be the worst thing that could happen, but she knew she had no right to interfere.

She picked up her cup to discover that the coffee, or chicory, or whatever it was, was cold and completely unappetising. She put it down in disgust and walked over to the window. Her eyes widened. A beautiful double rainbow arced over the rain-washed landscape.

She was taken up with the beauty of the scene: gazing at the shimmering arc, her troubled mind cleared. There was something she could do. Of course there was. She just needed a little more time. Mrs Wilson and her daughter would have to be patient for a while longer.

Two months later

Ada Wilson stopped and looked up the steep road that led to Hillside House. She dug the pencil-drawn map that had been sent to her out of her handbag and checked it hopefully.

'Let me see it,' her daughter said. She glanced at it briefly. 'This is the way. Can't miss it. In fact, I think that's the house up there.' She crumpled the map and tossed it into the ditch.

Her mother scowled. 'They didn't say the road was so steep. They could have sent a car to meet us.'

'Don't be daft, Mam.'

'Daft? What do you mean, daft?'

'Even if Miss Forsyth has a car she won't have any petrol, will she?'

'There are ways and means,' her mother said. She looked at the way ahead and sighed. 'Anyway, we'd better get a move on. The letter said we were invited for lunch. *Lunch.* I suppose that's her way of saying dinner. Well, we don't want to make a bad impression by being late.'

Janet grinned at her. 'Oh, we'll make an impression all right. Dressed like this especially for the occasion.'

Her mother scowled again. 'You just keep quiet about that. Leave it all to me.'

'Of course, Mam. Whatever you say. Now let's stop blethering and haddaway up this hill.'

Mother and daughter set off again. Ada had developed a limp. Her daughter looked at her and said, 'If you're suffering, it's your own fault for wearing those stupid shoes.'

'They're me best shoes. I want to look smart. This Miss Forsyth is some kind of lady.'

'What makes you think that?'

'That Mr Golightly, the solicitor. He told me at the funeral that I had no need to worry about Carol because, apart from the fact that her dad's insurance policy had left her well provided for, she was in a very good home for the duration of the war. He said Miss Forsyth was from an old and distinguished family.'

'That doesn't mean she has a title, if that's what you're thinking. I mean, she doesn't sign herself *Lady* Forsyth, does she?'

'Whatever the case, she must be well off. She lives in a big house and she can afford to take in a bunch of evacuees.'

'Listen, Mam, she'll be paid by the government just like anyone else who takes the kids in. I've heard that some do it just for the money and the vackies get nowt to eat except bread and marge.'

'That's outrageous! People taking advantage of those poor bairns. I would never do a thing like that.'

'Of course you wouldn't. You've got a heart of pure gold, haven't you, Mam?'

There was something about Janet's tone of voice that made Ada look at her daughter suspiciously. But Janet was now a good few paces ahead of her and Ada was out of breath. There was no more talking as she concentrated on getting up the hill.

Miss Forsyth answered the door herself. The woman who stood there was overweight and breathing heavily. Her face was round and her small eyes were almost obscured by reddened, puffy cheeks. A black felt hat with black feathers clipped to one side with a rhinestone pin was perched on top of dark hair permed to a frizz. Over the shoulders of her black coat she wore a tired-looking orangey-red fox stole with yellowing teeth in its sharp little snout. She also wore a pair of shiny black patent leather shoes with the most preposterous high heels. Her feet had swollen and folds of flesh hung over the sides.

The girl with her had hair just as dark as Carol's and there was a faint family likeness. However, a sour expression marred what could have been a pretty face. Her complexion was sallow and she wore a shapeless black coat that looked too big for her skinny frame.

Miss Forsyth gripped the solid old door with one hand. *Her letter alerted me but this is worse than I imagined,* she thought. Oh dear, was she a snob?

She had always striven not to be. She used to hate it when her mother would refer to someone as *not our kind of person.*

Mrs Wilson was looking at her expectantly. She realised she had been standing speechlessly for too long and pulled herself together.

'You must be Mrs Wilson and Janet?' she said, quite unnecessarily. *I'm twittering,* she thought.

'Yes, my lady,' the woman said and her daughter shot her a furious look.

'Oh, I'm not a lady,' Miss Forsyth said. 'At least, not in the sense of having a title. I'm simply Miss Forsyth.' *And I have no intention of asking you to call me Margaret, just as I will never get familiar enough to call you Ada,* she thought to herself. 'But please do come in.'

She stepped back and held the door while they entered. She didn't miss the cool, almost contemptuous, look the girl gave her. She felt deeply uncomfortable. *The girl knows,* she thought. *She saw my reaction and she has taken my measure. For Carol's sake I must try to put things right.* She was given an extra moment or two to recover her poise when Mrs Ellis appeared.

'Would your guests like a cup of tea?' the cook asked. 'And perhaps some sponge cake? Carol helped to make it yesterday.'

'Oh, I'm *sure* they would.' Miss Forsyth realised she was gushing. 'I mean,' she turned to face Mrs Wilson, 'would you?'

'Very nice, I'm sure. I could do with something after that walk from the station.'

Miss Forsyth sensed there was some criticism here but she was too flustered to try to work out

297

what it was. 'I'll show you to my little morning room,' she said.

'The *morning* room? Oooh, how delightful!' Janet said, attempting a posh accent. Her smile was false and there was no mistaking her hostility.

Miss Forsyth controlled a surge of irritation and soldiered on. 'I know it's a sunny day in June,' she said brightly, 'but we've lit a fire in there. This old house is a bit draughty even in the summer months.'

'My, my, how *trying* for you,' Janet said.

Miss Forsyth looked at her keenly. She saw an intelligent girl who should probably still be at school rather than working in a factory. She wondered if Janet herself had realised this, and if that was why she was so resentful. This did not bode well for Carol.

Chapter Sixteen

Miss Forsyth led the way into the morning room. Ada Wilson hurried in, blinking in the bright sunlight. 'Carol, pet,' she began, then she stopped and looked around in surprise. 'Where is she?'

'She's in the kitchen with the other girls. Mrs Ellis has been giving them a cookery lesson.'

'Really? Why does she need cookery lessons?'

'If these girls were at home I'm sure their mothers would be teaching them.'

'Even your own niece?' Janet asked.

'I beg your pardon?'

'Mr Golightly told us that one of the girls was your brother's daughter, and wasn't that nice for the others to be mixing with the upper classes.'

'I'm sure he did not say that,' Miss Forsyth responded sharply. Her patience was stretched tight.

'Well no,' Janet said. 'He just said "a girl like that". But it's obvious what he meant, isn't it?'

'I suppose it is, but I don't approve and I apologise. As for the cookery lessons, I'd like you to know that my brother's wife is a very good cook and I'm sure she would want Bridget to learn as much as Mrs Ellis can teach her.' *This is ridiculous*, Margaret Forsyth thought. *I'm letting this angry, resentful child provoke me.* She became aware that she was clenching her hands.

Janet hadn't done with her. 'Can *you* cook?' she asked.

'Much to my shame I am not very skilled in the kitchen, but the world has changed since I was the same age as my niece.' Not giving the wretched girl time to say any more, Miss Forsyth hurried on, 'However, it's time I brought Carol through to meet you. Mrs Wilson, if you and Janet would like to take off your coats, Mrs Ellis will put them in the cloakroom.'

'Who is Mrs Ellis?' Janet asked.

'You just met her in the hall.'

'Is she a relation of yours?'

'No, she's my ... my...'

'Chief cook and bottle washer,' Mrs Ellis said as she came in with the tray. 'Here you are,' she said. 'A nice pot of tea and some home-made cake.'

'Are you a servant?' Janet asked.

'Not that there's anything wrong with that,' her mother interjected hastily. 'A big house like this needs looking after. I mean, when Carol moves into her house in Seaton I'm sure we – I mean, she – will employ a daily woman. After all, she will be able to afford to, won't she?'

'I have no idea,' Miss Forsyth said coolly. 'And as for Mrs Ellis, yes, she works here, but to tell you the truth we are more like old friends.'

Mrs Ellis put the tray down on a small table near the hearth, then waited for the coats. Mrs Wilson kept her hat on. Mrs Ellis glanced at it and looked away quickly.

Miss Forsyth stared at her two guests. The mother's dress was rusty black crêpe which had seen many better days and hung unevenly round her ample form. One large shoulder pad had slipped forward, giving her a lopsided look. Janet was wearing a dress of scratchy-looking black wool that looked as though it had been cut down to fit by an inexpert needlewoman. Miss Forsyth wondered quite inconsequentially if Ada Wilson or the girl herself had done it.

'Do sit down and drink your tea,' Miss Forsyth said. 'I'll go and get Carol.'

Irene waited until Carol had left the kitchen with Miss Forsyth before she asked, 'What are they like?'

Mrs Ellis was putting a carrot cake in the oven along with a carrot flan. She glanced over her shoulder. 'Check that pan of stew for me and I'll tell you. And Hazel, you can clear everything away now and get the table wiped down.' She closed the oven door, put a hand in the small of her back and straightened up. 'Bridget, would you take a sheet of newspaper and wrap up all the peelings for Molly's blessed hens? Rita will be along to collect them.' She sat down at the table. 'How's the rabbit stew?'

'It's fine.'

Irene sat at the table and Hazel and Bridget, their tasks completed, joined her. They looked at Mrs Ellis expectantly. 'Go on, then, spill the beans,' Irene said.

She pretended to be puzzled. 'What do you want to know?' she said.

'Don't tease! You know what I mean. What are Carol's relatives like?'

'She won't like them.'

'Why not?'

'Mrs Wilson isn't a bit like her mother.'

'In what way?' Bridget asked.

'Mrs Clark was nicely spoken and dressed in a ladylike sort of way. She was obviously nervous when she came here, and wasn't quite sure how to behave, but she listened to Carol's father, who was a proper gent, and she minded her manners. Whereas Mrs Wilson...' she paused.

'Are you trying to say that Mrs Wilson is more like my mother?' Irene intercepted furiously. 'She dresses common and speaks rough? Is that what you mean?'

'Hold your horses, miss. You're always too ready to jump to conclusions. I meant no such thing. I don't think your mother is common. She likes to dress up a bit fancy like, and why not? She's a right bonny woman. And maybe she doesn't talk like Miss Forsyth does, but neither do I. No, pet, your ma's just as much a lady in her own way as many who would consider them-selves her betters.

'But this Mrs Wilson is an entirely different kettle of fish. She's got a mangy old fox tippet round her shoulders – the damn thing has one eye missing – and a great daft bunch of wilting feathers on her hat. I nearly laughed out loud. I'm sure she thinks she looks respectable, but her whole manner is what I would call coarse.'

Slightly mollified, Irene asked, 'And what about her daughter? Janet, isn't it?'

'Aye, Janet. As skinny and spare as her mother is fat and flabby. And although she's the same age as Carol, her discontented, pinched little face makes her look years older. And in my opinion, I don't think Mrs Wilson cares one jot about Carol. I think she's out to see what's in it for her.'

'What do you mean?' Bridget asked her.

'The lass won't be too badly off. Miss Forsyth told me her father had seen to it that she wouldn't be left penniless, and the house belongs to her now.'

'But it's been bombed,' Irene said.

'She'll get a grant to put it right. I can't help thinking that Mrs Wilson wouldn't have bothered to turn up if the lass had been left with nowt.'

'Poor Carol,' said Hazel.

Irene glared at her. 'What do you mean, *poor* Carol?'

'For goodness' sake, Irene!' Hazel exclaimed with a rare flash of anger. 'I know you don't get along with her, but she's lost her parents in the most tragic fashion and the only relatives that turn up probably don't care for her at all.'

Irene felt embarrassed. She admitted to herself reluctantly that she had deserved Hazel's reprimand.

Mrs Ellis looked uneasy. 'I've spoken out of turn. I shouldn't have said any of this, not to you bairns. I could be quite wrong about the woman.'

'I shouldn't think so,' Bridget said. 'It would take a very clever person to fool you, Mrs Ellis. But there's no need to worry, Hazel. My aunt may seem to be a trifle vague and unworldly at times, but she's a keen judge of character. She won't let Carol come to any harm at the hands of these two. I'm sure of it.'

When Carol entered the morning room along

with Miss Forsyth, Ada Wilson put her cup down onto the little table, slopping tea in the saucer as she did so. The tallest feather on her hat fell sideways and remained sticking out at an angle. She heaved herself to her feet and nearly sat down again as one high heel caught in the fringe of the rug. She righted herself and stretched her arms out in Carol's direction.

'Carol!' she said. 'My poor little niece.'

Carol was horrified. *Am I supposed to run into her arms?* she wondered. She tried to control a look of distaste and remained exactly where she was. Mrs Wilson put her arms down again and in the awkward silence her daughter spoke up.

'She's not your niece,' Janet said. 'You and her mam were cousins, not sisters. That makes you and Carol second cousins or something like that.'

Her mother shot her a furious look and Carol glanced at them both in dismay.

'All right, clever clogs,' Mrs Wilson told her daughter, 'but I want Carol to look on me as her aunt. Aunty Ada. That's more friendly than calling me Mrs Wilson.' She sent Carol a saccharine smile. 'Isn't it, pet?'

Carol remained silent.

Janet shrugged. She hadn't bothered to stand up and she returned her attention to the slice of sponge cake she was eating.

'Well, I want you to know that I'm very pleased to meet you, Carol,' Mrs Wilson said, 'but I must say I'm a little surprised.' She drew in her breath and shook her head slowly.

'Is something the matter?' Miss Forsyth asked.

'Well, I hate to say this, but I admit I'm upset

304

about the way Carol is dressed. I mean, the grey skirt will just about do, but the pink blouse and cardigan – I don't know what to make of it.'

'Oh, I see. You think she should be wearing black?' Miss Forsyth said.

'I certainly do. After all, her parents are hardly cold in their graves.'

Carol flinched but remained silent.

Miss Forsyth said, 'You exaggerate. And in any case, I do not believe that children should wear mourning clothes. We do not live in the Victorian age.'

'She's not a child. Carol is fifteen years old, just like my Janet, and I made sure that she went into mourning, just like I did. My Cyril is wearing a black band on his sleeve.'

'And how long do you intend to keep this up?'

'For six months, of course. It's a matter of re-spect. I thought a lady in your position would know that.'

Carol's eyes widened as she took in the hint of impertinence. Before Miss Forsyth had a chance to reply, she said, 'But you hardly knew my parents.' It was the first time she had spoken since coming into the room.

Mrs Wilson looked at her in surprise and then she adopted a sorrowful expression. 'I knew your mother when we were children, and even if we drifted apart after she ... I mean, as we grew up, as people do, she was still family. And family is important, wouldn't you say so, Miss Forsyth?'

'Yes, family is important. That is why I invited you here. I wanted Carol to meet her relatives. I wanted to give her a chance to get to know you.'

'Very good of you, I'm sure. But I have to say you took your time about it. It's weeks since I wrote to you.'

'Yes, and I do apologise.'

Mrs Wilson looked at her expectantly, but it was obvious that Miss Forsyth was not going to say any more.

Carol glanced from one to the other. She could hardly believe this was happening. Why had Miss Forsyth brought these dreadful people here? Did she think she would want to grow close to them just because they were some kind of cousins? The whole situation was a nightmare.

At that moment Hazel came in to say that lunch was ready.

Janet, who had quietly eaten every slice of cake, got up immediately and said loudly, 'About time.'

Carol thought she would die of embarrassment. She couldn't escape the appalling fact that she was related to Mrs Wilson and her daughter, and she couldn't imagine what Miss Forsyth must be thinking. She was utterly mortified.

'Hazel, would you show our guests to the dining room?' Miss Forsyth said.

As the three of them left the room, Miss Forsyth turned to Carol. 'I know this wasn't the original plan, I wanted you to have some time alone with your family, but would you mind if I joined you for lunch?'

My Family! She called them my family, Carol thought in horror. She was torn between embarrassment and revulsion. She did not want Miss Forsyth to spend any more time with these dreadful people, but nor did she want to be left alone with them. After an inner struggle, and almost choking on the words, she said, 'Oh, please do.'

Miss Forsyth frowned as if something was worrying her. 'Carol,' she said, 'I'm not sure what Mrs Wilson is going to say, but I want you to know I'm prepared.'

Her manner was slightly tense and Carol looked up at her nervously.

Miss Forsyth's features relaxed into a warm smile. 'Don't worry, dear child. You can trust me to do my best for you.'

She placed a hand on Carol's shoulder and they walked into the dining room together.

'What's happening in there?' Irene asked Hazel a little later.

'They're eating their lunch,' Hazel replied. 'They've just about finished the rabbit stew.'

'But what are they talking about?'

'That's none of your business, miss,' Mrs Ellis said. 'And that's why I chose Hazel to wait on table. She knows better than to spread idle gossip.'

'But you were gossiping before, weren't you?'

Mrs Ellis's cheeks turned pink. 'Yes, I suppose I was and I'm sorry for it.'

'Don't feel bad about it,' Irene said magnanimously. 'It's just natural to want to know what's going on.'

'Yes, pet, it is,' Mrs Ellis said, 'and I'm sure we're all wondering what they're talking about, but in this case, it's up to Carol whether she wants to tell us.'

'I'm just as curious as you are, Irene,' Bridget said, 'but I have to agree with Mrs Ellis. What do

307

you think, Hazel?'

Hazel almost laughed. Everyone in the kitchen was looking at her, and no matter what they had said, she could see the curiosity in their eyes. Even Mrs Ellis.

'Believe me, I couldn't tell you, even if I thought it was okay to do so,' Hazel said. 'Each time I went into the room Miss Forsyth nodded towards me and everybody stopped talking.'

'*Pas devant*,' Bridget said.

Irene scowled. 'What are you on about?'

'It's French. It means,' Bridget glanced at Hazel and hesitated. 'Don't talk in front of the children. *Pas devant les enfants.*'

'Or the servants,' Hazel said. '*Pas devant les domestiques.*'

Bridget looked uncomfortable. 'It's just an expression,' she said. 'I didn't mean that you were a servant.'

'I know that.' Hazel smiled at her.

'I'm sorry.'

'No need to be. *Ça ne fait rien.*'

Irene's scowl deepened. 'Talk French, why don't you?' she said. 'You know I don't understand a word of it.'

Mrs Ellis sighed. 'You know, Irene, sometimes you seem to be determined to be offended. I'm sure Bridget and Hazel weren't getting at you. Were you, girls?'

'Of course not,' they said in unison.

'Now,' Mrs Ellis looked at the mantel clock, 'I think they've had enough time to eat that stew. Let's hope they appreciate this chocolate pudding.'

Hazel cleared the dinner plates away and brought in the chocolate pudding. Carol flinched as Mrs Wilson used her napkin to dab at a spot of gravy that had dribbled onto her chin and then wiped her mouth, leaving a long smear of lipstick on the starched white damask. Janet had actually used her dessert spoon to scoop up every remaining drop of gravy on her plate and now she was cleaning the spoon by licking it before starting on her pudding.

'My, that was very good stew, even if it was just rabbit,' Ada Wilson said. 'I suppose you get a lot of those in the country?'

Miss Forsyth nodded her assent.

'And now a steamed pudding with chocolate sauce. What a treat! You're spoiling us. But then I imagine it's handy for you having all the girls' ration books.'

Miss Forsyth looked puzzled. 'I'm not exactly sure what you mean, but I trust Mrs Ellis to do her best for them.'

This was the one moment of light relief for Carol, who knew, along with the others, that ration books were a total puzzle to Miss Forsyth and that she was more than happy to hand over the responsibility to Mrs Ellis.

Ada Wilson's expression changed to one of censure. 'But I must say, I was disappointed to see Carol toying with her food like that. Is she always this picky?'

'Carol isn't at all picky, as you put it,' Miss Forsyth said. 'You surely must understand that she might be a little nervous today.'

'Why should she be nervous?'

'Because she's meeting you for the first time.'

'We're her kith and kin. She has no need to take that attitude with us.'

'What attitude?'

'She's hardly said a word since we arrived. She doesn't seem a bit pleased to see us.'

'Stuck up, in my opinion,' Janet interjected through a mouthful of pudding.

Carol ignored her. 'Why should I be pleased to see you?' she asked Mrs Wilson. It was the first time she had spoken since taking her place at the table.

Mrs Wilson stared at her. Janet's eyes widened in surprise and then she sniggered.

Carol dropped her head and looked down at the table. She realised how ill-mannered she must have sounded, and although she didn't care what Mrs Wilson and Janet thought of her, she did not want to behave badly in front of Miss Forsyth. Miss Forsyth had told her that she could trust her.

'I'm very sorry,' she said. 'That was rude of me. But Miss Forsyth is right. I am nervous. And of course I should be grateful to you for bothering to come and see me. I hope you'll forgive me.'

She looked up and saw that Mrs Wilson was frowning while Janet looked from one to the other with ill-concealed amusement.

'Well, I don't know what to say, I'm sure,' Mrs Wilson said. 'After all the trouble we've gone to, to be spoken to like that.'

'Go on, Mam,' the girl said. 'Carol has said she's sorry. And if she's going to be one of the family, don't you think it's time to tell Miss Forsyth what your plan is?'

'Your plan?' Miss Forsyth spoke sharply.

One of the family? Carol felt a surge of panic.

Mrs Wilson looked flustered. She turned to scowl at her daughter.

'Mrs Wilson,' Miss Forsyth said impatiently. 'What exactly is your plan?'

'I wouldn't call it a plan,' Mrs Wilson said.

Janet shook her head and sniggered, then turned her attention to her chocolate pudding.

'Well what would you call it?' Miss Forsyth said.

'Never mind what it's *called*,' Mrs Wilson said crossly. 'The way I see it is this.' She paused and made an effort to look sympathetic, shaking her head sorrowfully. 'Carol, the poor dear child, is an orphan.'

'That's true.'

'And she is a minor.' She stared at Miss Forsyth challengingly. 'She is under age.'

'Yes, she's under twenty-one.'

'So there's about six years to go until she can handle her affairs and make certain decisions.'

'What exactly do you mean?'

'Legal decisions. Matters to do with her house, the money in her bank account, that sort of thing.'

'You are quite right.'

Mrs Wilson looked surprised at Miss Forsyth's ready agreement and she went on more confidently, 'Well, it came to me that she should have a legal guardian.'

Miss Forsyth nodded as if in agreement.

'And obviously, as her nearest relative, that job should go to me.' She looked at Miss Forsyth expectantly.

Carol held her breath. She glanced at Miss Forsyth, who seemed to be quite calm and untroubled.

She said I could trust her.

'Have you spoken to Mr Golightly about this?' Miss Forsyth asked.

'Not yet. I wrote to him and told him I would like to make an appointment to see him. He wrote back and said that if it was about Carol's estate – that's what he called it – there was no point, as yet. He said nothing could be done until Brian and Anne's wills are sorted out. Apparently it's complicated because they have no way of knowing which one of them died first.'

Carol gasped and even Janet looked shocked.

'Really, Mrs Wilson, you should not be speaking like this in front of Carol,' Miss Forsyth said repressively.

'No? Well, I'm sorry if I've upset the child, but these things have to be settled. It's in her interest in the long run.' She became aware that everyone was staring at her and shifted in her seat uneasily. 'I've already told you that we would look after her house for her and be there to welcome her when she comes home.'

'Perhaps we should ask Carol what she wants to do,' Miss Forsyth said.

Mrs Wilson frowned. 'If you like.' She shrugged. 'Go ahead, then.'

Miss Forsyth smiled at Carol encouragingly. 'Carol, my dear, I thought it right and proper that you should meet your relatives. That's why I invited them to come here. I wanted to give you the chance to get to know them. I know this hasn't been a very long meeting and you must tell me if you want them to visit us again before you make up your mind.'

'What do you mean, make up her mind?' Mrs Wilson said.

'Whether she wants to live with you or stay here.'

Mrs Wilson frowned. 'Of course I wouldn't take Carol away from here until the war is over,' she said. 'And then I think it would be up to me to decide where she lives.'

'No, I don't think so. But, Carol, don't be afraid to tell us what you want to do. Do you want to live with Mrs Wilson?'

Mrs Wilson turned her frown into an ingratiating smile. 'Not Mrs Wilson, Carol, pet. Aunty Ada. I've already told you that.'

'Carol?' Miss Forsyth prompted. 'Don't be afraid to tell the truth.'

'I don't want to live with Mrs Wilson,' Carol said in a rush. 'And can't you be my guardian rather than her?'

'No, she can't, miss,' Mrs Wilson said. 'I'm a blood relative. She's not. It wouldn't be legal. Tell her.' She stared at Miss Forsyth challengingly.

'Nonsense,' Miss Forsyth said sharply. 'I could apply to the courts if I wished to and I would do so willingly, but there is no need. Carol already has a very satisfactory guardian.'

'And who might that be?'

'You seem to have completely forgotten that Mr

Clark had a brother who is living in Australia. Mr Golightly and I have been in touch with him. Luckily the air mail is still getting through.' She smiled faintly. 'Austin Clark is named in both Mr and Mrs Clark's wills as Carol's guardian. He had agreed to that when the wills were drawn up.

'He is much more closely related to Carol than you are. He and his wife are schoolteachers. They have no children and they would be overjoyed to have Carol join them. There would be no point whatsoever in your challenging the will.'

'Australia!' Mrs Wilson said. 'She can't go there. It wouldn't be safe. There's a war on. Goodness knows how many ships have been lost!'

'She doesn't have to go yet. Her uncle is happy for Carol to stay with me until the war is over. Then he hopes she will visit them and stay for a while. But they would leave it entirely up to Carol to decide whether she wanted to make her life there or stay in England.'

While they had been talking Janet had quietly swapped her empty pudding dish for her mother's. 'So that's it, Mam,' she said as she scraped every last drop of chocolate sauce up. 'You're not going to get your hands on Carol's bank account, nor move into her nice little house at the coast. So why don't we go home and get these stupid black clothes off?'

Ada Wilson, scowlingly deflated, did not put up a fight. She hardly said another word. She made a face when she drank her coffee but Margaret Forsyth could not blame her for that. As soon as Hazel had cleared the table, Mrs Ellis brought

314

their coats and waited to see them out. They left without further ceremony.

Janet trailed behind her mother long enough to wink maliciously at Carol and say, 'It's all right for some, isn't it!'

No plans were made to meet up in the future.

Miss Forsyth had risen from the table when the Wilsons had left. Carol was still sitting there, looking bewildered and desolate. Miss Forsyth knew it was time to explain her actions.

'I'm sorry if this has been difficult for you,' she said, 'but I could not let my own opinions or prejudices influence the way I handled this. Mrs Wilson and her daughter are your relatives and I had to give you the chance to get to know them. Although I did not think it likely, you might have got along well with them. If so, you might have chosen to stay with them rather than go to your uncle in Australia.'

Carol stared at her. 'I don't have to go there, do I? To Australia?'

'No, dear. As I said, your uncle wants to do whatever will make you happy, and it would make *me* happy if you stayed here with me for as long as you like.'

At that, the usually reticent Carol rose from her seat and hurled herself into Miss Forsyth's arms. 'Thank you,' she said. 'Oh, thank you.'

Margaret Forsyth held her close and vowed to herself that whatever the future brought she would do everything she could to protect this dear child.

Chapter Seventeen

December 1952, Christmas Eve

Paper garlands criss-crossed the ceiling from corner to corner in the outer office of Marion Grey's Secretarial Agency on the top floor of a large old house in Eldon Square. A bunch of holly hung from the central light fitting. Wine and canapés were set out on the table in the small kitchen. Maud Robinson, an elderly cousin of Marion's who had worked for her since she first set up the agency, was in charge of the refreshments.

Marion herself was drinking whisky. Sandra Walton, who was working temporarily in the offices of a wine merchant, said the wine that had been provided for the rest of them was a better than usual Liebfraumilch.

'You can drink it with anything, you know,' Sandra told them. 'You don't have to worry about changing the wine for different courses at a dinner party.'

They took her word for it.

Once the guests had filled their plates and taken a glass of wine, they drifted into the outer office where there was room to move around. Those who had been with the agency for a long time chatted like old friends, but, as is usual in the world of temping, some of them did not know any of the others. Marion asked Hazel to look after them and make them feel at home. Then she retired to her inner sanctum to top up her glass and light up one of her favourite black Russian cigarettes.

Most of the guests were female, but there were three men. They huddled together on the draughty landing at the top of the stairs as if they were prepared to make their escape at any minute. Hazel guessed that, before long, they would probably decant themselves to the nearest pub.

'Hazel? Hazel Stafford? Is that you?'

One of the men, who had just been to the kitchen to fill his plate, stopped in his tracks and stared at her. She returned his gaze but she didn't recognise him.

'You don't remember me?' he said.

'I'm sorry, I don't.'

'Of course, I didn't have a moustache when we knew each other. Although I remember trying very hard to grow one in the hopes that it would attract one of you girls.'

'Paul!' Hazel said. 'You're Paul Barton.'

'That's me! Fancy meeting up after all these years. I joined the air force after I left Withenmoor, you know. I'd intended to train as an accountant, but I hardly had time to settle into a job with a very good firm when I was called up for national service.'

'Poor you.'

'No, it was okay. I was posted to Germany.' He smiled broadly.

'You liked it there?'

'Very much. I took German lessons and stayed on after I was demobbed. I took any kind of job

I could get to support myself while I tried to write a book.'

'And did you write it?'

'I wrote several. All thrillers set in war-torn Europe. None of them have been published. But I'm still hopeful.'

'But now you've come home?'

'En route to America. I thought I'd try my hand at screenwriting. I've got this fantastic idea for a movie about spies. The trouble is that a lot of other people have the same idea or something similar. But my plot has a real twist in it. I'm sure no one else has thought of it. I've started work on it, you know, and–' He stopped when Hazel held up her hand.

'Paul, stop!' she said laughingly. 'I can't keep up with you!'

'Sorry. I do get carried away, don't I?' His smile was rueful.

'So how long are you going to stay in New-castle?' she asked.

'Until I've saved up enough money to take me to California.'

'Hazel? Can you spare a moment?' They turned to see Marion Grey smiling at them.

'Coming.'

'Catch up with you later,' Paul said.

Hazel had been pleased to see him but she was relieved to escape his onslaught of information. Marion led the way into her private office. There was a pile of brightly wrapped presents on her desk. The patterns on the Christmas wrapping paper varied but the parcels were of uniform size and shape.

Marion glanced at her watch. 'Seven o'clock. I think we should wind things up now,' she told Hazel. 'Folk will have things to do on Christmas Eve.'

Hazel glanced at her. She was longing to ask what this most private person would be doing over Christmas but, for all she had known her for years, she did not feel close enough.

Marion must have read her mind. 'It will just be Maud and me this evening,' she said. 'My son and his wife will bring their new baby to see me tomorrow.'

'You have a son and ... and a...'

'Granddaughter.'

Hazel could not hide her astonishment. 'I didn't know that you ... you were...'

'Married?' Marion smile was restrained. 'I was. Very happily. Warren died in the outskirts of Berlin just weeks before the end of the war.'

'I'm so sorry.'

'My son was eighteen, in his last year at school. Maud moved in to help me and she's been with me ever since.'

Marion raised her black cigarette to her pillarbox-red lips and inhaled. A moment later she blew out a cloud of smoke that momentarily obscured her face. When the haze cleared Hazel saw that Marion's smile was quizzical.

'Do you find it difficult to imagine me as a grandmother?' she asked.

'Well...'

'It's all right. You needn't answer that.' She laughed softly. 'And, of course, I imagine that I have no need to tell you that this conversation has been strictly confidential. For years I couldn't talk about it. I suppose I became secretive. I wear my wedding ring on a chain around my neck.' She paused. 'Hazel…'

'Yes?'

'I have long suspected that you lost someone too. Am I correct?'

Hazel nodded assent.

'You must have been very young.'

'I was. And so was he.'

'Then for God's sake move on. I was more than blessed that I had our son. And now I have a loving daughter-in-law and a grandchild. And maybe there will be more. Don't condemn yourself to loneliness.'

They looked at each other. Neither spoke. Then Marion stubbed out her cigarette and indicated the Christmas presents on her desk.

'Will you help me give these out? They're all the same, except this one.' She put one parcel aside. 'This is for you. You can open it later.'

They handed out the parcels and watched as they were opened. Everybody had been given a set of superior stationery: a thick pad of creamy white writing paper and matching envelopes. Hazel heard someone whisper, 'She'll have got a job lot,' but nevertheless most acknowledged that it was a handsome gift.

After thanking Marion, the guests began to leave. Hazel could hear them laughing and shouting Happy Christmas to one another as they collected hats, coats, scarves and gloves from an empty storeroom that had been commandeered for the purpose and hurried down the flights of stairs. The men were the first to go.

Back in her office Marion handed Hazel her present. It was also a writing set, but it was contained in a zipped, soft brown leather case. Inside the case there was a black and silver ballpoint pen and a little compartment to keep postage stamps in.

'It's beautiful, Miss Grey. Thank you very much.'

Hazel stared at the notepad and envelopes. Without warning, another writing set sprang to mind. Instead of a leather case, she pictured a shiny pale blue cardboard folder with a Scottie dog wearing a tartan collar on the front.

Marion had opened Hazel's gift of a scarf clip. She smiled down at the dark blue oval decorated with a Grecian lady in profile. 'Thank you, Hazel. It's very nice. How did you know that I would prefer the dark blue background to the more usual pale blue?'

'I didn't know. It's what I preferred.'

'Clever girl. Now off you go. I'm going to help Maud clear up and head home to sit by the fire with my knitting.'

'Knitting?' Hazel knew she sounded shocked.

'I was joking.'

Marion refused Hazel's offer of help and insisted that she leave.

Paul was waiting for her in the entrance. 'Come for a drink?' he said.

His smile was cheerful but it didn't quite reach his eyes. Hazel sensed an underlying need for company.

'I'd like to,' she said, 'but my mother will be expecting me.'

'Surely she won't mind if you stay a little longer. After all, some office parties go on for hours.' Paul laughed. 'Tell her you met an old friend, someone you haven't seen for years. Just one drink, and I promise you I won't attempt to lead you astray.'

Hazel couldn't help laughing. 'Okay, just one drink. But where shall we go?'

'The County. That's probably the nearest place I can take a respectable young woman like you.'

The lounge bar in the comfortable old hotel was crowded but Paul managed to find them a couple of seats at a table tucked away in the corner. As soon as Hazel was seated he asked her what she would like to drink.

'I'm not sure. I don't really drink very much.'

'But when you go out with your boyfriend – I mean, you must have a boyfriend?' It was a question.

'Yes, I do.'

Hazel wasn't sure but she sensed he was disappointed. 'Well – what do you drink when you go out together?'

Hazel thought of the dinner dances she had been to with Kenneth. She would leave it to him to choose a bottle of wine. Apart from that, she and her mother would sometimes have a shandy when they brought home fish and chips, made with pale ale and lemonade, but she didn't know if it would be appropriate to ask for one in these surroundings.

'Maybe I should just have a cup of coffee,' she said.

'Nonsense,' Paul said. 'Will you trust me to

order something for you?'

'All right.'

He grinned. 'As it's the cocktail hour I shall get us both martinis.' He vanished in the direction of the bar.

Hazel had never had a martini and she was afraid she wouldn't like it, especially when Paul placed the drink before her and she saw the glass contained three olives speared on a cocktail stick.

'Drink up,' Paul said.

She sipped it gingerly.

'Well?' he asked. 'Do you like it?'

'I do.'

'Well, if you drink that up I'll get you another one.'

She shook her head. 'I don't think so.'

'Why not?'

'You promised me you wouldn't lead me astray, remember?'

They smiled at each other and settled back with their drinks. Paul was soon talking non-stop about his years in Germany, a short stopover he had made in Paris, and his decision to go to California.

'If all goes well I'll probably settle there,' he said. 'Or maybe not. The trouble is that kids like us were thoroughly unsettled when we were uprooted and sent away from our homes during the war. I've met other former evacuees who have found it just as difficult to adjust to the post-war world as I have. What about you? Did you like coming back here?'

'I don't know what else I could have done.'

'You were the brightest in our little group. You could have headed for London. You would have got a job easily, made good money, started a successful career.'

'My mother is here in Newcastle.'

'Are you close?'

'Yes, we are.'

Hazel felt uncomfortable. The questions were becoming too personal. Paul did not seem to notice her unease.

'You're lucky,' he said, staring into his drink. 'I was never close to my parents. Oh, they weren't cruel or neglectful or anything like that. It was just that they had married so young that they were still teenagers when I was born. They were so entirely wrapped up in each other that I think, secretly, they were rather relieved when I was sent off to the country.'

'Surely not.'

'Maybe I'm doing them an injustice, but they certainly never objected when I decided to stay on in Germany.'

Hazel was curious. 'Are you staying with them now?'

'No. When Dad was demobbed they decided to move to Australia. Cost them ten pounds each – assisted passage.' He laughed. 'They became what the Aussies call Ten-Pound Poms.'

'Will you visit them?'

'Maybe I will if they ask me. But now I'm going to have another drink. How about you?'

Hazel glanced at her wristwatch. 'Paul, I can't stay much longer.'

'Just five minutes more – like they say in the song.'

He began to sing the popular lyric and Hazel

gave in. 'All right. But hush, people are looking at us. And make mine lemonade.'

When Paul came back with the drinks Hazel asked him why he had chosen to come back to Newcastle to work when he could have gone anywhere, even London.

'I've been keeping in touch with Gavin. Gavin Pritchard. Do you remember him?'

'Of course. You and he were the liveliest members of our special group.'

'As a matter of fact I'm lodging with him. Gavin has a flat in a big old house in Tynemouth. He works for an insurance company; he's doing very well. Anyway, I've been staying there for a few weeks, so that's how I know about the invitation.'

'What invitation?'

'To the coronation celebrations in Withenmoor.'

'Oh, that.'

'Are you going to go?'

'I'm not sure.'

'Why not? Is it because you have other plans?'

'Well, there is that to consider. My boyfriend's mother is having a little party on Coronation Day. A few friends will watch the ceremony on television.'

'And no doubt your boyfriend would be peeved if you don't go?'

Hazel sighed. 'Yes, but it's more complicated than that. There's my mother. She's invited, too, but she won't go without my father and I doubt very much if he would enjoy himself at Kenneth's house.'

'So your mother will demand that you stay with her?'

'She would never demand it. She would probably tell me to get along and enjoy myself but she would be hurt.'

'Poor you. I wouldn't be in your shoes.'

Hazel was surprised to have confided in Paul like this. She glanced at him and saw that he seemed to be genuinely sympathetic. However, she decided to move the conversation away from her own problems.

'What about you? Are you going to go?'

'Well, I haven't had a personal invitation. I think the old dear I was billeted with passed away not long after the end of the war, but Gavin's been invited and he said it would be okay for me to go along with him. He can't stay for the whole week but we'll be there for most of the festivities.'

'So you're going to go?'

'I think so. It will be good to meet up with old pals. Do you know anyone who'll be there?'

'Well, Rita Bevan and Jimmy Doyle never left Withenmoor, but as for anyone else, the only one I've been in touch with is Irene Walker, and she hasn't decided yet.'

'I remember Irene. Pretty girl, but she had a bit of a temper on her. But you were pals with her, weren't you?'

'We were billeted together at Hillside House.'

'Oh, yes, the rest of us thought of you as the posh lot. Are you still friends with Irene?'

'We keep in touch.' Hazel smiled. 'She hasn't changed much, but basically, she's okay.'

'So, what's her problem?'

'What do you mean?'

'Why hasn't she decided yet whether to go to

Withenmoor? Boyfriend problems?'

Hazel didn't think Irene would be too pleased if she told Paul the details of her problems with Ray, so, as briefly as possible, she told him about Irene's burgeoning singing career and how a week in the country might interfere with her engagements. Paul was surprised.

'Irene Walker heading for the bright lights, eh? Is she any good? Have you heard her sing?'

'I have. She's very good. She deserves to succeed.'

'That's terrific. I wish her well.'

'I'll tell her. But now I really must go.'

Paul rose reluctantly and led the way to the door. He paused before they stepped out into the cold night air.

'Let me know when you make your mind up,' he said. 'You can leave a message with Maud at the office.'

'I will.'

Hazel thanked him for the drinks and they crossed the road together to the Central Station. Hazel joined the queue at the bus stop; Paul was going to get the train to the coast. He had already turned to leave her when he stopped and came back.

'I nearly forgot,' he said. 'What about Carol Clark? She stayed with you at Hillside House, didn't she? I was quite smitten with her but she was a bit stand-offish. Do you know where she is now?'

'Yes, I do.'

He frowned; perhaps he was puzzled by Hazel's subdued response. 'Do you ever see her?'

'Now and then.'

Her bus had arrived and the queue began to move forwards. Paul caught at her arm.

'Do you know if Carol will be going back for the celebrations?'

'It's not a matter of going back. She's already there.'

'What do you mean?'

'Paul, I've got to go.'

Hazel disengaged her arm and stepped up onto the bus's platform. The conductor rang the bell and the bus pulled away. *Just in time*, Hazel thought as she made her way to the last vacant seat. She really couldn't have borne to talk to Paul about the path Carol's life had taken. It would have taken too long.

Hazel put her key in the lock, let herself in and was surprised by an unfamiliar sound. Laughter. She closed the door and stood in the darkness of the narrow passageway. A soft glow from the street lamp fell through the fanlight. *Of course, it's the wireless,* she thought. *They're listening to some comedy programme.* But her father hardly ever listened to the wireless; he thought most of the programmes were rubbish and did not find any of the comedians funny. Not even Tommy Handley.

She stuffed her gloves in her pockets, unbuttoned her coat, took it off and hung it up on one of the hooks on the wall. Ahead of her a narrow beam of light cut through the dimness. She looked round to see that her mother was standing at the living room door. At the same moment there was another burst of laughter and this time Hazel definitely recognised her father's voice – and one other. A voice that seemed familiar but that she hadn't heard for a very long time.

Her mother looked bemused.

'Is someone here?' Hazel asked.

'Yes, pet, you've got a visitor.'

'And did I hear Dad laughing?'

'You did.'

'But what ... who...?'

'You'd better come in.'

Hazel did not know what, or rather who, she was expecting to see, and for a moment she stared in bewilderment at the well-dressed young woman who was sitting at the table drinking tea. Bill Stafford sat opposite their guest, looking through a collection of colour photographs which were scattered across the flower patterned oilcloth. Hazel looked from one to the other in bewilderment.

The stranger looked up and sprang to her feet.

'Hazel!' she exclaimed. 'It's so good to see you!'

Hazel stared at her. The face was familiar; she should know who this was, but somehow the voice was different.

'Don't say I've changed that much,' her old friend said.

Suddenly Hazel realised who this was.

'Mavis!' she said. 'No, you haven't changed. I was thrown by the accent.'

'I know. That's what everybody's been saying. They say I sound like a Yank, but of course it's Canadian.'

'Sit down, both of you,' Joan said. 'I'll make a fresh pot of tea.'

Her father looked up and smiled distractedly,

then returned his attention to the photographs. Hazel looked at Mavis questioningly.

'I brought these to show you,' Mavis said. 'The lakes, the mountains, the city, the college I attended, the school where I work, the house where I live and the house we hope to buy, and the police station. A sort of snapshot of my life in Canada.'

'Why the police station?' Hazel asked.

'That's where Earl works.'

'Earl?'

Hazel's father looked up and grinned. 'Your old pal is going to marry a Mountie. What do you think of that?'

Hazel stared at her father. She had no idea why Mavis's photographs had put him in such a good mood.

'Look,' he said as he pushed one of the photographs towards her. 'That's him in his uniform. Fine figure of a lad, isn't he?'

Hazel looked at the photograph. 'He's very handsome.'

Mavis looked pleased. 'Well, the uniform helps, but he's not bad, is he? I wish you could have met him, but we couldn't afford for us both to come over.'

'He looks like a film star,' Hazel's father said. 'Pity about the horses.'

'What do you mean, Dad?' Hazel asked.

'Mavis told me the Mounties stopped using horses for regular duties before the war. Horses are just for ceremonial occasions now.'

Hazel's mother came back to the table with the teapot and an extra cup and saucer. Hazel shot her an enquiring glance. Her mother looked at her father and then shook her head as if to say, I don't know what's got into him.

Mavis didn't notice their bewilderment. 'Amazing, your dad wanting to be a Mountie, isn't it?'

'*What?*' Hazel said, too shocked to worry about polite speech.

'Yes. As a kid he was fascinated by stories of the Klondike gold rush. He would buy the ha'penny story papers. You know, stirring tales about heroes and villains, and that led on to stories about the Mounties. He loved the films. Of course all the movies were black and white in those days, so he told me he just had to imagine the red serge jackets and the brown leather riding boots.'

'He told you all this?'

'Yes. My photographs set him off.'

'I still remember some of those stories,' her father said. He sat back and stared into the mid-distance. '*The Golden River, The Haunted Mine, The Mountie Gets His Man,* then my favourite, *Scarlet Riders.* I was just a little lad, but I used to dream of going to live in Canada and joining the Royal Mounted Police.'

'You never told me,' Hazel's mother said softly.

'What would have been the point? When I left school there was a war on, and by the time it was over I was working to help support my widowed mother. Real life set in. The dreams faded.'

'Oh, Bill, I'm sorry.'

He looked at her and smiled. 'It wasn't your fault, Joan. And besides, it was just as well, wasn't it?'

'What do you mean?'

'If I'd gone off to Canada I would never have met you.'

Hazel stared at her parents. Her mother was shaken to the core, but her father gave no indication of having noticed her reaction. He turned his attention back to the photographs and arranged them in a neat pile, then handed them to Hazel. 'There you are, lass. Have a look at them. I think I'll be off to the Hare and Hounds.'

'Bill, it's Christmas Eve,' Hazel's mother said.

'I know that, but you three lasses will want to have a good old chinwag. It's best if I leave you in peace.'

He went through to the hall to collect his cap and overcoat, and a moment later they heard the front door closing behind him.

It seemed nobody knew what to say. Hazel and Mavis looked at each other and laughed. Then, 'Where shall we start?' Hazel asked.

'Shall I talk you through the photographs?'

For a while Hazel and her mother passed the photographs to each other while Mavis described what they were seeing. When they came to the picture of Earl in his uniform Hazel asked, 'So when are you getting married?'

'In the summer when the school's on holiday.'

'You're a teacher?'

'No, a school secretary.'

'Mavis, why did you stop writing to me?'

Her old friend couldn't meet her eye. 'I can't really explain it, and I'm so sorry. It's just that my life changed so much – I had an exciting new life in a new world. My old life, the old world, sort of faded.'

'With everyone in it, it seems.'

'Hazel,' her mother said, 'you're not going to quarrel with your old friend, are you?'

After a moment's silence Hazel said, 'No, I'm not. I shouldn't have said that, Mavis. I'm sorry. And I'm glad you've come to see us, really I am.'

'It's the first time I've been home and it'll probably be the last. I just wanted to see everyone before I got married.'

'What about your parents?'

'What do you mean?'

'Are they happy that you won't be seeing them again?'

'Earl and I want them to come and live with us. Our new house will be big enough to give them their own little apartment. They've already been out to visit us a couple of times and I think they like the idea. My mother's sister is there, of course.'

'So you'll be cutting all ties with your old life?'

'I suppose so.' Mavis shifted uncomfortably in her chair. 'But what about you?' she asked. 'What are your plans? Before you came back your mother told me you had a very nice boyfriend.'

Hazel glanced at her mother in exasperation.

'Don't look at me like that,' her mother said. 'It's natural for Mavis to want to know whether you plan to get wed or not.'

'And do you?' Hazel asked. 'Plan to get married?'

'Not in the immediate future.'

Hazel knew this was an unsatisfactory answer, but how could she tell Mavis that Kenneth and she had never really discussed marriage and that both their mothers were getting impatient with the situation? That wasn't how normal people behaved, was it? The magazine stories and the films that her mother loved best usually had a happy ever after ending. *And I'm not providing one for her,* Hazel thought.

'Oh, well,' Mavis said. She was clearly disconcerted. 'At least you ... I mean, your mother said you really enjoy your work.'

'I do.' They were on safer ground. 'I work for a variety of businesses and I meet some interesting people.'

'But do you never feel you'd like to get a permanent position rather than moving around all the time?'

Oh dear, Hazel thought. *I think I've just failed another test.* She smiled. 'This way I'm always learning something new.'

'They can't all be interesting – the places you're sent to.'

'No, they're not. But at least I know that I will soon be moving on.'

'I see.'

Hazel could tell that Mavis, on the verge of marrying and settling down herself, didn't understand at all, and she steered the conversation back to Mavis's wedding plans.

A short while later Mavis said she had better get back to her parents' house. They hugged each other and promised to keep in touch, but somehow Hazel could not see that happening. She was pleased to have seen the girl she had been best friends with when they were at school, but too many years had passed. They were both very different from the little girls they had been at the outbreak of the war.

Chapter Eighteen

December 1952, New Year's Eve

'I'm not so sure about this, Irene.' Leonard Walker sounded worried.

Irene was standing before the large mirror on the wall above the sideboard, applying another layer of lipstick. She glanced beyond her own reflection and saw her father staring at her. She turned to face him. 'What's the matter, Dad?'

'The Apollo's not the place it used to be when your mam and I used to go dancing there.'

She smiled at him. 'I know. It's all rock'n'roll now instead of the Charleston.'

He smiled. 'Less of your cheek!' But his anxious expression soon returned. 'What do you think, Edie?'

'The world moves on, Len. When we were Irene's age our parents probably felt the same about the new ways as you do now.'

'I don't mean new ways, Edie. I mean the Apollo itself. It's gone downhill. There's an altogether different crowd goes there now.'

Irene turned back to the mirror and powdered her nose. Ray would be here any minute and she wanted to be ready. He was always going on about having to be professional. When she was satisfied she turned to face her parents. 'What do you think?'

Edie surveyed the wide-skirted navy blue dress scattered with a pattern of white and yellow daisies. 'You look lovely, pet. You don't half suit navy, and that wide white belt really shows off your waist.'

Her father shook his head. 'And exactly how many petticoats have you got on? You might as well be wearing a crinoline. But, no, your mam's right, you look lovely.'

Irene looked at her parents. Her mother was wearing a new powder-blue dress and her father had on his best suit. 'Are you going to the club?' she asked them.

'No, we thought we'd see the year in at home,' her mother said. She gestured towards some food and drink set out on the table. 'One or two of the neighbours might pop in. We're getting a bit old for gallivanting.'

'Speak for yourself!' her husband said.

They smiled at each other but Irene sensed some sort of nervous tension.

'Do you want me to come home for midnight?' she asked. 'My act will be over long before then.'

'No, that's all right,' her mother said quickly. 'You stay on and enjoy yourself.'

Her father's worried look had returned. 'All the same, I wish you weren't going to the Apollo.'

The doorbell rang: Ray had arrived. Her mother picked up her own fur coat from where it had been waiting on an armchair and helped Irene into it. Then she handed her her vanity case. Ray was as smartly dressed as usual in yet another new suit and an expensive camel coat. He consulted a flashy gold wristwatch.

'Half past seven,' he told them, although the time was plain enough to see on the mantel clock. 'Doors open at eight. We'd better get a move on.'

'Ray?' her father began.

'Yes, squire?'

'The Apollo...'

'What about it?'

'I've heard it can get rough.'

'Have you?' Ray looked as though this really surprised him.

'Yes, I have,' Len said curtly and Irene could see her father beginning to lose his usual amused tolerance of Ray.

Perhaps Ray sensed this, too, because he adopted a concerned and reassuring tone. 'I can see you're worried about Irene's safety and that's natural. But I assure you I'll take great care of her. I wouldn't let anyone harm one hair on her pretty little head.'

The atmosphere inside the car was an unpleasant mixture of cigarette smoke and Ray's powerful new aftershave. He was humming a tuneless refrain as he drove which seemed to indicate that he was in a good mood. When they stopped at some traffic lights he reached for Irene's hand.

'You're very quiet,' he said. 'What's up?'

'Is Dad right about the Apollo?'

'What do you mean?'

'Don't play games, Ray. You must have seen how worried he was.'

The lights changed and Ray set off again. 'I did, and I told him not to worry. I'll look after you. And, Irene, this one's good money. You won't regret it.'

He resumed his tuneless humming, at the same time tapping out a meaningless rhythm on the steering wheel with his fingers. Irene turned her head to look out of the window. Tall Victorian dwellings rose on each side, giving the street the appearance of a dismal canyon. The old gas lamps had not been replaced in this part of town and each one revealed a small area of dilapidation.

Irene sank back into her seat and pulled the collar of her mother's fur coat up around her ears. She closed her eyes and took comfort from the lingering aroma of Californian Poppy.

The doors were not open and a crowd had already gathered in the draughty street outside the Apollo. They were boisterous and noisy. Irene wondered if they had come straight from the pub. A group of lads gave piercing wolf whistles whenever a couple of girls arrived to join the throng. Many of the girls had beehive hairdos and wore stiletto shoes with dangerously thin heels. Irene wondered uneasily whether they would appreciate her wholesome girl-next-door look.

Ray slowed down as they approached and then stopped and gazed at them thoughtfully.

'What is it?' Irene asked.

'Well, I was planning to draw up on the stroke of eight and have you arrive in style.'

'So?'

'From the look of it, they'll be too eager to get in from the cold. As soon as the doors open they'll make a rush for it. They won't stop to let you make a grand entrance.'

'So what are we going to do?'

'I'll park round behind and we'll slip in the back door. That's probably a better plan anyway.'

'Why?'

'From the looks of some of those lads, it's probably best not to let them get a glimpse of this car. Don't want it to be nicked, do we?'

'Oh, definitely not. We don't want anything to happen to your car!'

Ray glanced at her irritably. 'Don't be sarky, Irene. And for God's sake put a smile on your face. If you're going to make it in show business you've got to learn to be a proper little trouper. Don't let the success you've had so far go to your head. You've got a long way to go.'

'Thanks.'

'And never forget how lucky you are to have me to guide you.'

In spite of the coolness between them, Ray still came round to help Irene out and hand her her vanity case before locking the car.

'This way,' he said.

There were no street lamps in the lane. An exhausted looking moon cast a very pale light. Ray put an arm under her elbow and guided her over the greasy cobbles. The yard behind the dance hall was full of overflowing waste bins. Suddenly there was a flash of green eyes and a startled cat leapt from one of the bins and vanished into the dark. Irene trembled with fright, and Ray put an arm round her and pulled her close.

'Don't worry baby,' he said. 'A black cat crossing your path is supposed to bring you good luck.'

Irene had no idea how he could have known the

cat was black. All they had seen was a dark streak which had vanished in seconds. But, warmed a little by his newly caring tone, she turned to him and smiled.

'That's my girl. Now let's get inside.'

Ray knocked on a heavy wooden door and a few moments later a burly man in a dinner jacket opened it and stared out suspiciously. 'Ray?' he said. 'Why come in this way?'

'Miss Walker was a little concerned about the behaviour of the crowd waiting at the main entrance. A little overexcited, don't you think?'

'Really?' the man said. He looked her up and down. 'Think yourself too good for us, do you?'

'No, of course not,' Irene said. She turned to Ray and frowned in annoyance. Why had he said that it was her idea to come in the back door?

'Miss Walker is quite the rising star, you know,' Ray said.

'Oh, yeah? Then how come she was available to fill in for the opening spot at such short notice?'

'Because you're paying good money, Barney.'

'I was forced to, wasn't I? There was nobody else to be had. You struck a hard bargain for some kid I've never heard of.'

Irene, feeling thoroughly humiliated, tried to turn and flee, but Ray gripped her arm.

'Give her a break, Barney. She's just starting out, and once you hear her sing you'll know you've done the right thing.'

'Don't worry,' Barney replied. 'I'm hardly going to turn her away when there's no chance of getting anyone else. Not on New Year's Eve.' He stepped back and opened the door a little wider. 'Hawway

341

in, then. But she'd better be as good as you've made out, or you and me won't be doing business again.'

The lino-covered passageways behind the ballroom were narrow and maze-like. Irene was reminded of the House That Jack Built in the pleasure park at the seaside. Inside this decrepit fairground attraction there was a maze leading past distorting mirrors and on to a collection of very old waxworks depicting long-gone royalty, a weary Hiawatha in a drooping feathered head-dress and a child-sized model in a kilt and tam-o'-shanter holding a placard saying: *Rob Roy as a Boy.* The final chamber held an exhibition of old instruments of torture.

Irene tried to thrust these images from her mind as Barney stopped to open a door. No torture chamber; just a small, squalid room smelling faintly of mould.

'There you are, miss. It's not exactly the star dressing room, but then, you're not exactly a star, are you? Now I've got things to do before the group arrives.' Barney hurried away.

Irene gazed around the dimly lit room and her shoulders drooped. It was hard to tell what the pattern on the faded carpet had been. Splintery floorboards showed around the edges. The panes of the high window were painted black, probably a leftover from the days of the blackout. There was a curtained-off area for changing, a sagging arm-chair and a hard wooden chair set in front of the wooden board which served as a dressing table. A shadeless light bulb hung from a ceiling fitting.

Ray couldn't help but sense her dejection. He

brushed past her and pressed a switch on the wall beside the large mirror. The light bulbs framing the mirror sprang to life and he turned to smile at her. 'There you are. Plenty of light to help you make up your pretty little face.'

Irene cringed inwardly. 'Perhaps you haven't noticed,' she said, 'but my pretty little face already has make-up on.'

Ray sighed. 'Of course I've noticed, but you'll need to touch it up, won't you? And primp your hair a bit. Are you going to take your coat off?'

'I'm cold.'

'Don't worry, you'll warm up once the night gets going. Do you want me to rustle up a cup of tea or coffee?'

'Okay. Coffee. But wait a minute, Ray.'

'What is it?'

'You didn't tell me I was the supporting act.'

'Didn't I?'

'No. Neither did you say I was a last-minute fill-in.'

'It's not important. You've got the work. That's all that matters.'

'So who is this group that Barney mentioned?'

'A pop group. Kat and the Teds. That's Cat with a K.'

'I've never heard of them.'

'They're just starting up. Local kids. A good-looking girl vocalist and three lads. Guitar, drums and keyboard. The lads dress like Teddy boys. I'm told they're quite good. They write their own stuff and they should go far if they get the right management. Now I'll go and get your tea.'

'*Coffee!*' Irene called after him and sank down onto the hard chair by the dressing table.

She looked at herself moodily in the mirror. She knew she shouldn't be making a fuss. She knew by heart the many stories about the struggles some of the big stars had had when they were starting out. The trouble was, she didn't feel as though she was getting anywhere. She didn't want to go on forever being a copy of Doris Day. She wished Ray would let her introduce something new into her act, then maybe one day she would be a star in her own right with people writing songs just for her.

The coffee was bitter. She made a face when she tasted it and Ray said, 'Wait a mo, this will improve it.'

He took a leather-covered hip flask out of his trouser pocket and poured a few drops into her cup.

'What's that?' she asked.

'Irish whisky. Drink up, that should put a smile on your face.'

Irene wasn't too sure whether she liked the taste but it certainly warmed her up and she relaxed a little.

'Better get ready,' Ray said. 'The doors are open and they're coming in. All ready for a great night out. Listen. The band has started up. They'll be calling you soon.'

Irene slipped off her coat. 'Where shall I put it?' she asked. She looked round the room and frowned.

'What's the problem?'

'It's a good coat. Anyone coming in here might

nick it.'

'No one will come in here. Why should they? But give it to me. I'll hang it up behind the curtain.'

While Ray did so she sat down and leaned towards the mirror to touch up her make-up and tease her hair into place. She stood up and faced Ray.

'You look terrific!' he said. 'The spitting image of the star herself.'

Irene wished he hadn't said that but as he had obviously thought it would please her she smiled her thanks.

A moment later a younger version of Barney appeared in the doorway. 'Dad says you're on now, Miss Walker.'

Barney's son had the same heavy build as his father. He was the kind of man Irene's father would say would be useful in a fight. With that thought in mind, she followed him along the maze of corridors until they reached a door that led up to the stage.

Irene stood in the wings and looked out at what she could see of the dance floor. The band was playing a medley of the latest hits and the dancing had started. Round the sides of the floor, sharply dressed young men wearing jackets with velvet collars and crêpe-soled shoes stood with pint glasses of beer and called out to their mates or any passing girl they fancied. Many of the girls were dancing with each other and Irene didn't blame them.

Ray had vanished as soon as he had given Sydney, the bandleader, her music and Irene was left wondering what would happen next. Then the band stopped playing and she could hear some of the dancers shuffling back to their tables. The noise level rose. Sydney turned to look at her and gave her a wan smile, then he stepped forward and spoke into a microphone.

'And now, ladies and gentlemen,' he said, 'I want you to give a warm welcome to our new songstress, Miss Irene Walker.'

A mocking cheer went up. The bandleader waited for silence but the noise level increased. He sighed, raised his eyes to heaven and gestured for Irene to join him centre stage. There was a moment's silence, a smattering of applause and then a burst of laughter from a group of girls.

'Get her!' one of them hooted. 'What *does* she think she looks like!'

'Where do you think they found her?' another girl screeched.

'The ark, probably!'

By now more of the dancers were laughing then suddenly one of the lads shouted, 'Shut up and give the lass a chance!'

In a brief hush, the band leader said quietly, 'Look straight ahead. Don't look at them. Ready?'

Irene nodded and the band started playing 'Lullaby of Broadway'.

At first all went well. The dancing resumed and although nobody appeared to be listening to her at least they weren't complaining. In between numbers, Sydney said, 'You'll have to get used to this sort of thing, pet. Sometimes I wonder why they bother to have a vocalist in a dump like this. But it's the same in the classy nightclubs, we're just background noise.'

Irene was halfway through 'Moonlight Bay' when a fight broke out at the back of the hall.

'Keep going,' Sydney hissed. 'Barney and his lad will sort them out.'

Despite Sydney's advice not to look at them, Irene couldn't help glancing in the direction of the disturbance. The scuffle was soon over and she saw Barney and his son dragging two lads out by their collars. Just before they vanished through the door, she caught a glimpse of a man in a dark overcoat and a trilby hat with the brim pulled down to shade most of his face. He obviously hadn't come to dance and she wondered if he was a member of one of the criminal gangs. Perhaps he was in some sort of protection racket.

'Irene! Get on with it!' Sydney said urgently.

She turned to smile her apology and finished her song. There was no applause and no fans standing right in front of the stage to gaze up at her adoringly. *Never mind, those days will come,* she told herself.

'Game for one more?' Sydney asked.

She nodded.

'Okay, let's do "Bushel and a Peck".'

Perhaps it was the upbeat rhythm that brought more to the dance floor and raised everyone's spirits even higher. Soon the high spirits turned to irritation, then anger, and there was a great deal of yelling and pushing. And then the fighting broke out again. This time the trouble was not confined to the back of the hall. Individual skirmishes started on the dance floor itself.

On Sydney's instructions, Irene and the band

347

kept going, even though not one soul could have been listening to them. And then objects started flying – beer bottles, tankards and even shoes. It was obviously too much for Barney and his son to handle and they seemed to have vanished from the floor.

'He'll be calling the cops,' Sydney said, and at that moment a heavy glass pint tankard flew up onto the stage and caught him on the temple. Irene noticed the blood streaming down his face before she saw that her dress had been drenched with beer. Behind her the band were packing up and leaving.

'Time to go,' Sydney said. Cupping her elbow, he hurried her off the stage.

The musicians had packed up and vanished into the maze of corridors, leaving Irene to make her way back along the dimly lit corridors to her dressing room. Where was Ray? Thoroughly disorientated, she opened the wrong door and found herself in a larger dressing room. Ray was there with Kat and the Teds. At least, she guessed that was who they must be. They all looked what people called 'cool'. They smiled at her.

'Rough out there?' Kat asked.

'Bedlam.'

'Do you think Barney will get it under control?'

'I have no idea, but I'm not going to wait and find out. Ray? Can we go now?'

'Well...'

'*Please!*'

'What about you guys?' Ray asked the group.

'We'll hang on a bit longer then he'll have to pay us, won't he?' one of the boys said.

They all laughed.

'That's the spirit,' Ray told them. 'Now, like I was saying, you need someone professional to look out for you. Someone who knows the business.'

He had forgotten all about her. Irene backed out of the room and fled. She could hear the pandemonium in the hall behind her and also the distant clanging of the bells of police cars. She found her room and rushed in to get her coat and her vanity case. The vanity case was no longer on the dressing table. She tore the curtain aside to discover that the coat had gone too. She looked around, desperately hoping that she had made a mistake and that this was the wrong room. But then she saw her empty coffee cup on the dressing table with a faint smear of her lipstick on the rim.

Irene felt like weeping. Her vanity case with all her carefully chosen make-up and, much more important, her mother's coat. She was under no illusion that she would ever get them back. She wanted to go, but Ray was too busy talking to the pop group. No doubt he would be persuading them to sign up with him. Feeling utterly miserable, she found her way to the back door, wondering if she would be able to find her way to the nearest bus stop. Her dress was soaking and her hair was plastered over her forehead in damp locks. She smelled like a brewery and she was shivering with cold.

She had almost reached the door when she became aware that someone was coming up behind her. 'Ray?' she said, turning hopefully.

But it wasn't Ray. It was the man in the dark

overcoat and trilby.

She opened her mouth to scream but he shook his head. He stepped past her to open the door. 'Wait here, Irene,' he said softly. 'I'll take you home.'

She stood on the step in the doorway and watched him walk away. The air was frosty and she wrapped her arms around herself to try to stop the shivering. She couldn't understand why she was waiting instead of turning and going back to find Ray. Why wasn't she terrified? The stranger knew her name, but that didn't mean that he knew her. The bandleader had introduced her before she started singing. He hadn't sounded in the least threatening, but gangsters could be deceptive; she knew that from the gangster movies that she loved.

And then she remembered where she had seen him before. Or thought she did. Surely this was the same man she had glimpsed talking to her father in the station. If he knew her father he might want to help her. But it was more than that. Something stirred in her memory. An impossible thought began to take shape, but before it surfaced she saw car headlights sweep along the lane. The car stopped and a figure emerged from the gloom and crossed the yard towards her. He pushed his hat back and looked up and smiled.

'Terry!' she gasped. She fell into her brother's arms.

Terry made her put his coat on and settled her in his car. When he got in he didn't start up straight away; they just sat and looked at each other. Then Irene dropped her head in her hands and began to sob.

'Don't cry, Irene. You're safe now. It's over.'

She looked at him angrily. 'That's not the reason I'm crying. It's seeing you!'

'You're not pleased to see me?'

'Don't make a joke of it, Terry. All these years I thought you were dead and now you turn up out of the blue and expect me to be happy about it. Where have you been?'

'All over the place, but in London mostly.'

'What have you been doing?'

'This and that.'

Suddenly her rage boiled over. 'You let me believe that you'd been killed in the war! In my mind I thought you were some kind of hero.'

'I'm sorry.'

'Sorry isn't good enough! You owe me an explanation.'

Terry sighed. 'Yes, I suppose I do. I was called up but I never reported for duty. I'm no hero, Irene. I'm a deserter.'

'Why? Are you a conscientious objector?'

'No, I've no such principles. I'm a coward.'

Irene was shocked. She had no idea what to say. Her beloved brother, who she had idolised all her young life, was admitting to cowardice.

Terry turned away from her and started the car. After a moment Irene asked wretchedly, 'Did Mam and Dad know?'

'They couldn't fail to after the military police turned up at their door.'

'They let me believe you were missing in action.

Didn't they trust me enough to tell me the truth?'

'They were protecting you. It was best you knew nothing.'

'I saw you and Dad at the station.'

Terry was startled. 'When?'

'Just before Christmas.'

'You recognised me?'

'No, but now I know it must have been you. Dad looked worried sick.'

'He was. If they catch me it will mean prison. That's why I never went home. I came up to Newcastle on business now and then and dropped them a note to let them know I was all right, but if I'd been caught with them it could have meant prison for Dad too.'

'But you're taking me home now?'

'I was there earlier.'

'What's changed?'

'Nothing's changed. After I caught up with Dad in the station I got homesick. It's been a long time. And you know... New Year ... getting older and all that... I thought it would be nice to see the year in with them.'

'So that's why they decided to stay in tonight. It was a lie about neighbours dropping in.' Irene remembered thinking that her mother had looked tense. 'Did you intend to stay until I came home?'

'I was going to slip away straight after midnight.'

'Great!'

'Irene, I've told you, we thought it much better that you were kept in ignorance.'

'Thanks a lot!'

'But I still intended to see you, although I

didn't plan that you should see me.'

'What do you mean?'

'Why do you think I was at the Apollo? The plan was that I should slip in and see my kid sister wowing the crowd and then go back and tell Mam and Dad how great you were.'

'Well, that plan came to nothing, didn't it?' To her chagrin Irene felt the tears begin to well up again. She stifled a sob.

'There's a clean handkerchief in one of my pockets. Feel free to snivel all over it.'

Irene found the handkerchief and dabbed at her eyes. She examined it in the dim moonlight streaming through the windscreen. 'I've smeared mascara all over it.'

'Don't worry. And don't fret about what happened tonight. That manager of yours was an idiot to take you there. You've got to dump him.'

She sighed. 'And I suppose you'll tell me I should settle for life behind the cosmetics counter at Brownlow's?'

'Not at all. You've got real talent. You're streets ahead of some of the singers I've seen in the London clubs. But I think you should give up this Doris Day act.'

'And what should I do?'

'Keep your job at Brownlow's for a while and start singing lessons. Find the best teacher you can. And perhaps you should find a dance class too. Would you like that?'

'Sure I would, if I could afford it.'

'Don't worry about that. I'll take care of everything.'

'Can you afford to?'

'And some.'

Irene looked at him. 'Are you a thief, Terry? Is that what your business is?'

'No, I keep on the right side of the law. I deal in surplus stock. I started with a load of blankets that the army no longer had any need for. I'd been working – odd jobs – and I used every last penny I had and sold them at a profit. Then I went on to army and air force hats, scarves and gloves, anything I thought I could find a market for, and soon a whole new world of trading opened up. I dodge about a bit, got to keep ahead of the competition, but it's all completely above board. The only thing they could nick me for is being a deserter.'

'Don't you ever think of giving yourself up? Get it over with and start life afresh. Then you could come home.'

Terry stared ahead, frowning a little as if he were trying to remember the way. Irene thought he wasn't going to answer, but then he sighed deeply and said, 'I've thought about it, often. But it's no use. I don't think I could survive jail.' He turned to glance at her with a half smile. 'I'm a coward, remember.'

Irene wanted to scream at him not to make a joke of it, but she realised that, no matter what had happened during the years since they had last been together, her brother had not changed. He had always been a joker and always would be.

'Here we are, then,' he said. The car had stopped.

Irene half opened the door and looked out. They were in a back lane. 'This isn't where we live,' she said.

'No, but it's not far. I couldn't park outside our house, could I?'

'You still call it *our* house.'

'Yeah, it's still my home, even though I'll probably never live here again.' He sounded resigned.

'Terry!' she said suddenly.

'What is it?'

'Mam's fur coat! Someone at the Apollo pinched it.'

'I'll get her another one.'

'As easy as that?'

'Yes, as easy as that. Now come on, let's get home.'

Terry held her hand and they hurried down the lanes they had played in as children, then entered the house by the back door. Her parents were sitting by the fire. They took one look at Irene and rose from their seats in shock.

'For God's sake,' her father said. 'What happened?'

By the time Irene had stripped off, pulled a wet brush through her hair and washed herself to get rid of the smell of beer, then changed into a comfortable pair of grey slacks and a red sweater, Terry had told their parents what had happened at the Apollo.

Edie gave them each a plate with sandwiches and sausage rolls.

'You told me some of the neighbours might call in,' Irene said. 'This was all for Terry, wasn't it?'

'I'm sorry, pet. We thought it best to keep it to ourselves.'

'Terry told me.'

Her parents glanced at each other. They looked distressed, but Irene couldn't stop herself

'What would you have done if I'd come home before midnight?'

'I would have made a quick exit,' Terry said. 'But let it go now, Irene. We're all here together now and I don't know when I'll see you again.'

Irene nodded mutely and sat down. For a while no one spoke. Terry took a silver cigarette case from his pocket, opened it and offered it to Edie and Len. Edie smiled. 'I've given up,' she said. 'Irene persuaded me.'

'Did she, now?' Terry said and winked at Irene. 'That was good advice. What about you, Dad?'

'I don't smoke at home. It's not fair to your mam.'

Terry sighed and put his cigarettes away without taking one. Then, perhaps remembering the day Irene had told him she had given her cigarettes to Ted the gardener, he said, 'What was it like at Withenmoor?'

'You've been there. You saw the house. You met Miss Forsyth and the other girls.'

'Just the once. You seemed happy enough.'

'I was. Apart from missing Mam and Dad, that is. Miss Forsyth couldn't have been more kind. Hazel was pure gold. We still keep in touch.'

'What about the other two? Carol and Bridget, wasn't it? What happened to them?'

'Carol is still living in Withenmoor.'

'Was she Miss Forsyth's niece?'

'No, that was Bridget.'

'And what happened to her?'

356

'She drowned in the tarn.'

Terry looked shocked and Irene felt the old familiar feelings of suspicion and rage rise within her. She fought to control them because, as Hazel had reminded her countless times over the years, nobody knew what had really happened that day. They had all had to take Carol's word for it and there was no reason not to. Except for what happened afterwards.

The fire crackled and the heavy old mantel clock ticked solemnly. Edie filled their plates and Len said it was time for a drink. Then someone rang the bell and knocked on the door at the same time.

Terry stood up and Irene grabbed his plate of sandwiches before they fell to the floor. 'The cops!' he said. 'I shouldn't have come here. I'll have to go.' He made for the back door.

'Don't go out into the lane,' Len said. 'If it is the cops, they'll be waiting for you.'

'Coalhouse,' his mother said.

'They'll find me.'

'It's all you can do,' Len said. 'Get going.'

He snatched Terry's overcoat and hat from the chair by the table and thrust them into his arms. As soon as Terry had slipped out, Len went to answer the door. Irene and Edie held their breath.

'Don't think you're coming in here,' they heard him say. 'Irene doesn't want anything more to do with you.'

It was Ray. They heard him protesting but Len slammed the door in his face and came back into the room. 'Go and get your brother,' he told Irene. 'No doubt he'll be complaining about what

357

the coal dust has done to his Savile Row suit.'

The intimate mood had dissipated. 'I suppose I should think about going now,' Terry said. 'Here, Dad, take this.'

He reached into the inside pocket of his overcoat and brought out a bulging envelope. Irene suddenly realised where all her father's 'bonuses' had come from.

'It's too much, lad,' her father said.

'No, Dad, it could never be enough. I've let you down badly and this is the least I can do.'

'Well, at least take a drink, then.'

Len poured some sherry for Irene and Edie and whisky for Terry and himself. They stood and looked at each other, and tried to smile.

Then Edie said, 'Listen.'

The ships on the Tyne had begun to sound their hooters, and a moment later the church bells began to ring. Then, unhurriedly, majestically, the old mantel clock whirred into life and began to chime. They waited until the count of twelve was fading and raised their glasses.

'Happy New Year,' Len said sombrely. 'God knows when we'll meet again.'

Chapter Nineteen

Rita watched as Molly stirred the broth and moved her foot gently to disengage the black and white cat that was trying to twine itself around her leg.

'Come here, puss,' Rita said. She picked the cat up and dumped it in the basket. 'Stay there with your babies.' Ever since she had come here all those years ago it seemed there had always been a basketful of kittens of one sort or another.

She returned to the table and set out a bottle of sherry, a bottle of port wine and a couple of bottles of beer. Then she checked the plates of food. Thick slices of home-made bread, boiled-ham sandwiches, a dish of pease pudding, cheese straws, sausage rolls, mince pies and the remains of a large Christmas cake.

Molly turned and smiled. 'I hope you're hungry, lass. You've got enough there to feed an army.'

'Well, you never know who's going to drop in, do you?'

'I can tell you one who will come, for sure.'

'Who?'

'Angus Fairley with his blessed pipes. It's enough to wake the dead when he gets going.'

'With any luck he'll be half seas over by the time he gets up the hill.'

'Aye, they give him a drink or two at every house he calls at in the hopes he'll stop playing.'

Rita sat down at the table and looked pensively at the spread. 'We never did this at home, you know.'

'What? Don't folk go first footing in Newcastle?'

'Yes, they do. It's just nobody ever wanted to call at our house. There was never any food and Mam and Dad used to sit and drink together until they could barely stand. Then they would start fighting, falling all over the place, and hitting out at anyone who got in the way.'

'You mean you?'

'Aye.'

'Well, those days are long gone, pet, and you know your future is going to be full of happy days.'

They glanced at the clock. 'Just a minute to go,' Molly said.

Rita hurried to the door. As soon as the church bells echoed up from the valley below there was a loud rapping. She pulled the door open and Jimmy Doyle walked in bearing a basket containing bread, salt, a lump of coal and a bottle of whisky.

'Happy New Year,' he said and bent down to kiss Rita enthusiastically.

'You're cold!' she said.

'Of course I am. Standing out there until the stroke of twelve just so I could be your first foot.'

'And there's no one else we would rather have,' Molly said. She took the basket from him. 'Food, flavour, warmth and good cheer,' she said as she took out its contents. She put the coal on the fire and then opened the bottle of whisky and poured them each a tot. They raised their glasses and

Molly said:

'Here's to the bright New Year
and a fond farewell to the old,
Here's to the things that are yet to come and to the
memories that we hold.'

They drained their glasses.

Molly dished out a bowl of broth for Jimmy and set it on the table.

'This is good,' he said.

'Rita made it.'

'Go on!'

Molly laughed. 'She did. I've taught her all I know. You'll be all right there, lad.'

'Give over, Molly,' Rita said.

'No, pet, I've been thinking. If this great moon-struck lad is serious, don't you think it's time you set a date?'

'It's not for want of asking on my part,' Jimmy said as he reached for another slice of bread and spread it thickly with butter.

'I know, lad. And I think I know why she keeps putting things off.' She turned to Rita. 'You don't want to live at the farm, do you?'

Rita shook her head.

'So what's the answer, Jimmy?'

'I've promised to manage the farm for them until young Ian's old enough to take over.'

'But surely that doesn't mean you have to live there, does it?'

'Not at the farm. The Armstrongs would give us one of the cottages.'

'What about living here in this cottage? It's only

a mile away. You could walk that in next to no time.'

'Would you really let us live here?' Rita asked.

'Why not? This place will be yours one day. The cottage and the land. You're like a daughter to me, lass, and like a good daughter I would expect you and your man to look after me as I grow older. We'd all be winners. So what do you think?'

Rita and Jimmy looked at each other and smiled. 'I think we'd better set a date,' Rita said.

'Now fill a plate up, the pair of you, and go and make plans.'

There was a rap at the door and the first of their neighbours arrived. Soon the cottage kitchen was full of people determined to look forward to better times. Rita and Jimmy took their plates through to the sitting room where a small fire burned in the grate and a couple of old oil lamps burned low, casting a soft glow. They were content to sit quietly on the sofa for a while and then Jimmy said, 'Do you ever think back to what our lives were like before we came here?'

'I try not to. I know it's different for you, because your parents were kind and you had a happy life with them. Do you ever regret coming here?'

'Never. You know I was always meant to live in the country, unlike Joe.'

'And I feel the same way, so it's not surprising that we both stayed. And the only other one from our lot who's still here is Carol. Who could have predicted that?'

'I know,' Jimmy agreed. 'It was a strange chain of events, her parents both dying, then Miss

Forsyth adopting her.'

'Yes, that was after Bridget drowned.' Rita gave a little shiver. 'I can still hardly bear to think about it.'

The memory of that day was still horribly vivid. Rita had taken a basket of vegetables up to Hillside House for Mrs Ellis and she'd been in the kitchen when Carol had rushed in, soaking wet and half frozen to death. 'The tarn!' she'd said, gasping for breath. 'Bridget went out onto the ice and it gave way. I tried to help her, I just couldn't reach her.' Then Carol had collapsed.

Miss Forsyth had phoned for the police straight away, but she hadn't waited for them to arrive. Alan Sinclair had been there, and he'd raced up to the tarn with Miss Forsyth and Ted the gardener following on. They had been too late to save Bridget. She was probably dead even before Carol had set out to get help.

'It must have been such a terrible way to die,' Rita whispered.

'Don't think about it, sweetheart,' said Jimmy. 'I'm sorry I brought it up.'

They were quiet for a while and then Rita said, 'Anyway, where were we? What about your mam and dad? Will they mind about me?'

'Why should they?'

'I'm not exactly from a good family, am I? Me dad's notorious.'

'Mam and Dad wouldn't hold that against you. They're not like that. And in any case, I'll be able to tell them I'm marrying a woman of property.'

They both laughed. Jimmy took their empty plates and placed them carefully on the floor, then he drew her into his arms and kissed her. After a while Rita drew back.

'I'd better go through and help Molly,' she said.

Jimmy picked up the plates, but just as they stood up, Molly entered the room with a newly arrived guest carrying a plateful of food and a glass of whisky. 'You can sit in here if you like,' she said. 'Rita and Jimmy will be pleased to have a chat, won't you?'

'Of course,' Rita said.

Molly hurried away and the three of them smiled at each other hesitantly.

'Well, let's sit down,' Rita said. 'Shall I turn the lamps up a bit?'

'No, it's all right. I prefer it like this,' their visitor said. He held up his hands helplessly, a plate of food in one and a drink in the other. 'I wonder if you would move the armchair back from the fire a little. It's hot in here, isn't it?'

'Of course,' Jimmy said.

That done, they all sat down, their guest seeming to be quite happy in the shadows.

'I feel awkward,' he said. 'I'm the only one eating.'

Jimmy grinned. 'I'll soon put that right. Want anything, Rita?'

'No, but you go ahead and fill your plate, I know you want to.'

When they were alone Rita said, 'I'm glad you came. You never go anywhere. You keep to yourself too much.'

'I know.'

'You shouldn't.'

'I know that, too.'

'So what's different about tonight?'

'New Year ... memories ... happy days long gone. Do you understand?'

'I think so.'

'The coronation celebrations. Is she...?'

'I don't know yet.'

'You'll tell me?'

'Yes.'

'And you've never said anything?'

'I promised you, didn't I?'

He nodded.

'Although it went against my better judgement,' she said.

'It wouldn't have been fair.'

'No, you're wrong. What you've done hasn't been fair. Not fair at all.'

Rita stared at him but he turned his head away from her. There was more she wanted to say, but at that moment Jimmy returned and a droning sound started in the kitchen.

'Listen,' Jimmy said. 'No one could stop him.'

Angus Fairley had arrived and was greeting the New Year with his pipes.

Margaret Forsyth had invited a few friends to see in the New Year with her at Hillside House. The sitting room had been redecorated since the war, and although there was no new furniture, Carol had seen to it that there were splashes of colour provided by new curtains, cushions and rugs.

They were not really new, for there were no new fabrics to be bought, but Carol had searched through the trunks and chests in the unused rooms of the big old house and found curtains, bed linen, table linen and even bolts of cloth that had long been forgotten. The Forsyths had always been well off, and Carol was pleased to find that it was all good quality and, more importantly, in good taste.

She had found a woman in the village, Mrs Pickett, to do the sewing for her and who was skilled enough to know exactly what she meant. Mrs Pickett was also adept at altering Carol's clothes to suit the latest fashions and styling new clothes from the coats and dresses to be found in the wardrobes of Hillside House. Miss Forsyth had given Carol permission to take whatever she wanted.

Sometimes Miss Forsyth and Carol would go to the travelling cinema that visited the village hall with a collection of old and new films. When they'd seen *Gone With The Wind*, they had laughed together at the scene where Scarlett pulled down the green velvet curtains to make herself a new outfit so she could go and impress Rhett Butler.

Tonight Carol looked beautiful in a burgundy silk sheath. The dress was the colour of Scarlett O'Hara's ball gown, and Carol, with her translucently pale complexion and silky black hair, was at least as beautiful as Vivien Leigh. Miss Forsyth's adopted daughter was not only beautiful, she had willingly taken over the burden of running Hillside House and most of the financial affairs. And she had made it plain that she would never desert her.

Miss Forsyth sometimes worried about that. Any man would be proud to have Carol as a wife. Surely she would marry some day. She could only hope that if such a man appeared he would be happy to live here in Hillside House, for everything she owned would one day belong to Carol.

She looked across the room and saw that Dorothy and Charles Edwards had arrived. They accepted a drink and Charles immediately peeled off to go and talk to the new young GP and his wife. Dr and Mrs Crawford were not really new – they had been here ever since Alan Sinclair's father had died – but local people still called him the new doctor.

Margaret approached Dorothy with a smile. 'Have you heard from Grace? Is she coming back for the coronation celebrations?'

'She's going to stay with us for the whole week.'

'She'll be retired now, of course?'

'Only just. I think she feels at a bit of a loss. She loved teaching; Charles said she was a natural.'

'I can't imagine her sitting at home and knitting. I wonder if she'll find something to do.'

'It sounds as if she already has. She's very interested in the plight of refugees. She speaks both French and German, you know, and she's started lessons in Polish. They need people like Grace to work in Europe with the lost souls still languishing in the DP camps.'

'Poor displaced persons,' Margaret said. 'I've heard there are still thousands of them trying to trace their families. I fear some of them never will.'

Dorothy smiled. 'On a more cheerful note for this New Year's Eve, Grace told me that there are many weddings and births in the camps. There are people who are determined to make new lives for themselves.'

'And I'm sure Grace will do her best to help them.'

'And what news do you have?' Dorothy asked. 'Are Hazel and Irene going to come?'

Margaret shook her head. 'They haven't replied yet.'

'That's odd.'

'Not really. They have lives of their own, commitments, responsibilities. Perhaps I'm being selfish to expect them to want to come here.'

'Not selfish. They were part of your life for so long; they owe you much.'

'I don't expect gratitude. It was no hardship to have them here. It might sound strange, but those were some of the happiest years of my life.'

'It doesn't sound strange at all.'

A cloud passed over Margaret's face and she looked away. 'Until the day I lost Bridget, of course. Her father and mother had sent her here to me imagining she would be safe. They survived the war against all odds, only to lose their only child.'

'You can't blame yourself. It was an accident.'

'But I do blame myself. The girls didn't tell me where they were going that morning, but I should have asked them. It had been snowing, and snow landing on the ice slows down the freezing process. I would have told them the conditions weren't suitable. I failed them.'

Dorothy was obviously aghast. She looked at her old friend in consternation.

'I'm sorry,' Margaret said. 'I don't know what came over me. Perhaps it's the passing of the year. It makes you think of times gone by as well as the times to come.' Visibly pulling herself together, she said, 'I must go and see if Mrs Ellis is happy in the kitchen. I've asked her to join us at midnight, you know.'

Dorothy watched Miss Forsyth cross the room, smiling at her guests, including the present head-master of the village school and his wife and grown son. She stopped and beckoned Carol, who immediately hurried towards her.

It's so strange, the way Margaret has taken to Carol, Dorothy thought. The girls had been to-gether when the tragedy occurred, and Margaret might well have resented Carol because she had survived while Bridget had drowned. But perhaps Margaret was grateful for the desperate attempts Carol had made to save Bridget, endangering her own life in the process. Of course, Carol had lost her parents in the most hideous manner, and it might be that their grief and despair had brought them together. That must be it.

'Why so pensive?'

Dorothy focused on her surroundings to see that her husband had come to join her. 'Was I?' she asked.

'You looked as though you were brooding about something.'

'I wasn't exactly brooding; I was thinking about Carol and how much her life has changed since she first came here.'

Charles glanced across the room to where Carol was handing round a plate of canapés.

'I know what you mean. She was a strange little thing when she first came. She didn't fit in with the other girls and I suspect that was because she thought herself much better than they were.'

'In what way? I mean, she was bright enough, but certainly not as clever as someone like Hazel Stafford.'

'No, I don't mean in that way. I mean that she thought she was above them socially, and to be brutally honest she probably was.'

'Not that that sort of thing matters in the slightest,' Dorothy said.

'Of course it doesn't matter to right-thinking people, but it mattered very much to Carol. That's probably why she adapted so well to living here in Hillside House.'

'And that wouldn't have happened if her parents had survived the air raid,' Dorothy said.

'And if poor Bridget had not drowned in the tarn, Margaret might not have adopted her.'

They watched Carol for a moment. She was still doing her duty with the canapés and was offering the tray to Muriel Teasdale and her mother. Muriel had helped run the evening classes Dorothy had set up during the war. Carol was smiling at them, but suddenly she turned away abruptly. Dorothy thought that for a moment she looked far from happy. But, almost instantly, she was smiling again.

Charles must have noticed it too. 'Do you ever doubt Carol's sincerity?' he asked.

'What do you mean?'

'To put it crudely, do you think she's in this for what she can get?'

'She's not exactly poor, you know. She has money in her own right. Margaret told me she sold the house her parents left her, and soon after the war she inherited a tidy sum from her father's brother in Australia.'

'It's not the money, though, is it?' Charles said. 'It's this...' He paused and gestured round the room. 'It's this way of life.'

None of the guests stayed for much more than an hour after midnight. Carol was in bed by two o'clock but she could not sleep. At first the evening had gone well. She knew she looked good, Aunt Margaret was pleased with her, and she had genuinely enjoyed helping to entertain the guests – until Muriel Teasdale had spoiled everything.

'You must be looking forward to the coronation celebrations,' Muriel had said.

'I think we all are,' Carol replied politely.

'But it will be special for you, won't it?' Muriel had persisted.

'Special? Why?'

'To have your old friends here, Hazel and Irene. The three of you lived here together at Hillside House, didn't you?'

'That's right.'

'They will be coming, won't they?'

'Actually, neither of them has replied yet.'

'Oh, poor you. Never mind, there's still time, I suppose.'

'I suppose so,' Carol had said and turned away before the stupid woman could see how agitated she was.

The last thing she wanted was for Hazel and Irene to come and stay for a week, particularly Irene. Hazel was okay most of the time, but Irene had made her dislike of Carol plain from the start. It was probably jealousy on Irene's part, Carol thought. She must have known how common she was, how her accent jarred. Hazel had seemed to blow hot and cold. Sometimes she was perfectly nice and then at others she seemed to be watching and disapproving. And of course both of them were jealous that Bridget had chosen Carol to be her friend.

Bridget...

Carol tried, as she had done so many times before, to blank out all thoughts of what had happened on that long ago winter's day. It was nearly ten years now since she had found the skates in a trunk in one of the attics. She didn't say anything to the others, but waited until they were just about to go to bed and then caught Bridget on her own.

'I've found the skates,' she said. 'I think they would fit us. At least one pair of them would, and we can always take an extra pair of socks.'

'What skates?' Bridget said.

'Remember, last Easter you told me that your father and aunt used to go skating on the tarn when they were children, but the thaw had set in so we didn't do anything about it?'

'Oh, yes.'

Carol had been upset by Bridget's apparent lack of enthusiasm. 'Well, why don't we go skating tomorrow morning? It would be fun, wouldn't it?'

'I suppose so. But it all depends on the thickness of the ice. This has been a pretty mild winter so far.'

'Well, at least we could go and have a look.'

Bridget smiled resignedly. 'You're really keen, aren't you?'

'Mmm.'

'Are we going to tell the others?'

'There are only two pairs of skates.'

'They could come along and watch. And perhaps we could take turns.'

'Irene would hate it.'

'Yes, she probably would, but what about Hazel?'

'She wouldn't leave Irene on her own. You know what a goody-goody she is.'

Bridget raised her eyebrows. 'Sometimes, Carol, I think you can be a little spiteful. It isn't an attractive trait, you know.'

Carol felt herself flushing. She tried to hide her scowl.

'Oh, please don't look at me like that,' Bridget said. 'I'd love to come skating with you. We'll go straight after breakfast tomorrow.'

Carol had not been able to find any skate bags, so they tied the laces and carried the skates over their shoulders. They were wrapped up warmly with woollen scarves, pompom hats and gloves. Rita Bevan had begged balls of wool from anyone who had some to spare and she had been knitting and selling her creations to raise money for the refugee children. Miss Forsyth had bought a set for everybody in Hillside House, including Mrs Ellis and herself.

There had been a light fall of snow during the night, but in the morning the weather was crisp and dry. A keen wind lifted the snow from the branches of the trees and it blew about like the flakes in a snow globe. Carol felt exhilarated. Not only did she have Bridget to herself for a while, but she hoped she was going to surprise her with how well she skated.

She recalled the visits she had made to the ice rink with her father and how he had praised her and jokingly told her that Sonja Henie had better look out because Carol could prove to be a serious rival to the Norwegian film star. She found herself both smiling at the memory and unexpectedly feeling a pang of grief. She felt tears well up in her eyes.

'What's up?' Bridget said.

'Nothing. It's just the wind. It's making my eyes water.'

By the time they reached the tarn Carol had suppressed the bittersweet memories of her father.

'Look, we can sit on that outcrop of stone to put our skates on,' she said.

'I don't think so,' Bridget replied. She was looking out across the tarn.

'What do you mean?' Carol asked.

'We can't go skating today.'

'Why not?'

'I don't think the ice is thick enough.'

'How can you tell?'

'Well, I can't be sure, but the ice further out looks cloudy and I seem to remember only clear ice is safe.'

It had all happened so quickly after that. Carol put her skates down and joined Bridget at the water's edge.

'I'll test it,' she said.

'No, don't.'

But Carol ignored her and stepped onto the frozen surface of the tarn. She turned and smiled. 'It's perfectly safe.'

'Pack it in, Carol, and get off the ice. We're going home.'

Why hadn't she listened? Smiling and laughing, Carol had turned away from Bridget and ventured further out. She could never remember what she had heard first: Carol's shout of alarm or the frightening crunching sound as the ice cracked.

'Turn round! Come back this way!' Bridget called.

Carol turned round but she didn't move. She couldn't move. She was frozen with fear.

'This way,' Bridget ordered. 'You know this ice is safe.'

Carol just stared at her.

'All right, reach out for me,' Bridget said and she stretched her arms towards Carol.

The cracking sound grew worse and Carol realised there was water sloshing around her feet. At last panic made her react. She reached out for Bridget and grabbed both her arms. But instead of allowing Bridget to pull her to the bank, she panicked and pulled Bridget onto the ice.

'Okay,' Bridget said. 'We're both going to make a leap for it.'

And they did. But only Carol made it. At the same time as she landed on the bank, Bridget slipped backwards and fell onto the ice, which opened up at a frightening speed.

Carol's first instinct, and she would always remember this, was to go back onto the ice and reach for Bridget.

'No!' Bridget yelled. 'You'll make things worse. Get a branch or something. Get me something to hang onto.'

Carol searched the shore frantically but there were no branches to be found. The tarn was far above the tree line. She ran back to the water's edge, tears streaming down her face. There was no sign of Bridget. For one glorious moment Carol thought that her friend had managed to scramble out. She looked around frantically, but there was nobody in sight.

She's under the ice, Carol thought. Ignoring Bridget's orders, she sank to her knees, lay flat and edged herself forward. The ice cracked and groaned and the splinters spread towards her. Nevertheless she reached the gaping hole and peered down into the water. She thought she could see something under the ice, a red and white scarf drifting to and fro, but she could not reach it. Ice-cold water began to soak into her clothes.

Carol knew she had to get help. She edged back to the shore, stood up and ran faster than she had ever run in her life.

She remembered very little of the next few days. Mrs Ellis and Hazel had got her upstairs, removed her wet clothes and dried her. They had dressed her in dry clothes and then wrapped her in blankets before helping her onto her bed. She passed out. She had no idea how much later she had opened her eyes to see Alan's father, Dr Sinclair, looking down at her.

'You're going to be all right, Carol,' he said. 'You've been very brave.'

Brave? She couldn't make sense of that. She put the thought by until later.

She looked up at the ceiling and frowned as she tried to work out what the shifting patterns were. *A fire,* she thought, *they've lit a fire in the hearth.*

For the next few days, she wasn't sure how many, she stayed in bed and Mrs Ellis brought her bowls of warm soup. One day, as she was waking, she heard voices. Miss Forsyth was talking to Mrs Ellis. Carol had been dreading the moment when she would have to face Miss Forsyth. Before they noticed she was awake, she closed her eyes and kept them closed. What she heard next was puzzling.

'Poor, brave child, she risked her own life,' Miss Forsyth said.

This was the second person who had called her brave.

'Aye, it seems she did,' Mrs Ellis said. 'I wonder if she'll ever be able to tell us exactly what happened.'

'Maybe, one day, but I have no intention of making her relive it unless she wants to. It's enough to know that Bridget went out onto thin ice, and when it gave way, Carol did her best to rescue her.'

Did I say that? Carol thought. *Did I let them believe that it was Bridget's idea to go onto the ice and not mine? Did I omit to tell them that it only happened because Bridget was trying to save me?*

'I wanted to talk to her,' Miss Forsyth said, 'but I suppose we should let her sleep.'

They left the room.

Carol turned her face into her pillow and wept. She knew the answer to her own question. Some

377

instinctive source of self-preservation had led her to tell only part of the truth. She had deliberately not told them that she was responsible for what had happened. She could not bear to be blamed. Also, if the truth were known, Miss Forsyth might send her away from Hillside House. That she could not have borne.

She knew she must keep her secret.

And so she had for all these years. Miss Forsyth had believed her without question and so, miraculously, had Mrs Ellis. It was only Irene who seemed to question what had happened, and the wretched girl had voiced her suspicions to Hazel. Carol had heard them whispering in corners and seen how they stopped talking the minute they saw her.

It grew worse when Miss Forsyth formally adopted her. Carol knew in her heart that Irene, at least, suspected her of somehow deliberately killing Bridget, or at least not trying to save her. But Irene was wrong. It was wicked of her to think that. It had been an accident, hadn't it? And she really had tried to save Bridget. Carol often comforted herself with this thought, at the same time completely blanking out that it would never have happened if she had listened to Bridget and not ventured out on the ice in the first place.

Carol could only hope that Hazel and Irene would refuse Aunt Margaret's invitation to come back to Hillside House.

Chapter Twenty

Hazel was surprised when her mother told her that of course she must go to Kenneth's house for his mother's New Year party.

'Are you sure?' she asked.

'Well, he's got a car now, hasn't he? If you don't stay on too late he can bring you home and be our first foot.'

'But you'll be on your own until then.'

'Your dad will come home after closing time, and besides, I'll have to get used to being on my own when you get married, won't I?'

'Oh, Mam, are you dropping hints again?'

Her mother smiled. 'Perhaps I know something you don't.'

'What are you talking about?'

'I had a cuppa with Florrie Small the other day.'

Hazel struggled to make sense of this, then the fog cleared. 'You had your tea leaves read!'

'Yes, and she saw a wedding cake. That means a speedy and prosperous marriage.'

'Oh, Mam, how could she see a wedding cake in a collection of soggy tea leaves?'

'I saw it myself. You couldn't mistake the shape of it.'

'That's because she told you what to look for. I'm sure Florrie just makes it up as she goes along.'

'No, pet. It's an ancient art, going right back to China.'

Hazel sighed. 'And how much did she charge you?'

'Florrie never charges.'

'Really?'

'Really. But you can leave a coin on the table if you like.'

'And you left...'

'A shilling.' Her mother smiled. 'And it was worth every penny for a bit of fun. It's good to get out and have a bit of fun now and then.'

Hazel relaxed. 'So you didn't take it seriously?

Her mother sighed. 'I don't suppose I did, but I'd like to believe it was true. You've been very good to me, Hazel, but it's time you had a life of your own.'

When Kenneth called for Hazel he asked her mother if she would like to come too. She would be very welcome. But she refused politely and said she would be quite happy to sit by the fire and listen to the wireless, and that she wanted to be at home when Hazel's father came back from the Hare and Hounds.

'Are you sure? 'Hazel said.

'Get along with you.'

Hazel didn't know whether to be relieved or worried by her mother's unusual behaviour. But for once she didn't feel guilty about leaving her on her own.

They had only been at Mrs Gregson's little gathering for about ten minutes, but Kenneth could barely hide his displeasure. 'Just look at him,' he said quietly to Hazel.

'Look at who?'

'Arthur. The so-called tea planter. He's handing round the drinks as if he were the host here.'

'I think your mother asked him to.'

Kenneth scowled. 'She shouldn't have.'

'Why not?'

'That's my job. You and I could have gone to the dinner dance at the Grand, but I thought I should be here with her.'

'To keep an eye on Arthur?'

Kenneth's scowl deepened. 'Oh, I know what you think, but yes, that's exactly why I decided to be here. That man is a charlatan, and what makes it worse is that my mother is a very intelligent woman yet she doesn't seem to be able to see through him.'

'And if she could see through him, what is it that you imagine she would find?'

'That he's after her money and that he'd like to move into this cosy little house of hers and put his feet up for the rest of his life.'

Hazel put her hand on his arm. 'I think you're worrying needlessly, Kenneth. As you said, your mother is an intelligent woman. I don't think she would be taken in by a fraudster.'

'So why is she behaving like this?'

'Because he's charming.'

'Really?'

'And attentive, and, although you might not see it, he's quite handsome in a distinguished sort of way. No wonder your mother likes having him around. It's flattering for her. But do you know what? If he is what you say he is I'm sure your

381

mother will have worked that out by now, and even if they get married–'

'Heaven forbid!'

'She would never allow him to swindle her and she would never disinherit you.'

Kenneth nearly choked on his drink. 'Is that what you think of me?' he asked. 'That I'm only concerned that I might be left out of her will? Surely you know me better than that.'

'Yes, I do, and I truly believe your concern is for your mother and not for yourself, but I think you have to trust her, and if they do get married you should be altogether gracious about it and walk down the aisle with her and give her away.'

'Give her to Arthur?'

'And another thing, have you considered that Arthur's feelings for her are sincere and that they are genuinely in love?'

'Love? For God's sake, what's that?'

Hazel's eyes widened. 'It's what makes people get married.'

'Oh, I suppose you're talking about romantic love. That can lead to disaster. No, people get married because they have an initial attraction and then they grow to like each other; they get on well together and feel comfortable in each other's company.'

Hazel looked at him soberly. There was nothing she could say. How could she tell him that she would never feel comfortable in his company again?

Kenneth moved away to switch the wireless on. There was still an hour to go, but his mother liked to greet the New Year with the strokes of Big Ben.

Carol glanced around at the other guests. There were not quite as many as there had been at Mrs Gregson's Christmas party just over a week before. Effie and Cora, the sisters from next door, were here, and some other neighbours, Mr and Mrs Partington, who had been unable to come for the Christmas gathering because they had gone to stay with their son and his family in Edinburgh. There was Arthur, of course, and – unexpectedly – the editor of the local paper and his wife.

Hazel would have imagined that journalists and former actresses would have much more lively parties to go to on New Year's Eve, and she soon discovered she was right.

When Tim saw that she was alone he came hurrying over. 'I hoped you'd be here,' he said. 'I have a favour to ask.'

'If it's about your book...'

'It is.'

'I'm really sorry, but you know I told you that I couldn't help you.'

'Not when I'm writing it, I know. But what about when I've finished? Would you consider going through the manuscript and seeing if I've made any glaring errors? You wouldn't mind doing that, would you?'

Hazel stared at him, thinking, and then she smiled. 'No, Tim, I'd love to help.' Then she added quietly, 'It's time I faced up to my memories.'

Soon after this conversation, Tim and his glamorous wife hurried away. He explained that he was going to a civic function at the Rotunda Ballroom hosted by the mayor.

The New Year was barely an hour old when Kenneth took her home. He drove in silence. Hazel didn't glance his way but she could sense his displeasure. Usually when they had a tiff they were quick to make up, but this time Hazel didn't know what to say, and it didn't seem as if Kenneth did, either.

What a start to the year, Hazel thought, and she decided she must make some kind of effort. When he pulled up outside her house she turned to him and said, 'You will come in, won't you? My mother hoped you would be our first foot.'

'I've got nothing to bring.'

Hazel thought for a moment. 'A coin,' she said. 'A silver coin. That's one of the gifts that's considered good luck.'

Kenneth felt in his pocket and brought out a half-crown. 'Will that do?'

'It will, and even better, you're a tall, dark-haired man. That's perfect. Now go on, rap on the door.'

Her mother opened the door and smiled a welcome. 'Come in,' she said. 'Mind you let Kenneth step over the threshold first.'

They all wished each other Happy New Year, and Kenneth and Hazel said it again in the kitchen, where her father was sitting at the table with books and papers spread before him. Hazel thought the atmosphere surprisingly peaceful.

'Would you like a bowl of New Year broth, Kenneth?' her mother asked.

'Yes, please, Mrs Stafford.' He loosened his coat and sat down at the table. He looked a little awkward as he produced the half-crown coin. 'I

384

wish you prosperity in the days to come.'

'And you, Hazel? Would you like some broth?'

'Yes, please.'

'Sit down then.'

Hazel knew that Kenneth couldn't be hungry and guessed that he was trying to restore peace between them. Before her mother filled the bowls of soup, she tidied up the flimsy paperback books that were strewn across the table. Her father gave a resigned shrug, but instead of retreating to his armchair near the fire, he actually started a conversation with Kenneth about the Robledo brothers who were born in Chile but played football for Newcastle United.

Kenneth's eye was caught by the books.

'I've had them since I was a lad,' her father said, and he pushed three of them across the table.

Kenneth looked at them. He read the titles out loud. *'Ghost Valley, The Masked Mountie, Sergeant Young of the Yukon.* You like Mountie stories?'

'I used to. I was so taken up with the idea of them that I even thought I might go to Canada and apply to be a Mountie myself.'

'But you never went?'

'Family circumstances.' Her father looked wistful for a moment and then he smiled. 'But my life took a different tack and I can't complain.'

Kenneth didn't stay long. He explained that he did not want to leave his mother alone, though Hazel knew very well that Mrs Gregson was not alone. Arthur had assured Kenneth that when the party broke up he would stay and keep her company. Of course, this had the effect of making

Kenneth want to get home as soon as possible.

When he stood up so did her father. 'I'll see you to the door, lad,' he said. 'And then I'll lock up and go up to bed.' He paused at the door and looked back at the table. 'I know you two lasses will want to have a bit of a chat but don't be too long, Joan.'

He shut the door behind him and Hazel looked at her mother in amazement.

'I know,' her mother said. 'He's turning into a different man.'

'What's happened? He's not ill, is he? *You're* not ill?'

'No, pet. It's nothing like that. It's just since Mavis came along with those photographs, it's set him thinking.'

'But surely that would make him miserable – the fact that he didn't fulfil his dreams.'

'I think he's realised that they *were* just dreams and it's made him think about the way his life has gone. He's actually started giving me a peck on the cheek when he leaves the house. And tonight he came home before closing time.'

'Last night,' Hazel said. 'It's morning now. You must go to bed and get some sleep.'

'So should you.'

Hazel helped her mother clear the table and wash the few dishes. And then a question occurred to her. She looked down at the books on the table. 'Where has Dad been keeping these? I've never seen them before.'

'And I'm ashamed to say, neither have I.'

'Why ashamed?'

'When we married and set up house your dad

brought an old suitcase with him. He said it was full of things from his mother's house, old photographs and the like. He shoved it to the back of the cupboard under the stairs and I never saw it again. I never asked him anything about it.

'Oh, Hazel, it was full of his boyhood treasures and I showed no interest. There are photographs of his mam in her best bonnet and his dad in his uniform, and of your dad's little brother who died when he was only two years old. What kind of a wife have I been not to know what was in that case?'

'You've been a very good wife.'

'I took him for granted.'

Hazel was astounded. 'That's rubbish. *He* took *you* for granted. You kept the house clean, cooked good meals when you only had a few pennies to buy food; you went out to work to bring in extra money. How on earth can you say *you* took *him* for granted?'

'I expected him to be like every other working man – to work hard, to bring the wages home and put them on the table. I never asked him if he was happy.'

'And did he ask you?'

Her mother sighed. 'No, pet, he didn't. We got too caught up in the fight for survival. We've lived through hard times, and instead of bringing us closer as it did for some people, it drove us apart.'

'Oh, Mam, you shouldn't be talking like this on today of all days.'

'You're wrong, Hazel. We're supposed to make New Year resolutions, aren't we?'

Hazel nodded.

387

'Well, mine is to try and understand him better. I want us to be happy before we're too old to care. And don't worry. Although your dad would never put it into words, I think he feels the same way as I do.'

Hazel stood on her bedroom chair and reached for the shoebox she kept on top of the wardrobe. The lid was covered with a fine layer of dust; she couldn't remember the last time she had opened it. She sat down on the bed with the box resting on her knees, gathering the courage to open it. Eventually, she put the lid on the floor and stared at the contents.

The quiet was suddenly broken by raucous voices in the street outside. She leaned sideways and lifted the curtain. A group of boisterous young men, who maybe had celebrated too well, were making their way down the street singing 'Auld Lang Syne'. She let the curtain fall. She must have waited a full minute before lifting out the bundle of letters, tied together with a ribbon. She had brought them home with her from Withenmoor.

How many years was it since she had taken these pages out of their envelopes and sat and wept over them? Trusting herself to stay dry-eyed, she removed the first letter Alan had ever written to her from its envelope.

She read the letter now and studied the exquisite illustrations decorating the Shakespeare poem, reliving the emotions she had felt at the time. She had been surprised and elated that Alan had chosen to write to her when he returned to boarding school after the Christmas holidays. She had just turned fourteen and Alan was almost sixteen. They had been children. And yet she remembered her disappointment because he had ended the letter with *Yours sincerely* rather than *Love*. It seemed he had wanted them to become friends. And yet she knew now that, even if they didn't recognise it at the time, they had begun to fall in love.

There were other letters from school, and over the years, as they spent time together and grew to know each other, the letters began to tell of their developing feelings for each other. Alan had written of his plans for the future. He wanted to go to art school but his father had insisted on university. In the end he had gone to neither.

Hazel put the letters aside and took out an envelope containing photographs and another containing some of Alan's sketches. She looked at the drawings first. A farm dog, a startled rabbit, a basketful of kittens in Molly Watkins' kitchen. There were views of the hills, the tarn, the ruins of the ancient fort and settlement on the crest of the hill. The picture of the fort brought back bittersweet memories.

In some lights these tumbledown shapes could look dark and brooding, but the last time she and Alan had climbed up there before he went away had been gloriously sunny. The sky was clear, the air smelled sweet, a lark was in full throat and you could see for miles and miles across the countryside.

'Wonderful, isn't it?' Alan had said. 'Just think what it must have been like to live with this view.'

Hazel laughed. 'It's all right on a day like today, but imagine what it would be like when the rain never stops, or in the middle of winter.'

'Granted,' Alan said.

'I wonder why they decided to build up here in the first place?' she said.

'So they could see the enemy coming and could guard the pass.'

'Oh, of course. They were soldiers. They had to defend their territory.'

They had been quiet for a while after that. It had reminded them that Great Britain was at war and that Alan had declared it his duty to enlist now that he had left school. Hazel took the rug out of the haversack she was carrying and spread it on the springy turf. Then she took out sandwiches and a bottle of lemonade.

'Hungry?' she asked.

He turned and smiled. 'You bet.'

His own haversack contained his sketch pad and his camera, and after they had eaten Hazel sat quietly while he wandered about taking photographs and eventually sat down to do some sketching. The sun grew warmer; Hazel felt sleepy. She lay back and closed her eyes.

When she opened them again the sky had clouded over.

'Wake up, sleepyhead, I think we'd better get going.' Alan was packing his haversack.

He reached down and held out his hands to pull her up, and then he held her in his arms and kissed her. He was eighteen and Hazel was sixteen, and yet they knew in that moment that they were destined to be together for the rest of their lives.

Hazel put the sketches aside and reached for the photographs: snapshots of themselves and their friends. She studied the small squares of glossy paper with serrated white borders, seeing Irene, Carol, Bridget, Rita, the Doyle brothers. And the grown-ups: Miss Forsyth, Mrs Ellis, Ted the gardener, Molly Watkins. Hazel realised that these were the kind of snaps that Tim Gilbert might like for his book, but she knew she would never give them to him.

One of the snaps had fallen on the floor. Hazel picked it up and saw herself lying sleeping near the old fort. When Alan had had the film developed and shown her the photograph she had been cross with him.

'That was a really sneaky think to do,' she said. 'Taking my picture when I knew nothing about it.'

His face had fallen. 'I'm sorry. I should have thought. But it was such a happy day, wasn't it? A day to remember. The blue skies, the birdsong, the feeling of peace, of escape from the troubled world down below.'

'And the rain,' Hazel said. 'Don't forget the rain.'

Alan smiled. 'Well, we almost made it, didn't we?'

Hazel remembered the laughter in his voice and then their scramble down the hillside paths, trying to escape the gathering rain clouds. They didn't make it, and the rain was so heavy that by the time they reached Hillside House they were drenched. They burst into the kitchen, dripping all over the stone-flagged floor. Mrs Ellis took one look at them and pulled two large towels down from the clothes airer.

'You'd better get upstairs and change your clothes, Hazel. But as for you, young man, you'll just have to dry yourself as best you can. Then sit near the range and wait until the rain stops before you go.'

The next day, Alan phoned Hillside House and asked to speak to Hazel. 'I've got a beastly cold,' he said. 'My father said I'll survive but my mother won't hear of my leaving the house until I've stopped coughing and sneezing. Oh, and by the way, as soon as that happens my parents want to meet you.'

'I've already met your father, more than once.'

'That was when he had to make the occasional house call. But this is – I don't know how to put it – this is something personal.'

'What do you mean?'

'I've told them how I feel about you. Predictably they said we were far too young.'

'So why do they want to meet me?'

'Because I told them that, whatever they thought, you were the girl for me and if they would only meet you and talk to you, they would understand why.'

'Oh.'

'What's the matter?'

'Are you sure this is a good idea?'

'Why shouldn't it be?'

'We're so different. I mean, your father is a doctor and mine a labourer. Your mother went to university and mine works as a cleaner.'

'What's that got to do with anything?'

'Don't pretend it doesn't make a difference.'

'Not to my parents.'

Hazel usually trusted Alan's judgement, but this time she was not so sure, and when the day came that Alan called for her to take her to his home, she was very nervous. She need not have been. Dr Sinclair was his usual courteous self and Mrs Sinclair, although quiet, showed no sign of hostility. She was very pale and seemed to be tired. However, she began to talk about books and Hazel wondered if she was quizzing her. If so, she seemed to be pleased that Hazel was well read and had a keen interest in the classics.

After tea Dr Sinclair turned on the wireless to listen to the latest news bulletin. Another convoy had been lost in the North Atlantic. Of the thirty merchant ships that had set off for Murmansk, only two had got through.

'They should have had more air cover,' Alan said.

His mother sighed. She looked unutterably sad. His father glanced at her and turned the wireless off.

Alan and his father loaded the tea trolley and wheeled the used crockery into the kitchen. Hazel wondered if they usually did the washing-up or whether this was a ploy to leave Hazel alone with Mrs Sinclair. If so, she wasted no time. She looked at Hazel intently and said, 'These are strange times, aren't they? The world we knew will never be the same again.'

'I know.'

'Your generation has had to grow up more

quickly, before your time. And you will have to make sense of it all when the war is over.' She paused then said, 'You know he wants to enlist, don't you?'

'I do.'

'He intends to join the RAF. He wants to fly.'

'I know.'

'And there's nothing you and I can do except pray he comes home safely.'

Mrs Sinclair did not live to see whether her son came safely home. Hazel thought it a blessing that she was spared knowledge of the way he had died. She and Alan had four more weeks together before he enlisted. She opened the first letter he'd sent her when he was doing basic training. Or square-bashing, as he'd called it:

They first thing they did was give me a savage haircut, followed by medicals and vaccinations. We marched everywhere with people shouting at us. The drill instructors are the most fearsome men I've ever come across. Getting up at six o'clock in the morning is no different from school. Then the whole day is taken over by drill and lectures. The other fellows are from all walks of life but we have one thing in common, we want to fly.

Alan had illustrated the letter with small sketches: the face of a drill instructor contorted with anger, a mournful recruit peeling a mountain of potatoes in the cookhouse, Alan himself sitting on his bed polishing his boots. His letter was amusing and full of hope. However, he told her he missed her and asked her to write to him as often as she could.

Before he went on to flying training, he came home on leave. Hazel was astounded at the change in him. He was lean and fit and so handsome in his uniform, but most of all he had the confidence of a man with a purpose rather than the wistful dreams of a schoolboy.

After that, all his letters were strictly censored. All Hazel and his parents knew was that he was based at Castle Donington. Instead of getting used to it, every time he came home on leave it was harder to let him go. They walked the hills together, they talked of a possible future. Alan still wanted to go to art school and his father had come round to the idea, believing that his son had earned the right to follow his dream. Sometimes they talked of marriage, although they knew life would be hard while Alan was a student. Hazel assured him that she would be perfectly happy to go out to work and support them both, considering Alan was destined to be such a famous artist. Sometimes, on the way home from the tarn or the old fort, they walked in silence, simply holding each other's hands.

A year after Hazel had been invited to tea with Alan's parents, Mrs Sinclair died of cancer. Hazel and Dr Sinclair became close. They supported each other through anxious times. After D-Day in June 1944 the tide of war turned and Hazel and Dr Sinclair began to hope that their prayers had been answered and that Alan would come home to them.

Then, in 1945, a month after his twentieth birthday, the Hurricane that Alan was piloting on escort duty over Germany was hit by flak. Alan limped home across the Channel but then crashed to the ground in flames.

Hazel had been eighteen years old and she believed her life was over.

It was almost dawn by the time Hazel put her treasures back in the shoebox. She had never told her mother of her heartbreak but had simply talked of Alan in terms of friendship. It was Miss Forsyth who had supported her through the darkest days – kindly Margaret Forsyth, who had known heartache herself and who had never given her heart to anyone else.

'I loved him so much,' Miss Forsyth told her, 'that anyone else would have been second best. But you are very young, Hazel. Maybe you will meet someone one day and fall in love again.'

Hazel had eventually met Kenneth and she realised now that she had sleepwalked into a relationship that wasn't good for either of them. Whether or not she would ever fall in love again didn't matter. She would break things off with Kenneth and accept Miss Forsyth's invitation. She sensed that only by facing up to the grief she had suffered would she be able to move on.

She spent New Year's Day peacefully with her mother and father and found to her surprise that she enjoyed the lunch of roast capon and her mother's own recipe of sage, onion and apple stuffing. That evening she realised how tired she was and went to bed early, leaving her parents sitting by the fire.

On Friday the shops opened again, but as Hazel wasn't going back to work until Monday she decided to go to Brownlow's after lunch to see Irene. The January sales had started and Hazel had to hover in the background for a long time until Irene was free to talk for a few minutes.

They wished each other Happy New Year and Hazel said she'd like to have a chat.

'Sure. Why don't you have a look around the sales and we'll meet at the station café again as soon as I've finished work.'

Hazel followed Irene's advice. She didn't get anything for herself, but she bought a Gor-Ray permanently pleated skirt for her mother and a Fair Isle pullover for her father.

The station was very busy. It seemed everybody had been to the sales. Hazel and Irene met on the concourse then went to the café, where Hazel queued at the counter for a pot of tea and a couple of raisin scones whilst Irene found them a table.

'So what's this in aid of?' Irene asked when they were settled. 'It's not just for the pleasure of my company.'

Hazel smiled. 'Why wouldn't it be?'

'Because you have a look about you, as if you're going to quiz me about something.'

'That's true in a way.'

'You need some advice about make-up or the new beauty treatments?'

'When I do, I'll come to you, I promise. But I really want to know whether you've made up your mind about going to Withenmoor.'

Irene smiled. 'I have. I'm going.'

'Is that all right with Ray?'

'Ray is history.'

'Oh, no! What about your career?'

'I wasn't ready for it. Someone advised me to have singing lessons until I reach a professional standard. And that's what I'm going to do.'

'That's marvellous, Irene. Who gave you this advice?'

'Someone I trust.' She paused. 'And what about you?'

'Yes, I'm going.'

'And Kenneth?'

'I'm afraid Kenneth is history too.'

Chapter Twenty-One

June 1953

On Monday morning, the day before the coronation, Hazel followed Irene as they made their way along the corridor of the train. They were peering through the glass panels trying to find an empty compartment. Hazel didn't think they would have much luck. She was about to tell Irene they should settle for one that wasn't too crowded when Irene stopped so suddenly that Hazel bumped into her.

'What is it?' Hazel asked.

'Look who's coming our way!'

Hazel glanced ahead and said, 'Oh, no!'

Three of their fellow evacuees were walking towards them.

'Quick, run, before they see us.'

Irene took hold of Hazel's shoulders, turned her round and gave her a shove. Soon they were hurrying back the way they had come, almost breathless with laughter. In the next carriage, to their amazement, they came across a compartment with only one elderly lady inside. Irene pulled aside the sliding door and they almost fell in. Still laughing, they slid the door shut and hefted their suitcases into the overhead net rack.

'Joe Doyle, Gavin Pritchard and Paul Barton.

Remember what a pest Paul used to be?' Irene said.

'He wasn't that bad.'

'Maybe not, but I don't fancy having to talk to him all the way there.'

'Hello, Irene, hello, Hazel,' their fellow passenger said. 'I hope you don't mind having to talk to me.'

They turned round and stared at her. 'Miss Norton!' they said in unison.

'How wonderful,' Hazel said.

'What an opportunity to catch up,' Irene added.

They sat down opposite their former teacher, and for a while, as they tried to fill in the details of the years since they had last met, they didn't even notice that the train had pulled away from the station and begun its journey to Withenmoor. Then, strangely, they fell silent. Perhaps each was remembering that first journey more than ten years ago.

Hazel stared out of the window. The soot-stained rows of terraced houses were still there but every now and then there was a gap where a bomb had hit. Not much further on, the countryside was as breathtaking as ever, even though the skies were cloudy and a smattering of rain was beginning to speckle the windows.

'What happened to the lovely sunshine we had a couple of weeks ago?' Miss Norton remarked. 'And now we have this cold wind and rain. I hope it will be better than this tomorrow, although did you know that the sun hasn't shone kindly on any of the coronations this century?'

When they left the train at Withenmoor they went their separate ways. Miss Norton explained that she was going to stay with Mr and Mrs Edwards. 'But I'll catch up with you tomorrow,' she said and she waved goodbye.

Hazel and Irene set off up the steep road that led to Hillside House.

Carol stood at her bedroom window watching for the first sign of Hazel and Irene coming up the hill. This way she would be prepared, ready to face them – and face the past.

She remembered another time she had stood here watching the road apprehensively. It had been a cruel winter's day and the skies were so dark that she almost missed the first sight of them. Then, out of the shadows, a tall man and a woman had emerged. They were dressed in black. His bearing was upright. The woman, almost as tall as he was, walked a slight distance away from him. It was if they were alone in their private worlds of grief.

For this was Bridget's mother and father come to Withenmoor for their daughter's funeral. Carol had been spared the church service, but at some time that day, she had heard Bridget's father say to Miss Forsyth, 'We'll leave tomorrow, Margaret. And you can do what you like with this place. Father intended it for you and I shall never set foot here again.'

Before they left, Bridget's mother had sought her out. 'I understand you did your best to save her,' she'd said. 'I'm glad that she had such a good friend.'

I was *her friend,* Carol thought. *And I did try to save her. But I've never admitted it was all my fault. And now I must live with these memories for the rest of my life.*

Eventually she saw two figures battling their way uphill against a rising wind. She went downstairs to open the door for her friends.

Later that night Hazel and Irene sat in Hazel's bedroom talking about the day.

'It's as if time has stood still here,' Hazel said.

'Well, poor old Ted has gone the journey. When you were talking to Miss Forsyth, Mrs Ellis told me that for a while they had one of the Italian prisoners of war help in the garden until they found a local man who had just been demobbed.'

'Did Mrs Ellis tell you how she felt about the Italian soldier?'

'Apparently she took to him. She thought he wasn't getting fed properly at the camp and she introduced him to good, old-fashioned British food. She also said that Hilda Barton still hasn't got the knack of handling the vacuum cleaner.'

'Don't you think Miss Forsyth and Mrs Ellis look and talk as they always did?' Hazel said. 'It's wonderful to see them together, isn't it?'

'What do you mean exactly?'

'Well, they're even more like friends than mistress and servant. It's amusing the way they grumble away at each other. The war brought them closer. It changed everything. None of us were ever the same again, were we?'

Irene sighed. 'Do you ever think what would have happened to us if we'd never come here?'

'No. That would be pointless.'

'We all changed. Even me.'

'Really?' Hazel smiled.

'You encouraged me to control my temper.'

'And was I successful?'

Irene laughed. 'Not entirely, but I'm not as bad as I was.'

'I'll take your word for it.'

'And you ... you seemed to develop into the kind of person you were always intended to be.'

'That's deep.'

'But Carol has changed the most, hasn't she?' Irene said. 'She's even more la-di-da than she was when she first arrived. She acts like the lady of the manor.'

'Irene, don't...'

'But she doesn't look truly happy, does she?'

'Maybe she's just nervous about seeing us again. After all, you were often quite beastly to her, weren't you?'

'I suppose so. But it's more than that. I think it's her conscience that's bothering her. I'd love to know what really happened at the tarn that day. There was something evasive about Carol from the moment she walked into the kitchen.'

'She was distraught. Terrified.'

'Yes, but didn't you notice that she couldn't look anyone in the eye?'

'Irene, stop right now. We'll never know what happened and it's time to let it go. In fact, it's the perfect time to let it go.'

'What do you mean?'

'A new young queen, a new beginning, a new world...'

'Wow, Hazel, I never thought you were so sentimental.'

Hazel laughed. 'Well, I'm not usually, but some

times are special, aren't they? And as for Carol, it's obvious that Miss Forsyth, who did so much for us, loves having her here. It gives her a purpose, it makes her happy. And we want her to be happy, don't we?'

'Of course we do.'

Coronation Day was cold and wet and windy. Hazel gazed out of her bedroom window and thought it was not the right sort of day for a national holiday. They had an early breakfast of porridge and toast and then accompanied Miss Forsyth to church.

'As you know, I don't attend regularly,' she had told them the night before, 'but this will be a special service in our little church. Historic, even. Then we will be coming back to listen to the service from Westminster Abbey on the wireless.'

'Some folk will be watching it on television,' Mrs Ellis said. Hazel thought she sounded aggrieved.

'Really, Mrs Ellis, we've been through this ad nauseam. I just don't fancy all those cathode rays coming into the house.'

'That's what folk used to say about electricity, that it would leak from all the sockets if there was nothing plugged in,' Mrs Ellis retorted.

Hazel was surprised. Miss Forsyth's opinion about television was the first sign she had given that she was growing old. Or maybe she felt out of place in this fast changing world. Ironically, it was the staid Mrs Ellis who was prepared to welcome new inventions. Hazel was more convinced than ever that their old friend needed a young person to keep her rooted in the present. And that person was Carol.

After the coronation service most people hurried along to the village green, where Molly's Easter egg rolling had taken place the year Alan had helped them dye and decorate the eggs. The plan was to have a picnic and a fancy dress competition for the children, then a parade of floats entered by the cubs and scouts, the brownies and guides, the village football team and the ladies' afternoon tea club.

Unfortunately the rain began to pour down. Everybody gathered up their picnics and dashed into the village hall, which was already being prepared for the concert and dance that night. Hazel felt sorry for the little ones who had taken such trouble over their costumes. Some of them were near to tears, but they cheered up when Mrs Edwards announced that there was no reason why the competition should not take place here and now.

It was judged by herself, Molly Watkins and Muriel Teasdale. The first prize went to a little girl dressed as Britannia, the second to John Bull, and the third to a girl dressed as Dorothy from *The Wizard of Oz*. She had a snappy little dog with her playing the part of Toto. Everyone who entered got a consolation prize, then anyone under the age of sixteen was given a coronation mug.

The parade was abandoned. There was nothing else to do until it was time to meet for tea in Jack Armstrong's new barn. Dorothy Edwards announced that the coronation committee had hired a couple of coaches which would be waiting at the station to take anyone who needed a lift.

'What do you think?' Irene said to Hazel as they hurried through the rain back to Hillside House. 'Could you live in a place like this where everybody seems to know everybody, or do you feel more at home in town?'

'I don't know,' Hazel replied. The truth was that she didn't feel at home anywhere.

The rain stopped mid-afternoon and the party from Hillside House lived near enough to the Armstrongs' farm to walk there. Irene noticed that Miss Forsyth no longer strode ahead vigorously but was quite happy to bring up the rear with Mrs Ellis. After a while Carol, who had been walking with Hazel and Irene, dropped back and Miss Forsyth seemed grateful to take her arm.

Irene saw Rita the moment they entered the barn, putting food out on the trestle tables. They greeted each other enthusiastically. It wasn't long before Irene exclaimed, 'Rita, that ring! You're engaged!'

'Don't sound so surprised.'

'I'm not. I'm delighted. Who's the lucky man?'

'Jimmy Doyle. Who else?'

'And when's the wedding?'

'You're full of questions. In a year's time, as a matter of fact. Your old pal Rita Bevan is going to be a June bride.'

'I'm so pleased for you.'

'Aye. Well mebbees I'll invite you to the wedding, but now, how about lending a hand? Folk'll be ready for their tea.'

Irene glanced round the barn. Fresh straw had been spread across the floor and red, white and blue flags and bunting decorated the walls. On the tables there were plates of cooked meats, hard-boiled eggs, jars of pickles and dishes of salad. At a separate table there were bottles of beer and lemonade.

'Who's paying for all this?' she asked.

'The coronation committee,' Rita said. 'They've been fundraising for months. Everybody's welcome but we haven't got enough plates to go round, so we've borrowed them, and the cutlery, from the barracks near Carlisle. Molly's helping Mrs Armstrong to make up some containers of food to send out to anyone too ill or too old to get here.'

Irene gazed at Rita. 'You're very happy here, aren't you?'

Rita's smile was radiant. 'I bless the day that Molly took me in. But hawway, Irene, if you really intend to help me let's get a move on.'

When everything was ready and folk had begun to find places at the tables, Irene and Rita sat down for a moment on a couple of bales of straw. Rita glanced around. 'Have you seen Hazel?'

'Over there, look. She's talking to Miss Norton.'

'She looks very serious.'

'I imagine it was a big decision for her to come back, considering what happened.'

'Have you ever talked to her about that?'

'Hazel doesn't encourage conversations that get too personal.'

'Aye, you're right. I suppose I'd better catch up with her later.'

'You talk as if you don't want to.'

Rita frowned.

'What's the matter?' Irene asked.

Rita shook her head. 'Nothing's the matter. It's just that I won't know what to say to her. But let's not sit here blethering, it's time to get some food down you.'

She hurried off. Irene could tell that her old friend was fretting about something, but she had made it quite obvious that the conversation had come to an end.

After tea Miss Forsyth insisted her party go home to rest before going to the concert and dance in the village hall.

'I won't be staying very long,' she said. 'I don't mind admitting that after all the excitement today I'm exhausted.'

'Me, too,' Mrs Ellis said.

'But you must stay on at the dance, Carol,' Miss Forsyth said. 'I'm sure you'll have a lot to talk about with Hazel and Irene.'

Hazel noticed how strained Carol's smile was and she felt sorry for her.

The band consisted of a couple of local lads with piano and drums. Hazel went to have a word with them and a moment later Irene pretended to be surprised and reluctant when they asked her to come up and sing.

Miss Forsyth was delighted. 'You always had a beautiful voice, Irene,' she said. 'Remember the carol services?'

'I do.'

Hazel looked away. She remembered the carol singing only too well, especially the first occasion, when Alan had accompanied them on the piano. Then the walk home through the frosty streets.

She wasn't surprised when a little later Carol said she would rather go home with Miss Forsyth and Mrs Ellis. Irene was circulating, chatting to the many friends she had made when she worked in the village store. Nobody noticed when Hazel got her raincoat from the cloakroom and slipped out into the summer night.

The sky was clouded but a silvery light was reflected on the grey slate roofs and the drenched roads. The rain had held off, although the wind was blowing raindrops from the dripping hedges. Hazel walked away from the hall. Behind her the music and laughter spilled out into the peaceful streets of Withenmoor. Soon she was walking uphill, but she wasn't going back to Hillside House. Not yet. She needed to be alone. She looked up to where the ruins of the old fort crested the hill. She knew she had to go there, maybe for the last time.

The shadows lengthened and the wind began to blow the clouds across the sky. The light was deceptive, but as she drew nearer to the fort Hazel thought she saw a figure leaning against one of the tumbledown walls. Perhaps it was a ghost, she thought fancifully, one of the long ago soldiers who had guarded the pass.

Maybe she should turn around and go back. Whoever was there might not welcome company. Now he had dropped his head into his hands and the slight keening of the wind was enough to cover the sound of her footsteps on the ancient track. She felt compelled to go on.

She had reached the fort when his arms dropped to his sides and he raised his head to look down into the valley. He had not seen her. Transfixed with shock, she stared at his profile. A ghost indeed. Her heart beat painfully against her ribs.

'Alan!' she gasped, her voice strangled.

She thought she heard him sigh but he didn't turn to look at her. 'Hazel?'

'Why?' she asked. *'Why?'*

He was silent.

'I thought you had died in the crash.'

Still no reply.

'For God's sake, speak to me! Did you not want to see me again? Did you stop loving me?'

'No.' His voice was hoarse with anguish. 'It was *because* I loved you.'

She stared at him. A cold breeze lifted her hair but it was not the sudden chill that made her shiver. 'What are you saying?'

He turned to face her. She stared at him speechlessly. She had never known such heartache as that which flowed through her now.

'Now do you understand?' he said.

The left side of his face was quite normal but the right was marred with appalling scar tissue. His lip was drawn back from his teeth and his right eye was almost covered by a fold of skin. 'I walked away from the crash but not before I was severely burned. They did their best for me, but there's a limit to the surgeons' skills.'

Hazel felt her heart was breaking. 'Why didn't you tell me?'

'Surely that's obvious.'

'No, it's not!'

'I couldn't inflict myself on you. That wouldn't have been fair.'

She began to shake with anger. 'What you *did* wasn't fair. Did you have no faith in me? Did you think my love was so shallow?'

'You're angry.'

'Of course, I am!'

'You could have lived with this?'

'How can you even ask? I loved you and I still do, and you've wasted years, precious years, when we could have been together.'

She took a step away and turned her back on him to stare down at the village. After a while her anger receded a little to be replaced by bitterness. 'You came back here,' she said.

'Where else would I go? The people here accept me. The children have learned not to stare. When my father died I sold the house to the new doctor and I bought a cottage just a short walk from here.'

'So they knew. The others knew and they never told me. Your father actually wrote to me and told me you hadn't survived the crash.'

'In a way I hadn't.'

'He lied to me.'

'I begged him not to tell you the truth. In those dark days he would have done anything for me. Anything I asked. Can't you understand?'

Hazel, her throat constricted with grief, nodded silently. After a while she said, 'But the others, people I thought were my friends. Miss Forsyth... Rita... They betrayed me.'

411

'I made them promise. They agreed, even though they thought I was wrong. Miss Forsyth comes from a generation used to sacrifice, where men were expected to do the honourable thing. She respected my wishes.'

'But Rita?

'She berated me at every opportunity. But she made a promise, so she kept it.'

Hazel turned to look at him. She felt drained. Her voice was subdued. 'And your hopes and your dreams, Alan? What about your plans to go to art school? You were so talented, so gifted.'

He was silent for a moment then he took a step towards her, raising his right arm as he did so. 'It's not just my face, Hazel.'

She stared at his hand, or what was left of it. His fingers were truncated and fused together. She felt tears well up in her eyes. She took a step towards him. 'Alan,' she said, her voice ragged with emotion.

'Don't cry, Hazel,' he said quietly. 'I can still take photographs. Mostly of the countryside and the creatures who live here. I sell them to magazines. Some say I'm pretty good.' For the first time his voice softened and the left side of his mouth drew up into a smile.

She hardly dared ask but she said, 'And your drawing? Your painting?'

'I'm trying to use my left hand. I don't know if I will succeed.'

'But you'll go on trying?'

'I will.'

'Oh, my darling,' Hazel said, and she took him in her arms.

After a moment's hesitation, he put his arms around her waist and held her close. 'I'm sorry. So very sorry,' he said. 'Will you forgive me?'

Hazel looked up into the face of the man she loved, then she smiled and said, 'I might.' They regarded each other earnestly. 'What are we going to do?' she asked.

'We? I'm not sure what you mean.'

'Alan, now that I've found you, don't imagine for one moment that I'm going to walk away. You must know that we belong together.'

They held each other close, neither speaking, both surrendering to the joy of their reunion, until Hazel became aware that the moisture on her face was not just tears.

'It's starting to rain,' she said.

'The cottage isn't far. I'll light the lamps and we'll sit by the fire.'

For a moment Hazel was tempted by the intimacy the image evoked. Then, 'No, my darling,' she said. 'There will be time enough for that.'

The long summer day had given way to night and she turned to gaze down at the lights defining the streets of the village where they had once been so happy. Snatches of music and laughter were carried up on the strengthening breeze. She looked at him questioningly.

'Yes,' he said.

Then, hand in hand, they ran down the moonlit hillside towards the people and the world they loved. A world they would face together.

The publishers hope that this book has given you enjoyable reading. Large Print Books are especially designed to be as easy to see and hold as possible. If you wish a complete list of our books please ask at your local library or write directly to:

Magna Large Print Books
Magna House, Long Preston,
Skipton, North Yorkshire.
BD23 4ND

This Large Print Book for the partially sighted, who cannot read normal print, is published under the auspices of

THE ULVERSCROFT FOUNDATION